PRAISE FOR MARTIN L. SHOEMAKER

"Martin Shoemaker is a rare writer who can handle the challenges of dealing with future technology while touching the human heart."
—David Farland, *New York Times* bestselling author

"Martin Shoemaker's 'Black Orbit' is a more conventional *Analog* adventure, and a very good example of such . . . A really solid story."
—Rich Horton, Locus Online

"['Bookmarked'] is an exceptional example of how to discuss deep moral and philosophical issues while maintaining a tight narrative that brings the reader along. This story will be added to the required readings for my SF classes."
—Robert L. Turner III, Tangent Online

"In 'Brigas Nunca Mais,' Martin L. Shoemaker presents one of the best tales in the issue. A framed narrative about a love relationship told through the voice of the groom at a wedding on board a space ship, this tale delights by featuring dance as a central image and metaphor . . . A very enchanting story."
—Douglas W. Texter, Tangent Online

"What I did particularly enjoy [about 'Murder on the *Aldrin* Express'] was the excellent character development, and the heart and emotional depth brought to the story by its romantic aspect."
—Colleen Chen, Tangent Online

THE
LAST
DANCE

THE LAST DANCE

MARTIN L. SHOEMAKER

47N◉RTH

Text copyright © 2019 by Martin L. Shoemaker
"The Aldrin Cycler: A Foreword by Marianne J. Dyson" © 2019 by Marianne J. Dyson

Published by 47North, Seattle

www.apub.com

Amazon, the Amazon logo, and 47North are trademarks of Amazon.com, Inc., or its affiliates.

ISBN-13: 9781542007986 (hardcover)
ISBN-10: 1542007984 (hardcover)
ISBN-13: 9781542004312 (paperback)
ISBN-10: 1542004314 (paperback)

Cover illustration and design by Mike Heath | Shannon Associates

Printed in the United States of America

First edition

To Colonel Buzz Aldrin,
who convinced me to tell a story about a Mars cycler;
and to Tina Smith,
who convinced me there was more to the story.

It's a damn express train. Oh, I don't mean it's fast; I mean it goes from point A to point B on a fixed route, no stops in between. Then it circles around and goes back. I'm glad it'll take *us* to point B, but it never even stops at either end to explore. This prototype will only make one loop before it goes in for redesign; but they're already working on her sister ship, the *Aldrin*, and that one will be a giant express train from nowhere to nowhere, never stopping. What kind of captain worthy of the title would want duty like that when there are worlds to explore?

—Captain Nicolau Aames

Contents

THE ALDRIN CYCLER

FOREWORD BY MARIANNE J. DYSON

The *Aldrin Express* derives its name from Buzz Aldrin, whom most people know as the Apollo 11 astronaut who walked on the moon alongside Neil Armstrong in 1969. Not as many people know that Aldrin was the first astronaut with a PhD (from MIT), and his doctoral thesis was "Guidance for Manned Orbital Rendezvous." NASA selected him because of this expertise. The other astronauts soon nicknamed him "Dr. Rendezvous" as a result.

Aldrin's orbital mechanical skills were needed when the radar failed during Gemini 12. Aldrin did the calculations in his head while Jim Lovell piloted their ship during a rendezvous in Earth orbit. If a similar failure had occurred in lunar orbit, he could have helped Armstrong rendezvous with Mike Collins in the "mother ship" while out of touch with Mission Control.

After Apollo, Aldrin joined a chorus of space enthusiasts promoting plans to explore and settle Mars. Addressing one of the major obstacles to sustaining a settlement, he applied his rendezvous skills to the problem of the recurring fuel costs of transporting people to and from Mars. (Fuel typically accounts for 85 percent of the mass of a rocket.) He discovered a way to significantly reduce this cost by utilizing a circulating orbit and regular "gravity assists" from Earth. He described this plan, later named the Aldrin cycler, in "Cyclic Trajectory Concepts," published in 1985.

The Aldrin cycler reduces the cost in two ways. First, the mass of the transit habitat with its radiation shielding, recycling life support systems, communications equipment, and so forth is launched once and reused. Every reuse saves at least four supersized rockets' worth of fuel.

Secondly, like grabbing a pole to swing around and change direction, the cycler takes advantage of Earth's gravity instead of using fuel to travel from Earth to Mars. These opportunities occur every twenty-six months near the time, called opposition, when Earth is passing Mars. (Mars is then overhead at midnight, on the opposite side of Earth from the sun.)

Once on the orbital "track," the cycler never stops. To get on board, personnel and their luggage ride a "taxi" flight to rendezvous and dock with the cycler as it flies by Earth. About five months later, the cycler flies past Mars. The passengers get back in their taxi and ride it to Mars. A taxi from Mars might also deliver supplies or crew to the cycler during the flyby.

The cycler then continues outward past Mars's orbit (at 1.5 AU) to about 2.3 AU (where 1 AU is Earth's distance from the sun). It slows down and "falls" back toward the sun. It crosses Mars's orbit again on the way back, but Mars has already passed through that intersection and is not there.

As the cycler crosses Earth's orbit, Earth's gravity pulls the spacecraft toward it and speeds it up. The cycler then swings around Earth and changes direction back toward Mars—not using any fuel.

While passing by Earth, another group of passengers can taxi to the cycler. Aldrin wants this "outbound" cycler named *Armstrong*, after Neil.

The crew that rides the *Armstrong* to Mars must wait thirty-one months for it to fly by Mars again. Thus, they would be gone from Earth for the five-month trip to Mars, the nearly thirty-one months spent on Mars, and the twenty-one-month return to Earth, for a total time away of about four years nine months.

Alternatively, a second "inbound" cycler (which Aldrin would name *Conrad*, after Apollo 12's Pete Conrad) can be launched so that the flyby of Mars occurs when the cycler crosses Mars's orbit on its way inbound. The Mars crew would only have to wait twenty-five months on Mars to catch this cycler, and the trip to Earth would again be five months. Their total time away drops to about two years eleven months.

Crew serving on the outbound or inbound cyclers would return to Earth every twenty-six months with a flyby of Mars either five months or twenty-one months into each tour.

The Aldrin cycler is especially well suited to transport people and delicate items that can't be exposed to high acceleration, radiation, extreme temperatures, vacuum, or isolation during the long trip to Mars using other options. This cycler's primary drawbacks are that the flyby velocity at Mars is on the high side and the trajectory requires periodic corrections (at aphelion) to account for Earth and Mars not being in the same plane. Thus the search continues for orbital solutions that lower the rendezvous speeds (reducing taxi fuel requirements) via more gravity assists or increasing the flight time and using more cyclers. And maybe someone will figure out how to open a wormhole—but that's another story.

Before we hop on the *Aldrin* Express, I'd like to thank Martin for the invitation to "ride along" on this trip to Mars. Ever since we met at the 2013 WorldCon in San Antonio (just as "Murder on the *Aldrin* Express" came out in *Analog*), it was obvious that we shared a passion for space and an appreciation for Buzz's vision of human settlements on Mars. I expect our five-month trip to Mars will literally fly by as we continue to discuss and explore a wondrous future in space.

Marianne Dyson is an award-winning author and a former NASA flight controller (the topic of her memoir, A Passion for Space*). Her recent children's books include* Welcome to Mars: Making a Home on the Red Planet *and* To the Moon and Back: My Apollo 11 Adventure *coauthored with Buzz Aldrin. See www.mdyson.com for more information.*

A NOTE ON RANKS IN THE SYSTEM INITIATIVE

Many of the characters in this book serve in different branches of the International Space Corps chartered under the System Initiative, a future international space program built from the preexisting programs of the member nations. As a new service, it has its own rank structure, inspired by but different from the ranks of contemporary and historical services. To help the reader understand the chain of command, here are the ranks used in all branches of the System Initiative.

Enlisted Ranks

T-1	T	Trainee
E-0	R	Recruit
E-1	SR	Spacer Recruit
E-2	SA	Spacer Apprentice
E-3	SP	Spacer

E-4	AS3	Astronaut 3rd Class
E-5	AS2	Astronaut 2nd Class
E-6	AS1	Astronaut 1st Class
E-7	CAS	Chief Astronaut
E-8	SCAS	Senior Chief Astronaut
E-9	MCAS	Master Chief Astronaut

Warrant Ranks

B-1	BN1	Bosun 1
B-2	CBN2	Chief Bosun 2
B-3	CBN3	Chief Bosun 3
B-4	CBN4	Chief Bosun 4
B-5	CBN5	Chief Bosun 5

Officer Ranks

O-0	MID	Midshipman (Officer trainee)
O-1	ENS	Ensign

O-2LTJG	Lieutenant Junior Grade
O-3LT	Lieutenant
O-4LCDR	Lieutenant Commander
O-5CDR	Commander
O-6CHF	Chief
O-7CAPT	Captain (Commandant for ground posts)
O-8RDML	Rear Admiral
O-9VADM	Vice Admiral
O-10 ADM	Admiral
O-11 FADM	Fleet Admiral

Some of the incidents that follow predate the System Initiative, and some of the characters in this story serve in other forces outside the Initiative, so there may be some exceptions to this table.

1. The Inspector General's Office

From the memoirs of Park Yerim, Inspector General in the System Initiative

28 May 2083

"Can I get you anything, Inspector Park?" Matt asked.

I shook my head and came to my senses. I had been staring too long at the gray-brown door with the freshly painted sign, black letters on white: "Inspector General Park Yerim." This still seemed like a dream, a running-and-hiding-but-you-can't-escape dream. I had been feeling fight-or-flight urges ever since I had arrived on the *Aldrin* a week ago, escorted by Admiral Knapp, Admiral Morais, a host of other officers, Rapid Response troops from the Admiralty, and a pile of legal orders.

But the ache in my shoulder, hanging on nearly two weeks after I had bruised it, reminded me that I wasn't dreaming. I turned to Matt Harrold, my new assistant, sitting at what had been Chief Carver's desk just a week ago. Back when Nick Aames had been captain of the *Aldrin*, and my office had been his office, Anson Carver had been his second-in-command. He had occupied Aames's outer office as a buffer between

Aames and the rest of the world. Now that I was de facto in command, Matt had been assigned to be *my* buffer. I hoped he was up to the task.

"Soju?"

"Excuse me, ma'am?" Matt's face was blank.

"It's a Korean rice liquor," I said, missing the sweet hint of anise and the soothing effect of the alcohol. "I haven't had good soju since I left Seoul."

"I don't know if the ship has any soju. Would vodka do?"

Matt was still too new to recognize I was joking, in my cynical way. Like me, he had been selected more because he was available than because he was the best person for the job. When the *Aldrin* had swung through the Earth-Luna system at her high departure velocity, only a few stations and ships had been in position for rendezvous. So the System Initiative had crewed our mission from whoever happened to be in the wrong place at the wrong time. And so I found myself, barely three years in the Inspector General's Office, presiding over the biggest tangle of political and commercial and military interests of the decade: the investigation and possible court martial of Captain Nicolau Aames. I had, according to the Initiative, plenary powers to straighten out this mess; but I had no idea how. Soju wouldn't help, but nothing else would either.

"No, Matt, I'm fine. There probably isn't any good vodka on board either. Can you see if the ship's stores have anything for my shoulder? It's still sore from my collision on Farport. And something for a headache too. I'll be in Aames's— I mean, my office."

In the one-quarter gravity from the *Aldrin*'s spin, my feet still felt heavy as I crossed through the outer office. Like much of the ship, the bulkheads of the room were a sickening gray brown. When Holmes Interplanetary had owned this ship, the bulkhead color had been an interesting choice: ochre, the color of the Holmes logo. When the System Initiative had taken over the ship, they had repainted everything in government gray; but the orange shade bled through, giving everything a muddy color.

And then I entered "my" office, and the tone turned even darker. Aames had painted his office walls black, and all the trim was either black or gray. The carpet was dark gray, almost black as well. His chair was a navy-blue web, almost the color of my IG uniform, on a dark aluminum frame. Even his desk, a typical command desk with a touch display nearly three square meters in area, stood on a single black pillar. The recessed lights in the ceiling added to the glow from the touch display. Together they overpowered the faint light from the window.

That big picture window taking up almost the entire wall behind the desk. Aames had established his office in the rear ring of the *Aldrin*, along the rear wall, so that he could have that window. And that view: the Earth and Luna, each in three-quarter phase as the ship sped on its way to Mars in its cycler orbit. As the *Aldrin* slowly spun in space, the twin planets rotated in and out of sight twice per minute. Some might find that motion unsettling. I found it hypnotic. The only calming experience I had had aboard this ship. I stood at the window, staring at home, and I wished I were back there: Luna, Earth, Farport. Hell, any post but this one.

But wishing wouldn't change things. Staring wasn't getting me anywhere, so I turned away from the window and looked at the office. Along the spinward wall was a small sink and a shelf with glasses, wide plastic bulbs with narrow mouths to prevent sloshing over in the low gravity. I poured myself a glass of water, holding the glass antispinward of the faucet head to compensate for the Coriolis effect that curved the stream. I was careful to stop at the full line, or the water would spill out even with the tall neck.

I sat in the command chair and set the glass in a coaster molded into the desk's frame. The desk display was filled with virtual piles of my documents. Off in one corner was a cluster of notes from Aames's command, all neatly ordered. The office, like the desk, had been immaculate when I had assumed command, and I tried not to disturb anything more than my investigations required. I didn't feel comfortable putting any of myself into this room; I was only a temporary occupant, and either Aames or a new commander would reclaim it eventually. The sooner, the better.

Aames hadn't put much of himself into the room either. Besides the dark decor, the only personal touches were a battered old blue reader sitting on the desk—must've been older than me—and the hand-painted sign on the second door, the one in the antispinward wall. It was a bright-blue rectangle painted on the black background; and in very neat white lettering, the sign read: "São Paulo. Keep out." That was the door to Aames's cabin, where he was confined to quarters, pending the results of my investigation. The source of all this trouble was fewer than eight meters away. That door had never opened once since I had moved in to this office.

Forward of this ring were nine more identical rings, a stack of rings rotating on a central core. Each ring was sixty meters in radius, four decks deep with each deck measuring ten meters across. There was an outer cargo deck for storage and shielding, a main deck, a middle deck, and an upper deck. Each ring was divided into numerous cabins and passageways, so that the one large space became many small, even cramped, spaces. And over time that space filled up; every so often, the Cycler Consortium added another couple of rings in a complicated orbital rendezvous. The addition of the G and H Rings in the last cycle had brought the total usable deck space to twenty-seven acres: roughly the deck space of six old wet-navy aircraft carriers. The *Aldrin* was practically a city in space.

And of course, in the latest Earth approach, the Consortium had added the brand-new I and J Rings; that seemingly simple engineering feat had unfolded into the mess that I was privileged to clean up.

I folded back the flap in the left sleeve of my dark-blue uniform, revealing the suit comp that I wore like a gauntlet. With a swipe of my finger, I pushed my latest interview notes from my suit comp to the desk. Back in my own office on Farport, my comp would've automatically synced with my desk (a much smaller, less impressive desk than the one I sat at now); but I hadn't managed to set up the sync protocols with Aames's desk. Or for that matter with any computer system on the *Aldrin*. The ship's technical staff kept promising to fix that, but it never seemed to happen. It had been that way ever since I had boarded: the crew were never provably derelict in their work, and yet they managed to be politely uncooperative and incompetent. I had to push to get them to do anything outside of their routine ship duties. The message was clear: *We don't like you.*

The door chime sounded, and a window opened on the desk. Aames had a concealed camera outside the door, letting him see his visitors before he answered. The window showed Matt and a ship's officer—a heavyset, middle-aged woman of medium height in the gray uniform of the *Aldrin's* crew. Her hair had probably been auburn once, but now there was more gray than russet color. She wore a medical cross on her collar and an old-fashioned stethoscope around her neck. I tapped the desktop, and the door slid open.

Matt led the doctor in. "Inspector, Dr. Baldwin is here to see about your shoulder and your headache."

I frowned and held my palm up to halt them. "I only needed an aspirin, Matt."

Dr. Baldwin set a black medical bag upon the desk. Then she grabbed my arm, turned it wrist up, and found my pulse. "We don't work that way on the *Aldrin*," she said, her voice surprisingly deep. "It's diagnosis before treatment here." She put the stethoscope ends in her ears and held the cup to my chest.

I pushed her hand away. "Doctor, wouldn't a medical scanner be more accurate?"

She slapped my wrist with her free hand, and I let go. "Inspector, you may be in charge of everything else on this ship, but I still run the medical department. Scanners take battery power we don't need to waste as long as I have working eyes and ears. Now shut up and let me work, or you can keep your damned headache."

I could have had her up on charges for striking a superior officer, but I was too shocked to respond. Besides, then who would've seen to the medical needs of the crew and passengers? So I shut up and complied, breathing in and coughing and doing whatever else the doctor instructed. Matt stood by. I hadn't dismissed him, so he didn't know what to do. When I saw the uncomfortable look on his face, I waved him out. Matt seemed worried about me. Ever since we had arrived on the *Aldrin*, he had subconsciously been acting like a big brother—the big, strong American man protecting the tiny Korean farm girl.

Well, maybe I had made up that last bit, my own subconscious playing its own games. Matt couldn't know that I was a farm girl from outside Hongcheon, couldn't know how my rural manners and dark skin had made me an outcast all through school. The rustic clothes and stringy brown hair had been replaced by a crisp uniform and a regulation cut, yet sometimes I still felt like that little *chon tak* who ran away to space to prove herself. Matt—and pretty much everyone in the International Space Corps, to their credit—didn't care about where I came from, just how I did my job.

After checking the rest of me over, Dr. Baldwin finally got to my left shoulder. I had injured it in our rush to leave Farport for the *Aldrin*. She had me remove my uniform jacket and my blouse so she could look at the bruising. She had me lift and flex, and she probed, finding some tender spots. "It looks like you inflamed it from overuse right after bruising it. And somebody dressed it, someone competent, but not a doctor."

I nodded. "Chief Gale."

Dr. Baldwin snorted. "Figures. He's had a decent amount of field medic training, but he thinks he's a doctor. Your shoulder shows signs of acceleration stress, and the dressing didn't help there. Some anti-inflammatories would have, but it's too late for that. I think all it needs now is time. You can get dressed."

Satisfied at last, Dr. Baldwin pulled a small bag of pills from her pocket and held them out to me. "No more than three of these a day. I recommend you get more exercise—but take it easy on that shoulder—and more sleep. And do less meddling so we can do our jobs."

I took the pill bag and sighed. "Doctor, I have work to do, just like you. Please let me do it."

She crossed her arms. "I'm having a hard time doing *my* work with the Inspector General team and the Admiralty's shock troops all over the ship, disrupting operations, panicking the passengers, and putting the crew through an inquisition."

I rose, steaming. "An inquisition? This is a proper investigation by the Inspector General of the International Space Corps. And Captain Aames brought it on himself by refusing to surrender this ship under lawful orders."

"Sit down and watch that blood pressure!" Surprised at her tone, I sat. "This is a political witch hunt, driven by people whom Captain Aames rubbed the wrong way."

"From what I can tell, that's a long list. I have a string of complaints about him that would stretch from here to Farport, crew complaints in particular."

She sniffed. "No doubt mostly from the Space Professionals? No, I know, you won't divulge the complainants. The captain has drummed out plenty of crew in his career, malcontents and SP layabouts who couldn't measure up to his standards. Good riddance to them."

My headache was growing stronger by the second. I took a pill and a long drink of water, giving myself time to calm down. I set the glass back in the coaster, and then I looked back to the doctor. "You really believe that, don't you? You're not the only one. Most of this crew is intensely loyal to Aames. Why? What is there about him?"

Dr. Baldwin shook her head. "No thank you, Inspector, I'm not going to tell you anything that could be twisted into evidence for some court martial. You can't compel me to talk."

I pressed my fingertips together, feeling my pulse pound in them. "Doctor, do you know what 'plenary power' means?"

She nodded. "It means you can do whatever the hell you want, and the Admiralty and the Initiative will back you up. Unless you offend the wrong people, like Captain Aames did. Oh, you can't have me put out the airlock, but you can mete out all manner of administrative punishment. Even ruin my career." I was ready to agree, but she continued, "But I'm still not saying anything for the record. If you have a problem with that, then confine *me* to quarters. And hope that no one gets sick or injured between here and Mars."

I stood again, watching the doctor for any sign of disapproval. When she said nothing, I started pacing, my hands clasped behind my back. After crossing the office three times, I calmed down enough to go on. "Doctor, I know you're upset. Your whole crew is. I don't want to upset them more, but I have a job to do. I have to straighten out this mess in a way that placates everyone involved: the System Initiative, the Admiralty, the UN, the Holmes Trust, the Space Professionals, *and* your crew. I want to do that in the fairest way possible; but I can't if I don't have the whole picture. Right now I have official Admiralty charges and reports; I have complaints from the Space Professionals; I have amicus briefs from the Trust and a dozen shareholder groups; and I have noncommittal testimonies from your crew. What I *don't* have is your side, your crew's side. I don't understand the way Captain Aames works, and so I can't see the complete picture." I paused and looked her in the eye. "Let me be honest with you, Dr. Baldwin: if I go only by facts currently in evidence, the situation can't get much worse for your captain. The only reason I haven't filed a summary judgment and a recommendation for a full court martial is this crew seems certain that Aames is right and the facts are wrong. My instincts tell me that if a whole crew is united like that, they know something. Something I should know. But none of them will talk to me beyond official duties."

She held my gaze, not wavering a bit. "So what do you want from me?"

I tried to look trustworthy. "Off the record, tell me why you're willing to risk your career for Captain Aames."

I had made inspector pretty young compared to my peers, largely because I was very good at reading people. I saw by the upturn in her eyes that the doctor was convinced. "Off the record?" she asked.

"Off the record." I pulled off my suit comp and set it aside. Then I switched off the desk, turning the room suddenly dark.

Dr. Baldwin went to the sink and poured a glass for herself, then she leaned back against the desk. "Sit down, Inspector. Let me tell you a story from my first tour on the *Aldrin*. That's when I first learned how Nick Aames works."

2. Racing to Mars

Off-the-record account of Constance J. Baldwin, MD, Chief Medical Officer of the IPV *Aldrin*

Covering events from 25 June 2064 to 22 November 2064

I was thirty-four years old, in what should have been the prime of my medical career; but in fact, I was washed up, a victim of my principles and my temper. My life as a doctor was over—until Nick Aames unexpectedly swept in and threw me a lifeline, asking for me personally to be chief medical officer of the Mars cycler *Aldrin*.

And I hated him for it.

Oh, not right away. I had never met him, so how could I hate him? I was grateful. So as soon as I had dropped my gear in my office, I headed up to the bridge to thank him.

But when I got there, my image of my benefactor was shattered. As soon as the bridge door opened, I heard him berating his crew. "Howarth! Why are those mooring lines not reeled in? Sakaguchi, are those engines ready yet? We boost in two hours, people. Don't waste time. *Move!*"

I peered in through the door. Nick Aames loomed over his bridge, a redheaded, gray-clad vulture looking to swoop down on anyone that drew his ire. The bridge was arranged in the classic "mission control" layout, three rows of desk stations facing a main display, officers in gray uniforms manning each station; and at the rear was the captain's raised aluminum-and-web chair. The curve of the deck and the height of the chair combined to give Aames an elevation of nearly two meters relative to the front row of stations, so that he could look "down" upon each station and see the displays. He glared at everyone and everything around him, a scowl fixed in place. His uniform was immaculate, and his red hair and beard were neatly trimmed; despite the tone of his voice, his slouch and his attitude made him seem sloppy, just as I had heard from his detractors. When I saw the glare in his eyes, I decided that he was not sloppy, but rather *dismissive*: he was busy, and he had no time for anything but planning the maneuvers.

Chief Carver was a contrast to the captain: just as neat and trim, but his dark face was alert and warm as he greeted me at the bridge door. I saluted (still not comfortable saluting even after my academy training), and I introduced myself. "Dr. Constance Baldwin, reporting to Captain Aames."

Carver returned my salute, and he smiled just a bit. He was a charmer. "Welcome aboard, Doctor. We're glad to have you. Let me introduce you to the captain."

He walked over to the captain's chair, and I followed, trying to imitate his precision stride and failing utterly in the one-quarter gravity. Carver cleared his throat and announced, "Captain, Dr. Baldwin is reporting for duty."

I saluted again, but before I could say a word, Aames snapped at me without taking his eyes from the stations: "Is anyone sick here, Doctor?"

I was unsure what to do, so I held my salute; and I answered without hesitation: "No, sir."

"Have there been any injuries that I missed? Did someone call you to treat a bout of spacesickness?"

"No, sir."

"Then what the *hell* are you doing here? I do not tolerate spectators on my bridge, particularly during departure maneuvers. Get the hell off the bridge, Doctor, and back to your office where you belong."

And that was my introduction to Captain Nick Aames. I owed him for my second chance as a doctor. And instinctively, I hated him. I had the urge to knock him out of that chair, but I held my temper. Barely.

☾

I had signed aboard the *Aldrin*'s first full cycle to Mars and back. She had been through shakedown cruises in Earth-Luna space before then, but now she would begin a series of boost maneuvers to launch her on a cycler trajectory to Mars. After a flyby, orbital mechanics would sling her out and eventually back to Earth; and then, with skilled piloting, she would repeat that cycle, Earth to Mars and back, again and again with minimal fuel costs. All it took was time: five months out, twenty-one months back. I faced over two years under a captain whom I hated. My streak of career bad luck looked to stay unbroken.

I returned to my new office, a small space that smelled like a doctor's office should—disinfectant with a tang of medicine—but looked like the interior of a mud hut. Back then, the *Aldrin* was still owned and managed by Holmes Interplanetary, and they had painted the interior in their corporate colors, a hideous shade of orange brown. Oh, they called it "ochre"; but in my dark mood, "orange muddy" was all I could see.

"Suck it up, Connie," I said to myself. "You're still a doctor. You have a practice. That's enough."

I opened my old black medical bag and pulled out a clear plastic tube containing a sheet of ivory parchment: my medical diploma from the University of Michigan. I had almost left the tube at home—our mass budget for personal effects was *that* tight—but I couldn't make myself do so. I removed the parchment, unrolled it, and wondered how I was going to hang it. The frame had been too much for my mass budget, but I had no intention of going to space without that parchment.

I had worked too hard to get that diploma—and then fought too hard to keep it. I had reported sanitation violations at my hospital. They sued, and I countersued. The evidence was all with me, and I was vindicated. Eventually I won; but in the process, I lost. I had the court settlement on my side and a big damage award, but I also had a reputation as a troublemaker. One slimy investigator had pushed me too hard one night, trying to provoke a reaction; I had lost control, punching him when he had grabbed me in a restaurant. *Smart, Connie, really smart.* Witnesses had testified that I was provoked, so the police never pressed charges, but that became my reputation: the temperamental woman who punches men in bars. The hospital's PR flacks made sure that story was in all the media, and I was marked, a whistleblower with a temper. No one ever used the word "blackballed," but no hospital would grant me admitting privileges. Without those, no practice would accept me. I was locked out of medicine.

At first I was angry. Despite my natural temper, I had kept my calm throughout the court proceedings. (Punching holes in walls at night didn't count.) When I realized how screwed I was, I was angry enough to punch more than a wall, but I was smart enough not to make that mistake twice. Eventually I figured I was still young enough to switch career paths, so I used my settlement to fund my training in space operations and space medicine, and I also became a reservist in the International Space Corps. Then I sent applications to all the transport companies.

And then I waited. It seemed the blackballing went further than I had realized. I had good recommendations from my instructors at the academy, but I received no interview requests. *None.* I still read about shortages of doctors in space, but apparently the shortage wasn't enough to overcome my reputation. My medical career was over, it seemed, and I didn't have a backup plan.

But then out of nowhere, my fortunes completely reversed: instead of an interview request, I received a job offer from Holmes! But I was confused. I had applied there, yes, but I had never heard a word from them—until this offer.

I was torn between celebration and doubt, and doubt won. I didn't want to derail the job offer, but I hate not understanding. So I called their personnel director, and I asked her to confirm. She was very positive: "Yes, it's very unusual, Dr. Baldwin. But your academy record and your résumé are exemplary. And your instructors spoke highly of you, Mr. Quintana particularly." Quintana had taught our unit on emergency management. "That was enough for Captain Aames. He insisted we hire you. Our launch schedule is very aggressive, so we didn't have time for the customary rounds of interviews. I hope that's all right with you?"

Absolutely it was all right! And before I knew what was happening, I was on Farport, boarding a rendezvous shuttle, and looking forward to meeting the man who had believed in me.

That bastard, Nick Aames.

After the second *Bradbury* expedition, most people knew Aames by reputation. For a while he was a media hero. And he was also somewhat legendary at the academy, though a lot of people there were *not* fans. "Difficult," they said. "Sloppy." "Obstinate." "Insolent." "Arrogant." "Smug." And more often: "Arrogant bastard." "Smug asshole." I had written these off as jealousy or petty rivalries. Now I was ready to believe them. And worse.

Oh well. I had worked for tyrannical bosses, and I had put off hitting them for over two years (until I found out they were compromising patient safety, and then I hit them in the courtroom). I could put up with Nick Aames for that long. The boss didn't matter, only the patients did.

C

But soon I was as fed up with my patients as well as my boss. Or to be more specific, *a* patient: Anthony Holmes. He first came to my attention when my assistant, Dr. Santana, brought me the ship's medical report, a summary of the condition of the crew and the passengers. When he pushed it to my desktop display, I skimmed over it. I knew Santana's record, so I trusted he had done thorough work. But then I saw that one line was marked "Incomplete."

"Who's this 'Holmes, Anthony,' and why is his record incomplete?"

Santana whistled. "A hundred-twenty passengers and crew on board, and you zoom right in on the one incomplete. You're pretty sharp, Doctor." I nodded, acknowledging the compliment. "Anthony Holmes is the sole heir of Anton Holmes, chairman and primary stockholder of Holmes Interplanetary. In other words, he's the boss's son, and he damn well acts like it."

I pulled open Anthony's file and skimmed through it. Twenty years old. Overweight by Corps standards, but reasonably fit for a civilian. Excellent dentition and bone health, the best a billionaire's son could buy. Neurotransmitters all in optimum range, cardiovascular efficiency in the eightieth percentile for civilians of his age range. Therapeutic nanos . . . "Damn, he's a NoNan."

Santana nodded. "He refused to accept his nano injection. The admitting nurse insisted, and Holmes fired him."

"Fired him? Can he do that?"

"No, Doctor. Chief Carver stepped in and explained that the chief medical doctor has authority in all medical personnel decisions. But by the time that was settled, we were far behind on our passenger screening. The chief said we should deal with Holmes later."

I sighed. "And this is later." I tapped the "Contact" button on Anthony's file.

A few seconds later the channel opened, showing a young blond man with well-coiffed curls and an expensive smile. His face was on the heavy side of average, and his eyes were bright blue. "Hey, this is Anthony, what's up?" The voice was young, cheery, and didn't sound at all like a troublemaker's. I hoped this was all just a misunderstanding.

"Mr. Holmes, this is Dr. Baldwin—"

"Doctor." Anthony interrupted me. I hate being interrupted, and it didn't make me any happier when his cheer was replaced by an edge. "I expected this call. I've made my decision, so you're wasting your time."

I swore under my breath, remembering my bedside manner for difficult patients. Then I continued, "I respect that, Mr. Holmes, but they pay me to waste my time. Could you please visit my office after boosting so that we can discuss your treatment options?"

"Treatment?" He laughed, and then he sneered. It turned his pleasant face into something uglier. "I don't *need* that 'treatment,' Doctor. I've done my research. And I'm busy after boost. We're holding a launch party. You're welcome to join us, but you're not going to change my mind."

I shook my head. "Mr. Holmes, I have to be on duty for any injuries that come up in boost. It would be a lot easier if you could come here."

"Sorry, Doc, I just don't have the time." And he clicked off.

Damn! Save me from self-educated "experts" who think they're doctors.

But before I could get any angrier about Anthony, Chief Carver's face came up on the ship-wide comm. "Attention, all department heads: departure boost in fifteen minutes. Secure your areas. Departure boost in fifteen minutes. Level 1 boost alert."

Level 1: not even a quarter G, just enough to correct our course and inject us into our cycler orbit to Mars. I had trained all the way to level 5 in the academy. You would think level 1 would be a breeze, but because no one took it seriously, ships usually had *more* injuries at level 1 due to loose objects that no one had secured.

Not on the *Aldrin*. When the boost horn sounded, I kept an eye on the med feed on my desk, watching for red lights indicating injuries; but the board stayed green. Aames's crew didn't leave loose ends.

For nine minutes, the big fusion engines burned. Between the spin and the boost, the "gravity" pushed toward the aft curve of the outer wall. Passengers were strapped in, but boost-certified crew could move around as duties required.

At the end of nine minutes, the boost horn sounded again, and Carver returned to the comm as the boost ended. "All hands, we're clear of boost. All personnel are free to move around." He grinned and signed off.

I checked the medical board again: still green across the desktop. I flipped to my office status view. Everything was fully stocked, we had no patients in the infirmary, and all our paperwork was up to date.

I was still steamed, but I had a job to do; and no matter how I searched, I could find no excuse to delay any longer. So I headed to the passenger lounge and to Mr. Holmes's party.

☾

It was easy to find Anthony in the lounge. The kid was heir to several billions, no matter what currency you measured in; and that much money generates its own gravitational field, drawing in a crowd of syco-phants and a ring of nervous corporate bodyguards. I pitied the guards: no one could miss them in those ochre uniforms. I was glad we wore the grays of the Space Corps instead of those awful things. The kid and his crowd were a marked contrast to all of us: they wore a wide range of civilian attire. The kid himself was in a blue silk shirt and darker-blue slacks, both designer fashions. That outfit probably cost more than I would make that month.

I had to show my ID for scanning before the guards would let me within sight of Anthony, and they wouldn't let me any closer until they confirmed with him. A guard approached him, whispered in his ear, and pointed at me. Anthony nodded and waved me over.

I stood beside him, and he said, "Have a seat, Doc." I looked around his table but saw no place to sit. A crowd of passengers, young men and women bound for the Mars mission, occupied every seat. I just looked pointedly at them, and Anthony added, "Folks, can you give me a minute to consult with my doctor?" The passengers quickly stood and made room, and I sat down. Anthony held out a plate of little crusty buns that were maybe a couple centimeters across. "*Pão de queijo?* It's some Brazilian cheese bread." He gestured to one of the guards, a tall, bald, ebony-skinned man with a serious look. "Chuks, get the lady a drink."

The guard scowled—at Anthony, not at me—and I shook my head, holding up my hand. "I'm on duty."

Anthony laughed. "Doctor, it's all right. Dad won't mind."

I frowned and narrowed my eyes. "I don't answer to your dad, Mr. Holmes. The Corps rules are very clear. Now please, this is not a social call. I'm very concerned. You're at risk for muscle and bone loss, and also for low-level radiation effects. These are easy to avoid, but we really need to set up an appointment for your therapy nanos."

He picked up his glass and took a long drink. The glazed look in those blue eyes told me it wasn't his first. "Sorry to waste your time, Doc. Not gonna happen."

"My name is Dr. Baldwin." My voice was chill. Then I remembered that getting angry would make things worse, so I aimed for a lighter tone. "Let me assure you, the therapy is perfectly safe."

Anthony slammed down his glass, displaying his lack of space reflexes: the liquid in the glass lagged behind, then splashed to the bottom, and splattered out all over him and the table. "Shit!" Anthony said. From nowhere, another guard appeared with a napkin and started sopping up the mess. Ignoring the guard, Anthony continued, "Safe? I've read the NoNan reports, Doctor. Your 'therapy nanos' are associated with higher incidences of rheumatoid arthritis, schizophrenia, insomnia, peripheral neuropathy." He continued with the usual litany of unconnected symptoms, ticking them off on his fingers. He covered every one I had ever heard of, plus a few new ones.

I knew better than to interrupt a NoNan zealot in mid-zeal; though I wanted to tell him what an idiot he was, I let him ramble on until he ran out. Then, in my calmest, most reasonable voice, I responded, "Mr. Holmes, those 'reports' are pseudoscience promoted by celebrities trying to stay relevant and entertainment 'doctors' who know more about audience ratings than medical research. The NoNan literature has been discredited by every scientist who has reviewed it. I can assure you that the reputable studies do not show any significant correlation between therapy nanos and any of those symptoms."

Anthony shook his head. "'Studies' funded by the companies that manufacture nanos. What's your cut, Doc? How much do you get for jabbing me?" He grinned as he said that, but he was pushing my limits.

"Mr. Holmes, take your accusations and shove them. If you want a painful death, don't let me stop you."

I stood and started to leave, but he grabbed my arm to stop me. "Doc, relax."

My vision started to go red, and I felt my temple throbbing. I yanked my arm away and raised my voice so the whole room could hear. "Keep your hands to yourself, asshole, if you don't want them broken. Boss's brat or not." Anthony let go, but the dark-skinned bodyguard moved to stop me. He was a head taller than me, and in very good shape, but I fixed him with the glare I had learned to use on hospital lawyers. "Out of my way, or I'll see you in the infirmary." He stepped aside, and I stormed out for my office.

C

But I didn't get far down the passageway before I heard a deep voice calling, "Dr. Baldwin."

Still too angry to stop or turn back, I kept marching. I heard feet hurrying behind me, and I tensed, expecting someone to grab me and try to stop me. *Relax, Connie, you'll take their head off.*

But my pursuer was smarter than that: a flash of ochre clothes and dark skin swept past me, climbing halfway up the wall. In one smooth motion and without ever touching me, the tall guard had leaped in front of me. Despite his bit of acrobatics, he wasn't even breathing hard. He stood there, full of wiry energy, and that ochre uniform wasn't the least mussed. He *almost* made that color look good. Almost.

The guard held out a hand to stop me. "Doctor, please wait."

"I'm sorry. Mr. Chuks, is it?"

He straightened and smiled. "Major Adika, Chukwunwike Adika. Only my friends call me Chuks." He had a nice smile, but then it fell. "And overprivileged billionaire's sons. I have the honor of leading young Mr. Holmes's security detail."

I rolled my eyes. "I'm *really* sorry, Major Adika. You'll notice *he* grabbed *me*. I never laid a finger on him. I lost my temper, but I'm not a threat to Mr. Holmes." *As long as he keeps his hands to himself.*

The major nodded. "We had scanned you for weapons. Our bio-scans had read your heart rate and blood pressure, and our thermal sensors showed no significant increase in activity in your limbic system, so we judged you as nonthreatening." And then the major's smile returned. "But if in your anger you had slapped the young mister, we might not have noticed, officially. Some of us believe that the young mister gets away with too much because people want something from him. And his father, the brilliant businessman, has a blind spot where his son is involved." Then the smile turned to a broad, likable grin. "Should I ever choose to resign in style, I might slap him myself."

I had been prepared for another type of confrontation. My pulse had been racing. But the major's humor relaxed me. There was a lot more to this man than muscle. "Thank you, Major. That helps. Did you follow me just to apologize?"

"It is not right for a professional such as yourself to be treated so. An apology was required." His voice had a hint of an accent, and his word choice was rather formal. I suspected English was not his first language. "But no, that was only part of my reason. Doctor, is Mr. Holmes really at risk?"

I nodded. "You've had your therapy nanos. Were they explained to you?"

"Doctor, I and my team were selected for this detail because we all have space experience. Mr. Holmes Sr. wants us ready for any risk to his son. We all have been briefed on therapy nanos. But young Mr. Holmes's sources—"

"Are a bunch of quacks and kooks and attention-seekers who might get him killed. They play off the public's lack of science skills to inflame ridiculous fears. Those fears are harmless on Earth; but here and on Mars, therapy nanos are his best defense against a number of general metabolic ailments. I can't guarantee those will be fatal, but the risks are high. Unacceptably high, in my medical opinion. He risks decreased bone density and muscle tissue loss due to the low gravity, and cumulative effects of low-level cosmic radiation in open space. He'll survive, probably, but he risks painful, permanent injuries. And death can't be ruled out. Angry as he made me, I still can't put him through that without a fight."

The major added, "And if he gets injured or sick, you will have to put up with him in your infirmary." I laughed at that, and the last of my tension slipped away. He laughed as well—a good, deep, hearty laugh—and then continued, "Doctor, if you tell me his life is at stake, I will sit on young Mr. Holmes while you give him the injections." The major's grin grew. "I might even enjoy it."

I grinned back. The major should've been a doctor. He had a talent for putting people at ease.

But then I shook my head. "I'm sorry, I wish I could, but regulations and my code of ethics forbid me from performing invasive therapy on an informed, competent patient who refuses it. His behavior aside, Holmes is competent. Legally."

His face turned solemn, every muscle standing out in frustration. "Then I do not know what to do, Doctor. You cannot treat him, and I cannot protect him if he refuses to allow it."

By then I had decided how *I* would deal with the problem: I would pass the buck. It was a corporate political problem as much as a medical problem. "Let's let the captain deal with this. Perhaps he can persuade Holmes Sr., and then Holmes Sr. can persuade Junior."

The major looked doubtful. "No one has persuaded young Mr. Holmes against his will in years."

But I didn't see any other option, so I tapped the captain's icon on my comm.

Captain Aames's face appeared on the comm screen on my sleeve. He still had that casual air, almost—almost—*slovenly* in contrast to the alert bearing of Major Adika. But rank hath its privileges: if the captain wanted to be casual, it was his command.

His tone, however, was just as sharp as I remembered. "Dr. Baldwin, I hear you had an altercation in the passenger lounge. Do I need to rule that off limits to you? Do I have to worry that you'll assault someone again? Or can you behave as a respectable officer of this ship?"

"Captain, I don't know what you've heard, but—"

"What I *don't* need to hear, Doctor, are excuses. I have three complaints from Anthony Holmes: two about your behavior and one about his missing security chief. I don't need trouble with the boss right at this moment, nor with his son. Can you skip the excuses and explain yourself?"

So I explained everything that had happened. Occasionally I looked up at Major Adika for confirmation, and each time he was watching me carefully and nodding as I went. His intense stare unnerved me even more than the captain's glare.

I was careful not to gloss over anything, avoiding anything that might sound like an excuse; but when I was done, the captain snapped, "Is that it?"

"Yes, sir."

Then the captain leaned in toward the camera and raised his voice a notch. "And you chose to discuss a patient's private medical matters over *an open comm* in the middle of *a public passageway* where *anyone could overhear?* Do you know how much trouble Anthony could make with a breach of privacy claim? Why didn't you come to me in person?"

I clenched my fists, out of view of the camera, but not of Major Adika. He waved both hands palms down in a calming gesture, and that gave me just enough control to keep going. "Captain, you said you never wanted to see me on your bridge."

Captain Aames looked upward and snorted. "I'm not *on* the bridge, Doctor. I'm quite certain my schedule is posted, and it shows me in my office right now. Did you even bother to check my schedule?"

I swallowed my reply, because I knew he had me. "No, Captain, I did not."

Then Captain Aames surprised me with his answer: "That's better, Doctor. The facts. Don't pretty them up, and damn sure don't cover them up, and things will go much better here."

I was confused: ready to fight, and suddenly the fight was gone. Just like with Major Adika. Was I too defensive? Was I *looking* for trouble?

I would have to think on that later; right now, I seemed to have calmed the captain, and I wanted to build on that. "Understood, Captain. I'll head to your office immediately."

"No." The captain waved that idea away. "It's too late for that. If privacy has been breached, it's done already. No, I think I'll need to clear this up in person, so as not to further antagonize the boss's son. Wait for me outside the lounge, Doctor."

C

By the time Captain Aames reached the passenger lounge, Major Adika had gone back in. The captain didn't say a word to me; he just nodded and entered the lounge. On the doorstep he looked back at me for a moment and motioned with his head: *Follow me.*

So I followed. The captain strode directly up to Major Adika, presented his badge for scanning, and held his arms away from his side. Again I noted the contrast: the major was coiled energy, watching for trouble and ready to spring, while the captain was casual. Yet the captain was every bit as confident, and his eyes swept the room in the same fashion.

I noticed the major's aide subtly scanning for weapons as the major rescanned my badge. When the aide nodded, Major Adika let us approach the table. Again all the chairs were occupied by hangers-on; but Captain Aames cleared his throat and stared down at them, and they couldn't meet his stare. They quickly slipped away, and the captain sat down across from Anthony. I joined them, caught uncomfortably between two men I had already angered once that day. I could feel my anxiety mounting, and with it my temper.

Then a subtle movement caught my attention: Major Adika moved to stand near the table, just outside the circle of conversation but close by if there was any trouble. He stood poised in the low gravity, as if ready to spring, but with his arms lightly crossed in front of himself. He caught my eye and gave me a barely noticeable smile; and just like that, my anxiety blew away on the wind.

The table now held the remnants of a plate of nachos and soy cheese. Damp streaks showed it had been wiped clean at least once, indicating one or more spilled drinks. Anthony had had a few more drinks since I had left, and he was showing the signs. His body mass let him absorb a fair amount of alcohol, but his head was weaving, and his hands were unsteady. He looked at Captain Aames, startled as if he hadn't noticed our arrival. "Nick! Hey, how's things on the bridge, Cap? Chuks, we need more drinks here."

Major Adika didn't move, and Anthony didn't notice. He didn't have time: Captain Aames took control of the conversation. "Mr. Holmes, I understand there was an unfortunate incident between you and Dr. Baldwin earlier."

Then Anthony finally noticed me. "Oh, hey, Doc. No hard feelings, right? Get the Doc a drink, somebody. Look, Nick, it's no big deal." Anthony had a drink in his right hand and waved it around, gesturing with it as if making a point. "The doc just got a little, you know, hot. She's used to ordering patients around, and I don't take orders."

"I understand, Mr. Holmes. The doctor just didn't realize how strongly you hold to your NoNan views."

I began to get annoyed all over again. What happened to Nick Aames, the Terror of the Spaceways? Here he was, coddling the boss's son just like all the other ass-kissers. Aames could learn a thing or two from Major Adika.

And Anthony was lapping it up. "That's right, NoNan!" He raised his voice and stood. "NoNan, everybody. Say it with me. No! Nanos!" And just as he commanded, many civilians in the crowd joined in as Anthony stood. "No! Nanos! No! Nanos! NONAN!" Anthony waved his drink around, spilling it, and I barely dodged the alcohol.

The room broke out in scattered applause, and Anthony bowed and sat. As the applause died down, he waved his now empty glass at the captain. "No nanos, Nick. I'm keeping my body pure. And that's final."

The captain nodded and spoke calmly. "I understand. Dr. Baldwin has explained the risks if you decline therapeutic nanos?" I tried to answer, but the captain held up a hand. "Let him answer, please, Doctor. For the record."

Anthony stared into space. "She didn't, but that nurse guy, Floyd—"

"Carl Lloyd," the captain corrected.

"Yeah, Lloyd. He read off all the risks, all the usual nano company lies. I've heard them all before."

"So you were informed of the risks, and you're declining treatment. For the record," the captain repeated.

"Yes, and yes."

"So noted." The captain tapped a button on his comm, and Holmes's statement was recorded. *That was it? That would get me and him off the hook legally, but it wouldn't do a thing about the risks.*

But the captain wasn't done. "And now I think an apology is in order."

My jaw dropped. *No!* I couldn't swallow that much pride. No way would I apologize to that young punk, even if it meant my job.

Before I could object, Anthony blinked twice, and then responded. "It's all right, Nick. The Doc meant well. She doesn't have to apologize. We're good, right, Doc?"

I was ready to shout that we were not at all good; but before I could, Captain Aames raised his voice and said, "You've made a mistake, Mr. Holmes." He looked down at his comm. "It's you who are going to apologize to Dr. Baldwin for manhandling her, a professional and one of *my* officers. You're also going to apologize for your slanderous accusations."

"What?" Anthony leaned over the table. "You forget who you're talking to. You're outta line, Nick."

And before anyone knew what was happening, the captain reached out and swiftly slapped Anthony across the face. "That's *Captain Aames* to you, kid."

Everything happened at once. The room grew silent at the slap, so everyone heard the captain. The guards moved toward our table; but Major Adika held up one hand, and they stepped back. I noticed a very slight grin on the major's face.

Anthony rubbed his jaw. "What— Nick—" The captain raised his hand again, so Anthony corrected himself. "What do you think you're doing, Captain? Who do you think is in charge here?"

The captain checked his comm again, and then he pushed a file to the major's comm. "As of two minutes ago, *I* am. We just passed Earth's gravipause."

Anthony tried to focus. "Earth's what?"

"If you actually *belonged* in space, you would know that the gravipause is that point where the sun's gravitational pull exceeds Earth and Luna's combined gravity."

Anthony acted like he understood, but I doubted anything had penetrated all that alcohol. "That's interesting. But it's still no excuse to be insolent."

"You damn bet it's an excuse. According to my contract with your father's corporation, once the sun's pull takes over, I have plenary power here. I can do whatever I, *in my sole judgment*, decide is necessary for the safety of my passengers and crew and for the safe completion of our mission. I can dispense orders, regulations, and discipline as I see fit."

Major Adika nodded. "He's correct, Mr. Holmes. This contract is very clear. He can't have you flogged or keelhauled, he can't violate your fundamental rights, but he has practically the powers of an old British sea captain when it comes to the smooth operation of this ship."

Captain Aames glared at Anthony. "And smooth operation requires proper respect for my officers and crew while in performance of their duties. You will apologize to Dr. Baldwin. Now."

Anthony scowled. "I will not."

As quick as before, Captain Aames reached out and slapped Anthony again. Then he lowered his voice so that only the three of us could hear. "If you make me slap you again, kid, I'll pull your pants down to do it in front of all your adoring fans. Now, apologize to the doctor. Make sure everybody hears it." Then he sat back and waited.

Martin L. Shoemaker

Anthony stared, a mix of emotions struggling across his face: defiance, fear, anger, and shock. I might've felt sorry for him if he hadn't angered me in the first place. Finally he leaned back in his chair, looked around the room, and raised his voice. "I am sorry, Dr. Baldwin. It was disrespectful to accuse you of taking money from the nano companies. And I was wrong to grab you like I did. That was no way to treat an officer of this ship." He paused, looking down at his empty glass. Then, even louder, he added, "What are you all looking at? This is supposed to be a party. Bartender, a round for the house."

The noise picked back up again, though it sounded a bit forced. Under the rattle of glasses and the buzz of conversation, Anthony added, "Happy now, *Captain* Aames?"

The captain ignored the scorn, but he laughed haltingly. "Kid, your entire fortune couldn't make me *happy*. But for now, I'm satisfied with your apology."

Anthony was surly, and he didn't try to hide it. "I suppose now you're going to force me to take therapy nanos."

Captain Aames shook his head. "No, that would be a clear violation of your fundamental rights. I can't force you to accept invasive therapy against your will. But I can take other measures for your own protection. Dr. Baldwin?"

I sat up straighter. "Yes, Captain."

"Doctor, what was the preventive therapy for musculoskeletal loss and incidental radiation exposure *before* we perfected therapy nanos?"

"Captain, it involved tripling the recommended exercise regimen. That provides sufficient muscle growth and bone development to counter the losses. And a good, healthy, active metabolism can repair most low-level radiation damage. Assuming he stays healthy otherwise."

"I see. And has the kid even started the standard regimen?"

I checked Anthony's chart. "Not yet, Captain. Of course, it's still early in the day."

"Nonsense, Doctor. Never too early for exercise." The captain stood. "On your feet, kid!"

"Fuck off." Anthony tapped his comm, but then he looked puzzled. He stabbed with his finger, but still nothing happened. "Hey! Why can't I call Dad?"

The captain replied, "I cut off your outbound communications."

"You can't do that! You can't violate my rights."

"I can't *violate* them; but in the interests of ship operations, I can regulate and restrict them. We only have so much communications bandwidth, so I have to meter it. You will get *one* fifteen-minute call, once per day. Your slot is *after* your workout. Now *on your feet.*" And with that, Captain Aames reached down, grabbed that expensive blue shirt, twisted it into a knot, and easily lifted Anthony in the low gravity. He set the young man down on his feet, looked him over, and sneered. "Drunk. Flabby. Out of shape. We'll have to do something about that. Kid, the running track is one ring up, but you can start running *now.* Get up there and give me some laps."

Anthony looked indignant. "I'll be your boss someday."

"Only if I can keep you alive that long. Now move!" The captain raised his hand again, and Anthony flinched. Then he stumbled through the crowd. Major Adika moved ahead of him, clearing a path, and Anthony ran to the door.

"That's a start," the captain called after him. "But faster!" He turned to me. "Doctor, shouldn't you be supervising his therapy?"

"Yes, Captain." I didn't see why I needed to watch the kid run, but I wasn't ready to cross Captain Aames. I got up and headed to the door just in time to see Anthony bolt antispinward, toward his cabin; but the major grabbed his arm, spun him around, and shoved him spinward toward the ramp to the upper ring. Adika grinned as they passed me.

I started jogging as well, using the long, loping low-gravity stride we had learned in lunar training. I had gone only a few meters when a bit of gray appeared in my peripheral vision. Turning my head slightly, I saw Captain Aames jogging beside me. "Best you can do?" he asked.

And then he pulled ahead of me, rushing to pass the major and catch Anthony. He prodded the kid all the way up the ramp and onto the big running track. The track was a third of a kilometer, completely circling the upper ring. When I reached the top of the ramp, I saw Anthony stumble up ahead, and the captain catch him, then coax and prod him, demonstrating the low-G lope. Anthony struggled with the stride, but Captain Aames got him moving.

I was still adjusting to the lope myself, so I lost sight of them; but I could see Major Adika, so I rushed to catch up with him. Then as my stride adjusted, we both picked up speed until we were up with the captain and the kid. The captain had thrown off his uniform jacket somewhere, and his shirt showed sweat stains. I decided that was smart, so I threw off mine as well.

The captain set a reasonable pace, especially in one-quarter G, but Anthony soon showed signs of fatigue. That only made Captain Aames more persistent. "Slacker! Are you *that* soft, kid?" He cajoled and taunted to keep Anthony moving.

Sometimes the captain moved ahead and loped backward, keeping right in the kid's face as he tossed out casual insults. "Your problem is you can't pay someone to run for you. Do you ever do *anything* on your own?" *That* spurred the kid onward, though he didn't have breath to respond.

After fifteen laps, I slowed down. I was in okay shape, but I didn't run much. The major dropped back with me, though I'm sure that was just courtesy: he didn't show any signs of strain. Anthony attempted to slow down as well, but the captain pushed him even harder. Soon they were out of sight again, and I enjoyed my leisurely run with Adika.

Not long after that, the captain and Anthony passed us. A little later, they passed us again, moving faster this time. The kid was looking pale, and I raised my hand for the captain's attention, but he pointedly ignored me. It gave me some comfort to see that the captain's shirt was drenched with sweat. He wasn't a machine after all.

Halfway around the ring, we had to dodge around a mess on the track. I smelled stomach acid, and I saw bits of undigested soy cheese in the puddle.

The next time around, the captain and Anthony had finally stopped. Aames stood and supervised as Anthony, shirtless, sopped up the vomit with an expensive blue silk rag. The captain called, "Halt!" and Adika and I came to a stop. Anthony looked up from his work, panting, and glared at Aames. The captain returned the glare and then turned to me. "Doctor."

I recognized the command in his tone, so I dropped to my knees, grabbed Anthony's wrist, and felt for a pulse: 180, high but not danger- ously so for his age and health. His respiration was labored, but already it was slowing. I leaned my ear to his chest. His heart sounded busy, but good. I didn't have my bag, so I couldn't check BP or electrolyte balance, hardly any of my routine checks; but I had enough data to give a preliminary answer. "He's fine, Captain. He'll feel it tomorrow, but he's fine."

"You bet he'll feel it." The captain paused for breath. "Major Adika?"

The major snapped to attention, his broad chest rising and falling steadily in that damp ochre shirt. "Yes, Captain."

"Major, this has been fun, but I can't spare this much time day after day, even for the health of the kid. He needs three runs per day, Doctor?" I nodded. "Since he's such an *important* kid, I can take time to run with him third watch every day. Major, can you handle first watch?"

Major Adika nodded. "Yes, Captain."

The captain turned back to me. "Doctor, this is therapy, so we need medical supervision. I need you to take the second watch."

"Yes, Captain. I'll need to trade watches with Dr. Santana."

"Don't bother me with details, Doctor, just do your job." He held down a hand to Anthony, but the kid ignored it. The captain snapped his fingers twice, and finally Anthony got the message. He took the hand, and the captain pulled him to his feet. "So, kid, that'll be your routine from here to Mars: a half-hour run, once each watch. Except fourth watch, we'll let you sleep through that one. You'll need it. Doctor, should that be a sufficient substitute for therapy nanos?"

I smiled and nodded. "It should, Captain."

Again looking at Anthony, the captain continued, "Three top officers watching out for your health. That's how important you are. Does that sound good, kid? Or would you like to get those injections now?"

Anthony couldn't stand straight, but he lifted his head enough to glare at the captain. "No, *Captain*." And without another word, he staggered down the ramp to the middle deck. Major Adika ambled after him. Aside from the sweaty shirt, you might never have known that the major had worked out.

I waited until they were out of sight down the ramp, and then I spoke up. "Captain, you know he's going to call his father immediately."

The captain turned and stared at me. "Did I ask for observations, Doctor?"

"No, Captain."

"Good!" My eyes widened. I had expected recrimination, not praise. "Don't look so shocked, Doctor. I expect you to bring things to my attention when you think they're important. You can expect me to chew you out when I think you're wasting my time. And I expect you to push back because you know you're right. I expect you to fight me until we know what the facts are. I don't need a bunch of yes-men for officers. I need the whistleblower who gave up her career because she knew she was right. That's who I hired; is that who I got?"

"Yes, Captain."

"That sounds rather timid to me, Doctor. Are you ready to fight me when I'm wrong?"

"YES, CAPTAIN!"

"That's better." The captain nodded, and his tone softened. "You're right, Doctor, he'll call Anton Holmes. Not immediately, he's too exhausted. But eventually. And then Anton will call me. And then, I don't think the kid will like the outcome."

"Understood, Captain. But might I ask one favor?"

"Spit it out, Doctor."

"Captain, I would dearly like to listen in on that call from Anton Holmes."

Again his tone softened, and he sounded amused. "Doctor, it would be my pleasure. Besides, I may need the kid's physician to back me up."

☾

When the time came, I wasn't the only one waiting for the call. Major Adika joined us. The captain's office was decorated in tasteful dark shades: black walls, big black desk with a touch-display surface, dark-gray carpet, and brushed metal accents. The navy-blue chair provided a spot of color that drew attention to its occupant. It was such a relief from the ochre throughout the ship, I felt the urge to hide there through my entire tour. But that would've meant hiding out with Captain Aames; despite our new détente, I wasn't ready for that. He still struck me as volatile and demanding, and I didn't need that kind of stress all day long. I didn't know how Chief Carver could handle it.

Behind the captain, a massive window showed Earth and Luna slowly spinning past, over six light-seconds away. I stared at the dwindling planets, and I thought about escape: all my past mistakes, all the wreckage that had been my career, it was all just a microscopic point on that little blue dot in the distance. I might make all new mistakes here on the *Aldrin*, but this really was a second chance for me. I was determined to make this work.

My thoughts were interrupted by a chime from the desk. A beat-up old e-reader sat in the middle of the desk. Captain Aames slid it to the side, and then he waved us to stand behind him. He tapped the desk's surface, and a woman's face appeared in a window in the center of the glass. She said, "Incoming call from Anton Holmes, Captain."

Aames nodded at the desk. "Put him through, Miles." The woman's window moved aside, and another window appeared, showing an older man who was recognizably a relative of Anthony Holmes. The hair was the same dark blond, but short and bushy and with many gray bristles. The face was thinner, harder, and more serious; but the bone structure was the same, and he had the same intense blue eyes. Those eyes were narrowed at the screen, though he probably couldn't see us yet.

"Mr. Anton Holmes," Miles said, "Captain Aames can speak to you now. Please remember that the light-speed delay is six seconds one way, twelve seconds round trip. Mr. Holmes, please begin." Experienced interplanetary hands can speak in parallel, each person making points while listening to older points as they arrive; but for most people, it was simpler to wait for each statement, and for one party to control the discussion until passing control to the other. Miles had just given Anton Holmes control, so we had a twelve-second wait for him to begin.

The woman disappeared, replaced with the view from the captain's camera, a narrow focus that showed only him, not the major and me. After a pause, Holmes spoke. "So, Nick, I understand you had a problem with my son."

The captain responded. "Your son was drunk before we reached the gravipause. He grabbed my doctor. He's lucky she didn't belt him. She has a history, you know." He looked up at me, eyebrows raised as if daring me to protest.

Twelve seconds later, Holmes rolled his eyes. "I think you're making a big deal out of nothing. Can't we just start over, pretend this never happened?"

Aames nodded. "We can start over . . . with a new captain, and with you fulfilling the cancellation clause in our contract. That would be five years' salary, payable immediately, plus a commission on each trip for that period. Would you like to invoke that clause?" He paused, but not long enough for Holmes to take control. "But wait. There's no qualified captain aboard, and we can't turn back now. That would be a mess, wouldn't it?"

Twelve seconds later, Holmes was exasperated. "You can't be serious. You would quit over such a small matter as this?"

"No, but unless you fire me, I'm going to run this ship my way. You can remove me, but you can't second-guess me. Either I'm in charge here, or you are. But I won't be your figurehead. And it's *not* a small matter. Do you still insist on sending Anthony to Mars?"

"Damn straight I do. This is a *Holmes* mission to Mars, and there's going to be a Holmes leading it."

The captain sighed. "You forget, Anton, I've been to Mars. I know Mars. He's not ready to go there, and he's damn sure not ready to lead any mission."

"Oh, I know that." Holmes leaned into the camera and lowered his voice. "It's just symbolic for the media, and a notch for his résumé. He won't do anything but give speeches. It'll just be a quick down-and-back on a fast drop shuttle as you approach. The shuttle will bring him back before you pass. It will be purely ceremonial. Adika will keep an eye on him the whole way, and there won't be time for him to get into trouble. I may be too busy to go myself, but by damn, there's going to be Holmes footprints on Mars. That will be worth a lot of points on the stock market, and also in boardroom battles."

"I still think it's a stupid idea, but it's out of my hands once we reach the Mars gravipause. My only responsibility is to get him there safe and healthy. That's not going to happen if he suffers bone and muscle loss and radiation symptoms. Since he's being a stubborn ass about his therapy nanos, hyperexercise is what my doctor prescribes. Isn't that right, Doctor?" And he widened the frame to show me and the major standing behind him.

"Yes, Captain," I answered. "This is the recommended non-nano therapy for a space traveler of his age and health."

Aames turned to the major. "And is young Mr. Holmes in any physical danger?"

Adika shook his head. "Mr. Holmes, I agree with Captain Aames: your son has no business on Mars, and our security team will be very busy keeping him alive. But here on the *Aldrin* with this exercise program, he is perfectly safe."

Aames continued, "So in the best expert opinion on-site, this is in Anthony's own best interests. May I proceed? Or should I clean out my office?"

In the twelve seconds it took to respond, Holmes's glare intensified as he listened. Finally, he sighed, but he had a look of determination. Billionaires are accustomed to doing things their way. "All right, I'll talk to him. Are you satisfied, *Captain?*"

Aames smiled at the camera, but it wasn't a warm smile. It was awkward, like he wasn't used to smiling. In a way it looked almost predatory. "Quite satisfied, *boss.* Now is there anything else? Or can I go back to running my ship?"

"No, nothing else. Get to it." And just like that, the image cut out.

"He's a busy man," the captain said, swiveling his chair to face the major and me. "That conversation probably cost fifty-thousand dollars of his time, plus bandwidth charges. We should feel privileged. Do you feel privileged?" Before we could answer, he continued, "So, Doctor, Major, we proceed according to plan." Then Aames grinned at the major, showing real warmth for the first time that I had seen. "Just like Luna, eh, Chuks?"

Major Adika grinned back. "Just like Luna, Nick, except this time we are on the other end of the stick. I believe Sergeant Fontes would laugh to see us now."

"No, thank you," the captain answered, "I heard enough of his laughter in Lunar Survival School." For a moment he stared out the window, back at Earth and Luna. Then he turned back to his desk. "Let's hope our 'recruit' is no more difficult than we were, eh?"

Adika shook his head. "He is not difficult, but he will never be ready for a dangerous place like Mars."

The captain nodded. "That's why he has you watching over him. He couldn't be safer. But enough of this. I have work to do, and so do both of you. If you don't, I'll find some. Get out of here."

So we left his office, returning to the world of awful ochre in Carver's office, the gateway to the captain's sanctuary. Chief Carver was on the bridge, so we were alone; but I waited until we were safely out of Carver's outer office and in the passageway before I turned to Major Adika. "You said only friends call you Chuks. I take it you know Captain Aames?"

Major Adika smiled again. I could get used to that smile. "Doctor, we have a saying: 'Space is vast, but the Space Corps is not.' If you stay in the Corps long enough, you will be amazed at how many people you will meet. You could not possibly remember them all. But one does not forget Nick Aames. Though many would like to." And he laughed.

I could get used to that too.

The next day, when it was time for my run with Anthony, I tracked him down in the lounge again. I expected the bodyguards to let me pass, since they had already screened me twice the day before, but they were more professional than that. They were cordial and courteous—the major even gave me one of those big smiles—but they scanned me as thoroughly as they had the first time. Then they let me through.

Anthony was sitting at the same table, but alone this time. A few passengers waved at him as they passed by, but none sat down. As they walked past me, I heard muted giggles and comments under their breath, including the word "brat."

I sat down at the table. Anthony stared down at a glass of what looked like tomato juice. Without asking, I picked it up. "Hey!" he objected, reaching for the glass.

But I pulled the glass away. "Doctor's orders. I need to know what you're drinking." I took a sip. It *was* tomato juice, reconstituted, without any hint of vodka. I set the glass back down. "Good choice."

Anthony took the glass and stared into it again, slumping in his chair. I sat down next to him, took his wrist, and started checking his vitals. He was silent and sullen as I worked. He had some pallor, nothing bad, but he looked like he had been kicked around. I guess he had, in a way. Despite myself, I started to feel almost sorry for him. Sorry enough to fudge the truth a bit. "It seems your pulse is a little erratic, Mr. Holmes. I'll sign a doctor's slip excusing you from this afternoon's run, if you'd like."

Anthony shook his head. "No." And then I saw something of his father in him, the same steel behind the blue eyes. He drank the rest of the tomato juice, set down his glass, and rose. "Let's go." He led the way to the upper ring, and a guard trailed us, taking a position at the top of the ramp. We started running; and as we ran, I saw another guard at the top of each of the four ramps. We had the ring to ourselves.

Anthony took off at a very fast pace, much too fast to maintain for a half hour even in our gravity. I rushed to catch up with him; but when I did, he put on more speed. I had to run all out to catch him again.

Anthony kept going as fast as he could for as long as he could, barreling forward as if Captain Aames were still chasing him—or something worse. I could see he was getting tired and sloppy, and I worried he might hurt himself.

Eventually he slowed down. I was relieved, because I couldn't keep up that pace much longer. But though he slowed, he remained at a running pace, not a jog. Whatever reserves he had wouldn't last long.

When I saw Anthony's face getting red, I called out, "Enough." And I halted, but he kept going. "Stop!" I shouted. This time he stopped, and I walked forward to check him over, a guard running up as I did. The guard, a tall Asian woman, paid no attention to me. Like me, she was worried about Anthony.

His heart rate, respiration, and temperature were all dangerously high. "That's enough, Mr. Holmes. Don't make me get rough. You've got to pace yourself, or you're going to make yourself ill, maybe injure yourself."

Anthony leaned against a wall, head resting on his arms. The guard put a hand on his shoulder, but he shook it off. "Leave me alone," he panted. "I can do this."

"You can't do anything if you keep this up. Don't argue with your doctor."

But Anthony shook his head. "He thinks . . . I can't do this."

"Captain Aames?" I looked around as if the captain might be listening. "That man's a closed one, Mr. Holmes. Don't assume you know what he's thinking. He's manipulative, and that might be exactly what he wants. If you try to outthink him, you'll only hurt your head."

"Not Aames."

"What, those people in the lounge? Is that what they were laughing about?"

Anthony glared at me. "Laughing. Billionaire's son getting what's coming to him." His breathing was becoming more regular. "Phonies. But not the first. Always want something from me, but I see through them."

"Then why do you care what they think?"

Anthony straightened and snarled. "Not them, my dad! He thinks I can't do this. He thinks I don't have to." His breathing was even, but now he hesitated for a different reason, choking back his emotions. "He thinks Aames is just punishing me for grabbing you." He swallowed. "Doctor, I'm so sorry. I was drunk, and I was completely out of line. It won't happen again."

"Damn straight it won't, next time I'll punch you for sure." But I smiled as I said it. "We can pretend it never happened, Mr. Holmes, if that will help with your father."

"Please, call me Anthony. When people call me Mr. Holmes, it usually means they want something."

"All right, Anthony. Call me—"

Anthony held up a hand. "I'll call you Doctor. The captain wants me to respect his officers." He tried to smile, but it faded, and he shook his head again. "But it won't help with Dad; he just wants this over. He thinks I should just put up a show for a while, and Aames will get bored. He says not even a week, just a few days. He says, 'Put in a minimum for a few days, satisfy Aames. Even you can do that.' *Even you.*"

I turned away, and so did the guard. It looked like Anthony was about to cry, and we didn't want to make things worse for him. Looking toward the wall, I replied, "Anthony, you *can't* do this if you keep pushing this hard. You're on the edge of exhaustion. But you can, you *will* do this if you just build up. At your age and in your condition, you can keep this up all day, once you work up to it. But if you go trying to prove something to your dad, you're going to prove him right. If you want to prove him wrong, you're going to have to work smarter. Can you do that?"

"Yes, Doctor."

He sounded more in control, so I turned back to him. "We'll finish this half hour, walking. You've already overexerted yourself this watch. Then I'll set up a pace schedule for you, building up gradually as you go; and you will stick to that pace no matter who tries to push you harder. Tell them it's doctor's orders. Understood?"

Anthony managed to smile at that. "Even Captain Aames?"

"You let me handle Captain Aames. Just concentrate on your work-out plan, and you'll show him. And your dad."

"Yes, Doctor." And we started walking. And talking. And despite myself, I found myself coming to like him. Anthony drunk was obnoxious, but Anthony sober was a pretty nice kid.

Not that I would call Anthony a kid to his face, not like the captain did. I could see his pride was mostly a defense, and it could be easily battered. But he *was* a kid. Not chronologically—I had known twenty-year-old soldiers and EMTs and astronauts who were by no means kids—but in terms of experience. Poor Anthony at twenty had never had to do anything, not anything hard. Oh, he had been places, symbolic trips to half the world. He had been on aid missions as a front man for the Holmes Trust, and he had done symbolic spadework for the cameras; but it was never real, never anything he *had to* do because the job had to be done and he was the only one to do it. It was all just tourism masquerading as effort. And this Mars expedition was more of the same: Anton wanted to "expose" him to the world, but Anthony never even had to finish a job. As soon as the media attention drifted, Anton would whisk him back home while other people did the hard work. This one little thing, this ninety minutes of running every day, may have been the most sustained effort Anthony had ever put forth.

☾

I had just dropped off to sleep that night when my comm chimed. I lay in bed, eyes closed, and called out, "Comm, answer. This is Dr. Baldwin, is anything wrong?"

Captain Aames's voice came through the comm, and my eyes snapped open in the darkness. "Baldwin, what the hell's up with changing my orders for Anthony Holmes?"

I was glad my comm camera was off so the captain couldn't see my face. "I changed *my* orders, Captain, because in *my* judgment he can't handle the way he was pushing himself. He's out of shape; he needs to work up to that pace. Otherwise he'll break down before he ever gets to Mars."

"Good. If that keeps him off Mars, that's better for everyone."

"What? I thought you were doing this to get him ready for Mars."

"Doctor, I'm not interested in getting him ready. I just want to test him and find his limits. And if those limits keep him off Mars, so be it. Let me test him."

"Captain, he can do this. Give him a chance."

"You can give him a chance if you want, Doctor. Not my concern."

"But his health is my concern. This little game of yours isn't. My order stands. Comm off."

I pulled my covers over my head. It took nearly an hour for me to calm down enough to fall asleep.

C

Monitoring Anthony's progress was most of how I passed my time at first. Our work in the infirmary was light: periodic screenings, treatment of minor injuries, monitoring of health and nutrition, and lots of paperwork to send back to Earth. We were staffed to cover unexpected emergencies, which meant we had plenty of time to cover normal operations.

We were a week out from the gravipause when I came into the infirmary and found Dr. Santana with a patient: Major Adika. The major sat on an exam table, shirtless, as Santana ran a scanner over his shoulder. I couldn't help staring: Adika's muscles were even more impressive without the shirt; but more impressive yet were the scars.

Then I noticed the major smiling at me, and I realized that I was staring. "Excuse me, I have work to do." My face felt warm as I ducked into my office.

I found myself reading the same page of the same routine report for the third time and still not noticing what I read, when Dr. Santana came into my office. There was an odd smile on his face. "Dr. Baldwin, I think you should see this patient."

"What? Push me his chart. Is there something wrong?"

Santana's smile grew. "No, Doctor. I think *you* should see *him*. He asked for you. Personally."

I flushed again. "Oh. Thank you." I stood, felt my hair to see if it was out of place, and walked back into the infirmary.

Major Adika still sat on the exam table, still shirtless. I fought to keep my eyes on his face so as not to get flustered. "So, Major, what's the problem today?"

Then he smiled, and I got flustered despite my plan. "I think I have pulled a muscle in my shoulder."

Those muscles? I can't believe that. But I resisted saying that out loud. "How did this happen?"

"Oh, it was a foolish thing. I was sparring with the captain in the gymnasium, and he got the better of me with one of his capoeira moves. He sent me tumbling, and I grabbed a grip to stop myself; but I failed to account for the ship's spin, and I felt a pull. Or possibly a tear."

"I see. Well, Dr. Santana has already examined you, but let me take a look." I pulled out my scanner and ran it over his shoulder. As I did, I got a close-up look at those scars. One ran from his right clavicle almost to his spleen. Another crossed his left bicep like a tattoo. There were smaller scars all over his torso, including one circular red tear in his right deltoid that I was sure was from a bullet. "This isn't your first injury by any means, Major. You've lived a dangerous life."

"Mine is a dangerous profession, Doctor."

"Are there a lot of attacks on Mr. Holmes?"

"No, but I have been a bodyguard for only a few years. Before that, I was in Initiative Security, Rapid Response Team. This job is a vacation after that."

"Uh-huh." I lowered the scanner. "Well, Major, you're correct: it's a muscle pull, nothing torn. I prescribe a few sessions of massage and some analgesic cream." I looked back to his face. "But I'm not sure why Dr. Santana couldn't have prescribed that."

Adika put his shirt back on, and the big grin came back. "But then I would be asking Dr. Santana if he is free for dinner tonight, not you. He is a very nice gentleman, but I would prefer your company, Doctor."

Again my face felt warm, but I kept my voice steady as I answered, "I would like that, Major."

"Please, call me Chuks."

☾

After that, Chuks and I spent a lot of time together, as our duties allowed. I learned to appreciate his quiet humor, his enthusiasm for space, his dedication to duty, and his gentle strength. He was a good man, and comfortable to be with. He was proud of his homeland, Nigeria, and proud of his warrior heritage. Although he was powerful and skilled and capable of great violence, he saw restraint as the mark of the true warrior: violence was a tool he used to protect the weak and defend what he believed in, not an end in itself and not something that drove him. Knowing how hard it was to restrain my own temper sometimes, I was impressed with how well he had mastered his own. He could be passionate in his mission, but he was always in control.

I learned that incredible body of his, including that roadmap of scars that hinted at the violence in his past. These fascinated me from a clinical perspective: How had he suffered that cut in that spot? How had he survived a deep trauma like the long scar across his chest? Who had shot him in the back, and why? But he refused to talk about these past missions, preferring to leave his past buried. The only scar he commented on was on his calf: a nearly perfect impression of human teeth, both upper and lower jaws. When I asked about that, he laughed and said, "It was a performance review that got out of hand." But when I asked for details, he refused to say more.

But I didn't mind. I had secrets—I never explained how I had landed on the *Aldrin*—so I could hardly fault him for his own. These secrets only intrigued me more. The only real disagreement we had regarded Anthony: I was getting to like the kid and see potential in him; but Chuks kept cautioning me. "His enthusiasm never lasts, Constance." Normally, "Constance" bothered me. It was such a formal name, and it didn't feel right to me. I was just Connie. But when Chuks said it, he imbued the name with a softness, a quality that made me feel special.

We sat in an observation room, curled together on a couch, staring out at the stars as they spun by. "You've known him longer, Chuks, but I just see something there. I think he's changing." I didn't tell Chuks about my conversation with Anthony and his determination to show his dad he could do this. That was private, not my secret to share. But after that, I believed in Anthony, and I wanted to support him. "And I don't think Captain Aames would push him like this if he didn't believe Anthony could do it."

Chuks shook his head. "You do not understand Nick Aames yet, Constance. He tests people, tests them to the breaking point. If they pass the test, he raises the bar. If they break, then he is satisfied because he knows their limits."

I looked into his eyes. "I thought the captain was your friend."

"He is. But it is difficult being Nick's friend. He tests his friends too. It is just what he does."

"Some friend." I frowned. "Well, maybe he doesn't believe in Anthony, but I do."

Chuks wrapped his arms tighter around me. "You are a good woman, Constance. Despite your temper." I glared at him; but then he smiled, and I did too. "I just don't want you to be hurt when Mr. Holmes returns to form."

Over the next few weeks of running, my faith in Anthony grew as he shaped up well. Thanks to the exercise and a carefully selected diet, he quickly dropped his excess weight, and that made the running easier. Soon I was able to lift my limits and let him set his own pace. I was glad that *I* was getting a good workout too: it was the only way I could keep up with him.

As his body shaped up, so did his mood, and not just because he had more stamina. The passengers who had laughed at him soon forgot his embarrassment, but they didn't forget his power and influence. They began trying to curry favor again; but with his new confidence, Anthony also became more discerning. He was quick to cut out the obvious toadies and focus on the ones who were willing to treat him as just one of the crowd. And one way he selected his companions was by inviting them to run with him. The sycophants soon gave up on that, while those who stuck with it grew closer as they challenged each other to faster paces and longer runs. It wasn't long before I gave up on keeping up and concentrated on my own pace. Soon we had six regulars who joined us each day, four scientists and two bodyguards. We ran for a full hour, followed by dinner in the lounge; and they were *friends* to Anthony, perhaps the first true friends he had ever had.

And sometimes we had another companion: at least once a week, Captain Aames joined us even though it wasn't his watch to run. Then I *completely* gave up on the race, and I just hung back and watched. The captain still pushed and still taunted, but Anthony found it easier and easier to keep up. The captain still won every race, but their times got faster every week.

On the days when the captain joined us, he also dined with us, and he even put dinner on his tab. I won't say he let his hair down, but he showed a shrewd appreciation for morale and unit cohesion. He sat with us, inquired as to experiments and preparations, and listened to jokes and stories. He programmed the lounge's music system with his own eclectic mix of classic waltzes and Brazilian lounge songs. And every week at some point, he stood and said, "Ladies and gentlemen, ship's duties call, and I must go. Let the real party begin." He would leave then, usually with a plate of pão de queijo; and after that, just as he said, the celebration started and the drinks were ordered. But Anthony never again drank like he had that first day, and he would stop if I commented, or even just gave him an odd glance. He was determined not to lose control again.

In the tenth week of racing, however, Captain Aames broke the routine. He stayed at the table long past his usual departure, and he signaled the waiter for a round of drinks. Anthony ordered his usual, the house beer, and slowly sipped it. The captain watched him, not judging, just watching. Finally he asked, "So, kid, are you ready for those therapy nanos yet?"

Anthony almost spewed his beer. The captain had sucker-punched him there. Then he took a long drink. I suspected that was to give Anthony time to think of his answer. Finally he set down the half-empty glass. "No, Captain. I'm still not interested. I think Dr. Baldwin is doing a fine job of keeping me healthy *without* polluting my body with unnatural machines."

The captain almost smiled at that. "Unnatural machines. Ah, yes . . . Doctor, I completely forgot we had an expert on nanomachines here."

Anthony tightened his grip on his glass, but he kept control. "Not an expert, Captain. I've just done my research."

"Yes, yes, your research. I forgot. Don't be so modest, kid, it sounds like expertise to me. So tell me: What is the activation frequency of a salt-ion scavenger nano?"

Anthony hesitated a second. "I'm not sure, Captain. The . . . sound frequency—"

"*Light* frequency, kid," the captain interrupted. "Modern nanos are generally activated by specific spectral signatures. Try this one: What's the orbital period of Phobos?"

"Oh, I know this one!" Anthony was so eager to answer, he ignored the fact that this wasn't a nanotechnology question. "Approximately 7.7 hours."

"Approximately will get you dead in space, kid. Okay, back to nanos: How many generations of sintering nanos can you get out of a typical batch before they start to degrade?"

"I don't know, Captain. We have specialists on the mission to deal with that sort of issue."

"Specialists, yes." The captain nodded. "And what is your specialty, kid?" He let the question hang in the air for almost three seconds before turning to the rest of the runners. "Oh, that's unimportant right now. We have all of these experts with us. Isn't it fantastic that we have all these experts on this mission, Doctor? Savoy, what's your specialty?"

Laurence Savoy, a tall, shy Frenchman with dark, curly hair, blinked. He wasn't used to the captain's attention. Finally he stammered, "Atmospheric chemistry, Captain."

Aames nodded. "And you, Meadors?"

Minnie Meadors, a tall blonde from Boston, was quicker with her answer: "Astronomy, Captain. Seven hours, thirty-nine minutes, fourteen seconds."

"What? Oh yes, Phobos. You must love the viewing from here."

"It's phenomenal, sir. A dream come true."

"Enjoy it, Meadors. It only gets better as we approach Mars. This is a chance most astronomers will never get. And you, Krause?"

Katherine Krause, a short, sturdy German woman, replied eagerly, "Geology, Captain. I'm counting the days to my first field survey."

"I look forward to your reports. And Martinez?"

Jerry Martinez, a medium-height, muscular Hispanic male, answered with a big smile, "Software engineering, Captain." He pointed a finger around the table. "As soon as we land, they're all going to think up new requirements for their systems, things they never thought of before. Somebody has to reprogram all their gear to meet those new requirements."

"Excellent. You should talk to Chief Carver. He pulled out some software wizardry on our previous Mars mission." He paused. "Of course, a big factor in our survival was cross-training. Did I tell you about that, Doctor?"

I wondered where Aames was going with this, but I played along. "No, you didn't, Captain."

The captain nodded. "We lost some good personnel, but we had the essentials covered, thanks to cross-training. Say, does your mission have a cross-training plan?"

Meadors shook her head. "No, Captain, but that's an excellent idea. I'll bring it up with the mission planners."

Aames shook his head. "Don't bother. I already suggested it, fourteen months ago, but they rejected it. They said that was 'Old Space' thinking, and they have a 'New Space' mission plan. But now it seems like your people have a lot of leisure time." He slapped his leg. "That's it. I'm making an executive decision. You'll all start cross-training seminars for your team. And for my crew as well, since many of them hope for a Mars mission someday."

The runners stared at him, openmouthed. Finally Martinez spoke up. "You're serious."

"Deadly serious, Martinez. Deadly. The seminar sessions will be recorded so crew on other shifts can follow along. I'll expect each of you to organize the seminars for your field and to present me syllabi and progress reports to review. Martinez, you can start with software engineering on Mondays. Everyone should know more about programming and how to communicate with programmers. Meadors, you'll do astronomy on Tuesdays, Krause and geology on Wednesdays, and Savoy and atmospheric chemistry on Thursdays. I'm sure I can talk Major Adika into teaching Martian survival on Saturdays, and we can all take a break on Sundays."

Anthony looked at the captain and swallowed. "And Fridays?" But I was sure he already knew the answer.

Aames stared right back at him, but those blue eyes didn't flinch. "On Fridays, you're going to teach us everything there is to know about nanotechnology. And when we have questions, you'll find the answers and teach us those. And repeat, and repeat, until we're all as expert in the subject as you are." And then he leaned in, almost into Anthony's face. "Unless you think you can't do it, kid?"

Anthony held the captain's gaze, and he kept his voice low and level. "I can do it. Captain."

"That's what I like to hear! Doctor, if the kid needs any help, see to it that he has supplemental reading. Oh, and kid, I expect you to be an active participant in *all* of these seminars. Can you do that?"

This time there was steel in Anthony's voice. "Yes. Sir."

Aames leaned back. "Good, good." He looked around the table. "That goes for all of you. If this is going to work, I need you to set examples for the rest of your team." At last his gaze returned to Anthony. "I expect you to be *leaders*, not spectators. For the good of the mission." Then he placed his palms on the table and stood; and just like any other week, he said, "Ladies and gentlemen, ship's duties call, and I must go. Let the real party begin." And he left.

As soon as the captain was gone, Anthony drained the rest of his beer. Then he stood to leave as well.

I was worried. The captain was pushing too hard, and this was completely out of nowhere. I was afraid all the work we had done might be lost in this one blundering move by that—by that tyrant, Nick Aames.

I looked across the lounge. Chuks stood in a corner with a good vantage on the room. He had his earpiece in, so I was sure he had heard the conversation. He looked at me, frowned, and shook his head. I had learned to read his face and body language: *I am sorry. The bar has been raised.*

But I wasn't ready to give up hope. I went after Anthony and saw him down the hall. "Anthony, wait." He kept walking toward his cabin, so I ran to catch up. "Anthony, stop. Let's talk." But he kept walking, so I kept pace. "Anthony, you've come so far, you're doing so well. Don't let—" I looked around to see who might be listening. A guard stood a discreet distance away, so I lowered my voice. "Don't let the captain's pigheadedness undo everything you've done here."

Anthony just kept walking, not looking at me, but at least he answered, "I'm not, Doctor. He can't break me that easily."

"But then where are you going? What are you going to do?"

"To my room. To study. I have a seminar to prepare, Doctor." And then he did turn and look at me. "I look forward to your supplemental reading list."

That stopped me in my tracks, but he kept going, back stiff and straight and walking with an easy stride. For the first time, I really saw his father in him.

☾

But as determined as Anthony was, he still needed a lot of help for this challenge. I ended up spending my spare time tutoring him, not just recommending reading. He was bright—his father's genes ran true there—and he had the benefit of a very expensive education and private tutors; but he had never had to work at learning. Material that came easy to him, he blew through. When a topic proved too tough for him, though, he just turned to something else. No one had ever expected him to have the discipline to see his way through a hard part, and no one had taught him the analysis and study skills to master a subject. Now suddenly he was "enrolled" in five graduate-level studies, plus *teaching* one, and Captain Aames expected him to sink or swim.

And he wasn't sinking, but only because he spent all his nonexercise time studying. He even stopped showing up for dinner after workouts, until I put a halt to that.

"Doctor," he protested.

But I answered with a phrase he was learning to hate: "Doctor's orders. You need some downtime, or you're going to have a breakdown." He accepted my order, grudgingly, but the dinner conversations became more like an extension of the seminars. He kept probing his friends for answers, desperately trying to keep up with their work. His alcohol consumption dropped to almost zero, but I made a point to buy him a glass a night just to relax him. When he refused the first glass, I threatened to write out a prescription.

Anthony's determination was infectious. If Aames wanted to break him, then I was determined to keep him whole. But that had a cost: our tutoring time meant less time with Chuks; and though Chuks was a good man and tried not to show it, he resented it. "Constance, you will only be disappointed," he said one night; but I read disappointment in his own face. "You waste our time. In the end, Mr. Holmes will lose interest, and you will have accomplished nothing."

Our time. I bristled at that. "It's *my* time. If I want to spend it tutoring, I will. You don't own me."

"I don't want to own you, Constance, I want to protect you."

"You're not paid to protect me; you're paid to protect Anthony. Is my tutoring a danger to him?" Before Chuks could answer, I stormed out of the observation room. I was tired and frustrated, but that only made me more stubborn: if I had anything to say about it, Anthony would master his studies.

☾

Eventually Anthony's hard work and my tutoring paid off. He started asking smart questions in the seminars. When it was his turn to lead a discussion, he was always prepared, though I noticed he had a trick of delegating the more technical parts to the experts in the room, then synthesizing their responses into new insights.

In Chuks's Martian survival seminar, Anthony was often the first one with the right answer to any challenge. It turned out the one topic that really did interest him was Mars itself. He had to know everything about it; and in every other seminar, he managed to turn the topic back to "How will this help a team to survive and succeed on Mars?" Chuks was harsher with Anthony than with the other students, always dissecting his answers and pointing out weaknesses and mistakes; but Anthony just studied harder, and soon there were no weaknesses for Chuks to find.

And in his own seminar, Anthony quickly grasped how limited his "research" had been. He devoured my supplemental reading, until I had to call up more from Earth. He kept challenging the scientific consensus on nanotechnology, but his arrogance and confidence were gone. He now demanded that each precept be challenged and defended. He worked with the discussion leaders to explore nanos from the ground up. He asked Lieutenant Copeland, supervisor of the *Aldrin*'s nano labs, for permission to observe the labs; and after Captain Aames intervened, she approved him. Several weeks later, Anthony asked for permission to run some experimental batches. That approval took longer, and the captain demanded stringent oversight; but in the end, Anthony was approved to test a new design for waste reclamation nanos. His first two batches made an unholy stink, but Lieutenant Copeland said they showed promise. His third batch produced no odors, and his fourth batch improved on the efficiency of our stock nanos. Copeland agreed to put them through further testing.

We were about four weeks from the Martian gravipause at that point. The next Friday, when I showed up for Anthony's seminar, I was surprised to find the classroom almost empty. There were usually a dozen students, plus another dozen watching via comms. This time, the only people in the room were Captain Aames, Lieutenant Copeland, Chief Carver, and Chuks. I didn't look at Chuks. My temper had passed since our last argument, but something else was wrong, and I wasn't sure what. As Anthony grew more capable, Chuks became more distant, but he didn't explain why. I wondered if he resented being wrong. Then I refused to believe that such a good man could be so petty. Then I grew angry at myself: Did I really know Chuks was a good man after only four months?

Captain Aames was not big on saluting except when on station, so I wasn't surprised when he spoke before I could salute. "Just in time, Doctor. Have a seat. Mr. Holmes should be here any minute."

I sat in the seat that he indicated, making me the last person in a semicircle around the podium. Aames gave me no instructions, so I sat quietly.

When Anthony came in the door, I could tell he was as surprised as I had been; but he had practiced being unflappable in front of the captain, so he just walked up to the podium. The lights automatically lowered around us, and a big ceiling spot came on, pinning him in its beam. In the spotlight I could see just how much the exercise regimen had done for him. He was leaner, he stood straighter, and he carried himself with confidence. He looked every inch his father's son, only more at ease.

Anthony wore a forced smile as he said, "It looks like my lesson notes won't be needed today, so instead let's get right to it. Are there any questions?"

The captain never looked up from his desk as he asked from the shadows, "Mr. Holmes, what is the activation frequency of a salt-ion scavenger nano?"

Without missing a beat, Anthony answered, "There are many variants, Captain. The prime variant on this Mars mission has a primary activation spike in the ultraviolet C range at 210 nanometers, and a secondary spike at half power in the visible spectrum at 560 nanometers. We also have a variant with three spikes at 240, 500, and 614 nanometers. We have designs for other variants, but none in production. I can look those up if you'd like."

The captain looked at Lieutenant Copeland, and she nodded. Then he answered, "Unnecessary. How many generations of sintering nanos can you get out of a typical batch before they start to degrade?"

Again Anthony's response was immediate. "It's a trick question, sir. Sintering nanos are almost always destroyed in use, sacrificing their own component atoms to fabricate some new part or tool. So looked at that way, the answer is one. And sintering nanos are not self-replicating, so the answer is also one from that perspective. But if you look at the seed nanos that construct the sintering nanos, those are typically good for at least fifteen generations. In a pinch, you can push them to twenty, but the reliability of the sintering drops to the high-risk range above fifteen." Copeland nodded, and Anthony added, "And the orbital period of Phobos is seven hours, thirty-nine minutes, thirteen-point-eight-four seconds. Dr. Meadors rounded to the nearest second. During the course of the *Aldrin*'s rendezvous with Mars, that error will add up to almost forty-seven seconds. If you had had a discrepancy like that on the second *Bradbury* expedition, you and the other survivors would be dead right now."

This time the captain did look up, straight at Anthony. His eyes gleamed in the reflected light. "You think you're pretty smart, huh, kid?"

"Try me." Anthony smiled. "Captain."

"Okay, kid, tell me about your waste reclamation nanos."

"What about them, sir?"

"Everything. From concept to production to testing. Convince me that we should risk this Mars mission on some billionaire's son's hare-brained scheme."

And Anthony set out to do just that. He started explaining the history of reclamation nanos, the nanochemistry behind them, and the current state of the art. He was just summarizing the articles that inspired his new approach when Chuks interrupted him. "Mr. Holmes, you are stranded on Mars in the Elysium quadrant during a meteorological survey. It is early spring in that region. Your shuttle is incapacitated, and your water stock has been contaminated. Where is your best place to scavenge water, and why?"

That brought Anthony to a halt. He was deep in the middle of nanotechnology, and suddenly he was fielding a question on Martian survival. I was sure he was stalling when he asked, "How long do I expect to wait before rescue, Major?"

But Chuks smiled, and I knew Anthony had done well. "Two days, Mr. Holmes. Possibly less, depending on weather conditions."

Anthony didn't smile, but I saw confidence in his eyes. "For two days, Major, I wouldn't even try to scavenge subsurface water, though there's probably some in the area. For such a short trip, I would scavenge from the shuttle's cooling system. It would be easier to scavenge from the meteorology station, but we might need that station functioning at optimum in order to do local weather forecasts and bring my rescue shuttle in. If my landing shuttle was damaged so as to lose all cooling water, *then* I would scavenge just the minimum fluid from the station. I wouldn't even try to set up subsurface reclamation in only two days. I brought enough water with me for that period."

Chuks nodded. "Very good, Mr. Holmes." And he looked at me with a strange sadness on his face. "Please continue enlightening us about nanos."

And that was how it went. Anthony presented an informal paper on his reclamation nanos, answering questions, particularly from Lieutenant Copeland; and every so often, someone would pepper him with questions on other subjects. Chuks tested him on Martian survival. Chief Carver probed him on software requirements and verification. The captain questioned him on chemistry, astronomy, mathematics, and geology. And I questioned him on just about anything we had studied.

After an hour of this, Anthony was sweating, but still going strong. I ducked out and found him some water, and he just kept going.

After three hours, Anthony had thoroughly covered the planning, design, generation, and testing of his waste recycling nanos; he had also answered practical questions from across the range of Mars mission disciplines. He looked tired enough that I was ready to open my medical bag, but he was smiling as he asked, "Any more questions?"

The captain looked around the semicircle, and we all shook our heads. He shook his as well. "No, Mr. Holmes. Lights." The room lights came on. Aames stood, walked to the podium, and looked at the rest of us. "Ladies, gentlemen, I have one question for you: Has Mr. Anthony Holmes mastered the material presented in his seminar courses?"

As one, we answered, "Yes, Captain."

"Very well." He turned to Anthony. "Mr. Holmes, congratulations." He took Anthony's hand and shook it. "While it has no force outside this ship—and not here, while we're between the gravipauses—in the judgment of this review board, you have earned a doctorate of areology with a specialization in nanotechnology. We would be honored to attest as much should you wish to apply to any graduate or postgraduate program back on Earth. And who knows, maybe someday we'll have an *Aldrin* University, and you'll be our first doctorate recipient, retroactively." They shook hands again. "You've exceeded my highest expectations, Mr. Holmes. That doesn't happen often."

They stood at the podium like that until finally Captain Aames pulled his hand away. "So do you have anything to say for yourself?"

Anthony nodded. "Yes, sir, Captain." He turned to me. "Dr. Baldwin, I'd like to set up an appointment to get my therapy nanos as soon as possible."

The captain raised an eyebrow, and then he turned around and returned to his seat. "I suppose I'm going to start losing our races now."

Anthony blinked. "Sir?"

"Think, man, you're half my age. And in better shape than me, at least now. The only reason I've been winning is you have a handicap: you don't have half a million little machines constantly rebuilding bone and muscle damage. Your musculoskeletal damage has been slowed by exercise, whereas mine has been reversed by the nanos. Without that edge, I wouldn't stand a chance against you. I would've been eating your dust for at least the last month. With all your studies of nanotechnology, you hadn't figured that out?"

"No, Captain. I just figured you were that good." Anthony hesitated, but finally he blurted out, "You cheated, Captain?"

"*No one* is that good, Mr. Holmes. It's not cheating to know your subject, do your homework, and use your resources. It's smart; and if you're half as smart as you think you are, you'll learn to do it as second nature. When you have an edge out here, you take it. Your mission and your survival may depend upon it."

"Yes, Captain."

"When you take the nanos, it will be a relief. I can stop trying so hard, because I know I'll lose in the end. Aside from Major Adika, you may be the healthiest person on this ship."

"Thank you, Captain."

Aames turned to me. "Doctor, you should be able to accommodate Mr. Holmes immediately, shouldn't you?"

I picked up my bag and stood. "Yes, Captain. Right away." I started for the door.

But Anthony just stood at the podium, staring at Captain Aames, a big grin on his face. The captain stared back and asked, "Is there anything else, Mr. Holmes?"

Anthony nodded. "You called me man, sir."

The captain's eyes widened. "I did?"

"Yes, Captain. 'Think, man, you're half my age.' You didn't call me kid, you called me man."

Captain Aames genuinely smiled, the first sign I had that he knew how. "So I did. Was I wrong?"

"No, Captain." Anthony saluted, turned, and left for the infirmary.

☾

After I gave Anthony his injections, I traced down Chuks in his cabin. He let me in, and I threw my arms around him without saying a word. He kissed me, and we stood like that for a while. I just wanted things to be right between us, whatever that would take.

But when I pulled away, I saw sadness in his eyes. "Chuks, what's the matter? He did it! Are you that sorry to be wrong?"

He shook his head. "It is nothing, Constance. Life changes, that is all, and change always brings good and bad."

"What could be bad here? We should be proud."

"I am proud. Do not worry, I am just being foolish. Tomorrow will bring what it brings. Tonight we are together. We should celebrate."

And we did, and it was very good, and eventually his fantastic smile returned. But I couldn't forget his sad expression, and I couldn't stop worrying what might have caused it.

☾

Three weeks later, the review board and Anthony met in the classroom again. We were joined by Savoy, Meadors, Krause, Martinez, and a number of other senior mission personnel; the rest of the mission watched on the comms. Captain Aames directed a revised briefing on the mission plan, with each department head going through a grilling much like Anthony had. It wasn't Aames's mission, and he wouldn't be going down to Mars; but as the commander of the second *Bradbury* expedition, he was the local expert on Mars, *and* he had plenary powers between the gravipauses. If he wanted to be briefed, he would get briefed.

At last all the departments had reported to the captain's satisfaction, and he reclaimed the podium. He looked around the room. "Ladies and gentlemen, this looks like a very professional mission plan, and you've got answers to every question we can imagine. Now for the bad news: when you get down there, Mars is going to raise questions you *can't* imagine. Nothing in our evolution or experience can prepare us for Mars. Until you're there, you won't understand that. But if any team is ready for Mars, you are."

At this rare bit of praise from Captain Aames, Chief Carver and I and other ship's officers rose and applauded. This team had earned that.

When the applause faded and we all sat down again, the captain continued, "But you're not ready. Remember that, keep your wits about you, and you'll survive until the *Collins* arrives to pick you up. Never forget: Mars is going to surprise you. Now, are there any last questions?" Anthony raised a hand. "Yes, Mr. Holmes?"

"Captain, I've been thinking."

"It's about damn time," the captain said. Everyone laughed, including Anthony.

He continued, "Captain, I don't think I want to do a down-and-back on the drop shuttle. I respectfully request to be reassigned as permanent staff for the mission."

The captain looked around at the mission heads, and they all nodded slowly. "Are you sure? There's no turning back on this one. It will be fourteen months before the *Collins* arrives."

Anthony smiled. "I'd like to put this new degree to good use. Fourteen months is a good start on that."

Aames turned to me. "Doctor, is he in physical condition for the mission?"

I rose to attention. "He is, Captain."

The captain turned to Adika. "This would mean your team has to stay through as well. Are you all right with that?"

And suddenly I understood why Chuks had been so sad: he had known this was coming. He knew Anthony, and he knew how much Mars meant to him; and he knew that once Anthony qualified for the mission, he would insist on going.

I had looked forward to the long voyage home and a lot more time with Chuks. Selfishly I hoped he would say no, and we could still be together in the coming months. But then I got angry with myself. Anthony had earned this, he deserved this, and it was the natural outcome of all our efforts. So despite my anger, I was proud when Chuks stood as well and answered, "Captain, my team would enjoy the chance to spend more time on Mars, but the mission plan does not allow enough spare rations for that many. I believe there's enough buffer to safely cover myself and Mr. Holmes."

I would miss Chuks, but his plan made sense. I looked at him, and I smiled: *I understand. I'm proud of you.* He smiled back, and it was a perfect blend of his sad look and his big smile.

The captain stared at Chuks. "Major, that would do a lot to lower the risks in this mission." He turned his stare on Anthony. "Mr. Holmes."

"Yes, Captain."

"You would have to understand one thing: if you do this, you're not Anthony Holmes, the boss's son. You're bottom of the totem pole. You will do what you're told when you're told by whoever tells you. These people have been training for this mission for three years, some of them for longer. Their whole lives, even. You've had four months of cramming. That's not the same. You're not an expert, you're a nobody who *might* become an expert if you come out of this alive. The way to do that is to follow orders. Can you do that?"

"I wouldn't have it any other way, Captain. I'd *like* to come out of this alive."

Captain Aames looked at his comm. "All right, under those terms, I think you'll make a hell of a Mars explorer. I support you in this decision."

Anthony shook his head. "You support me? So am I authorized to go or not?"

The captain shook his head. "I *can't* authorize it, Mr. Holmes. As of three minutes ago, we passed the Martian gravipause. I'm not in charge anymore. You're the boss's son. If you want to go, who am I to tell you no?"

3. Modus Operandi

From the memoirs of Park Yerim

28 May 2083

Dr. Baldwin took a long drink, then concluded her story. "Of course, if Captain Aames had really wanted to stop Anthony, he would've found a way. When the safe completion of a mission is concerned, Nick Aames *always* finds a way. He let Anthony go to Mars because Anthony was ready."

I resisted the urge to grab my comm and make notes. I had promised Dr. Baldwin this was off the record, but I found myself regretting my promise. All my investigations for the past week had yielded facts, but not reasons. Not motivations. I looked up at the black door with its forbidding sign: "Keep out." That had been the unstated message everywhere I went on the *Aldrin*. Now, for the first time, I had a glimpse into the minds of the crew, and of their captain. The door was ajar, and I wanted to stick my foot in and pry it open. Or at least keep it from closing.

"So Captain Aames helped Anthony, and that's why you like him?"

"Like him?" Dr. Baldwin laughed. "I can't stand him. Nick Aames is not a likable man."

"Huh?"

"I don't like him; I trust him, as much as any commander out there, to get us through a mission alive and successfully. I also respect him as a commander. I'm grateful to him for my job, and for letting me run my department my way—after we clashed a few more times over who was in charge of the infirmary. And Chuks, for whatever reason, likes him; so for the sake of peace in my marriage, I put up with him on social occasions. But I'll never like him. He has so many layers of crust, it would take a surgical laser to get through them; and I don't believe what's inside is worth the effort."

"You've confused me, Doctor. I thought the point of your story was that Captain Aames challenged Anthony Holmes to get him ready for Mars. That seems pretty admirable."

"Then you weren't listening, Inspector. Nick Aames didn't give a damn whether Anthony succeeded or failed; he just wanted to test Anthony, to know if Anthony was ready. He would've been just as satisfied if Anthony had washed out. Either way, Aames would've had his answer."

"The way you told the story, he was happy with the answer."

"Happy? Let's say pleased. Captain Aames is pleasantly surprised when someone exceeds his expectations, and he expected Anthony to fail. But just because you passed his test won't stop Aames from testing you just as hard the next day. The test is never really over, he just thinks up new questions."

I frowned at the thought. "That sounds awfully stressful. Surely after all these years you could find a better job."

"A better job? Probably. But Chuks likes it here. And Chief Carver makes things a lot more bearable around the captain. If it weren't for him, I might have quit half a dozen times over the years. Plus there's this: I know that every single spacer on the *Aldrin* has met the exacting standards of Nick Aames. I can't think of a safer post in the Corps."

Dr. Baldwin packed up her bag to leave; but just as she reached the door, I spoke. "One more thing, Doctor."

"Yes?"

"I don't suppose I could borrow a surgical laser?"

Dr. Baldwin laughed and left, while I pondered what I had learned. Captain Aames was a conundrum, but now I had a small glimpse inside: Aames was demanding as hell and had a talent for pissing people off and driving them away; but Dr. Baldwin took that as a challenge, and she rose to it.

And when I turned the desk back on, it looked like she wasn't alone. One of the amicus briefs in my pile was coded: "From the Office of the Mayor, Maxwell City, Mars. Subject: Urge You to Dismiss All Charges Against Captain Aames." I pulled open the brief, and a video window opened in Aames's desk, brightening the room. The face that appeared was that of a man in his late thirties, with a lean and muscular look. He had close-cropped blond hair and bright-blue eyes that stared out of the screen. A caption beneath him read: "Mayor Anthony Holmes, Maxwell City." I tapped the "Play" button, and Holmes started speaking.

"Inspector Park, I understand you have been assigned to investigate Captain Aames on some preposterous insubordination charges." Holmes waved a hand at his desk. "Oh, I've read the classified summary, and it's nonsense. I'm sure if you dig deeper into the facts of the matter, you'll find a bunch of button-pushers who've had it in for Nick for years and have jumped on this opportunity to get rid of him. If it would help, I can arrange to appear as a character witness—by televisit, of course, since I hope you can dismiss this matter long before the *Aldrin* reaches Mars. I hear through the grapevine that you're under a lot of pressure in this matter, Inspector, and I would hate to add to that. But the people of Maxwell City would very much appreciate it if you could clear this up and get Captain Aames back to work. We would see it as proof that the System Initiative still puts safe and successful missions ahead of politics." Holmes looked through the screen and directly into my eyes, and I saw the personality that had won him three terms as mayor. "And I would see it as a personal favor, Inspector. Nick Aames is a difficult man, but that old bastard made me what I am today. Feel free to contact me if you have any questions." The video ended, and the room darkened again.

That was one side of the story. The other side was in the virtual pile of reports, charges, and briefs from the System Initiative and the Admiralty and the Space Professionals. They wanted Aames's head, and they didn't try to hide it.

As if on schedule, my comm chimed with a message: *Incoming call from Adm. Frank C. Knapp, Intl. Space Corps.* Knapp was in charge of the Admiralty troops who patrolled the *Aldrin*. He had a temporary office in the H Ring, and no one dared notice that that put him as far from Aames as he could possibly be and still have air to breathe. On the list of admirals whom Nick Aames had crossed, Admiral Knapp was at the top.

I pulled open the call, and my comm showed Admiral Knapp: old but still healthy, extremely fit in his black Admiralty uniform, and a shock of gray hair framing a lean face with high cheekbones and bright eyes. Those eyes were known to spear into subordinates and make them squirm. Knapp was very pleasant socially, and he knew how to court favor politically; but he expected immediate results from those who answered to him. "Park, why haven't I seen an interview with Captain Aames yet? We have enough flag officers to empanel a court, but they're all sitting on their asses, waiting for you to do your job."

"You'll have it when it's ready, Admiral. I'm not going to rush." Fortunately I did *not* answer to Admiral Knapp. The IG is an independent office with a separate chain of command. Knapp could bluster and intimidate, but he could give me no direct orders. In fact, my plenary power meant that technically *I* could give *him* orders, though I could never imagine doing so.

Knapp slapped his hand on his desk. "Stop dragging your feet, Inspector. This case is open and shut. If you give these people time, they'll cover up all the evidence. Just issue the charges, notify the panel, and get out of our way. Or do I have to march back to A Ring and walk you through it?"

Suddenly a bit of Dr. Baldwin's story came back to me, and I decided it was a perfect reply to Admiral Knapp. "You can remove me, but you can't second-guess me. Either I'm in charge here, or you are. But I won't be your figurehead. If you have a problem with that, take it up with Admiral Reed." Admiral Justin V. Reed was the head of the Inspector General division, and hence my boss—well, boss's boss, to be precise. "Unless I'm formally relieved, Admiral, I'll carry out my duties as I see fit."

Knapp trembled, and he looked ready to leap through the comm, but he answered in a very even voice: "I shall call Admiral Reed. Count on it, Inspector." He cut off before I could reply.

I wasn't sure where I had found the nerve to defy Knapp. Oh, I was in my rights, of course. I had seen Reed once have an admiral thrown in the brig to remind him of the independence of the IG. But I was the most junior of inspectors, with a lot less clout than Admiral Reed. Still, something in those words of Nick Aames had reached me. I *wanted* to have that sort of conviction; and with the right words to support me, I had it, if only for a moment.

Still that left one unanswered question: *Why hadn't I interviewed Captain Aames yet?* I didn't want to say it to Knapp, but I really didn't have an answer. There was just something unnerving about the man and his attitude, sulking there behind the black door of his cabin like Achilles in his tent. He had such a reputation in the Corps that I was intimidated without ever having met him; so I worked around the edges of the problem, gathering facts and interviewing admirals and crew. Anything I could do to postpone confronting the heart of the matter. Avoidance was part of it, but I suspected I had another, unconscious reason, and I had to work that out. I couldn't avoid Aames forever.

Meanwhile everyone wanted something from me, but they all expected different outcomes. I felt trapped, like giant external forces were pressing down on me, trying to push me in different directions at once. Like a spaceship with all its attitude jets firing at once, so it couldn't go anywhere, just spin in place and shake itself apart. Somehow I had to balance out all these forces and find a course that didn't lead to disaster.

I wasn't sure why I was making this so difficult. There was a quick way to deal with it, to put it all behind me, and I would have the support of the Initiative and the Admiralty as well: just find sufficient grounds for a court martial of Nick Aames, empanel a court from the officers who had come aboard with me, and turn responsibility over to the panel. It would be out of my hands then: let the panel do their fact-finding, problem solved.

Yeah, right. *One* problem solved, but a larger problem launched. If I read the mood on the *Aldrin* correctly, a judgment against Aames could lead to mutiny unless the crew was managed *very* carefully. Hell, some of the admirals were ready to charge them with mutiny already, since they had cooperated with Captain Aames when he had refused to relinquish command. The only thing stopping those admirals was that the *Aldrin* was already on its trajectory to Mars, and there was no way to replace the crew at this point. So tensions were high, and the crew was on edge.

And more than that, damn it, I refused to be pressured! I hadn't chosen this job, I was just a junior inspector general, but I was the only IG who could rendezvous with the *Aldrin* before she left for Mars. I could feel *that* force, too, my superiors watching to see if I would screw up. But there was one more force: my own stubborn pride. I had a job to do, and I was going to do it right. Prove that I deserved this assignment. More than anything, that kept me going; but my job still felt like a battlefield, an uneasy truce between North and South, just as Korea had known for generations. And there, standing in the demilitarized zone, was I.

That night, that metaphor moved one step closer to reality.

The first indicator I had of the trouble was my comm chiming in the middle of the night. I checked the clock: I had been asleep less than an hour. The doctor's pills had done their job, soothing the ache in my shoulder and enabling me to sleep soundly for the first time in two weeks. Somebody had better have a good explanation for waking me.

Then the comm screen lit up, and I sat up in my bunk and brushed my hair out of my face. "Admiral Reed." I wasn't sure what time it was where Reed was, but he looked like he always did: black uniform neatly creased, brass polished, face as clean as if he had just shaved. His bald head glinted from an off-screen light.

And as usual, his broad face bore a scowl. After a thirty-second light-speed delay, he responded. "Park, get out of bed. I need a report on this fight immediately!"

"Fight?" But in a separate window, my comm was already showing the details. *Fight in E Ring between Admiralty troops and off-duty* Aldrin *crew. Three in infirmary with minor injuries. Commander Adika has arrested three Admiralty troopers and one Spacer 1st Class. Situation peaceful but tense.* After that came a separate note: *I warned you. —Dr. Baldwin.* "Admiral, it looks to be settled already."

Another delay, and then Reed looked angrier. "Settled? They've imprisoned three Admiralty troops! The admirals are heating up the airwaves, demanding authority to pacify the ship. Is there a reason I should tell them no?"

I shook my head; and then, rethinking, I nodded. "Yes, Admiral, there's definitely a reason. This ship is a uranium pile just waiting for the right neutron to set it off. We need to calm things down, not escalate them. Those troops can't run this ship, so we need the crew to cooperate. Let me talk to Adika, find a way to handle things."

After the delay, Reed looked doubtful. "You're still pretty new, Park. I've received some complaints from Admiral Knapp. He thinks you're wasting time, and maybe getting influenced. Park, don't let a bunch of mutinous spacers push you around."

I thought again of Dr. Baldwin standing up to Aames, and of Aames standing up to Holmes. "Respectfully, Admiral, I'm not going to let anyone push me around and stop me from doing my job. Not spacers, and not admirals. Now I have to go meet with Adika."

Reed eyed me skeptically; but finally he said, "Carry on, Park. Dismissed."

☾

By the time I got to Matt's office, Commander Adika was there waiting for me.

As I had dressed and then traversed the ring, I had thought about this meeting; and the more I thought, the more it seemed like slow caution was the wisest course. We were in a cycler orbit to Mars, and there wasn't anything that would change that, so we were in no hurry. Maybe some time would let tempers cool, so that whatever I decided, the outcome would be more restrained. And with more time, I could better understand the true situation.

As soon as I saw Adika, my first thought was that Dr. Baldwin had not exaggerated her husband's stature. The man was tall, dark, imposing, and impressive, standing at attention like a massive onyx Atlas holding up the world. His posture showed confidence and readiness, and his eyes swept the room as if he were on guard duty.

I could see Matt was nervous about supervising a superior officer, especially one who could snap his spine with one hand. He stood nervously, looking from the commander to me and back. "Do you need anything, Inspector?"

"No, Matt, we'll be in my office."

Matt looked at Adika and raised an eyebrow. "Are you sure, Inspector?"

"Yes, Matt. You're dismissed." I knew he was trying to protect me, but I was sure I was safe. I had read Adika's record, and he was no threat unless under orders.

Adika and I entered my office, and the door slid shut behind us. The commander stood before the desk as I sat. His face, carved from stone like the rest of him, betrayed no emotion as he looked at me. Those eyes were piercing, and I suspected he could read people as well as I could. He would have to, in his job.

I pointed at the guest chair. "Take a seat, Commander."

Dark-brown eyes looked down at me, and he frowned. "Is that an order, Inspector?"

I shook my head. "There are no orders here today. It's an invitation, Commander. I would like you to be comfortable for this discussion."

"If it is all the same to you, I would be more comfortable standing."

Stone. Absolute stone. He revealed none of the charm that had swept Dr. Baldwin off her feet. I was his opponent, and he would show me no weakness. He showed only patience: I had made a move, and he would wait to find out what I wanted, wait all day if necessary.

I decided I needed to reduce the tension. "As you wish. But feel free to sit at any time. Please relax and get comfortable, Commander, and explain this fight to me."

His face impassive, Adika reported, "At approximately 2140, three off-duty Admiralty troopers—Rodriguez, Scithers, and Watkins—entered the public lounge on E Ring. The bartender served them drinks; as the night wore on, they drank more, and they became louder and belligerent. At 2245, she cut them off, and they took exception to this. They grew louder still, and they started insulting the *Aldrin* and Captain Aames. Some off-duty ship's crew took exception to this, and words were exchanged. Words turned to blows. When I arrived to break things up, your Admiralty troops had holed up behind the bar as a defensive position and were throwing bottles at crew and passengers."

I shook my head. "They're not *my* troops, Commander. Who threw the first punch?"

Adika's face remained stone. "I cannot say, Inspector."

"Oh, bull! You have video records, you know who's at fault."

He nodded slightly. "I have my records, and I will reveal them if ordered to do so. But respectfully, Inspector, it is you and the Admiralty who are at fault. You created this situation."

I sighed. "Not me, Commander. I don't like it any more than you do." I paused. "But I understand what you're saying. Tempers are ready to blow at any minute. If we don't prevent that, then we are at fault. *We*, Commander, and that includes you. I've read your record; you're just the man to defuse this situation. What do you recommend?"

Adika stared down at me. "You mean besides clearing Captain Aames of all charges?" I glared at him, and he continued, "Separation and cooling off. Aside from official duties, confine all Admiralty troops to G and H Rings. Confine *Aldrin* crew to A through D. Treat E and F as a demilitarized zone: passengers only except for troops and crew on duty. Give everyone time to see reason."

"And the three Admiralty troops you have in your brig?"

"They committed their offenses between the gravipauses. Legally, that means that it is Captain Aames's responsibility to decide punishment for them. Since the Admiralty has seen fit to deprive the captain of his lawful command, I shall have to hold the men until he returns to duty and decides what to do with them."

I shook my head. "Nice try, Commander, but unacceptable. I need you to turn those men over to me. Now. Or there will be no cooling off."

"Turn them over to you? So you can turn them loose with no consequences for their actions?"

I looked in Adika's eyes, trying to read him. "I'll have them confined to quarters for the duration of this trip when not on duty. And I'll have them reassigned to barracks work in H Ring. No chance they'll come into contact with crew again. And this will go into their permanent records. But that's the best I can do."

Adika inclined his head slightly. "It is acceptable."

I nodded and made notes on the desk. "Done. Thank you, Commander." I thought I saw surprise in his eyes, if only for a moment. I think he expected me to argue with him more, but I couldn't. I needed him on my side. If Dr. Baldwin was right, Commander Adika knew as much about Aames as anyone on this ship.

So I looked up from the desk. "Next subject: I want to speak with you off the record about Captain Aames."

"Constance said you might, but are you sure that you really do? You might not enjoy a frank discussion."

"To hell with what I enjoy." His eyes widened a bit. Finally, a sign of life inside the stone. "I'm here to learn, I'm not on a pleasure cruise."

"If I speak frankly, Inspector, you may learn true things, but things which will show that I do not approve of your work. No one in the crew does."

I sighed. "Commander, *I* don't approve of my work. I didn't volunteer here, I was assigned. I have orders and duty here. Looking at your exemplary record, I know that duty matters a great deal to you, yes?" He nodded. "Well, I take it very seriously as well. I hope you can respect that." He nodded again.

"But I'm not sure precisely what my duty is here yet," I continued. "Before we go approving and disapproving, help me to figure that out. I might surprise you."

For the first time, I saw just a hint of that Adika charm, a slight upturn at the corners of his mouth. "Then you have not decided to charge Captain Aames?"

I pointed to the virtual stacks on the desk. "That's the problem. You're a commander, you understand regulations. You know the facts in this case leave me little choice: they all point to charges. And a conviction."

The corners of his mouth turned back down. "If you go with the facts as recorded, Inspector. I see no other choice for you. But it is still wrong."

"Relax, Commander, nothing is decided yet. Off the record—remember?—I have larger responsibilities than just the facts. And as you said: 'the facts as recorded.' The situation here is more complex than we can see if we only look at logs and records from the Admiralty. The *Aldrin's* crew knows truths that aren't in those records; or they think they do, which results in the same discontent across this ship. I need to understand what the Admiralty believes and what the crew believes, and then I need to extract a set of facts that *I* believe. And *then* I can make my finding. Only then."

With that, Adika sat: still straight as a rod, but it was the first sign I saw that the commander could relax. "Inspector, I was not present on the bridge during the incident. I was not privy to any information there, and the captain is not in the habit of sharing his decision-making with me. He gives orders, and as his security chief, I execute them. I cannot shed light on the incident."

"Yes, but I don't care about the incident right now. I'm after a larger view, and as security chief, you know the mood of this crew better than anyone. You know how much trouble we could have if things go badly for Captain Aames. I'd rather avoid trouble for the sake of the mission, but I can't let that stop me from doing my job."

"That is the proper view of an officer."

"But if possible, I have to head off potential problems. So I need to ask you—*off the record*—if I should find grounds to proceed against Captain Aames, and if the court should judge him guilty, are we looking at worse than tonight's little fight? Could we possibly see a mutiny here?"

Adika almost nodded, just a half tilt of his head forward and back. "Inspector, one cannot say for certain, but I would rate the risk very high."

"I see. So you think this crew is that lacking in discipline?"

"No, Inspector." He shook his head emphatically. "I think this crew has that much trust in their captain, trust that he and they have followed the proper course for their mission."

"I see. Is there something we should do to prepare for that risk?"

Adika frowned. "I'm not sure I should say, because in the event, I might be leading the mutineers. Off the record."

My eyes grew wide. "Commander, I've studied your file. You have one of the finest records in the International Space Corps, dating all the way back to your time in the Rapid Response Team. I would not expect you, of all officers, to consider willfully violating Admiralty orders."

"Inspector, my oath is to three things, in order: safety of the mission, success of mission goals, and faithful execution of lawful orders. If those orders compromise the safety and success of the mission, then they are not lawful, so they are not binding upon me. You swore the same oath, you know it is to principles, not to men; but if I *were* to swear an oath to a man, it would be to Nick Aames, who every day demands we live up to those principles. If the Admiralty orders this crew to do something that will jeopardize this mission, you can trust that we will not do it. Removing Captain Aames is a high risk to this mission."

I rolled my eyes. "Bah. I don't buy it. Aames the Perfect. Aames the Observant. Aames the Challenging. I heard it all from your wife. She doesn't like him, yet even she has fallen under his spell."

At that, finally, he smiled. "Constance likes Nick more than she will admit. But they are too much alike, and that gets on her nerves. They both have high standards, and I live to satisfy them."

I slapped my hand upon the desk, making the old blue e-reader bounce. "You all treat him like some legendary figure, wiser than the Initiative and the Admiralty put together. With all due respect, he's just one person. No one is that good. He's just a man, as flawed as any of us. I don't understand this man and how he can inspire such fanatical loyalty. You all know this isn't real, it's a myth. Aames wasn't born fully formed as some sort of . . . some sort of super captain."

"Yes, Inspector, it is a myth, one he cultivates to keep the crew striving to improve. I have known Nick Aames since he was a raw officer trainee. I am well aware of his flaws and how he has learned to work them to his advantage." Adika looked closely at me, and suddenly I felt as if I were under a microscanner. "You are sincere? You wish to understand the captain?"

"I do. If it will help me to understand the situation on this ship, I do."

Adika leaned back, relaxed at last. "Then let me tell you of when I first met Nick Aames. Back when he was not such a pleasant fellow."

4. Working Out

Off-the-record account of Commander Chukwunwike Adika, Chief of Security of the IPV *Aldrin*

Covering events from 20 April 2046 to 10 June 2046

I first met Nick Aames in Lunar Survival School. That was back before the System Initiative consolidated most space services into the International Space Corps, back when almost every major nation had their own competing program; but no matter where else they competed, agencies wanted their best cadets to study under Sergeant Fontes. Under the best survival training in the system. Luna, the United States, Russia, India, China, Australia, the Celestial Arch, and numerous commercial space agencies all sent their best students to Tycho to study under Sergeant Fontes. He had taught at LSS for a generation, since before the war where the Free Cities gained their independence. If you go to LSS today, you still will learn a curriculum designed by Fontes.

I attended as a member of the United Nations Orbital Patrol: Chukwunwike Adika, the first Nigerian recruit, determined to make my people proud—as well as my father, a state governor who expected great things from his children. My brother was already an undersecretary in the Ministry of Justice, and my sister was regional vice president of the largest software company in Africa. I was no scholar and no diplomat, but I was tall and strong and fast and clever. I saw myself as heir to a long tradition of Nigerian warriors. The UNOP (the predecessor to our Orbital Defense Corps today) was a chance for me to make my mark where my siblings could not, where even Father had not: on other worlds.

Nick was serving in the United States Unified Space Service. That marked us as friendly competitors at the school; but for Nick, the emphasis was on *competitors*, with no *friendly* in evidence. He always had to be right, no matter the consequences, and he did not care who was wrong or how that made them look.

Fontes fostered that competition. He wanted us constantly wary, constantly alert, and he was not averse to using any tool that could motivate us. On our very first day, we twenty students gathered in the gymnasium—a square fifteen meters on a side and five high—for what we assumed would be an introductory briefing. Instead, when Fontes arrived, he immediately began grilling us. He paced in front of us, a blocky man with dark-olive skin and pepper-gray hair, and looked up at the ceiling as he asked, "What are the two biggest risks in space? Mr. Hazeltine?" And he turned his cold stare upon Rick Hazeltine, a new recruit from the European Space Agency.

Hazeltine, a short, thin blond man who scarcely looked old enough for space service, cleared his throat. Then he answered, "Ummm . . . vacuum and radiation?"

Fontes continued to stare until Hazeltine blinked. "Someone else. Miss Barnes?" None of us had met Fontes yet, but he already knew us all by name. Because we came from so many services with so many different rank structures—Adelle Barnes was from the Australian Space Research Institute—we were all "Mister" or "Miss" at Lunar Survival School. There were only three "ranks": student, instructor, and Fontes. Unless you *really* made a mistake; then Fontes would use your first name, as if you were some child who needed extra supervision.

Barnes, a sturdy brunette half a head taller than Fontes, looked suddenly small. "Vacuum and cold?"

Fontes looked up at the ceiling again, as if pleading. "This is going to be a long six months, isn't it? All right, just the top risk. Anyone?" He looked down at us. Some hands were raised. "No, none of you Loonies or Archers, you grew up knowing this. I want to see what the Downies know."

Downies was a scurrilous slur against we who came from Earth, and it spurred the students to speak out. Voices came from around the room: "Heat." "Energy." "Vacuum." "Asteroids." "Cosmic rays." I even spoke up with what I thought was a more sophisticated answer: "Coronal mass ejections." But Fontes only glared at me as he glared at the others.

Then on the far edge of the crowd, a short, red-haired American with a neatly trimmed beard spoke in a loud, rough baritone that cut through the clamor: "Ignorance and human incompetence."

We all paused to see how Fontes would react, and we knew from his smile that the American had scored. "We say uncertainty and human error, but that's close enough, Mister Aames." Fontes leaped in the low gravity and landed precisely in front of Aames. "How did you know? You have a friend who's been through LSS already?"

"No friends, Sergeant." Aames shook his head.

"Aames has no friends, class!" We all laughed. It was a weak joke, but I thought Fontes expected laughter. He leaned closer, his eyes boring into Aames's. "Then tell me, Aames, how you knew the two biggest risks in space?"

Aames stared right back, unblinking. "Easy, Sergeant: those are the two biggest risks *anywhere*. The world is simple, it's people who screw it up."

At that Fontes laughed, a rolling bass rumble that filled the gymnasium. "You're a hardened cynic, eh, Aames? That'll serve you well. Ladies and gentlemen, you can all learn from this."

I leaned over to whisper to Hazeltine, but Fontes had very sharp eyes and seemed to see everything at once. "You have something to add, Mister Adika?"

I shook my head. "No, Sergeant." My face burned. I did not want such attention on my first day in LSS.

But Fontes was unrelenting. "Out with it, Adika. It might be something important."

I glared, not at Fontes, but at the short American whom I somehow blamed for my embarrassment. "Sergeant, I was saying that I could think of one more critical risk: arrogance."

C

Lunar Survival School was as hard as Fontes could make it, but Nick seemed determined to make it harder. We all understood that any training mission could be deadly. Fontes said, "Luna doesn't play nice, so we don't either." We all learned to double-check every reading and every piece of equipment; but Nick triple-checked everything, his own work and everyone else's. He thrived on the stress, and he pounced on even the slightest deviation from procedure.

I learned this the hard way on that very same day during suit-up drills. We had all arrived on Luna in spacesuits, and I had already trained in them during UNOP Basic Training. I saw the suit-up drills as merely remediation for those students who were new to space, but I had not accounted for Sergeant Fontes. This was a serious drill, more thorough than I had ever seen in UNOP. And I also had not accounted for Nick Aames.

We paired up to dress ourselves and inspect each other; and as we paired alphabetically, that put me with Aames. For this drill, we each dressed ourselves in hard suits, each pair in a suit locker. (In later drills, we would dress each other, as well as simulated injured crew; and we would drill in both hard and soft suits.) Then we inspected each other. I am very tall for a Nigerian, just over two meters. Even in modern space-craft, I feel cramped. Aames, on the other hand, is barely 1.7 meters. He had to use a step stool to inspect my helmet and hoses. And he took inordinately long at the job, prodding and tapping and pulling at seals. Finally I had had enough. "Are you finished, Aames? We should be on the regolith by now."

"We'll breathe vacuum if we rush, Adika. I'll let you know when you're safe to go out."

And Aames kept working. I was almost ready to lift him off the stool and shout "Enough" when Fontes appeared in the doorway of our locker. He stood there in his own suit for several seconds, watching us, arms folded across his chest. Finally his patience grew thin. "Are you going to take all day, Mister Aames?"

Without looking away from his work, Aames answered, "I'm almost done, Sergeant. There's a lot of suit to inspect here."

Fontes drummed his right fingers on his left forearm. "A bigger suit doesn't take longer to inspect."

At that, Aames stepped down from the stool. "Yes, Sergeant, it does." I saw Fontes's eyes narrow through his visor; but then Aames pushed a report out, and it showed on my comm, announced by a chime. A matching chime told me Fontes had received it as well. Aames continued, "Adika's larger suit has more places for dust to hide. We can't avoid dust, but we have to fight it every chance we get. Dust buildup will abrade the suit and eventually wear a hole. Here." Aames indicated a point on my side, under my left arm. "Dust. And here." He pointed at the back side of my right arm. "Neither would likely be an issue today, but over time it adds up. If Adika doesn't learn to clean his suit better, he'll be a liability for the rest of us."

I glared at Aames, livid. The very idea that *I* would be a liability! I prepared to argue with him.

But before I could get a word out, Fontes nodded. "Not bad, Mister Aames. Are there any other exceptions in Mister Adika's suit?"

My temper rose still further, though I dared not show it in front of Fontes. They treated me like some sort of child. For an instant I was back home, back at the big dining table in the state house where my father and my illustrious brother and sister looked down on me—me, who towered over all of them, though they never seemed to notice—while they discussed my future as if I had no say in it.

Aames pointed at another item in his report and spoke, pulling my mind back to Luna. "Here, Sergeant. Adika's torso casing is three degrees out of alignment with his pelvic casing. It looks like the suit is a little tight for him, and he had trouble adjusting it." I *had* had trouble, but I would not admit it to Aames now. "That subtle twist would fatigue him over time, especially when combined with the joint pressure variances."

Fontes nodded. "Very thorough, Mister Aames." Aames didn't smile at the compliment. Fontes continued, "And do you know how long it would take for these fatigue effects to manifest?"

Aames frowned and punched at his comm. "I'm not sure how to calculate that, Sergeant. Roughly three hours?"

"More like four to six. And how long is this exercise?"

"Two hours, Sergeant." I grinned. Aames had gone too far, and had made himself look like a worried woman. Fontes started to speak, but not before Aames could add, "*If* nothing goes wrong."

That stopped Fontes before he could correct Aames; and instead, he agreed. "If nothing goes wrong, yes." He looked at me. "Mister Adika, file that report away. Study it. I'll want a paper in the morning on the precise risk percentages posed by your suit. And in the meantime, I'll see about getting you a suit that fits." He looked me up and down. "Somewhere."

Then Fontes looked back to Aames. "You were right this time, Mister Aames, but don't be a smartass about it. One of our most important rules here is: being a smartass is hazardous to your health. It makes you arrogant; and Mister Adika was right, arrogance is risky out here.

Don't assume you'll be right the next time." He looked at his comm. "Now, have you been inspected? We're holding up the excursion."

Aames shook his head. "I haven't given him a chance yet. I was making my report." And then he stood, legs slightly parted, arms slightly away from his side, and waited for my inspection.

I set to work quickly, but also nervously with Fontes watching me. I carefully went through the checklist, and also through Aames's notes. I did not waste time, but I did not miss any item on the list. I found some minor exceptions, all well within tolerance but still large enough to note. As I reported each one to Fontes, I watched Aames's face, grinning inside my helmet where he could not see. With my eyes I tried to say, *See? You are not perfect either, you smug American.* But despite my efforts, I saw no resentment in his eyes. In fact, I saw almost . . . satisfaction. The more I reported, the more his face relaxed.

At last I finished my report. "That is all, Sergeant. I judge his suit is fit for duty for this excursion." Fontes nodded and turned toward the passageway.

But Aames did not move. "Check my boots, Adika."

Fontes turned back, and immediately my face grew warm again. I had looked at his boots during my inspection, but not as closely as I might have. I was too rushed, and the boots were so low and my head so high, and it was difficult to lean over in my suit. I tried to treat this oversight as a triviality. "Your boots are in order, Aames."

Aames refused to move. "*Check* my *boots.*" And he lifted his right leg and planted his right foot on top of the step stool. As soon as I got a closer view of the boots, my heart raced. The strap near the top of the boot was twisted 180 degrees. The clasp was closed, but the polymer fabric showed stretch marks and abrasions.

I was angry and chagrined, but I was also disciplined. I knew my duty, no matter my feelings. I looked up at Fontes. "I must amend my report, Sergeant. Mister Aames's suit is outside of safe configuration in two particulars: boot strap twisted, boot strap strained. There is a significant risk that the strap could break or come loose during heavy activity, and the result would be a dangerous pressure loss." With my last words, I looked at Aames. I wondered at that moment if I would save him if I found him with such a pressure loss.

Fontes made a note on his comm. "That's a solid report, Mister Adika. And now I've had enough of waiting for you two. Both of you unsuit. You'll spend today's drill down in Excursion Services, getting your suits refitted and doing repairs." He looked up at Aames. "What the hell is up with you, Mister Aames? You *knew* about the strap?"

Aames pulled off his helmet and nodded. "Yes, Sergeant, and all of the other exceptions with my suit. If you check the appendix to my report on Adika's suit, you'll find the full details there."

Fontes pulled open the appendix and read for several seconds. Then he looked up again. "What. The. Hell. Aames? Do you think this is some kind of game?"

Aames shook his head. "No, Sergeant, just inspection. I knew how to inspect a suit, but I had no way to know if *Adika* knew how to inspect a suit. So I gave him things to inspect." He looked at me, his face betraying no emotion. "You need work, but you passed."

Fontes slapped Aames on the shoulder, rattling Aames's hard suit. "*I* decide who passes here, Aames. If you ever pull anything like that again, I'll invent a whole new punishment duty specifically for you." He looked at both of us and shook his head. "I've wasted enough time on you two. Get down to Excursion Services. Now."

He turned and left, and we unsuited in silence. Aames was done first, and he headed to ExServ. My anger churned in my gut: he had cost me two excursion hours, and there would be a mark on my record on my very first day.

I ran past Aames, slowing just long enough to give him a rough shove and a message. "Remember what Sergeant Fontes said, Aames: 'Being a smartass is hazardous to your health.'"

C

Aames had been right, of course, and those exceptions could have been deadly in the wrong circumstances. He never deliberately sabotaged a test again, but he remained ruthless in his inspections and his peer reviews. He was scornful and belittling in his critiques, and he made no friends as a result. This seemed not to disturb him, as he showed no interest in getting to know his classmates, and that made him even more of an outcast.

Some thought Nick was currying favor with Fontes. If so, he had a foolish way of going about it, since he continued to argue with Fontes and the other instructors. Nick followed their rules, but he always pointed out how he would do things differently if he were designing the protocols. At first Fontes doled out punishment duty for Nick's impertinence, but he soon realized that Nick took this duty as just another learning experience. Nick saw an opportunity to supervise details of his work and that of others. It was more reward than punishment.

So even the famous Armand Fontes eventually surrendered to the stubborn Nick Aames. Since Nick insisted on finding fault with everything, Fontes turned it into a new assignment, a new form of lesson. He made Nick put his findings in writing: official incident reports, change requests, and action plans. That kept Nick busy, but not busy enough. He still found time to critique our work; and because of our names, because of an accident of the Roman alphabet, I was the most frequent subject of his reviews.

I did mention I was proud, did I not? Nick was not the only young fool at LSS, as I hope I have made clear by now. I was proud, young, full of life, and full of myself. As I have matured, I have learned restraint. A warrior uses force for a purpose and does not let it drive him; but back then, I saw force as a way to win respect. After my embarrassment that first day, every report by Nick only made me angrier. Every report led to an assignment from Fontes: more research, more writing, more time with my head buried in my comm. Being more interested in action and strategy and planning, I hated the studies, and those assignments took up most of my spare time. Every hour of lost sleep made me hate Aames just a little more.

And on top of it all, Father's spies were as efficient as ever. Somehow word of my disgrace and my additional assignments got back to him. He messaged me, and I feared he would be angry; but it was worse: he was *pitying*. He offered to send me tutors. Personal tutors, at Lunar Survival School. What could be more embarrassing? But he was not worried about *my* embarrassment, only his own. He could not let his son fail out of LSS. His political enemies would use me against him.

I snapped off my comm without answering. And I went back to my studies, but I could not concentrate. All I could see was the judgmental face of Nick Aames.

C

One day in a survival exercise, I made just another small error, despite my increased diligence. I neglected to check a seal when assembling an emergency stretcher. The LED sensors around the edge said the seal was complete, and I was in a hurry to get our "patient" to medical care; but there was a bandage caught in the seal. The bandage was translucent enough for the LED to penetrate and read as a seal, but there was a small air leak. And naturally, Nick Aames was the one who checked the pressure and found the leak. After yet another of Nick's stinging incident reports and another assignment from Fontes, I had finally had enough. I would show this tiny little man with the red hair that no American could push around a Nigerian.

So the next evening I found Nick working out alone in the LSS gymnasium, as I knew was his habit. The rest of our classmates were wrapped up in duties or studies, but Aames was ahead of his work, as usual. We would have this room to ourselves for a while, long enough that I could corner Nick and teach him some respect.

Aames was running on a lunar treadmill, pulled down by elastic bands to keep him from bounding off the track. "Aames," I said, closing and locking the door behind me.

"I'm busy, Adika," he said, not breaking stride.

I shook my head. "We must have words, Aames. Now." As I approached, Aames came to a stop and detached the bands. I stood in front of him, my arms held loosely at my side.

Aames lifted a towel from the treadmill display and wiped his face. "Make them fast words. I have reports to file."

"I do not think it will take long." I shifted my weight, ready in case he tried to run past me. "And I have had enough of your reports. You will cease inspecting my work, and you will keep a civil tongue when you address me."

He pulled the towel away. "Fontes assigned those reports. Take it up with him."

"This has nothing to do with Fontes." I flexed my knuckles. "You must learn some respect."

Aames stepped down from the treadmill and walked over to me, hands on hips, not breathing hard despite his workout. "I *must* learn, eh?"

"You must." I looked down at the short little man, and I smiled. "And since I have seen that you will only learn the hard way, I—"

I had expected to banter with Aames, threaten him to make him respect me, and then bruise him just a little to take some satisfaction from his surrender; but Nick Aames did not know how such dominance games were played. I never finished my threat. He threw the towel at my face, and instinctively I blocked it, harmless though it was. Then without visibly flexing his muscles against the weak lunar gravity, Aames sprang backward, one foot flying up and catching me in the chin as he tumbled. The foot caught me entirely by surprise—my Earth reflexes simply could not conceive that such a short man could kick as high as my head—and I was lifted completely off my own feet. I flew backward, slowly falling as I smashed to a halt against the far wall.

The wind was knocked out of me by the impact, but I did not let it slow me down. I sprang back to my feet and leaped back toward Aames, determined to make my own use of the low gravity. But as I arced through the air, Aames danced away. It was the first time I had seen the graceful, acrobatic art of capoeira, and I did not know what to make of it. Compared to the wrestling styles I had learned in Nigeria and the *savate de rue* I had learned in the UN, Aames's moves seemed delicate, almost fanciful. I fought back the urge to laugh—just as Aames suddenly reversed course, sprang back at me as he rolled sideways, and kicked me in the side of the head with *both* feet in rapid succession. This time I fell to the ground, stunned.

As more proof that I was young and foolish, I believed then that size was the measure of a warrior. It was beyond my comprehension that this tiny American had struck me *three times* with such humiliating blows, without me once returning the attack. I was unfamiliar with Aames's style of fighting, I was unfamiliar with the low gravity, and I was growing blinded by anger.

My head rang with the kicks, but I recovered quickly, breathing deeply to try to master my temper. I assessed the situation. We both wore the shorts and shirts that were standard off-duty wear in the controlled environment of LSS. There would be no loose fabric to grab. My height was no advantage when Aames could easily leap over me. Instead I crouched low, minimizing my target area as I backed toward the door. I spread my arms out for a wider reach. Whatever tricks Aames might pull, I blocked his only way out. He could not evade me forever.

Still, I was not willing to wait while he made me look foolish. I tried to taunt him into a rash move. "You are a good dancer, Aames, but we do not dance. We fight! I am Chukwunwike, the strongest of my city, the strongest of my unit. You are just a little American, nobody at all. Come closer, and I will toss you like a sack of rice." But Aames ignored my challenge. He spoke not a word, standing ready but staying out of reach. "Come, man, are you afraid? You have exhausted your stock of tricks, and now you can do nothing but run?"

Still he said nothing. I started slowly edging toward him, trying to trap him against the wall; but just when I thought I might have him, he did another backward spring, bounced from his hands, and planted both feet on the wall. Then he bounced off and up and over my head, landing halfway across the room. He ran for the door.

Sensing weakness, I called after him, "You are a typical little American. You think you are the king of the world, until someone stands up to you. Then you run home like a frightened child. Run home to the women, Aames, and leave space to men. Run home to your mother and grandmother."

Something clicked. Somehow I had finally gotten to Aames's weak spot, whatever it might be. In an instant, he snarled and turned and leaped at me feet first; and for the first time he miscalculated, jumping too high and falling too slowly and giving me time to see the kick coming. I stepped aside at the last instant and grabbed Aames around the waist. We fell to the ground.

I had expected that this little man, this—this *dancer* would not know what to do when grappled, but Aames surprised me again. He fought like a jackal defending its home, all frenzy and energy. I held on, my strength and my reach finally giving me the advantage. Still he refused to surrender. He squirmed, he kicked, and he punched, and I realized that I could not let him go without risking injury. I tried to subdue him. As he twisted, I wrapped my legs around his torso, my arms around his legs, and I stretched him out. I would hold him there until he submitted. But no, he continued to wriggle and fight, despite all my advantages. I squeezed my legs, hoping that would make him yield.

But Aames proved to be a jackal in another way: he had teeth! I felt a tearing pain in my calf as Aames bit into my leg. Hard. I tried to squeeze the air out of him, but that only made him bite harder.

Squeeze, bite, squeeze, bite . . . I thought we might be locked there in a stalemate until Fontes would appear and throw us both out of LSS, but finally Aames worked free a hand and tapped twice on my side. He released his bite, and he went limp.

Nick Aames had surrendered. And what did I have to show for it? A set of bloody teeth marks. You can still see them to this day.

I let Aames loose, and we stood. I didn't feel triumphant, I felt spent. I had won the fight, but had I taught him respect? I did not see it. I still saw defiance in his eyes.

Then I heard pounding on the door. How long it had been going on, I could not say. I had been too focused on the fight. But as soon as I noticed it, the pounding stopped, and the door opened. Fontes strode in, followed by Barnes. Immediately he set into us. "Adika! Aames! I couldn't believe it when Barnes told me the gym was locked. What the hell were you two doing in here?"

I looked at Aames and down at myself, and I wondered how there could be any question: bruises, torn clothes, and blood running down my calf. And worse, if Aames demanded that the surveillance video be shown, it would be clear that I had provoked the fight. With one request, one well within his rights, he could ruin my career. I caught my breath as I tried to word an apology and hoped my father would not disown me when I was expelled from LSS. I hoped he would not lose his standing in the government.

But before I could speak, Aames answered, hardly breathing heavily at all: "Combat training, Sergeant. Mister Adika was teaching me UN hand-to-hand techniques, and I was showing him some things I learned in São Paulo."

Fontes looked down at my calf. "They teach biting in São Paulo?"

"They teach *survival*, whatever it takes. In some districts, São Paulo is as dangerous as Luna."

Fontes scowled. "Combat training isn't in the curriculum here, Nicolau."

Aames sneered back. "It should be, *Armand*. Sometimes survivors are in a panic, and they need to be subdued." And then he looked at me. "*Without* serious injury."

I looked at Aames in wonder. In his place, as angry as he made me, I would have informed on him without a moment's hesitation. Why had he covered for me? But I realized that any delay looked suspicious; so I turned back to Adika, I nodded, and I found my voice. "Yes, Sergeant Fontes. Mister Aames was explaining that to me. So we decided it is never too soon to start training."

Fontes frowned at both of us then. "And for that you needed to lock the gym?"

Aames spoke up again. "Adika had a lot to teach me. I needed time to consider it."

Fontes still looked skeptical. "Maybe we need to check surveillance." I opened my mouth to explain—somehow—but then he waved his hand and shook his head. "Never mind, I don't see any permanent damage, so I'll let it slide. You'll both see an infraction in your records, but not enough to get you booted. If I caught you fighting, now . . ."

Fontes stared at both of us just long enough to be sure that we got the point. Then he continued, "Barnes, you have your gym now. Aames, you owe me some paperwork. Move."

"Yes, Sergeant."

I was unsure how to react: I was still angry with Aames, but I was also grateful to him for not turning me in. At last I gave him a tentative smile; but he only stared at me, face like a carven mask, and left the gym. I was sure he would look back, but he never did. He had already forgotten me.

Fontes had not forgotten, though. He turned to me. "And Chukwunwike, I have a dirty yeast vat down on the third level and a wire brush with your name on it. If that vat isn't clean by 2300, that'll be another mark in your record. Go."

I went, following my comm map to the yeast vats. I was grateful that Aames had saved us both from far worse punishment. I was glad that I would not embarrass my father. But still I was not happy. I had entered the gym with wounded pride; and now my pride was confused, not assuaged. Aames had proven far too difficult to subdue, as if my size and strength were somehow less significant than awareness and determination. I had exhausted myself, so the anger was spent, but I did not know how to feel next. Yet Aames had shown no emotion at all, as if the fight had never happened. And where I would have held a grudge, he seemed simply not to care. As if the evening had meant nothing to him.

Then as I scrubbed the yeast vat, an anonymous message came in on my comm; and when I read it, I laughed until the echoes poured out of the vat. It was a single sentence: "If you ever do that when it puts a mission at risk, I won't go so easy on you next time."

When I finally tamed my laughter, I felt good, even with the throbbing pain in my calf. I did not fear the little American, but I was learning to like him.

5. BEDSIDE MANNERS

FROM THE MEMOIRS OF PARK YERIM

2 JUNE THROUGH 5 JUNE 2083

I looked at Adika. He still sat perfectly straight on the edge of the chair. "He lied for you? Everyone gives me the impression that Nick Aames never lies."

Adika's big grin returned. "I thought of that, years later, and I went over his words. Not a single one was false, precisely. They were valid interpretations of the facts. He just failed to put them in context."

"So that was it?" I asked. "An adolescent male bonding ritual, and you became fast friends?"

Adika shook his head. "It was not a bonding ritual, and there was nothing fast about it. We were not friends. But Aames puzzled me. I just could not understand his behavior.

"And so I studied him: not as an opponent, merely as an object of my curiosity. And in time I realized: none of this was personal to him at all. Not the inspections, the reviews, the constant testing. It was not about proving himself better than anyone, it was not a dominance game. It was not even malicious, though his lack of tact can seem like malice. It was simply about being *right*. Nick Aames is absolutely obsessed with being right, and correcting himself *or others* when they are wrong. He has that sense we see in children, but most of us outgrow: everything must be right, must be in order, or he cannot be at peace."

I looked around the office. I could see Adika's point: except for the hand-painted sign and the e-reader, everything here looked very ordered and polished, each black piece of furniture precisely placed within the room. There was a sense of dark unity in the design. But still . . . "The world is *not* an orderly place. He can't have much peace."

"Ah." Adika smiled. "And now you know. Like I did, you just got a glimpse into the heart of Nick Aames. He must have everything right, and he knows he never will. This is what makes him so difficult. He is *always* disappointed."

I thought about that. Adika's description was nothing like I had heard from Aames's detractors; and yet it fit somehow. It wasn't the whole of Nick Aames, but it was a piece of the puzzle I hadn't even realized was missing. It was like I had placed a jigsaw piece, and suddenly what I thought was a horse became a zebra. I wondered what the picture would become when I found more puzzle pieces.

"So you understood him? That changed your relationship?"

Adika shook his head again. "I am sorry, Inspector, you are looking for simple transitions, a switch turning on or off, when reality changes over years. I still do not truly understand Nick even today. And our relationship is always changing. But I can tell you the one crucial change that let us get through Lunar Survival School without killing each other."

"Oh?"

"I asked him for help."

"Huh? Captain Aames does *not* strike me as helpful."

"That is because people so rarely ask him. They know that he will pounce on every little mistake, and that is too much stress for most people. He makes himself unapproachable, unless you have the hide of a rhinoceros. But when I realized I was over my head with my studies, and I knew that Aames was ahead of the class, I swallowed my pride and I asked. And without hesitation, without making me beg, he readily answered my questions and helped me with my assignments. Oh, he was as abrasive as ever when I made a mistake. He has so little tolerance for error. But asking for help meant I wanted to be right, like he does. In the pursuit of knowledge, he becomes almost enjoyable to be around, like a large dog who will growl if you approach him incorrectly but will join you in the hunt. With his help, I turned my academic problems around, and I managed to graduate from LSS. Not with honors, but with my dignity intact."

I pointed at his record on my comm. "More than intact, Commander. You've had an incredible career. You could have your pick of top assignments. And yet you've settled for security chief on a transport. That's practically retirement for a man of your talents. What sort of influence does Captain Aames have, that he could talk you into this?"

Adika leaned forward and looked right in my eyes. "Inspector, you interviewed Constance about Nick, and now you have interviewed me. If you listen carefully, our answers are there. The one question *I* have is: If you truly want to understand Captain Aames, why do you not interview him?"

I had kept wondering that myself; and eventually I had found an answer, something more sensible than just me being intimidated by Aames's reputation. "I will when I'm ready, Commander. When I'm ready, and when I'm sure I can do so without prejudice."

"Prejudice?"

I nodded. "You must know that Captain Aames has a difficult reputation throughout much of the Corps. It's not something you can miss as you rise through the ranks. And during my preparation for this assignment, I heard from admirals and bureaucrats and astronauts and port authorities who all admonished me not to trust Aames, not to let him escape responsibility for his actions. Oh, sure, I also knew him as the hero of the second *Bradbury* expedition; but even that he turned into a mess before he ever got back to Earth. So by the time I set foot aboard the *Aldrin*, almost the entire picture—the entire *negative* picture that I had of Nick Aames—came from his enemies. That has to color my judgment and my reactions when I meet him. Everything I will hear from him, I will hear through that filter. And I *hate* that. I pride myself on my objectivity. As much as Aames demands to be right, I demand objectivity. So since I can't unhear those stories, the closest I can get to balance is to hear the other story from his friends."

Adika laughed sharply, just once. "I'm not sure Nick has friends."

"But— But you're his friend."

"I try to be, yes. But being Nick's friend is a serious undertaking, requiring much effort. We are classmates, shipmates, and brothers in the conquest of space; and on good days, we are friends as well, as much as Nick is able. But Captain Aames is not a friend you turn to for comfort in times of trouble; he is a leader you trust to guide you out of that trouble." Adika rose. "Or at least he was, and will be if you and the admirals will let him do his job. But I have a job to do as well, Inspector, if I may?" He snapped to attention.

I nodded. "Dismissed, Commander. And thank you."

☾

That seemed like a good plan, a way to get the full picture before I made any final decisions; but before I could follow through, I had paperwork to fill out and reports to file. Plus because I now had oversight of the *Aldrin*, I had to read every ship's report of any significance, looking for evidence—or signs that evidence was being concealed. Knapp was still making noises about cover-ups, and even though he irritated me, I couldn't ignore the possibility. Every time he filed a complaint—and that was several times a day—I had to drop everything and investigate it, even though not one had proven valid. So I had Matt and the investigative team pulling every report, highlighting anomalies, and pushing them to me for review so that I could stay on top of events. Since my team was thorough, the list of anomalies piled up.

I was still buried in paperwork two days later when Matt called my comm. "Inspector, we have another incident."

I sighed. "What's the admiral's problem now, Matt?"

"It's not Admiral Knapp, ma'am, it's Commander Adika. He sounded rushed, and he had to cut off, but he said he needed you to resolve a dispute on I Ring."

"I Ring? That's not open yet."

"It is now, ma'am. Admiral Knapp accelerated the schedule. That's in my report from yesterday."

Yesterday? I was still wading through reports from three days ago, so I hadn't seen yesterday's. I hurried out to Matt's office and spoke to him directly. "All right, if he calls back, tell him I'm on my way. And call if you learn anything more."

"Are you sure I shouldn't go with you, ma'am?" Matt seemed to be constantly watching for threats to me. There was enough tension on the *Aldrin* to justify his concern.

But if there had been a hazard, Adika would've warned me, I'm sure. "No, Matt, if you leave that desk right now, the reports will bury us. I've got this." I left Matt's office and headed for the cross tube.

The eight rings of the *Aldrin*—ten now, with I and J added—all rotated on the central hub, a zero-G zone where manufacturing and power generation took place. To allow speedier travel between the rings, they were also joined by four cross tubes. These could be sealed at each ring to contain pressure or gas leaks; but when I entered tube 3, I keyed in my override code that opened all the seals in it so I could race to I. In the low gravity, I had an easy run, using the loping stride that I was taught in Basic: push ahead with the rear foot, sail through the air, bend the front leg at the last minute to push ahead again. I had practiced enough to stay low with a steady cadence, slowing only briefly at each ring to call out, "Coming through, clear the tube!"

So I wasn't breathing heavily at all when I came to an abrupt halt at the hatch to I Ring. That hatch *was* sealed, though, and blocked by a gray-uniformed *Aldrin* spacer first class. I stood in front of him, tried to look commanding despite my short stature, and said, "I need to get into the I Ring."

But the spacer ignored my attempt to intimidate him, and he shook his head. "I'm sorry, Commander Adika ordered me not to let anyone else aboard I."

I tried again, letting some anger into my face. "Spacer, I'm Inspector General Park, I go where I choose. And Commander Adika called for me."

At that the man blinked. "I'm sorry, ma'am. The uniform . . . the light . . . I thought you were with the Admiralty." That was probably fair: in the low light, IG's navy-blue uniforms looked a lot like Admiralty black. "The commander specifically said to keep out Admiralty troops." The spacer tapped out a sequence on the hatch controls, and the hatch opened as he spoke into his comm: "Commander, Inspector Park is at tube 3." He paused. "Yes, sir, I'll tell her." He looked back to me. "Inspector, he's waiting for you at tube 4."

I entered the ring and was momentarily disoriented. The I Ring was no larger than the rest; but with no bulkheads in place, it looked spacious. The upper deck plates were missing as well, so the only ceiling was nine meters up. With the far bulkhead nearly ten meters away, the space looked like a giant metal cavern, curving off in both directions. It took me a moment to realize that the wall panels and deck plates were bolted against the side bulkheads, waiting for installation. I also noticed long strips and sheets of white tape across the panels, the bulkheads, and the floor.

Though the sights before me were confusing, the sounds left me no question where to go. Tube 4 was nearly ninety meters away, but I could hear the shouts echoing through the ring. I loped again toward the noise, coming upon a black-uniformed work crew as I went. They were unbolting wall panels and floor plates and setting up the decks. Some set the panels in place, some bolted them down, and some stripped off the white tape and wiped the panels clean. That small stretch of the ring was quickly coming together, already looking more like a place than a shell. I dodged around them as they worked, and I continued toward the next tube.

When I got to tube 4, I saw the sources of the shouting. I recognized the tall, thin man in Admiralty black: Chief Horace Gale, a British officer working under Admiral Knapp. On the rendezvous shuttle that had brought us to the *Aldrin*, Gale had used his field medic training to check my shoulder, and during our conversations, he had blatantly tried to prejudice me against Captain Aames. The two men had a history of bad blood. In fact, Gale's distaste for Aames may have been my first reason to learn more about Aames for myself. Although Gale had his good points, I didn't trust him. Even though he knew his way around a spacecraft, I thought him a phony: he used perfect BBC English with the admirals but slid into cockney with the spacers. If Gale hated Aames, that was one mark in Aames's favor.

Gale shouted now, more cockney than BBC: "Get out of my way, Bosun. We have work to do."

The target of Gale's wrath was a woman in *Aldrin* gray: taller than Gale, a sturdy build like she could toss him completely around the ring. Her red-blonde hair, cut in a short military style, blended almost invisibly in to her angry red face as she shouted right back: "You're not doing any work here. Get them off my ring, Gale."

Between them stood Commander Adika, massive hands on their shoulders, holding them apart. Around them stood eight spacers in black and six more in gray, all eyeing each other warily.

Gale glared at the woman, blood in his eyes. "*Chief* Gale, Bosun Smith!" Smith. I knew that name from my research, though we had never met. She was one of Aames's most loyal spacers. "And you're interfering with orders from Admiral Knapp."

"Shove your orders!" Smith answered. "Your crew is not qualified for this job. They're a hazard to this ship. If you won't stop them, I will." She twisted out of Adika's grip, and I thought she might punch Gale. Gale took three steps backward, fear in his face. He expected the punch as well.

I decided it was time to take charge. "*Enough!*" I shouted over both of them, hoping I sounded like an authority figure, not a little kitten caught between wildcats.

Fortunately Commander Adika backed my play. "*Attention!*" he shouted, and his deep bass echoed from the walls. Gale and Smith both instinctively straightened to attention. "Inspector on deck!" Everyone froze.

I looked with a silent thanks at Adika, but he stared straight ahead, not catching my eye. "Commander Adika." Then he looked down at me. I continued in a more even tone, "Since you're the only one not shouting, tell me what's happening here."

"Inspector, at 1013 ship's time, I received a call from Bosun Smith informing me that Chief Gale and his work crew had entered I Ring ahead of our work schedule. She informed me that the work crew were not certified for this work, and so they put the ship at risk."

Gale had started to interrupt, rushing to get his point in. "They do—"

"Chief." I cut Gale off. He looked sullen, but he shut up. "Continue, Commander."

"I called you immediately, Inspector, since interactions between the crews are your jurisdiction. When I arrived with my security detail"—he glanced at the *Aldrin* crew around him—"the work crew was already deploying, and Chief Gale and Bosun Smith were already arguing. I stationed guards at the tubes to keep the situation from escalating, and I have been trying to keep Gale and Smith apart until you could arrive."

I nodded at him, and I turned to Gale. "All right, Chief, is the commander's account accurate?"

Gale again spoke in a rush. "She's completely out of line, send—"

"*Chief!*" Again I cut through his chatter. "You will slow down, and you will address me as Inspector or ma'am, or I will have words with Admiral Knapp."

Gale looked like he was close to violence, his face trembling at my rebuke. But then he regained control and started over. "*Inspector*, Bosun Smith is out of line. My crew has installed rings at Farport for years. They're thoroughly certified at habitat ring power-up and setup."

"*Not* on the *Aldrin*," Smith snarled, causing Gale to flinch. I turned my glare on her as she continued, "Sorry, ma'am, but we're all in danger. The *Aldrin* is not Farport. Ring setup on a cycler is different. If you get it wrong, the whole ring could blow."

"Oh, bollocks." Gale took a step toward Smith, but stopped when she narrowed her eyes at him. Adika planted a massive hand in Gale's chest, and Gale slapped at it ineffectually. "They're just obstructing us. When I'm in charge here—"

I wheeled on Gale. "Chief, shut up!" I turned back to Smith. "The setup is that different?"

Smith nodded. "Thousands of pages of variances, ma'am. We've learned what works in space and what only works in mission planning. As we speak, they could be doing irreparable damage."

That was enough for me. "Chief, get your people out. Now. We'll sort this out in my office." Gale started to speak, and I stuck my finger right in his face. "*Now*, Chief. Commander Adika, if the Admiralty crew are not in the tubes in one minute, your guards are authorized to carry them out."

I think I saw a flicker of a grin on Adika's face. Gale, meanwhile, glared at me but backed down. He spoke into his comm. "Work detail, drop what you're doing. We're going back to our station. Chief Gale out."

Gale's crew took his order literally: I heard an echoed *whoomf* as somewhere antispinward several wall panels fell softly to the floor. And give them credit for speed: it was fewer than thirty seconds before they came around the ring in a steady lope-march.

The man at the rear of the crew was holding a big, loose ball of the white tape. As he came into view, he called out, "Chief, what do we do with this? It stinks, and the tape won't let go."

Smith turned at the word "tape," and her eyes popped wide. "Shit!"

That got Adika's attention, and he turned as well. That impassive stone face suddenly showed fear. "FIRE!" His shout boomed throughout the ring. "Evacuate! Now! Evac now! FIRE IN THE RING!"

Gale started to argue, but one of Adika's guards grabbed him around the waist and really did carry him into tube 4. That was the only clue I needed: I started pushing my way to the tube, but the entry was already crowded.

Suddenly I heard several loud pops from antispinward, followed by a whooshing sound. Again Adika shouted, "FIRE!" I turned toward the sound, and I saw a yellow glow where the ring curved out of sight. My heart raced and panic flooded my brain as I saw flames rolling into view. Some flowed along the deck plates, swirling as if hovering over the floor. Others chased up the walls, following the lines of white tape and then spilling like hot plasma into the open space, as if the air itself was aflame. I suddenly felt a wave of hot air. A tinge of some strange odor made my head spin.

I thought I might faint, and Adika picked me up. From his arms, I saw the spacer in the rear stumble. Whatever fumes I was breathing, he was getting a lot more, how much I couldn't guess. A big tongue of flame reached out from the main fireball, straight for him and that damned ball of white tape. I winced, not wanting to see him engulfed.

Adika tossed me to a guard, and he *ran*, faster than I had ever seen in one-quarter G. He reached the spacer, three steps ahead of the approaching flames, grabbed the tape ball, and with one hand ripped it loose from the man as he tossed him spinward with the other. Then he turned to fling the ball away.

But before Adika could let loose, the flame reached him, and the ball went up like a dry pine tree. Flames washed over him, and he screamed—in pain or defiance, I couldn't be sure—as he pulled back his arm and *threw* the burning mess. That didn't stop the flames, though: his uniform was fireproof, and he had no hair to burn, but the air around him was a fog of burning fumes. I hoped he wasn't breathing those in, or he would burn from the inside out.

The guards passed me hand over hand toward the tube. "Stop. Wait. Adika!" But they were too disciplined for that. Soon I was at the entry. I had just enough time to see Adika come running out of the flames like some demon from hell, swathed in hellfire, then tumble and roll to get free of the fumes. He scooped up the fallen spacer and rushed to the tube; but his stride was uneven, and he weaved side to side.

Adika's guards were coordinated and skilled, but not gentle. They prodded and pushed us all into the tube, shouting "Make room! Move!" the whole time. From the first popping sounds, it took fewer than twelve seconds for them to bundle everyone in; but in that time the air had turned hot enough to burn my throat, making me choke.

Last in the tube was Adika himself, his flesh raw with second-degree burns, maybe worse. "MOVE!" He tossed the spacer ahead and spoke into his comm, but it was half-melted, so he moved to the wall panel. He half shouted, half coughed: "Clear. Seal it." Then he punched a code into the panel, and the hatch slid shut.

The air immediately started to cool, and I breathed a little easier. "You can put me down," I said to the guard who held me. He did, but he kept prodding me forward.

I ignored the guard, squeezing back to Adika as the guards pushed the others out. Adika needed medical care, and I was certified as a corpsman. I could try to treat those burns until medics arrived.

But though he was staggering, Adika was still pushing me forward, still croaking out warnings: "Move. Out of the tube."

"Commander, you need to—"

But I never finished my sentence. A creaking, straining sound from the hatch made me pause; and before I could ask what it was, the hatch tore free and blew inward with a massive boom that deafened me. The blast of hot air blew me off my feet as it threw the last guards clear of the tube.

The last thing I saw was Adika, once again clothed in flames, reaching down and lifting me from the deck. I cried out, and I lost consciousness.

C

I woke slowly, in darkness. I heard a voice. "Inspector?" Dr. Baldwin? Yes, Dr. Baldwin; but her voice was flat, toneless.

"Ye . . . yes."

"Inspector, stay still." Her voice came from above and to my right. "You have first- and second-degree burns, including some scalding in your lungs, and you've breathed in some nasty fumes. But you're going to be okay. We have new skin patches in progress and therapy nanos in your lungs and larynx. You can talk if you keep it short."

"Eyes . . ." Something covered my eyes.

"Yes, your corneas were burned, and your retinas too. We've already repaired the corneas, and we grew you some new retinas, but your eyes are going to be sensitive for a while. We covered them so you didn't look into the light. Would you like to see?"

I tried to nod, but I couldn't feel if my head moved or not. *Good drugs.* I must have succeeded, because Dr. Baldwin continued, "Let me turn down the lights, and then I'll remove those pads. Later I've got some dark glasses you'll need to wear for a few days."

I heard Dr. Baldwin walk away, then back to my bunk. She put a hand over my eyes. "I'm going to pull the pads away, then lift my hand. If you say no, I'll cover your eyes again. Are you ready?"

"Mmmhmmm."

"All right." I felt her reach under her hand, pull some tape from my face, and pull out the pads. "One." Her hand lifted slightly, and I saw a bit of light, unfocused. "Two." Her hand rose higher, and I could see light between her fingers. "Three. How's that?"

I saw dim lights, colors, and a vague shape. As my eyes focused, the light grew sharper, making me wince; but then the pain dropped to just a dull throb. My eyes adjusted further, and the shape resolved into the face of Dr. Baldwin.

That face had aged a decade since our conversation. Lines were etched into it. Gone was the sardonic smile, replaced with a grim line that refused to be a frown, but I was sure one was nearby. And her eyes: even in the dimmed light, I could see that they were puffy and red.

Then I remembered: "Adika?"

Dr. Baldwin turned and looked behind her. "He's . . . right across the aisle." She turned back to me. "His burns were much more severe, deep tissue. His lungs are— We're printing new ones. We've got him on oxy-nanos and detoxers to take the strain off what lung tissue remains. And the toxins are all through his liver, but we'll . . . we'll clean that out, get some stem cells in there to replace the damaged tissue. He . . ." She fell silent.

I tried to speak again. "Sorry."

Her eyes flared. "Don't you be sorry!" I thought she was angry, but there was something else. Hope? Determination? No, pride. "He was doing his duty. That's all he ever wanted. Don't you . . ." She trailed off again.

My throat felt a little better, so I tried a longer speech. "Okay. Not sorry. Thank you. And him. Good man."

Dr. Baldwin nodded, and then turned away. I could hear soft sobs, and I lowered my eyes. If she didn't want me to see her cry, I would respect that. Finally she turned back. "The best, and don't you forget it." Then she forced a smile. "He'll pull through. I'm not done with him yet. Or with you. Are you more awake now?"

"Yes."

"All right, I'm going to raise your head a bit." Dr. Baldwin touched a panel on the bed, and the head end rose up. "I want those nanos to get deeper into your lungs. Is that okay?"

I wasn't sure what she was asking, but nothing felt wrong. I nodded again, and this time I actually felt the fabric of the pillow as my cheek scraped across it.

"And here are your glasses." She put dark glasses on me, and suddenly it was easier to see. I hadn't realized my eyes were straining; but now they relaxed, and the throbbing started to fade. I looked around. Already Dr. Baldwin's forced smile had faded. She was back to her impassive face, almost a mirror of Adika's when he was on duty. "Now I have other patients to see on other decks."

"Doctor." I stopped her. "Were there deaths?"

Dr. Baldwin nodded. "But don't worry, you can catch up on reports when your eyes get better. In the meantime, the bed and your glasses are both voice controlled, except for medical overrides. If you call out, the comm will summon me or Dr. Santana or one of the medics. There's a lot going on in your body right now, and some of it will feel pretty strange, so don't be afraid to call." She turned and left for her office; but from across the infirmary, she called back, "Do you feel up to a short visit? Matt Harrold is tearing himself up with worry." I nodded, and she spoke into her comp. "Nurse Lloyd, tell Ensign Harrold he can have five minutes."

Dr. Baldwin left just as Head Nurse Carl Lloyd came in, leading Matt. "Here you go, Ensign. Five minutes." Then he walked to check on patients in the next ward of the infirmary, giving us as much privacy as he could in the open compartment.

Matt looked down at me and tried to smile. "How are you feeling, Inspector?"

I gave him my best smile. "Like someone tried to blow up a spaceship with me in it. But the *Aldrin* has good doctors. They're taking care of me."

Matt nodded. "The best doctors. I pulled their records." He looked down. "It was the only thing I could do: make sure you were getting the best care. Inspector, this team has top ratings in emergency medicine and recuperative therapy. It's just like everyone else on this ship: some of the highest ratings in the Corps. It's almost suspicious, like the records are faked."

I shook my head. "I don't doubt they have the skills to fake the records, but they would have to infiltrate databases on three worlds to do it. You were thorough in pulling and analyzing records, Matt. Did you see any inconsistencies, any signs that the records had been tampered with?" Matt shook his head as well. "They're really that good, I think," I continued. "Aames selects the best who'll put up with him, and he makes them better."

Matt nodded again. "I'm glad he did. You need the best doctors so we can get you back to work. Admiral Knapp has been burying me in demands for status reports. I'll be glad I can tell him you're awake. And so relieved for you too."

I was touched by Matt's loyalty. I really hadn't earned it. I hadn't had time. He was just naturally loyal to his duty and his command, and I was the beneficiary of that. But I decided I would try to deserve that loyalty in the future.

Matt sat on the edge of my bed, and we talked for a couple minutes more, reviewing some of our IG business before Lloyd came over and tapped Matt on the shoulder. Matt didn't argue, just nodded and stood, saluting me. I saluted back, still a novel experience for me. "Dismissed, Ensign. And thank you." Then Matt and Lloyd left.

Now what? I was tired, an all-over weariness, but not sleepy. I tried to reach around for the bed controls, but I found I couldn't move. Even trying gave me throbbing aches all up and down my arms. Looking closer, I could see that my arms and torso were in a plastic cocoon. It must be growing the skin patches that Dr. Baldwin had mentioned. A little experimentation told me that my legs were free. I must not have been burned there.

So I was immobile. Then I remembered what Dr. Baldwin had said: my glasses had voice control, so I could read or watch a vid if I wanted to. But my eyes didn't feel up to that much work yet. So I lay there and wondered what to do next.

"Pretty boring, huh, Inspector?" A voice came from my left. I turned my head to see who was there, but I couldn't move enough to see past the corner of the mattress.

Still, the voice was familiar. "Bosun Smith?"

Smith answered, her voice slurred, "Call me Smitty. If we're gonna be roommates . . . not so formal . . ."

I hesitated. Already on this case, I had let too much informality in. It could color my judgment, and I couldn't afford that. But here, in this half-dark room, trapped in a shell with nanos knitting new skin and crawling through my lungs, with my rescuer across the room on his deathbed, I needed a friend. Or something like one. "My name's Yerim."

"One hell of an introduction, Yerim. Next time throw a party. We don't burn out rings at a party. Usually . . ."

I laughed. It hurt a bit, but it also felt good. "You're in good spirits, Smitty. Must be better off than me."

At that Smith laughed in turn; but it was a raspy, painful laugh that turned to several seconds of coughing. Finally she spoke. "Burns . . . most of my body. Face too. Is why talking funny. Skin mask on face. Ribs cracked where hatch hit me. Thought I was dead yesterday. But I'm feeling much better now. If this is a contest to see who's getting out of bed first, we're neck and neck." Then the humor drained out of her voice. "And way ahead of Chuks."

She fell silent, and I looked for a way to change the subject. Slowly what happened was coming back to me. "Smitty, what happened in I Ring?"

Smith snorted. "Exactly what I said. Gale's crew doesn't know the *Aldrin*." I waited for her to continue. "Farport is at LaGrange 2. Practically stationary. Habitat rings are slid in, gentle thrust. Dock and done. Then the crew comes in, sets up, cleans out the packing waste, ready to go."

"But the *Aldrin*?"

"We dock with the rings in flight. Our orbit is fixed. Rings have to be boosted to matching vector. Docking is harder, more impact. Everywhere more stress. So our interior panels are bolted down tighter. And the fixtures and fasteners and accessories are taped down with stronger tape. Boost tape, it'll stand up to anything short of launch from Earth."

"But?"

"But it's nothing at all like packing tape at Farport. Adhesive is practically a weld. Strong stuff. But when the bonds are broken, residue is toxic. Flammable as hell too." Smith laughed again, triggering more coughing. "Heh. Flammable as hell. Joking even when I don't try. Anyway, smallest spark will set it off. Procedure on *Aldrin* is: set up all the panels, evacuate air from the ring, *then* the crew comes in again. In suits. And cleans up the tape. Takes a lot longer, but the only way."

"And so Gale . . ." I shook my head in disgust.

"I knew Gale's crew were setting up. Didn't know they were stupid enough to pull tape. If I'd known, I'd probably be up on charges right now. Cracking the skull of an officer. Again."

I smiled a bit. "Those charges would've landed on my desk, Bosun, and they might've gotten lost there. I was tempted to crack Gale's skull myself, *before* this incident."

Another coughing laugh from Smith. "Oh, the famous Gale charms didn't work on you? Good company, then. He's a worm, but he knows how to play the game."

I shook my head, though she couldn't see it. "If this is a game, he just made a bad move."

"Damn straight. I Ring may be beyond repair. Air expanded, pressure blew the hatches. Probably not the vacuum seals, those are strong, but we'll have to check every single one in ultrasonic detail. Two months lost, minimum, and we're already behind. And then . . ."

I knew what she meant. "And then Adika. And casualties."

I heard her swallow. "Yeah. Chuks. Damn, wish Gale were here. I'm all clamped down here, but maybe I could spit in his eye or something."

I giggled, just once. "My legs are free. I could kick him."

That brought a spasm of coughing laughter. Finally Smith regained control and said, "You're all right, Yerim, for an officer." Then she coughed one more time. "But I'm a little tired. Think I'll sleep now, okay?"

"Okay . . . roomie."

After one more coughing stretch, Smith fell silent. Soon I heard a slight snore from my left. The steady in-and-out rhythm made me aware of just how tired I was too.

I was thinking I should try to dim the room lights; but before I could figure out how, I was asleep as well.

☾

I woke again, this time to the sound of hushed voices.

The lights were still dimmed, but someone had pulled my glasses off as I slept. So I went through the entire experience again: too-bright lights, eyes adjusting, throbbing pain. But the pain wasn't as bad this time, and my eyes focused more quickly.

I saw two figures past the foot of my bed, their backs to me. One was clearly Dr. Baldwin, her heavy frame sagging and her graying hair disheveled. Next to her stood a man, slightly shorter than her, his hair appearing a dark shade of red in the low light. He wore a crisp, clean uniform in the gray of the *Aldrin*'s crew; and on his shoulders were the gold bars of a captain.

Nick Aames had finally left his cabin, but it was no time for my interview. This was a private moment I was never meant to see, and I just wanted to be somewhere else. I didn't want to intrude. But my curiosity was stronger than my embarrassment, and I strained to hear their words.

Listening closely, I heard Dr. Baldwin. "Nick, he . . . he . . ."

The captain pulled Dr. Baldwin in tighter, and she turned to him and started sobbing into his chest as he rubbed her back. "Hush. Hush, Connie. He's been hurt worse than this before. One time on Luna . . ." He looked down at her face, and suddenly he cut off his story. "You don't need to hear that story again. But don't worry. Chuks is strong as a rhino, and he's got the most stubborn doctor in the solar system. You two will pull through this together, and he'll have a few more scars for his collection."

"But I don't know—"

"I do. The patient will recover. But his doctor needs her rest." And Captain Aames put his arm at her back and guided her across the infirmary to her office.

I lay there in the silent dim light. The tingling I felt wasn't new skin, but some deeper chill. Soul deep. Adika had said, *"But Captain Aames is not a friend you turn to for comfort in times of trouble."* And yet here Aames was, when Dr. Baldwin needed just that. And I wondered: Did any of his friends, did *anyone* really know this man?

I was still wondering, staring at the office door, when suddenly the door reopened. Before I could pretend to be asleep, Captain Aames came through, and he looked right into my eyes. As the door slid shut behind him, he held my gaze. His beard and mustache were neatly trimmed, his face looked freshly scrubbed, and his eyes were alert, though slightly moist.

Aames turned away and looked down at Commander Adika for a few minutes, his eyes swinging from the bed to the readouts and back. He looked back at me and raised an eyebrow—in question or in accusation, I couldn't tell. Then he looked past me as if I wasn't there, and he strode past me to Smith's bed.

Aames might ignore me, but I couldn't miss this chance to study the man whose fate was in my hands. I turned my head to follow him. I still couldn't see Smith's bunk, but I saw Aames lean over, turn on a small light, and shake the bunk. "Bosun," he said. His voice wasn't loud, but it was louder than anything else in the infirmary, and firm. In that room, it was a shout. "Bosun, officer on deck." Then he straightened and looked down at the bunk.

I heard a faint scrape to my left, maybe Smith shifting on the bunk. Then she spoke. "Captain. Apologize. No salute. Hands tied down."

Aames's tone was dismissive. "Then stop trying, you idiot, you'll rip something loose. And that stupid face mask, no wonder you can barely talk. Dr. Baldwin says it should have done its work now. Would you like it off?"

"Yes, Captain."

Aames leaned over the bunk again; and when he rose, he had a plastic shell in his hands, rounded and roughly fifteen centimeters across. In the light from the small lamp, I saw a moist sheen on the inside of the shell. "There, Bosun, do you think you can respond properly to a superior officer now?"

"Sir, yes, sir!" Her voice was still rough, but not slurred.

"That's better, Smith. Now Dr. Baldwin tells me you might be fit for duty in three to four days. Has she told you that yet?"

"No, sir."

"Well, that is *unacceptable!*" Aames slapped the bed monitor with a fist. "You're stronger than that, Bosun. I trust you will be at your duty station in two days. Is that understood?"

"Sir, yes, sir!"

Aames's tone softened. "That's good, Smith. We need you." Again he looked over toward Adika. "Now more than ever."

"It's all right, Captain," Smith answered. "We've survived worse than this."

Aames turned back to her bunk. "We sure as hell have, Bosun. We'll get through this. Unless Horace Gale blows us all up first." He looked at the door, but then turned back. "Is there anything you need, Smith?"

Smith paused. "My throat's pretty dry. A bulb of water, please, Captain?"

Aames swiped through her chart on her bunk controls. "Dr. Baldwin has you cleared for liquids, so I see no reason why not." He navigated smoothly through the darkened infirmary and over to the wall. I heard water pouring, and then he returned to Smith's bunk and held out a drinking bulb with a straw. "I would tell you to take this, but I guess you need your hands free for that. Here."

Aames leaned over and held out the straw, and I heard a sound of sipping, followed by a contented sigh from Smith. Aames remained there as she sipped some more, until finally I heard the whistling sounds of a dry straw.

Aames stood and set the bulb by Smith's bunk. "How's that, Smith?"

Smith sounded almost herself when she answered, "Sweet as Martian Springs, Captain."

"Yes, sweet as Martian Springs." And then Aames surprised me: he stood straight and snapped a salute to Smith, as if returning her own. Then he spun on his heels and strode out without another word.

As soon as the door slid shut behind Aames, Smith spoke to me. "We know the answer now, Yerim. I win. I'll be out of this bunk the day after tomorrow. Captain's orders."

"You can't mean that," I protested. "If the doctor says you're not ready, he can't order you back to duty."

"Relax." I could almost hear her smile. "He read my chart. He knew what he was saying."

"But he said three or four days."

"No, he said it *might* be three or four days. I'll bet the doctor also said it *might* be two. He wanted to push me, without any actual risk. He's always pushing."

"But how do you know?"

"I *know*," she said, and then went silent. That was the end of the subject.

My mind raced. This man was such a conflict: at once demanding and supportive, first irritating and then considerate. And manipulative, and she knew it! And yet she calmly agreed, as if . . .

And then it came to me. Smith had served under Aames as long as anyone in the Corps. She of all people knew how difficult and demanding he could be, yet she kept reenlisting for his crew. It made no sense to me, but then suddenly it made perfect sense.

I breathed in, then slowly out. I wanted to approach this carefully. Finally I spoke. "We're off the record here, Bosun, so you don't have to answer. But I have to ask: Do you love Captain Aames?"

"Well, if we're off the record, *Inspector* . . ." Smith sounded hurt, as if I had insulted her. But then she laughed. With a drink in her and no face mask, she didn't cough, and her laugh sounded hearty and healthy. "Sorry, Yerim, I couldn't keep that up. I'm not insulted, it was just an act. You're pretty funny. And that, well, it's just the funniest thing I've heard in a week. I've heard of ships where the crew loves their captain, but that ain't the *Aldrin*. Captain Aames ain't the lovable type. We respect him and trust him. On a good day. On a bad day, we hate him, and we try to stay out of his way. But we still trust him."

I shook my head. "I'm not talking about the crew, I'm talking about you, personally. Let me be blunt: Smitty, are you romantically attracted to Captain Aames?"

"Me? In love with Nick Aames?" Her laugh was louder and longer this time, echoing across the infirmary walls. "Not a chance. He ain't my type."

I turned toward her voice. "Are you sure? He's a powerful, driven man. Lots of women find that attractive."

Smith paused before she answered, "I'm sure he's not my type, ma'am, because *you* are." I hesitated, not sure how to respond. My face grew warm in the darkness, and I was glad she couldn't see my embarrassment. But she laughed again as if she had seen. "Don't worry, Inspector, you're also about twenty years too young for me, and you're on the wrong side of the captain's case. I'm not gonna make a pass at you." But then her voice softened a bit. "Although maybe, when this is all over . . ."

I swallowed, flustered, and wished I had a drink of my own. "Let's keep this professional, Smith." But then I paused, and Smith said nothing, as if expecting me to say more. And to my surprise, I did, very softly: "For now."

Smith made no response, and I rushed forward to my next point. "But then I find your loyalty puzzling. You've served more terms under Captain Aames than anyone. He has written you up for more infractions than I can count."

"Yep," she said, back to her usual jovial tome. "He has also written me a number of commendations; and though his performance reviews are harsh, he has consistently given me more positive reviews than negative."

"So you're loyal to him because he's fair?"

She laughed again, and some of the tension drained from the room. She had a nice laugh. "Captain Aames is completely unfair. Just like life. It's another way he tests you. No, Yerim, I'm loyal to him because I trust him more than anyone else to keep us alive and to fulfill the mission."

I nodded. "Yes, he does have an impressive record."

"Record? Records are written by bureaucrats who don't know the half of it. If you knew . . ." Smith trailed off.

"If I knew what?"

"It's nothing, Yerim," Smith replied. "I like you, but you're the inspector general. I can't say anything you might turn against the captain if you took it wrong."

I frowned in the semidarkness. I really wanted to hear Smith's story. There was so much to learn about Aames, and she knew him as well as anyone. So I decided. "Tell me, Smitty. Please. Help me to understand. This will be off the record, just between roomies."

"Off the record, huh? Well, I hope it's not just the meds, but I trust you. Okay, let me tell you what *really* happened on the second *Bradbury* expedition."

6. Not Far Enough

Off-the-record account of Chief Bosun Sheila Smith, Senior Enlisted of the IPV *Aldrin*

Covering events from 15 September 2059 to 30 May 2060

The first thing you should know about the second *Bradbury* expedition is I lived to tell you about it. That should be obvious since I'm telling you about it, right? But I had a drinking buddy back at the Old Town Tavern in Tycho Under, and practically every one of *his* stories ended with, "And then I died in the mess." We would have to buy him a beer before he would give us the real ending, so I've got no patience for that sort of trick. It's one of the oldest jokes in the history of bar stories, and it's just not that funny. Call me unimaginative, but I think the person telling the story has gotta be alive.

So yeah, sorry if it spoils my ending, but I lived through it. And so did Chief Carver, and Chief Gale, and near a dozen others. But we were the lucky ones. A lot of our shipmates died there on Mars or up in orbit.

Did I say lucky? No, it wasn't luck, it was Captain Aames. That was our only real luck the whole trip: Nick Aames was in charge, and he kept us alive.

DESCENT STAGE

Lander 2 dove through the Martian dust. A rumble like distant thunder sounded from the hull. "Watch your speed, Carver," the captain's voice blared across the radio. "You're dropping fast. Use some juice if you have to! I don't want to scrape you all off of Mars."

But it was Chief Maxwell who answered, safe in control bay 2 up on the *Bradbury*: "I'm on it, Captain." And sure enough, I bounced against my seat and then up against my straps as the lander suddenly *kicked* upward. "Doppler says there's a clear pocket behind this gust, we just have to slide over to it. Then we'll have better tracking."

The expedition had started fine. The eight-month trip out on the *Bradbury* was routine for a crew of experienced spacers: maintenance, training, experiments, and briefings. Or let's call them what they really were: indoctrination sessions. Oh, the brass were subtler than that, but that's because the System Initiative hired the best headshrinkers in the business to make the indoctrination subtle, make it seem like a *good* thing. And it was all the fault of Masha Desney and Bennie Cooper.

I could hear the captain's sneer in his response. "Good for you, Max. Glad *somebody* is awake over there. Carver, open your damned eyes! Or are you planning another collision here?"

That was unfair to Carver—young Anson Carver, his lieutenant junior grade bars still new—but "fair" isn't a word you use to describe Captain Aames. He wants your best, and he'll push till he gets it—or till you break. Carver had a collision during pilot training, and now Aames brought it up any time he wanted to push the man. A glance at Carver's helmet monitor showed a sheen of sweat on his dark-brown forehead, but his eyes were focused and steely, and he didn't let the captain's taunt shake his concentration. Carver wasn't going to break, I was sure of that. In fact he was doing pretty well, considering he had a few more distractions than Max did. Our landers used the system invented by the first *Bradbury* crew: a pilot in a skinsuit on the lander was paired with a copilot up on the *Bradbury* so they could share both local and global views of the Martian approach. Carver hung suspended by straps in the pilot pod, while Max did the same up in the ship. Though they used the same piloting gear, there was one key difference. Engineers tell a bacon-and-eggs joke: the chicken is *involved* in breakfast, but the pig is *committed*. In this landing, Carver was the pig in the frying pan, and Maxwell was the chicken back on the *Bradbury*, watching us and wondering if we would fry.

Commander Cooper's First team had devised this system, and Cooper had used it to rescue Desney, his second-in-command, after she had violated mission rules and landed on Mars. International mission planners had intended the crew to teleoperate robots on the Martian surface, preparing the way for future landings. No landings were approved for that mission, but the splintered crews on the First had all schemed to land on their own, chasing their own national prestige and influence. Of them all, Desney finally pulled it off, but crashed in the landing. After Cooper had unified his crew to rescue her, the floodgates were opened. The First crew rewrote their mission plan completely, with multiple surface excursions and piles of samples and data returned.

The distant rumble outside continued. On Earth, wind whistles; but on Mars, the thin air only propagates long sound waves, and even those don't travel far. The deep sounds of the wind were almost peaceful to terrestrial ears. But the winds were too faint to provide lift. We had to drop on power or on chutes.

"All right there, Ensign Smith?" Lieutenant Gale called across the cabin at me.

"All right, Lieutenant." I appreciated the concern, but not the tone behind it: *Poor girl, can you handle this stress?* The whole flight, the British officer had been overly concerned with my welfare, and I was sure he was trying to get me into his bunk. Hah! If I were going to turn to men, it wouldn't be to a snake like Horace Gale. He was a phony, a whole different person with the officers than with the enlisted. The

Initiative chose him, and Captain Aames didn't wash him out, so I would trust him. I even liked him, after a fashion: our crew was chosen for compatibility on a long mission, so even an asshole like Gale had his good points. But I didn't have to like him *too* far.

I smiled back at Shannon Lopez on the seat behind me, and she grinned. She had done her own share of rebuffing Gale, and we had joked about it on many occasions. Of course, she had rebuffed me too. If she was involved with anyone in the crew, it was Ahmad Razdar; but if so, they had been pretty discreet about it, even in the cramped confines of the *Bradbury*.

I rubbed my shoulder where the straps had caught me, but carefully so that Gale wouldn't notice. There was probably a bruise there, but it couldn't wipe the giant grin from my face. Yeah, we might die at any second, but I simply didn't believe it. After years of training and travel, *I was going to land on Mars, just like the First!*

I had watched the reports from the first mission, wanting to know everything about them, and I hadn't been alone. The public on Earth couldn't get enough of the First crew, those brave explorers who conquered another planet. But it had been a lousy career move no matter what the public thought. Behind the scenes there were massive shakeups across the national agencies.

The captain came back on the radio. "Max, hold off on that clear pocket if you can. We may need it for lander 1. Weaver says that may be the only solution that works for us, and we don't want you getting too close." There were six of us on lander 2, and six more including the captain on lander 1. We were the ground teams who would gather data, run experiments, and build facilities on Mars. (*On Mars!* I still got a thrill from that.) Max and Weaver and Koertig and Uribe remained behind on the *Bradbury*, running experiments of their own, tending the hydroponics and other ship's systems, and maintaining contact with Mission Control. Oh, and serving as our copilots.

"Captain," Carver answered, "that clear pocket's followed by two more. We can go for landing pad A or C, but C's got more clear air." There was an implied question there, a lift in Carver's voice. *Bad mistake, Carver,* I thought. *Never hesitate with him.* With Captain Aames, it's okay to not know, but say so.

And of course the captain pounced. "Choose one, Carver. I'm busy with my own lander. Max said you were a pilot, was he wrong?"

"No, sir," Carver answered. At least Carver was smart enough not to argue, just go back to his piloting.

So the first *Bradbury* expedition had been a dead end for its crew. They're celebrities, and publicly they're heroes; but unofficially, they're blackballed. Not a one of them has ever served on another Initiative mission, transport, or post. The only work they can find is with the transport companies and other private ventures. So what the Initiative screened for on the second *Bradbury* expedition wasn't Mars experts, but discipline and loyalty to the mission. They wanted us to follow the rules, while they would teach us what we needed to know about Mars. That's why none of us had any real experience with Mars. Or with Mars landings.

Chief Maxwell came back on the radio. "Deece advises we go for C, Lieutenant." Decision Control, or Deece, was the expedition's AI. She ran simulations and models to advise us on our decisions. "We'll need to boost to hit it without getting deep into the dust." I could just barely see Carver nod in the control pod, and then I felt a sudden push from behind as he applied some thrust from the main engine.

"Keep an eye on that dust storm," the captain said.

Gale cut in. "Deece's model says it'll miss us."

"It's not the model I'm worried about, Horace," the captain answered. He used Gale's first name any time the lieutenant annoyed him—which was often. "I'm looking at the real storm, and it's not following the model. It's already in the Coprates quadrangle, and it could turn our way at any time." Our landing pads were in the heart of

Coprates, in a fairly even stretch of Solis Planum. If the storm was in the quadrangle, Captain Aames was smart to be concerned. We needed visibility, both eyes and instruments, for a safe landing.

The Initiative particularly wanted a commander who wouldn't embarrass them again, so they had selected Captain Nick Aames. That may surprise you, given his reputation these days. He's seen as a loose cannon who has contempt for the rules, but that's not how he is at all. He has contempt for *stupid* rules, especially if they endanger the mission. But he respects safety rules, established procedures, and the chain of command as long as they serve the mission. When he throws out a rule, he has a damn good reason.

And he's all for discipline: it helps a crew to keep focus. He rode us until we knew every detail of our own specialties *and* had cross-trained in at least two others. He inspected every nut and bolt on the ship, once a month, and he launched surprise inspections any time he thought he might catch us slacking off. His ass-chewing skills were legendary, and we learned to avoid them.

If he went too far—he is Nick Aames, after all—we turned to Chief Maxwell. Max had served with Nick on three missions before Mars, and they understood each other. If you took a beef to Max, he could make you see it the captain's way, so the reprimand didn't sting so much; and if Max decided you were right, he could intercede with the captain. Sometimes. He had for Carver, convincing Captain Aames that the young computer programmer should cross-train as a pilot.

Suddenly a gust blew up, all visibility was lost, and I hoped Max knew what he was doing. Otherwise Carver, Gale, and I, and our three shipmates were gonna end up spread across the Mars-scape. But before I could even wonder if we would live, the lander dropped rapidly and slid back to a level altitude, and the air was suddenly clear all the way to the surface. "Nicely done, Lieutenant," Max said.

"Thanks, Chief. I think we have clear air all the way from here."

"This is Mars, lad. Never assume." But Lieutenant Carver had it right: with Maxwell's assistance, we rode the jets down to landing altitudes. It was still a pretty wild ride—not my wildest ever; someday I'll tell you about a bull-riding contest outside São Paulo—and the rumble never stopped, but Carver had it under control. Soon the red hills of Mars were everywhere outside the portholes, and Max came back on the radio. "Beacons show that landing pad C is three degrees starboard. Adjusting course." The robots from First had constructed landing pods and ground facilities. Those were often obscured by the blowing sands of Mars, but radar and radio beacons guided us down.

The captain came back on the radio. "Lander 2, we caught an unexpected sand front. If we keep this course, we can't see strip B, and radar shows soft ground off the edge. I'm boosting out of this approach, and we'll circle around for another try. Looks like you'll beat us down. Weather permitting, we'll rendezvous at your position."

Max answered, "You have enough fuel for another pass, Captain?"

"If I didn't, I wouldn't be making the pass." Even Chief Maxwell wasn't immune to the famous Aames scorn.

"Chief," Carver cut in, "I'm taking us down."

"All green from here, Lieutenant," Max added. "Helmets, everyone." I pulled my helmet down from the ceiling, put it on, and turned the latch that sealed it in place. That was SOP: it would suck to survive a crash but then asphyxiate on Mars, so we landed in our EVA suits.

The helmet dulled the sound from outside, but only until I tapped on the external helmet microphone. Then I heard a high-pitched white noise outside as the lander tore through the thin atmosphere. Next came clunking beneath us as the landing gear dropped into place. Carver and Max called readings and adjustments back and forth as we swiftly descended to the Red Planet—but not so swiftly as to crash. Looking around Carver's seat and his big helmet, I could see lander complex A out the front window: a landing pad, an automated propellant factory, a crawler garage, and some smaller structures. The main facilities were all subsurface for radiation shielding and environment control. All these structures had been constructed by the robots of the first expedition, guided by the crew in orbit. Well, until the day Masha Desney broke protocol and landed here, right where we were landing. After that, the First crew did a lot of the work themselves on the ground. Once they had broken protocol, they rewrote all their mission rules.

We continued our powered descent to the pad. There was a brief moment of panic as the port side dropped, a burst of adrenaline as Max compensated, and then suddenly I felt two swift jolts as the lander touched down, bounced, and settled onto the pad. The lander filled with cheers, and Max came on the radio: "Ladies and gentlemen, welcome to Mars!"

The captain's voice cut through the cheers. "Good flying, Lieutenant." I saw a wide grin on Carver's face, all white teeth, looking as if his dark face might split. I understood his grin: a word of praise from Captain Aames was a rare treasure. But as quick as that, the moment was past, and the captain was pushing again. "Gale, get your people unstrapped and out. I want that lander under cover. I don't like the long-range Doppler readings."

"Yes, Captain." Gale reached for his strap.

But then a female voice cut in, steady and warm: "Do not unstrap. Model analysis in progress. Do not unstrap."

"Yes, Deece," Gale answered, relaxing back into his seat. "Everyone remain seated." Deece was another consequence of the first expedition. The Initiative wanted to have oversight on every decision, but they couldn't do that effectively with a twenty-minute light-speed delay, or even longer if the *Bradbury* was behind Mars. So they installed high-end artificial intelligence to do their overseeing for them. Deece's job was to monitor every action, feed it into her scenario model, and advise us whether the action complied with the latest revised mission protocols; but she tended to blur the line between "advise" and "command." We all resented her for that (well, maybe not Gale, he was such a suck-up), but we were stuck with her.

Not that I have anything against AIs, mind you. I've met some great ones back in Tycho, programmed by real pros; but they're not *human*, and no amount of programming will change that. They just don't see things the way a human would. And Deece? Her programmers *weren't* real pros, if you ask me, and she was a pain in the ass. Too limited, unable to adapt to changes outside her training.

The captain was no happier with Deece than I was. "Damn it, Deece, that front could turn this way and bury that lander in dust." That was another reason for the subsurface facilities: we could lift the hatches, drive the lander into the pit, and close the hatches, shutting out the dust.

Deece was as unflappable as only an AI can get. "I have updated weather models from DC Command, Captain, and they still show no immediate danger. Under those conditions, Initiative protocols say the lander and crew must remain ready for immediate liftoff in case of an unforeseen threat. Until I assess the situation, I advise the crew to remain strapped in."

Deece's plan made sense, according to her protocols. Taking off from Mars is a lot easier than landing. To take off, you just have to miss the ground, and then keep missing. But to *land*, you have to miss it, but just barely; and then barely miss it again and again until you can hit it on your terms, not Mars's. With solid rocket boosters, we could lift clear of the worst dust storms in under a minute.

But Nick Aames had no intention of running away from Mars without a fight. "Fine, stay strapped in for now. But Carver, drive that bird over to the shelter pit. Let's not waste any more time than we have to. Now I have my own landing to complete, so stop chattering in my ear."

The lander started taxiing. The landing pad was half-buried in shifting sands, so Carver had to navigate by pattern recognizers and deep radar. If it weren't for Deece, we could've hoofed it over and prepared the pit, but instead we waited. Carver was just dropping the wheels to the pad when Captain Aames announced, "Lander 1 is down on landing strip B and heading for the nearest shelter pit."

Of course, that was the moment when Deece pronounced her judgment: "Model suggests no urgent threats that would require immediate liftoff. Recommend crew prepare to shelter lander 2."

"Thank you, Deece, we would've never figured that out." The captain's sarcasm was wasted on the AI, so he continued, "Max, take over the taxi. Carver, unstrap and be ready with the rest of them. I don't like that storm front. It's picking up speed. I want all hands prepping the shelter pit."

"Yes, Captain." Gale had already unstrapped and was crouched near the floor hatch. "All hands, get ready and strap on your toolkits. We don't want to waste a minute when we reach the pit."

So it was with a distinct lack of ceremony that I first set foot on the Red Planet: Gale opened the hatch as Max coasted us to a stop, and one by one we dropped down to the runway. It was a slow drop, thanks to Mars's low gravity. I had a moment to savor the feeling: *I'm on Mars! Right where Masha took her first step.* Then I had to bounce out of the way of the next spacer, just as we had trained.

As soon as I was in the open air of Mars, I heard yet another rumble, this time from the soft wind scraping past my bodysuit and my helmet. Our leggings and sleeves were soft pressurized tubes with gasket-fitted joints; but the bodysuits were hard, fitted shells that protected our vitals, and the helmets were hard polymer bubbles. Both were good protection against hazards.

I weaved a bit in the first real gravity I had experienced in months. The mactory deck of the *Bradbury* spun to create low centrifugal gravity, and we each exercised there daily; but as weak as Mars's gravity was, it was still more than double what I was used to. So I leaned against the lander's leg as I looked around to orient myself. Just east of the landing pad was the propellant factory, a small egg-like dome that ran on wind and solar as it automatically mined the Martian surface for perchlorates and other compounds that it shaped into propellant disks. These could be loaded into our booster tubes to help us escape Mars, when the time came. On the other side of the pad was the crawler garage; and beside it was an access turret, concealing stairs down into the shelter pit. Between the garage and the factory were the two metal plates of the pit hatches.

Gale was already working on the pit latch by the time I joined him. The latch was designed for manual operation. With the long time between missions and the blowing Martian sands, we couldn't trust that automated systems would hold up. So Gale was running a blower, clearing the hatches of sand, and I crouched down to unhook the latch. The hatches were designed to be opened easily from above: two large metal covers on hinges, locked together by a big circular compression latch. All we had to do was unhook the pair of meter-long handles in the latch, raise them up, and use them to turn the latch plate. When we turned it 180 degrees, the covers would be unlocked. We could lift them, and the lander could roll down the ramp and into the pit.

Or at least that's how it was supposed to go. I unhooked the handles easily enough; but when I tried to pull the first one up, it raised half a centimeter maybe, and then it wouldn't budge. I felt a slight scraping vibration through my gloves, and then—nothing.

I tried the second handle: same thing. "Lieutenant, there's sand in the shaft housing. These things won't budge."

Gale nodded. "Lopez, Van der Ven, Pagnotto, help her out." My shipmates joined me, two of us on each handle as we pulled. Elvio Pagnotto and I pried our handle for all we were worth. The months in low G hadn't weakened us, thanks to a ruthless exercise regimen on the trip out, but raw strength wasn't cutting it. I pulled with my arms and pushed away with my legs, trying to pry the handle from the ground.

Suddenly my grip slipped, and all my leg strength threw me violently into the Martian air. Despite myself, I yelled out loud. The sky and the horizon spun crazily as I rose and fell, and I noticed more sand whipping by, moving faster. I wondered if I would damage anything when I crashed.

Fortunately Carver was on the ball. He loped after me, caught me, and set me down. "You all right, Ensign?"

I smiled through my visor. "Except for my dignity." I spoke into my radio: "Lieutenant Gale, those things are stuck tight."

Captain Aames came on the line, and we all heard his exchange with Gale: "The latches are fine here, Gale. You must have more sand in the system for some reason. You'll have to clear the housing from underneath. Move, people. That front is picking up speed."

"The models—"

Aames cut in. "Screw the models, Horace! Look at the horizon."

I did, and I saw a growing cloud of sand. Again, I heard Aames's voice: "Move!"

Carver had caught me right near the access turret, so we set to work on it. The door was partly blocked by sand, but we were able to clear it. The space inside was five meters across, with flooring along the west half and the east half open into the pit. Into that opening led a circular staircase made of tall steps protruding from the shaft wall. On Earth, these tall steps would be almost a ladder, with just a thin handrail to separate us from the two-meter central shaft; but here on Mars, the steps were easy to descend, even with a suit, an environment pack, and tool kits. When we reached the bottom, the shaft ended at an open pressure door. Beyond that was a short, wide tunnel ending in another open door. The tunnel could serve as an airlock, if needed; but the doors had been left open, since neither end was under pressure.

The tunnel opened out into the pit. Light panels in the ceiling automatically came on, showing us the artificial cavern with its ramp to the surface at the far east end.

"At least the solars worked," Carver said.

"Uh-huh." The light panels, powered by a solar generator station on the surface, were bright enough to illuminate the entire pit.

A mechanical lift sat beside the ramp. We would use that to reach the hatches from below. Supply and tool cabinets lined the walls, as well as fold-out benches. A pressure door on the far side of the pit from the turret led to a shelter beyond.

But already the shelter had a problem: the main pit area was ankle-deep in loose dust. "Lieutenant Gale," Carver radioed up, "the seals have failed. There's a lot of sand down here. That's probably how it got into the housings."

"A lot? Can we get the lander down?"

"Yes, Lieutenant, it'll just make things messy."

"Messy we can handle. Get to work, you two."

Trudging through the loose, powdery sand all around our feet, we set to work on the hatches. Despite the sand, the lift still worked, raising us up above the ramp and then extending out so we stood at the underside of the hatches. Everything looked different from underneath, but Captain Aames had drilled us on all the first expedition's equipment. We knew how this system worked.

The handles below were much like the handles above, so Carver and I tried pushing up while Van der Ven and Pagnotto pulled from above. No go. We would have to clean and lube the shaft housings. Looking at them, I knew that would be impossible in their current position. "Lieutenant, pull the handles down. We can't fix them like this."

So we changed direction, Van der Ven and Pagnotto pushing down while Carver and I pulled. We had to hook our boots into the lift rails, or all we would do would be to pull ourselves up in the 0.38 G. We were panting and sweating, but eventually we pulled the first handle down. Carver and I each took a shaft housing, pulling them apart and cleaning them out and applying lubricant from our toolkits. Then we put them back together, and Carver radioed up to Gale, "Handle one is done, Lieutenant. Moving on to two."

But then Captain Aames came on the comm. "No time, Gale. Get your team down into that pit. Now!"

Deece's even, soothing voice answered, "My model shows the storm will not reach the vicinity for ten-point-three minutes."

"Your model is wrong, Deece. We're past the limit now. Gale, you're about to be buried. Move!"

"Yes, Captain," Gale answered. And moments later we saw dim light from the turret as the upper door opened and our shipmates came scurrying down amid billowing clouds of sand.

Gale was the last into the turret, pulling the door shut behind him, and the dust whirls died down. Gale looked around and shouted, "Bloody hell, Carver, you weren't kidding. There's sand everywhere. Everyone look around, find that bad seal."

We searched all around the pit, but we found nothing.

Finally Shannon thought to check the turret. "Here it is, Lieutenant." Gale climbed up the spiral stairs to join her on the floor above. There was no room for anyone else up there, but Van der Ven and Pagnotto looked up from below. "See here? It looks like something cracked the joint between the carbon panels. The panels are cracked, too, but vacuum resin sealed those." An epoxy-like compound, VR turns rigid in vacuum. The turret walls had a VR core to automatically seal leaks, but it was a new VR formula for the Martian atmosphere. It didn't harden quite as fully as the real stuff, but the seal was good enough if you didn't stress it. The same compound flowed between the inner and outer shells of our bodysuits.

Gale looked at the joint. "Maybe erosion, or radiation made the seal brittle. There's a quarter-centimeter gap here. Good job, Lopez. Get some seal tape on that. When the storm passes, we'll have to reweld that seal." Gale came back down the steps.

Carver called across the pit, "Lieutenant, the lander's registering dust piles. It's starting to get buried. Our own seals could develop problems."

"Damn. Deece, what's the storm model say? Can you launch the lander, get it away from the storm?"

"Analyzing." Deece paused for several seconds. "There is time to boost above the storm front, but we would have to refuel at the orbiter."

Captain Aames broke in on the comm. "Gale, that model's wrong. Look at the live images."

Gale checked his comm. "Captain, dust is high, but within the safety margin for a launch. If we wait, it won't be, and we'll have a lander crippled by dust. Deece, boost. Now."

If Captain Aames had any response, it was lost in the subsonic rumble of the solid rocket boosters igniting. The hatch plates rattled, and I was glad the lander wasn't any closer.

I noticed Carver looking at his own comm. Suddenly his eyes grew wide. He shouted something, but the shout was buried by the engines and the rattling hatches. Frantic, Carver punched a warning on his comm, and it popped up on my heads-up display: *GET UNDER LIFT! EXPLOSION!* Then he scrambled for the edge of the lift. I didn't wait, leaped after him, and I saw that Gale and the rest were diving for cover under it as well.

The engine rumble had diminished a bit, surely a sign that the lander was boosting skyward. I rolled up in a crouch just in time to see Shannon bolting down the stairs.

Then a much louder sound wave shook the entire pit, an explosion that quickly deafened us. The ground around us shook, ceiling panels fell, and the turret collapsed on Lopez. I tried to run to her, but Carver held me back. Then the ceiling fell in, and the lift dropped on us, and everything went dark.

And then I died in the mess.

Ground Control

I know, I know, I promised I would never use that joke. But you seemed awful tense, so I wanted to lighten the mood.

Well, all right, maybe I'm the one who's tense. I still don't like to remember that cave-in. It *felt* like I died: a crushing pain in my side, everything went dark all at once, and then I went unconscious from the shock. I *could've* died in the mess.

And there's another reason I don't like to think about it: Shannon was killed instantly. And Fadila van der Ven's left leg was caught in the lift mechanism and crushed. His suit's auto-tourniquet kicked in immediately, so he survived; but the leg was already a lost cause from the knee down.

I knew none of that at the time, though; I was too far out of it. The first I knew was a voice on my comm. "Smith. Smith, what's your status?"

It took me a moment to clear the fog from my brain. "Captain?"

"Report, Smith. Your suit shows you're injured, but not critical. Can you move?"

I flexed my legs and arms, trying to move; but something metal—the lift platform?—pinned me down, and the effort made my left ribs spasm in pain. Something soft around my legs and arms made movement difficult. Sand?

But I didn't need to move, the suit was on voice control. "Suit, lights." Nothing. "Suit, *lights*." Still complete darkness. "Lights, damn it! Lights!" I started breathing rapidly.

But Captain Aames kept his voice steady. "Calm down, Smith. Your suit comp says your lights are on." As captain, Aames had a circuit for each of our suits, and could check on our status, both mechanical and physiological. "If you can't see the lights, you're probably buried in sand. Now report: *Can you move?*"

I slowed my breathing, trying to dispel my panic. Claustrophobes don't last long in a spaceship, so I could handle a little sand, a little darkness. Gingerly, I tried my right arm again. It was definitely stuck between sand beneath and around it, and the metal lift platform above; but I could wiggle it back and forth. I couldn't feel the grains through my suit, but I could feel the powder give if I pushed. Maybe if I pushed enough . . . "*Ow.* Sorry, Captain. I think I'm trapped under the lift, and my ribs are pretty sore. But I can move a little. If I take it easy on these ribs, I can dig out."

"Be careful, Smith." Aames sounded almost empathetic. "Your suit says those ribs are only bruised, but suit comps can't always diagnose breaks. Your seals are intact, and you've got plenty of air, so take it slowly. Carver and Gale have dug free already, they'll get to you soon enough. There are others in front of you."

"Others?"

And as I dug—it felt more like pushing than digging, and the powder was getting looser—the captain told me about the others: about Van der Ven and his leg; about Pagnotto, who had proven it's *not* impossible to get a concussion in a helmet, just damned hard; and about poor Shannon. She had been a good friend, and I cried at the news, but not so as Nick could hear me. He thinks I'm strong, and I didn't want to let him down.

Then the captain made me feel even worse. "So they can help you dig out, but first they have to amputate Van der Ven's leg."

Then the sobs came, despite my efforts to control them; but I didn't have time to cry, so I kept digging. When I could speak without choking up, I decided to change the subject. "I think I see light, Captain."

Then Pagnotto's voice cut in. "Smith, I see movement. Is that you?"

"Elvio, yes, I'm almost out." Sand slid from my visor, and I saw the wreck that had been the shelter pit. The surface hatches were intact, and though dozens of ceiling and wall tiles had fallen all around, the bulk of them were still in place. A few of them hung down, swaying in a breeze. Damn. That meant we had a much bigger leak than before. Sand swirled around in occasional eddies.

Most of the light panels were out, and the swaying tiles and swirling sands cast shifting shadows; but through them I saw Elvio sitting on a wide bench folded out from the wall, waving to me. I couldn't see his face through his visor at this distance, especially not in the flashing light, but his suit had a prominent European Union flag painted across the chest.

Elvio pushed up with one arm and wobbled to his feet. "Wait, Smith. I shall come help."

"Negative," Captain Aames ordered. "Pagnotto, you're not even supposed to be sitting, much less working. Rest, and that's an order."

"*Si*, Captain." I saw Pagnotto collapse slowly back to the bench. Then he lay sideways. I couldn't see Shannon's body anywhere around. Gale and Carver had probably taken her into the shelter.

"What happened, Captain?" I asked. "What went wrong with the lander?"

Nick snorted. In my mind I could see the sneer on his face. "It was that damned AI."

"Captain," I whispered. Some people think AIs have feelings, but they don't. I wasn't worried about "offending" Deece. But she represented the Initiative planners here on Mars. Criticizing her felt kinda like insubordination.

"She can't hear; I cut her out of the ground loops." Now that *was* insubordination. But before I could raise an objection, the captain continued, "Her models from DC Command have been getting more and more erratic. Her programming is fine, but her premises are flawed. The dust was thicker than she accounted for; and when the lander took off, she shifted east for better visibility. Right over the propellant factory."

I stopped, stunned, my arms and head just clear of the sand. "Oh, fuuuuuck . . ."

"Yep. The entire propellant store went up. Max can't get a clear image through the storm, but the factory's probably a total loss."

That certainly explained this collapse. The automated factory had reported enough stored propellant for twelve trips to orbit—more than our mission plan called for, even. A lander *could* get to orbit again without refueling, but only if it could avoid maneuvering too much. Each lander had enough propellant on board for one launch, but not enough for future launches.

I couldn't bear to just lie there. I needed to do *something*, so I resumed digging as I asked, "So lander 2 was lost?"

"Negative. As big as the blast was, the lander was still boosting faster. She was rocked, but she kept going."

"Rocked? Any damage?"

"We can't tell yet. The trajectory's a little unsteady, so maybe. Maxwell and I are tracking her approach to the *Bradbury*. The team there can check her out when she docks."

I swallowed, and I realized that my throat was dry. I turned my head in my helmet, found my straw, and bit the end to open the bite valve. I sucked at the straw, but I got nothing. "Damn."

"Problem, Smith?"

"No water, Captain. I don't understand, my drink bag should have plenty of water."

"It shows empty on your readouts. Maybe when the lift fell on you, the bag burst. Now leave me alone, Ensign, I have to follow this approach."

I tried to pull myself free of the sloping mound of sand. Meanwhile I needed a distraction. "Can I listen in, Captain?"

The captain hesitated, then he answered, "All right. But don't chatter in my ear. I've got to keep an eye on Deece."

He cut me into the command loop, and I heard Chief Maxwell arguing with the AI. "—angle's too wide, Deece. Weaver, got those cabins sealed yet? We may have a collision! Deece, you need to boost higher."

Deece's calm voice contrasted with Max's tension. "All models indicate this approach vector is within acceptable parameters."

Captain Aames cut in. "Damn it, Deece, boost already."

"Yes, Captain. Boosting."

I couldn't see the approach readouts, but Max and the captain could. Max responded. "Too late, Deece, you're too fast. Abort."

"Models indicate—"

Max didn't wait for her to finish. "Abort! Captain, request control."

"Deece, turn control over to Chief Maxwell."

Deece's calm response gave me a chill. "I cannot do that, Captain."

Max's voice grew louder. "She's definitely too fast, Captain."

Aames's voice was coldly precise. "Deece, that's an order."

Deece replied, "Captain, you are under stress due to the trapped crew. Chief Maxwell is also under emotional stress. Psychological models indicate that your judgment is compromised. I am most competent to make this approach."

The captain answered, "This is Captain Nicolau Aames. Override sequence: one; code: one-one-A. Transfer control."

"Got it, Captain!" Max shouted. "All hands, brace for impact. Trying to pull away. Thirty meters, seven meters per second . . . Twenty, six-point-three . . . Ten, six-point-oh . . . Five . . ."

A horrible feedback squeal came over the comm, and then silence. I held my breath, stunned.

But then the silence broke. Static filled my ears, and then went down without completely going away. Through the static, Captain Aames was calling, "Max . . . Max, respond . . . Max, Weaver . . . *Bradbury*, Aames here, anyone respond."

There was only more static. As I listened for a reply, I managed to dig out enough sand below me that I was suddenly free, sliding slowly on my belly to the floor. I lightly rose to my feet and inspected my suit for scrapes, tears, or other damage. Eventually the captain stopped calling, and the static was quiet enough that I could hear Pagnotto softly moaning on the local channel. I stepped carefully around fallen tiles, plus one light panel that swung on a cable almost reaching to the floor. I had to be careful in the piles of sand: several times I felt debris beneath my boots, chunks of tile and rock and loose parts, large enough to trip me if I stepped on them wrong. I walked over to Elvio to check his suit diagnostics. "Captain, why's the comm so staticky?"

"Think, Smith, check your band. Your comm system automatically switched from SHF relay off the *Bradbury* to low-frequency ground wave."

"But that would mean . . . Sir, it's antenna failure, it can't be any more than that. Six meters per second isn't *that* fast."

"Maybe." But the captain sounded doubtful. "It depends on where lander 2 hit. My last reading before the comms cut off was an emergency alert from engineering, a fragment of a data packet. My suit computer is trying to reconstruct it."

Captain Aames fell silent, and I let him work while I saw to Pagnotto. Judging by his suit readings, he was conscious, but his eyes were closed. "How ya doing, Elvio?"

His eyes flickered open, but it took several seconds for them to focus through his visor. "I have felt better, Ensign. My head aches, my neck throbs, and a thousand pins stab my feet. And also, *ho vomitato*."

I checked Elvio's vomit bag. It was half-full, and I also saw some around his mouth and neck. "Heh. You look like I did after that pub crawl in Munich. Why aren't you in the shelter? We could get your helmet off and clean you up."

But my attempt to lighten his mood was a misfire. "I do not wish to see surgery."

Of course. Gale and Carver were in the shelter, amputating Van der Ven's leg. I silently agreed: we could wait outside awhile. I dug further into Elvio's suit diagnostics. The suit had diagnosed concussion, cervical acceleration-deceleration, but no signs of hematoma. That last was a small comfort, at least: I didn't relish the idea of catheterizing his brain. He tried to bear up under the pain, but he still moaned repeatedly.

The suit comp recommended sedation and rest, but emergency protocols had kicked in. In an emergency, an injured crewman might still do vital work, while an unconscious crewman was just one more problem. So the comp flashed a question: *Sedate? YES or NO.*

I tapped "YES," and then watched Elvio quickly slide into sleep. I welcomed the silence as his moans subsided. But the silence dragged out, and I got worried.

Then I was more than worried. Over the comm, the captain whispered a single curse in Portuguese: "*Porra.*"

If Nick Aames was shaken, I was scared. "What's the matter, Captain?"

"That data packet was an alert from the reactor system. Cooling was offline, and temperature was already in the red. Indicators of a critical failure in progress."

"Critical? That fast?"

"Or not. With the collision, there could be a subcritical failure, explosion, decompression, maybe other failures as well. We can't know, but we can hear the result. The *Bradbury* is offline."

"But our food . . . our tools . . ."

"No need to do an inventory, Smith. The bulk of our consumables were up there."

I swallowed, my dry throat painful. "Then we're dead."

"You're mighty talkative for a corpse," Nick replied.

I couldn't believe his scorn in this situation. "It's only a matter of time." I couldn't keep a half sob from creeping into my voice.

"You don't know that, Ensign!" Then Nick's tone changed. "I've seen you in bad times, Smitty: bar fights, rescues, battles with incompetent officers. I have seldom seen you lose, and I have *never* seen you give up without a fight. Am I wrong?" I had only heard that tone a handful of times in all the years I had known him: he was trying to be comforting, in his awkward way.

I tried to steady my voice. "No, sir."

"Of course not. I count on you for that. Yes, this situation is bad, but we're still alive. Our best chance to stay that way is to keep our heads together. We need all of us, every single one, with our heads in the game. Panic now *will* kill us."

A little stronger, I answered: "Yes, sir."

"This isn't a hopeless situation, Ensign. That new Holmes prototype, the *Collins*, is due to orbit Mars in eight months. If we can hold out, we can catch a ride home."

"Sir, at their approach speed? They'll be almost impossible to catch."

Nick sounded indignant. "Are you questioning my piloting skills?"

"No, sir." But I had doubts, whether I said them out loud or not. Like the *Aldrin* today, the *Collins* was on a cycler orbit, with a high-speed pass before the trip back to Earth. When the *Aldrin* passes a planet, she rendezvouses with special high-speed transfer shuttles, orbits perfectly timed to intersect her course. But the *Collins* was a prototype. Mars had no transfer shuttles back then.

"Good. Trust me, we'll make the rendezvous, but only if we last that long."

"But eight months, captain? Without the *Bradbury*?"

"We don't know that. Plus we have survival resources in this shelter pit, and some should be salvageable in yours. We need to know what we have to work with if we're going to make a plan. I need you to do a complete inventory. Check it against the computer's manifest, and don't overlook *anything*. I'm going to send you an annotated manifest with the items we *must* have. I don't care how much sand you have to dig through, but find those items! Then find anything else you can. We're going to have to stretch our resources further than they were ever intended, so we don't know what could prove useful. When you have that inventory done, report back to me."

"To you, sir? Not Lieutenant Gale?"

"Oh, inform Gale, of course. But inform me first."

"Yes, sir."

Again Nick's tone turned confidential. "I'm going to need you to keep an eye on things, Smith. Van der Ven's out, and Pagnotto's concussed. I can't tell what's up with Carver, but he's awfully quiet. And Horace . . ."

"I know, sir." Gale had always had trouble with Captain Aames. He was always looking for the easy answer, the fast answer. Gale had powerful friends in the Initiative, so the captain was stuck with him for political reasons, but we all knew there was friction there.

"I'm not sure you do, Smith. This is more than just his usual lazy attitude. Gale's a nervous wreck from the surgery. It's one thing to do virtual medical training, it's another to saw off your friend's leg without even a doctor to supervise, so I'm going to cut Gale a little slack this time. But that means you're the only one I can count on to hold it together there. If trouble comes down—"

"*More* trouble, you mean."

"If trouble comes down, I trust you to handle it. Don't let rank slow you down."

I tried to smile. "Have I ever, Captain?"

"That's the spirit, Smith. I knew I could count on you. Now get to work. For the next eight months, there's no such thing as spare time. We'll have to use every second to stay alive."

"Yes, Captain."

The comm went silent, and I had a brief shudder of panic, of *aloneness*. Elvio was with me, Gale and Carver and Van der Ven were just beyond the pressure door, and Captain Aames was only a comm call away; but there in the flickering light, buried beneath the surface of Mars, and doubting any of us would live through this, I felt alone, cut off from humanity. I'm not proud to say it, but right there, I collapsed to the floor and just sobbed in my helmet.

After a while, I found myself staring at the shifting shadows from the swinging light panel, and I realized I had no idea how long I had been staring. Damn. *"We'll have to use every second to stay alive,"* the captain had said, and here I was wasting who knows how many minutes wallowing in self-pity. If Nick Aames had been there, he would've kicked my ass for sure.

Well, the captain wasn't there, so I would have to kick my own ass. "Take an inventory?" I said to the silent comm. "Yes, sir." I pushed myself up from the floor—wincing a little at the pain in my left ribs—and began searching the shelter pit. This wouldn't be easy with all the devastation in the pit, but I appreciated a challenge to keep me busy.

I started by stacking the tiles and fragments into neat piles, clearing the floor and making it easier to work. I used my suit comp to keep a verbal inventory, counting off each tile or partial tile and describing its condition. I also kept an eye open for falling tiles: even in the low gravity, a tile that fell from the ceiling could damage my environment system. *Further* damage it, I should say. I had confirmed that my water bag had burst. Most of my drinking water was now soaked into my skivvies, mixing with the sweat I was working up. Eventually I could reclaim it if there was a working cycler in the shelter; but until then, the work was making me mighty thirsty.

With the floors cleared up, I started my search in earnest. Looking around, I could see that most of the wall cabinets were sealed, so I could assume their contents were intact. I had a manifest somewhere in my comp. "Suit, show me the manifest for this pit." My heads-up lit up with a display of the pit's contents as of the last computer inventory, as well as a map that overlay the scene in front of me, highlighting where to find stuff. There was a lot we could use in there: spare lander parts that might be adapted to other uses, food concentrates, electronics, almost everything from the captain's notes. There were even spare air bottles, filled by a little catalytic compressor that extracted oxides from the soil. I checked my own O2 levels and Elvio's: both were low, so I swapped in bottles from the compressor.

Then I checked the manifest for—*Yes!*—water bags, also from the catalytic compressor. I found one, swapped it into my environment pack, and sucked on my straw. I tasted water at last! It had a high mineral content and a definite tang of iron. "Martian Springs," the first expedition had dubbed it, but I didn't care: at that moment it was the sweetest thing I had ever tasted. I bit the valve harder and sucked as fast as I could. Even as I did so, I felt dampness spreading through my skivvies. There was definitely a leak in my environment system, but hydration was doing wonders for my spirits.

Captain Aames was right: we were a bunch of smart engineers and survivors, and we could do wonders with all these resources if we didn't panic.

The cabinets that had sprung open in the shaking had spilled their contents into the sand. I would've killed for a vacuum to scoop up the sand, or maybe a good old pitchfork to sift through it. I already knew there was debris under there, and you could hide a lot more under that artificial beach.

Then I remembered something from the manifest: a tool cabinet in the east wall contained "excavating tools." I opened that entry to look at the details, and it included a hand vac. Unfortunately, the tool cabinet was behind the collapsed lift, so it took some digging and scraping to get to it. I almost got stuck between the lift and the wall, and I gasped in pain at one point when my ribs got pinched *again*; but eventually, I emerged with the vacuum and a big grin on my face. It felt good to have a triumph, no matter how small.

Now what to do with all this dust? There was no way to get rid of it all, and no place to put it. Even trying would exhaust my air faster than the compressors could replace it. But I really didn't need to move *all* of it. What was most important were the areas near the spilled cabinets. After those, we could work on the other areas in our spare time. I just needed to sift the cabinet areas for valuable supplies.

I ran the hand vac over the pile. It left large items behind, but it picked up small items along with the dust. I had to check the interior filter frequently, pulling out small treasures and setting them aside as I dictated: "Suit, inventory: one box bolts, five millimeters, count twenty." It might not seem like much, but that box of bolts was on the captain's special list. Victory!

Another box, another item from the list. "Suit: one box washers, five millimeters, count twenty." I added two coils of wire and another box of washers; then I pulled parts from the filter, shook the dust from them, and set them on a shelf so I wouldn't lose them. I was like an old forty-niner panning for gems more precious than gold, only without water.

Damn. Why did I have to think about water? The air from the compressor was drier than what we had brought with us, and I really wanted a drink; but I knew I should control my water usage, especially given my leak.

So I put water out of my mind, and I concentrated on my vacuuming and sifting. It felt good to have something to do, something that occupied my mind and gave me tiny reasons to hope. Every small discovery made me think: *How can this help us survive?* Could those nuts and bolts help us to seal the shelter pit and build a better shelter? Could those wires help us build a radio that could reach the *Collins*? Every discovery was ripe with possibilities, and those possibilities kept me working. Well, those, plus my determination not to disappoint Captain Aames.

Soon I had enough salvage to fill a shelf, so I started another shelf and kept working. After about an hour, I saw the pressure door to the shelter open, and Carver and Gale came out in their suits. They helped Pagnotto through the pressure door, and Gale went in with him. Then Carver looked at what I was doing; and without saying a word, he found another hand vac and started searching the dust along the far wall.

We worked for two hours that way, in silence other than our inventory counts. I tried making small talk, but Carver was having none of it. A few times I caught his face through his visor, and his eyes looked hollow. The captain was right: this situation was dragging Carver down to a very dark place. That wasn't good for him, and it wasn't good for the rest of us either. We needed every hand; but worse, despair could turn contagious. I tried to get him to open up, but I had no luck.

Slowly our eyeball inventory lined up with the computer manifest. A few small parts might remain lost in the dust; but if there was anything critical buried there, we would find it when we needed it. So as Carver was sifting by the last spilled cabinet, I turned my attention to the access turret. Carver and Gale had cleaned out enough debris to recover Shannon's body, but the shaft was still mostly filled with collapsed tiles and the wreckage of stairs. Fragments of the turret roof lay beside the shaft, including one large chunk that was stained with blood. I also found shards of Shannon's helmet. Our helmets were light but incredibly strong. A normal impact couldn't shatter them, but they were never designed to survive a falling roof.

I started stacking and inventorying the stairs and tiles, and immediately saw the source of the wind and all the sand. The ceiling shaft was jammed with wall panels and roof fragments; but there were still large gaps, and my suit lights showed constant swirls of red Martian dust. The surface turret was just *gone*, completely swept away by the explosion of the propellant factory. Nearly three hours later, the sandstorm was still blowing strong. The pit was a sealed area, so the storm was mostly held at bay, but some wind and dust still found their way down the shaft. I knew that if I could clear the shaft, there was a secondary hatch I could seal against the storm. I stopped wasting time on inventory and stacking, and just started pitching debris out into the pit. I kept a watchful eye, as several times I dislodged pieces that then caused others to fall from above; but in the low gravity, I had plenty of time to dodge them.

This was the hardest work of the salvage operation so far, and the ache in my ribs returned. The inner arc of the stairs was supported by a metal rail, parallel to the guardrail like a giant DNA model with thin support posts joining the rails. In some places the stairs had fallen from the rails, but in others they were still attached; and the rails themselves were twisted out of shape, tangled between themselves, and knotted up the central shaft. If it weren't for those, I might have just climbed to the top through the center; but instead I had to clear a path. The metal rails were designed to support astronauts in suits in Martian gravity, so they weren't as thick as they might have been on Earth. With effort, I could bend and twist them a bit, trying to clear a path. Eventually, though, I had to take out a wrench and disconnect the stairs (carefully counting and pocketing the bolts) so that I could twist and pull the rails apart.

I cleared a path as high as I could reach, but the stairs went up almost three stories. There was a ladder set into the far wall of the shaft, so I climbed that as far as the wreckage allowed. Then I used tethers and carabiners to attach myself to the ladder so I could clear more debris. It was awkward at first, my feet planted on a rung as I leaned out on my tether, but I adjusted quickly. That was my undoing: I got cocky, and I misjudged my ability to spot and dodge falling debris. When I freed up one stair, the entire rail structure shifted; and before I knew what was happening, a ceiling tile came loose, smacked me in the back of my helmet, and dazed me pretty bad (though nowhere near as bad as Pagnotto). Naturally my feet slipped from the rung, and I fell free, my tethers pulling me back so I slammed against the wall. *Woof!* The air was slammed out of me, my ribs stabbed with a jolt of pain, and again I bumped my head on the cushioned rear of my helmet.

I hung there on the side of the shaft, blinking, not able to think clearly for several moments. Then a voice cut through my fog: "You okay up there, Smitty?" I looked down. Carver stood at the bottom of the shaft, looking up at me with worry.

I shook my head. *Ow!* That was a mistake. "I'm okay, just stupid. Not watching what I'm doing." Then I had an idea: Carver was talking, so I would try to keep him that way. "Lieutenant, can you help me out here?"

"Sure, Ensign." His voice lacked enthusiasm, but at least he showed a little life. I would settle for small steps.

Carver reached for the rung. "You need me up there?"

"No, I have another idea. I can drop stuff, and you can toss it out, keep the shaft clear. But I need something else, something more important. Can you be the eyes in the back of my head? As I work, can you watch for things that might fall?"

"I can do that. Just a second." Carver backed out to the edge of the shaft. "All right, I've adjusted the zoom on my helmet camera, and I've patched in a motion-sensing algorithm. If anything even wiggles up there, we'll know it."

"Good idea, Carver. What would we do without your computer smarts?"

"Yeah." He spoke only that one word, but so softly I could barely hear it. I could tell that the brief flash of light in his mood had left, and he was falling back into darkness. All because I had mentioned computers. Of course! Carver was the chief programmer on the expedition; and Deece, the chief program, had doomed us (unless Captain Aames could whip up a miracle). Carver was blaming himself: for the failure of the mission, for Van's leg, for Shannon.

I carefully felt backward and up with my feet until I found a rung. Then I felt back with my right arm—I tried to use my left, but my ribs said no—until I found another rung. I pulled myself back up, got my balance, and went back to work.

As I unbolted a stair from the rail, I decided to do a little direct intervention with Carver. It has never been my style to let people wallow in their troubles. Never tiptoe when you can charge in! I needed to get Carver to focus, shake him up, so I "accidentally" dropped the bolt. "Heads up, down there!" I watched the bolt slowly accelerate, leaving him plenty of time to pick it up on his motion sensor and step safely out of the way.

Carver stretched out one gloved hand, and the bolt fell neatly in his palm, his fingers wrapping around it. "Got it."

I grinned, though I doubt he could see it from there. "Make sure you count that, Lieutenant."

"One bolt," he answered, holding it before his visor, "one centimeter, slightly stripped." Then his voice took a lighter tone. "Apparently coated with butter."

"Sorry, Lieutenant." But I wasn't. I had him talking again, and I was going to take the opening while I had it. "We all make mistakes, huh?"

His helmet swiveled slightly as he shook his head. "There's mistakes, and there's . . ."

I wouldn't let him tail off now. As I worked, I kept at him. "Look, Lieutenant, things are damn bad here, but you'll only make them worse by blaming yourself." Carver grunted in acknowledgment, so I just kept going. "We don't know yet what exactly went wrong. I've worked with Nick—Captain Aames, I mean—on a half dozen after-action reports, and even he never finds one avoidable cause. You've read the same reports: the cause is *never* just one thing, because we would catch anything that big. It's always a dozen things that were *almost* perfect, but the tiny imperfections stacked up."

"But it was *my* tiny imperfection."

"We don't know that, Lieutenant. And right now, I don't give a damn. I only care about surviving the next few hours until Captain Aames comes up with a plan to get us through the next few days, and then the next few weeks."

Carver was getting irritated. "What plan's he going to come up with, Smith?"

"I don't know. That's why he's the captain, and I'm just a noncom. But I trust him. He *will* come up with one. And it's going to depend on all of us keeping our heads in the game. We have to rely on each other to get through this, all of us. Including you, Lieutenant."

I wasn't intentionally echoing the captain, but I realized I was on the same track. He had a way of influencing you, hammering and pushing you until you learned to see things his way.

But Carver was slipping away again. "I don't see what good any of this is going to do us. Nuts? Bolts? Gaskets? They're not going to change anything. Don't you understand, Smith? I've *killed* us."

Before I could answer, Captain Aames cut in, and I realized I had never closed my channel to him. "If you can whine like that, you're not dead yet, Lieutenant Carver. Neither are the rest of us, and we're not giving up. You will *not* let us down, and that's an order. Understood?"

Carver sounded sullen, which was better than depressed. "Understood. Sir."

"Knock off the attitude, Carver. Now. We don't need you blaming yourself and marinating in self-pity when there's work to be done. If you want to have a breakdown, wait until you get back to Earth."

Carver sounded controlled, but pissed. "Sir, yes, sir."

"Lieutenant, I want you to understand something. Right now I don't give a damn about who's to blame for getting us in this mess, I only care about who's going to get us out. Are you on the solution team?"

More firm this time: "Sir, yes, sir!"

"Good. Because if you're not on that team, then do us all a favor: step out on the surface, and leave your air bottles behind for someone who'll actually do their damn job. Is that your plan?"

"Sir, no, sir!"

"That's more like it, Carver. You're third-in-command on Mars right now, and I need you to act like it. Chief Maxwell put a lot of faith in you, Lieutenant. Don't let him down. Aames out." There was an audible click as the captain's channel closed.

I didn't say a word. I didn't want to push Carver one way or another, just when it seemed the captain had the young lieutenant back on track. So I just climbed a few rungs higher and attached my tethers to the highest rungs. Finally, I had clear access to the secondary hatch, but still the stair rails blocked it from closing. They were supposed to collapse down so we could close the hatch, but they were too twisted for that.

So I started work on the top bolts. When I had them half-loosened, I called back down, "Lieutenant, I have to drop the rails to close the hatch. They're kind of tangled and twisted. We'll need to clear the shaft once they fall, but you may have some trouble getting them out through the tunnel. Are you ready?"

"Yes, Ensign." His answer sounded neutral: not depressed, but without the fire Aames had ignited.

"All right, here's the first one." I released the last bolt on the lower rail. I had already removed and dropped the support posts that had connected it to the upper rail, so it started falling, caught up briefly on the upper rail, and then slid lazily free, dropping and eventually reaching the bottom of the shaft. It landed with a low crash, the sound barely reaching me through the Martian atmosphere.

Carver called up, "All right, let me drag this out." He started pulling and sliding the tangle through the short tunnel and into the pit.

Once the lower rail was clear, I set to work on the top rail. Soon I called down: "Top rail coming down." I released the last bolt and dropped the rail. I also pulled down and dropped some debris from the turret, mostly shards of wall tiles and bits of wiring that hung down into the opening.

Without even watching the debris fall, I took my chance to stick my head up into the ruins of the turret, so I could see just how bad it was. To my surprise, the damage was so bad, it was good: the turret had been almost completely swept away by the blast. A few fragments had fallen into the shaft and gotten caught, and a couple of wall panels had collapsed in a coincidental lean-to that covered the opening; but it looked like we would have no trouble escaping the turret when we decided we were ready.

I dropped back down into the shaft and set to work on the secondary hatch. It was an entirely manual mechanism, a hinged plate under the west floor of the shaft that swung down when I unlatched it. In the Martian gravity, it should have been little effort to swing the plate up to cover the hole in the east half and latch it in place; but my ribs objected to the twisting I had to do, and I dropped the plate before I could latch it. Then I had to dodge the plate as it swung by once, twice—and I caught it. Thanks to the Martian gravity, it swung slowly, but I was taking no chances with my ribs. This time I was more careful as I lifted it into place and latched it closed. Then once it was latched, I pulled out a handle that let me turn and tighten a pressure seal. At last, we were sealed off from the storm. My mouth was almost dry by then, and the new water bag was already empty. I was ready to get to the shelter and get another drink.

But when I looked back down the shaft, I knew I would have to wait a little longer for water. Carver was having trouble with the top rail: it was more tangled, and the twisted coils didn't want to fit through the tunnel. He tugged and pulled and tried to compress it; but no matter what he tried, it kept hanging up on the tunnel edges. As fast as I dared, I dropped down to help; and with the two of us compressing and pulling and pushing, we slid the rail out into the pit.

By the time we cleared the shaft, Carver and I were both puffing (though at least the ache in my ribs had dulled). It's never smart to overexert in a suit, so I waved Carver over to sit on a bench. But he shook his head inside his helmet, and he refused to sit. He paced and he stamped, and once he even slammed a wall tile.

Finally, I checked the captain's circuit to make sure we were alone. Then I had to ask: "Something wrong, Lieutenant?"

Carver turned away. "He's so rough on me."

Yeah, I had seen this coming. "He's rough on everyone, Lieutenant."

"Yes, but he seems to have a target painted on me. Especially during flight training. I did so well with Chief Maxwell. He was patient, he showed me what I needed to do to improve, and he insisted I had what it takes to be a pilot."

I smiled. "Max is special, Lieutenant. He's a great second-in-command, he understands his crew perfectly. He said plenty of good things about your flying." Then I worried: Would thinking about Max bring Carver down again?

But Carver was still on his rant. "Him, maybe, but not Captain Aames. Nothing I did was *ever* good enough for him. You should've heard him chew me out after my collision."

I laughed. "Half the ship heard, Carver."

I couldn't see Carver's face, but I imagined him scowling. "Yeah, that did wonders for my respect among the crew." I snorted, and he turned to glare at me through the visor. "What?"

"I've served with the captain long enough to know he wouldn't waste time chewing you out if you weren't worth it. He'd have kicked you off this expedition." Carver looked doubtful. "He could've done it, screw mission planning. If he had wanted you gone, you'd be gone. But him and Max, they're a team. They both have the same goals, they just go at it from different angles. They both want you to be your best." Carver was silent in response. Absorbing or doubting? I couldn't tell. "And we all need our best from each other right now. You want respect? All right, straighten up, take the criticism like a grown-up, and show that you've learned from it."

"What?"

"Look, Carver. Aames is only as rough on you as you need him to be. You get better, the chewing out will happen less often."

"How good do I have to get so the chewing out stops?"

"Heh. I'll let you know when I get that good."

CRAWLER

Carver and I entered the pressure door to the shelter. The airlock is large enough to let a rescuer carry an injured spacer, and protocol is to pair up if possible when using the lock. The extra person takes up more volume, meaning it takes less air to pressurize the lock, and so less energy to pump air in and out. We were cramped in the lock, but again, there were no claustrophobes on that mission.

Once we were through the airlock, we entered the dustlock, an almost futile effort to keep the Martian sand out of the shelter. The iron oxides of Mars aren't as insidious as the fine crushed basalts of Luna, but they can still play hell with mechanical and electrical systems. So in the dustlock, we took turns vacuuming off each other's suits, then swabbing them down with electrostatic cloths, and then finally vacuuming the floor. When all that was done, we stripped out of our suits and down to our skivvies: loose white underclothes, mine soaked with sweat and leaked water. My ribs gave one more brief twinge as I unbolted and opened my bodysuit, but then they suddenly felt better. Examining the inner shell of the bodysuit, I saw where it had been dented, right into my ribs. And that part of the shell was where the water supply ran through. The impact probably split a valve.

There would be time for suit repair later. We had had a long day already. We hung the suits in a locker next to Pagnotto's suit and Gale's helmet.

But for all that cleaning effort, when I padded barefoot into the shelter, I still felt the grit of sand beneath my feet. And no wonder: when Gale and Carver had brought Van der Ven in for the amputation, they hadn't taken time to unsuit; and since Van's suit had doubled as a tourniquet, they had left it on until they had started the operation. Now his suit lay piled in pieces on the floor by the exam table, where Van still lay, unconscious. Gale was also still in his suit as he moved back and forth between Van on the exam table and Elvio on a bunk nearby. He wasn't a doctor, but he and Van der Ven had both cross-trained under Dr. Koertig. It figured one of our field medics would also be our first patient.

I crossed to the exam table and looked at Van's medical comp, and then at him. We'd all had basic medic training, so I could see that Van was stable. He had lost blood, but the suit's auto-tourniquet had minimized the loss. He was still low, so Gale had given him two units of null plasma, and now he was on a saline drip with painkillers. Gale and Carver had amputated his left leg just below the knee. The stump was wrapped in fresh white bandages, probably half the bandages in the shelter. Van was dozing fitfully, and Gale had used restraints to hold him down. In the low Martian gravity, it would be all too easy for him to toss right off the table.

The shelter was made up of three rooms: a workroom, a utility room to the east, and a bunk room to the west. Each room was no bigger than a large ship's cabin, so we didn't have space for clutter. I stooped down, and my ribs weren't so bad now that the bodysuit wasn't pinching them. I started picking up Van der Ven's suit as I turned to Gale. "We can watch your patients, Lieutenant. You should unsuit. We need all the elbow room we can get."

"I know what I'm doing, Ensign," Gale snapped. But he headed to the dustlock. By the time I brought the pieces of Van's suit into the lock, he was mostly out of his own suit: his sleeves and bodysuit and boots were off and in the locker, and he was unsealing his leggings. I noted that he hadn't bothered vacuuming anything. I glared at him, pulled the hand vac from its wall socket, and started vacuuming Van's suit. Gale just glared back, hung up his leggings, and went back into the shelter.

I thought of making a smart remark, but then I remembered the captain's words: *We need all of us, every single one, with our heads in the game . . . Gale's a nervous wreck from the surgery . . . If trouble comes down, I trust you to handle it.* So I decided I could cut Gale a little slack too. I finished vacuuming and wiping Van's suit. I also found a pair of surgical gloves and some biodegradable wipes, and I used those for the grim task of cleaning out the lower left legging. There wasn't a lot of blood in there, thanks to the auto-tourniquet, but it was still a mess. When I was done with the blood, I started on Gale's suit, which had some exterior blood smears along with its coating of dust. And yes, Pagnotto's also needed cleaning. I could hardly blame Gale there, since his priority had been Elvio's concussion.

Once I was done with the suits, I turned to the dustlock itself, filling the hand vac by the time I was finished. Then I decided there was no sense in half measures: I swapped a new bag into the vac, returned to the shelter, and started vacuuming all around the exam table and the bunk. Then I went around the rest of the room, obsessively hunting every grain of sand.

But before I could finish with the sand, there was something else I had to deal with: more blood, on the table and on the floor . . . and Van der Ven's severed lower leg. It lay in a gray plastic tub under the exam table. Around it was a thin pool of blood, speckled with fragments of bone. I found myself staring at the coarse black hairs on the pale white calf, and also at the big hairy foot with its enormous toes. We had often kidded Van about his giant Dutch toes. Now I had to dispose of them.

I knew what I had to do, of course. We had trained for this and had been conditioned for it, but there's a difference between training and doing. If Gale and Carver could rise to the occasion and perform the surgery, the least I could do was the cleanup. So I took several more biodegradable wipes, used them to swab the table and the floor, and tossed them in the tub with the leg. Then I applied some antiseptic and used more wipes to sanitize all of the surfaces. When I couldn't avoid it any longer, I took the tub back to the utility room, I opened the large chute to the nanomolecular composter, and I dumped the tub's bloody contents in. Then I took more wipes, used them to clean the tub, and tossed them into the chute as well. After one more round with antiseptic, I tossed in the last wipes, and then I closed and sealed the chute. The composter's screen lit up, asking me what the remains were. It even provided a helpful dropdown menu, so all I had to do was check "1 human leg, partial," "<1 liter human blood," and "biodegradable wipes (with antiseptic)." Then the composter did the rest, selecting the ideal mix of nanomachines and the ideal temperature to break down Fadila van der Ven's lower left leg into component elements and nutrients that we would try to stretch out for the next eight months.

I'd done what I'd had to do. It was all according to protocol. But when I stopped and thought about what I had done, I fumbled open the chute just in time to add more organics to the composter. Then I closed the chute again, opened the dropdown menu, and added "<0.5 liter human vomit" to the list.

After a few minutes, to be sure my stomach had settled, I stepped away from the composter, and I looked around. Suddenly I noticed, over in the corner, another pile of uniform pieces and a shattered helmet. And just like that, I remembered Shannon. With work to do, I had put her out of my mind for a while, concentrating just on the next minute and how we would survive. Now here was her uniform, but . . .

I held down my gorge this time. And much as I hate him sometimes, just at that moment I had the urge to go embrace Gale, to try to comfort him. Suddenly I felt deeply for him and his cold, dazed attitude. I had gotten sick just disposing of Van's leg; but Gale . . . Shannon's body was nowhere to be seen because, while Carver and I had been out scavenging in the pit, Gale had done his job. I know you've heard stories of what an ass Gale is, including from me, and you're gonna hear worse. So right now I want to say this as clearly as possible: Gale's an ass, but under that, he's also a spacer. I'm not sure I could do all he did that day.

So then I went back to cleaning one more time: hauling Shannon's suit to the dustlock, wiping off the blood and vacuuming off the sand, and hanging it in a locker. Then I went back to the utility room and cleaned up the blood and the sand where the suit had lain. More wipes went into the composter, and I tried not to think about what was decomposing in there.

And then, finally done with cleaning at last, I looked down at myself. My sweaty white skivvies had become red: rust-colored dust streaks mixed with darker-red smears. Van's blood. Shannon's blood.

Great. We were all extremely healthy, the best that modern nanomedicines could make us, but blood was still an infection risk. And it was on my arms and knees too. I stripped out of my skivvies, scrubbed down with yet more antiseptic wipes (while wondering just how many were stashed in the shelter), and added the wipes to the composter. Then I hung my skivvies in the laundry cabinet, where a combination of cleaning fluids and nanomachines would scrub them clean, separate the wastes, and pipe the organics into the composter and the water into the shelter's reservoir. Shannon's skivvies were already hanging in the cabinet, halfway through the cleaning cycle.

I pulled a survival blanket from a shelf and wrapped it around myself. Not that I much cared if I went around bare-assed, usually, but I never did on duty. And it looked like we would be on duty for the duration. Plus I may have been feeling sympathy for Gale just then, but I was in no mood to deal with his leering. So I turned the blanket into a makeshift toga, and I returned to the workroom.

Gale was at a desk near the dustlock. He was on the comm with Captain Aames, and they were going over my inventory and making notes. Carver was tending to Van and Elvio. I was ready to collapse, but I was too well trained to go off duty without being relieved—or to interrupt the conversation between Aames and Gale. So I crossed to where Gale could see me out of the corner of his eye, and I stood at ease.

Finally Gale noticed me. "Captain, hold a bit. Yes, Ensign?"

I stood straighter. "Lieutenant, I'm done cleaning the shelter, and I could use a rest." I didn't add: *And so could you.* Rank hath its privileges, but sometimes it doesn't hath a lot of sleep.

"What?" Gale looked ashen and drawn, as well as unfocused. I pictured the composter again, and I managed not to shudder. "Oh, yes, Smith. It's been a bad day. Get some sleep."

"Thank you, Lieutenant."

I turned to leave, but the captain's voice stopped me. "Smith, have Carver check those ribs first. Your suit comp shows repeated abrasions and constrictions there. I want to know how bad those injuries are before you hit the bunk."

"Yes, sir."

"And Smith, I know you're tired. I hate to do this. But two hours. We can't spare more time than that right now."

"Yes, sir. Two hours. I'll make good use of them."

"All right. Dismissed." Aames and Gale went back to their planning, and I went to see Carver. He nodded, having heard the discussion, and he gestured at a bench folded up against the wall. Without saying a word, I pulled down the bench, sat down, and unwrapped my toga so Carver could examine my ribs. If Gale wanted to leer, let him. I wasn't going to violate the captain's orders.

But Gale was too busy in his conversation to notice, and Carver was too much of a nice guy to leer. Instead his eyes were like a quantum wave function: they moved from my face to my ribs and back, somehow without ever once crossing the territory in between. I almost laughed, and I suspected his dark skin hid a blush. He examined my ribs with a hand sonic, probed them with his fingers (making me gasp in sudden pain), and finally injected me with a small dose of osteo-nanos to help heal some hairline fractures that had shown on the sonic. Then he taped up my ribs, stood up straight, and looked discreetly away as I rearranged my toga to cover myself. Finally he spoke, subdued but no longer defeated. "Try not to smash those ribs again, Ensign, and you'll be fine." He managed a slight smile.

"Thank you, Lieutenant." I stood. "I'm not going to smash anything but my bunk for the next two hours." Then I walked to the water reservoir, filled a flask, and sipped at the straw as I went into the bunk room and found myself a bunk. "Martian Springs," I whispered. The water was just delicious enough to keep me from falling immediately asleep; but as soon as the flask was empty, I closed my eyes, and I was out.

☾

I woke to the sound of snoring: two tones, out of sync and off key. Carver and Gale were both asleep in bunks across the room. One of them should've been watching over Van and Elvio; but with all we had been through, who could blame them for catching some rest?

I checked my comp. In less than ten minutes, Captain Aames would send his wake-up call. I hadn't gotten enough rest, not with that dream. I thought about ten more minutes of sleep, but I decided against it. I thought how easy it would be to cocoon, to try to hide from our troubles and let depression and sleep wash over me until the end came; but I was afraid that dream would return, and it had wrung me dry. Besides, I knew the captain expected better of me than to just give up. He wanted my best, and damn it, I would give it to him.

I sat up, tightened my toga, and got up from my bunk. I went into the workroom, and I saw that the lieutenants hadn't forgotten their patients: they had set up a camera on a tripod, and it swiveled slowly back and forth between Van der Ven on the table and Pagnotto on the bench. I stepped in front of the camera and waved my hand at it. "Hello?"

"Good morning, Ensign Smith," came the deep rumble of Ensign Chukwunwike Adika. The big Nigerian had been a late addition to our crew, replacing Danita Williams after she had broken both legs in a training accident. We didn't know him that well, even after the months in transit. He was a very private man. But Aames gave Adika his highest recommendation, and the ensign was always calm and polite.

"Good morning, Adika. I guess." I looked at Van's diagnostic read-out. He had a slight fever, but his heart rate was steady, and he slept. "How are they doing?"

Adika paused. "They are no worse. I only wish that I could say that they are better."

I nodded as I looked at Elvio's readings. He was also asleep. "It's early. Give them time." I wasn't convinced time would be enough for them, though.

"And speaking of time, Ensign, I do have other duties here. Do you relieve me?"

I nodded. "I relieve you, Ensign. I'll watch the patients."

"Thank you, Smith. Adika out." The camera light turned off.

I checked the medical readings again, and I saw no immediate problems. So I went to the utility room, opened the laundry cabinet, and pulled out my skivvies. They were clean and maybe not as white as when they were new, but white enough. I dropped the blanket and pulled on my clothes. Then I folded the blanket, hung it in the laundry cabinet, and returned to the workroom.

I walked over to the reservoir for another flask of water, but the flask was only half-full when a dark hand reached over mine and turned off the tap. I jumped a bit: Carver had come up so quietly, I hadn't noticed him at all. I looked at him, and he shook his head. "Sorry, Ensign, we're on temporary rationing until the compressor and the composter can catch up. The captain says our patients have first priority for water, especially Van der Ven. He lost a lot of blood. We need to keep them both well hydrated."

I understood. The composter was an efficient recycler, but nowhere near 100 percent, and the compressor needed time for the catalysts to tease out water from the soil. Our mission plan called for installing many more catalytic compressors as well as other improvements over the First's systems, but all of that gear and a treasure trove of tools and raw materials had been lost to us along with the *Bradbury*.

And what about Maxwell, Weaver, Koertig, and Uribe? And Shannon, and Van's leg. I had no right to complain by comparison. So I took my half flask of Martian Springs and told myself to be grateful as I sipped it very slowly.

A voice came from the bunk room. "It's a bloody waste of time, if you ask me. And water." I looked up and saw Gale in the doorway, leaning against the frame and staring over at Van. "Pagnotto's going to make it, but Van der Ven . . ." Gale shook his head.

In shock, I looked back at Van. Once I reassured myself that he was asleep, I wheeled on Gale and spoke in a low, calm voice. "Keep it down, Lieutenant. He might hear you."

"I doubt he's hearing anything." Gale turned his eyes from the exam table. "He's too far under. And he won't be with us long."

Carver glared at Gale. "You don't know that, Lieutenant. The odds of post-op infection are low. There's nothing on Mars that can infect him, we're all pretty sterile, and we cleaned the area thoroughly before the procedure."

"Then explain his fever."

Carver blinked. "Probably his body still adjusting to the damage and the loss. Maybe some of his therapy nanos are rebalancing."

"Maybe." Gale snorted. "And maybe we're just losing him."

"So what? You want to just let him die? Just—" I almost said: *just drop him in the composter.* But that wasn't fair. Damn it! I was pissed off at Gale, but I couldn't let that make me forget that five hours earlier, he had saved Van's life *and* performed his first surgery ever. Not to mention dealing with Shannon. This disaster had been harder on him than on me. So I tried for a more calming approach. "I'm not ready to give up on Van der Ven."

"Of course you're not." Gale looked down at his feet. "You're just like Captain Aames. He never knows when to give up, and that attitude's contagious. He gets people to believe that nothing's impossible if you push a little harder. Well, some things *are* impossible. Sometimes it's time to stop pushing and just make do with what you have. And we don't have enough to keep Van der Ven alive."

"You don't know that."

"Look, Smith, it's all about our resources and how far we can stretch them. Will they stretch far enough for the *Collins* to get here? The captain has some crazy idea we can actually rendezvous with them. That is never going to happen, but they'll drop off a package of colonizing supplies. We can use those and keep going until there's a real rescue. But we can only do that if we can make our resources stretch that far."

"And we will."

Without looking up, Gale shook his head. "I know the captain thinks so, but I don't see how. Even with the most stringent rationing, I don't see all of us stretching our resources past six months. That's not far enough, not if we have to support people who are going to die eventually anyway and who can't carry their share of the load."

I bit back my instinctive reply and instead said, "I'm glad it's Captain Aames in command. He'll see it differently."

Gale kicked his bare foot against the doorjamb. "Yes, Captain Aames, he'll push us to do the impossible. And he'll kill us all." He sighed. "But you're right, we already have his decision: 'Every one of us is essential to our survival,' he said, and that's that. He promises to make life hell for anyone who suggests otherwise. And we have his orders: we're to keep Van der Ven comfortable and healthy and get him ready for the trip."

I looked up. "Trip?"

"As soon as the storm lifts, the captain wants us to consolidate with lander 1 at landing pad B. He says it will be easier to maintain one shelter instead of two, especially as this one is damaged. He has prepared a list of equipment and supplies, and we are to load these into the crawler for a trip across Coprates quadrangle." Gale swiped a finger across his sleeve comp, and my own comp beeped. "Carver and Smith, get that list together and into the crawler, while I see to our patients. Start by inspecting the S3 cable."

"Yes, Lieutenant." Synthetic spider silk is a miracle fiber for space travel: stronger than steel, at one-tenth the mass, and flexible as optic cable. Its one drawback is it can develop microscopic flaws that will cause it to unravel under stress, so it has to be inspected on a regular basis. The coils there in the shelter had been uninspected for nearly two years, so Carver and I ran it through the scanner very carefully. We rejected three out of ten coils, then we packed the rest into a travel case.

After the S3, most of the captain's list was out in the pit, so we had to suit up for that work. That gave me a chance to inspect the damage to my suit. Looking at the crumpled shell, I felt lucky that some minor fractures were all I had suffered. Our bodysuits were made of a semi-rigid polymer, individually fitted to each of us. The shell would absorb impact and shield us from most of it, but it might crack under enough pressure. That's what had happened to mine. Fortunately the vacuum resin between the layers had been good enough to save my life, sealing up the cracks and keeping my air in.

I had Carver double-check, and we both certified the bodysuit for use even with the cracks; I scavenged Shannon's water system, patched up my environment pack, and asked Carver to inspect my work again. When we were both satisfied, we suited up, buddy-checked each other, and returned to the pit. There we gathered up the rest of the captain's list: tools, spare parts, water bags, medicine, dozens of other items all went into the travel case. When it was full, we started on a second case, and then a third. By the time we were finished, we had five of the cases, each a meter square by half a meter high. They were made of a light polymer, extruded on-site by robots from the First, and they were easy to handle even when they were fully loaded.

With our cases packed, it was time to load the crawler, a low enclosed platform designed for medium-distance travel when it was safer to drive than to risk flying in storms. The video from the crawler garage showed that the building had survived the worst of the explosion: one wall was collapsed, but the rest had held, as had the roof. The crawler itself looked intact: an ugly rectangular box, three meters by five and two high, squatting between eight giant wire wheels. The reactor and the power train were all embedded in the understructure, designed to survive anything that didn't destroy the entire crawler. The whole structure was low, its center of mass below its axles, all to make it as stable as possible in case of Martian storms; but a pilot turret, a sensor tower, a winch, and cargo racks rose up above the box structure that housed the crew compartment with seats and bunks. Six could ride in comfort, twelve in a pinch.

The vehicle looked functional, except for the sensor tower, which had twisted and bent beneath the wall panel. Communications and radar were probably out, but we would find out soon enough. In deference to my ribs, Carver took the surface duty. He climbed the ladder to the surface, opened the lock, and climbed up into the ruins of the turret, crouching down between the two leaning panels. I watched the feed from his helmet cam on my screen as he peered through the cracks between the panels and out at the Martian surface. "Looks like the storm has passed, Lieutenant."

"For now," Carver said. "I wish Van der Ven was up to making a weather forecast. Or even Deece." Captain Aames had been unable to contact Deece or anyone on the *Bradbury*, so we had lost our eye in the sky.

"Nothing on the horizon, though, right? We should have time to pack and get crawling?"

Carver paused before he answered, "Nothing on my detectors. We're good for now." With that he pushed the panels aside, watching them slowly fall to the ground, where they blew up lazy clouds of dust that blocked his vision. Dust is different on every world. On Earth, it rises quickly, gets caught up in the thick atmosphere, and then slowly settles and blows away. On Luna, it sprays in fine jets, with no atmosphere to make it swirl into clouds, and then falls in smooth arcs like a volley of very tiny rocks (which is exactly what it is). But on Mars, the thinner atmosphere let it fly farther before air resistance took over; and then the lighter gravity let it hang in the air for far longer. With the winds died down for the moment, there was little to disperse the dust. And so Carver kicked up a great fog of dust all around him, and he had to wait over a minute before he could see his surroundings again. Then he had to brush his visor clean before he could walk the twenty meters to the crawler garage.

I watched through the helmet cam as Carver approached the garage. He walked in near-total silence in the still Martian air, the only sounds his own breathing and the faint buzz and clicks of his suit. He reached the west wall and opened the big garage doors, a pair of polymer panels that swung out from the center on big wire wheels. The southern door stuck halfway open: the south wall had partially collapsed, and the doorframe had warped from the stress. Carver leaned into the door and pushed. "Careful, Lieutenant, watch your footing," I called. Carver just nodded, braced his feet, and pushed harder, and the door swung farther open. It was wide enough for the crawler to emerge, but it would be a bitch to close again.

Inside the crawler waited, the south wall leaning against it. The rear end faced the door, showing the winch and the main airlock. I called out, "Do you need help getting it free, Lieutenant?"

Carver peered in between the panel and the vehicle. "Negative, Ensign. This'll be light work."

"I'll keep an eye on you, just in case."

The comm clicked, and Captain Aames cut in. "I'll keep watch, Smith. Get those travel cases out and ready to haul up. The radar looks clear for now, but don't waste any time. There could be another front over the horizon. Without the *Bradbury*'s meteorology reports, we can't be sure when the next sandstorm will be."

"Yes, sir." I went back and started moving the cases to the shaft. They were easy to lift in the Martian gravity, but still massive to move around, so I worked up quite a sweat hauling them. By the time the last case was in the shaft, a length of S3 cable hung down from above. Looking up, I saw the crawler's winch hanging over the opening.

I pulled down more of the S3 cable. There was a cargo clip woven into its end. I threaded the clip around the first case and through loops shaped into its sides, and then I hooked the clip back onto the cable.

Then I tugged twice on the line running upward. "First case is ready, Lieutenant."

"Aye, Ensign," Carver called down, and the cable pulled taut, lifting the case up the shaft. When it reached the top, Carver swung the winch around, lowered the case onto the crawler roof, and unhitched the case. Then he turned the winch back and lowered the cable again, and I started on the second case while he secured the first.

In this way, we loaded up all of the cases. By the time Carver was securing the fifth, Gale walked into the shaft, supporting Van der Ven beside him. He held out a survival harness, a web of S3 cables with holes for arms and legs. "Smith, lend a hand here."

"Yes, Lieutenant." Van had his left arm across Gale's shoulders, hand wrapped into the fabric of Gale's left sleeve. I bent down so he could brace his right arm on my shoulder, and then he lifted his right leg. I took the safety harness and threaded his leg in, up to the knee. Then I whispered to myself, "Don't be squeamish," and I pulled the harness around the stump of his left leg, tugging the harness up to his crotch. Van put his foot back down and let go of my shoulder, and the three of us managed to get his arms into the harness as well. We adjusted it snug around him and hooked the cargo clip in the back, and Carver activated the winch to pull Van up the shaft.

While Van was going up, Pagnotto walked into the shaft and over to the ladder. Gale called out, "Stop, Ensign. You're going up on the harness."

Pagnotto turned back. "I am much better, *Tenente*. I can climb." I agreed, Elvio looked very steady after his rest.

But Gale had his own ideas. "I'm sure you can, but we're *all* using the harness. The power use is minimal, and it's the safest approach."

There was no arguing—Gale was in charge; but Pagnotto made a point of donning the harness without help. After him, I rode the harness up, and then Gale. We each took our turn in the crawler's one-person airlock.

While we were waiting, Carver got on the comm to Captain Aames. "Confirmed, Captain, the sensor tower is inoperative. It would take a day to repair, even with replacement parts."

"You're not waiting a day, Lieutenant," Nick replied.

"Understood, sir. That means we'll have no radar, no meteorology, and visual limited to what the pilot can see from the turret. And no comms, sir, unless we stop periodically to step out and report."

"Negative, Carver. We don't know how soon another storm may come. Do not stop unless there's bad news to report. Good news can wait."

"Yes, sir." Then it was my turn in the lock, and I lost the comm signal. Carver came in right after me, taking up the rear. Once we were all inside, Gale pulled himself up into the pilot turret—an easy task in Martian gravity—and sat in the pilot chair. I could just see his feet sticking down into the main cabin and resting on a padded footrest that jutted out underneath the chair.

So we began our trip across Coprates quadrangle. We didn't go at our top speed, since Gale had to scan the Martian surface for hazards (especially with the sensor tower out), but we made good time. Since I had nothing better to do for four hours, I took off my helmet and lay back on my bunk. The wire wheels were great shock absorbers, so the crawler ride was smooth. Soon the steady hum of the motor hypnotized me, and I grabbed another chance to sleep.

☾

I woke feeling more rested. The hum still filled the cabin, but it was dark, the only light being the faint glow of instruments and the weak Martian sunlight leaking down around Gale's legs as he drove.

I checked my suit comp: I had slept a little over two hours. I could use more, but it was a good start, and I was too keyed up to go back to sleep. So I sat up and looked around the darkened crawler.

As soon as I did, I knew there was trouble: only one other bunk was occupied. Elvio slept soundly right across from me, but he was the only one there. The crawler wasn't big enough to hide anybody, but Van and Carver were nowhere to be seen.

I didn't want to wake Elvio; so I got up, walked carefully forward so as not to lose my balance, and stood underneath Gale, peering around the footrest and his boots. "Lieutenant," I whispered loudly.

Gale sighed, and then spoke in a low voice, without taking his eyes off the Martian landscape. "Yes, Ensign?"

"Lieutenant, what the hell's going on? Where are Van der Ven and Carver?"

"I don't know what you're talking about, Ensign." Still he didn't look down at me.

"Bullshit!" I said too loudly, and Elvio shifted in his sleep. I lowered my voice again. "Gale, you have complete system displays up there. No one left this crawler without you knowing it. Stop playing games, and tell me what happened."

Gale sighed again, and this time he did glance down at me between his legs. "All right, *Ensign*, I've had enough of your disrespect. But if it will quiet you down and keep you focused on survival . . . Yes, a little more than an hour after we left, Van der Ven slipped into the airlock and abandoned the crawler."

"What?" Again Elvio moved, and I tried to calm down. "Why the hell would he do that?"

Finally Gale looked straight at me, a sneer on his face. "I assume because unlike you, Smith, he understands that he is a liability. We cannot save him, and we'll doom ourselves trying. And since he is a better spacer than you, he chose to make the decision you and Aames and the rest were too soft to make: to cut himself loose."

"Impossible! Van's not a quitter."

"I only wish he had had the foresight to leave his oxygen behind. We could use it more than him."

I was stunned. Gone was Gale the manipulator, Gale the letch: the face I saw was cold, calculating, only interested in himself. Of course stress brings out the hidden side of people, but this change, I never would've guessed. I couldn't speak, couldn't think of a response. Finally I managed to ask, "And Carver?"

Gale shook his head and looked back to the horizon. "He woke a little later, and he asked many of the same questions. When I gave him the same answers, he demanded that I turn the crawler around."

"Hell, yes! What the fuck are you waiting for?"

"As I told him, *Ensign*, I do not take orders from my junior officers. Nor from you. Van der Ven made the right decision, and who am I to undo his sacrifice?"

I wanted to scream, but I held back. "And so Carver went after him?"

Gale nodded. "And good riddance. We cannot know when a storm may come, so we cannot waste time on his heroics. The lad lacks the temperament to be a good officer. We shall face some very difficult choices before this is through, and Carver cannot make the hard decisions. Better that we're rid of him now. Besides, that's more consumables for the rest of us."

"More consumables?" I shouted despite myself, and Pagnotto stirred. I made one more try to calm down. "Gale, turn this crawler around. Now."

Gale didn't look down. "Smith, I have had quite enough of your insolence. This discussion is closed."

That was the end of my self-control. I reached up, grabbed his boots, and yanked downward. Gale hadn't strapped into the chair, so he dropped to the floor, hitting both his tailbone and the back of his head on the footrest. The bodysuit protected his backside, but his head hit hard. Still, the padding protected him from any serious damage, so he was only staggering when my punch landed on his jaw. I was used to fighting in Earth's gravity, so I hadn't expected my punch to send him clear across the crawler and into a wall. The impact there added to his punishment, and he slid to the floor, semiconscious.

That finally woke Pagnotto. He looked down at Gale and then up at me. "Ensign?"

"Don't worry, Elvio." I bent down and checked Gale's diagnostics. I had done no permanent damage—not that I cared much right at that moment. "The lieutenant just slipped."

Elvio looked down and nodded. "In my time, I have seen many such slips. I am sure he shall be more careful in the future."

"Maybe, but just in case . . ." I lifted Gale up and stretched him out on a bunk. "He really should rest, for his own good. Can you make sure he stays there? I have to turn the crawler around."

"*Sí.*" Elvio nodded. "But why do we go back?"

So I told him the story. I didn't mention the fight, but Elvio was smart enough to fill in the missing details. When I was done, he waved me away. "Go, Ensign. Drive. No one will interfere, I promise."

So I climbed up into the pilot turret and wheeled the crawler around in a wide turn, coming back to our tracks. They were still visible, so we didn't have storm winds yet. Looking at the horizon, though, I couldn't be sure what was coming. How close were those dust clouds? Had my temper doomed us all? A crawler was a safe place to ride out a dust storm, but did we have enough air?

As I drove, I tried to call the captain. No luck—the comms were dead, just as Carver had said. I tried calling him and Van as well, but nothing. I had made my move, and now I would have to see it through. There was no one else to turn to.

Gale said Van left the crawler a little over an hour out, and we had traveled nearly two and a half hours. So I had at least an hour to drive. Maybe less, since I could drive faster, knowing the terrain was safe. But not too fast: I didn't want to miss any signs of Van and Carver. I wondered if maybe I should go back down and sedate Gale to keep him out of trouble. But no, Elvio would handle things down below. He got along with Gale better than I did since they had both come up through EU training and knew a lot of the same spacers, but I had seen the disgust in his face when I told him about Gale abandoning Van der Ven.

I pulled up our route map, and I estimated where Van might've gotten out. There was no sign that the crawler had stopped or even slowed near the hour mark; but at about one-eighteen, the track stopped for about as long as an airlock cycle. Carver must've persuaded Gale to stop long enough to let him out. I knew Van had left prior to that, so I sped ahead to that point.

As I drew close to the spot, I looked out, blinked my eyes, and looked again. "Anson Carver, if you were a woman, I could kiss you." I slowed the crawler nearly to a halt. Off to the side, just south of our tracks, stood a crude arch of flat Martian stones: two slabs standing and a third stacked on top of them. It was a clear message: *I was here.*

Once I slowed down, I could see Carver's tracks. He had made a point to walk beside the crawler tracks, so we could see where he went. He had even dragged something to make a clearer track—which was good, because the winds were picking up. Already the crawler tracks were blurred.

What should I do? If I went too fast, I could miss something important. If I went too slow, the tracks could be wiped out when the dust arrived. I settled on fast, but not top speed.

And sure enough, there came a point where I had lost the tracks. *Damn it.* I brought the crawler to a halt.

"Any problem, Ensign?" Elvio called up.

"No." I thought long before I continued, "We just have to backtrack a bit." I put the crawler in reverse, low gear, and let the computer's dead reckoning keep us on track as I scanned for tracks.

There! Of course I had lost the track: it suddenly turned north, crossed the crawler tracks (getting completely obscured in the process), and continued on the other side. Only there it ran more or less straight north, following a broad, indistinct track. That had to be Van, crawling.

The two tracks led quickly into some foothills, and from there into some low mountains.

I stopped the crawler again. The slopes were terrain the crawler could handle, but not well. I was torn: I wanted to rescue Van and Carver, but I didn't have the right to endanger Elvio. Nor even that rat bastard, Gale, even as mad as I was.

I turned off the motor, climbed down from the turret, and grabbed my helmet. "Elvio, I'm headed into the hills to help Carver with Van. Can you handle things here?" I glanced at Gale.

"*Si.*" Elvio nodded. "We have an understanding, I think. *Tenente* Gale shall not give me trouble. We shall be here when you return."

"Thank you." I put on my helmet. "But don't wait too long. If we're not back in an hour, we've run into trouble that's too big for us. Don't come try to help, just get yourself and Gale to pad B." Elvio nodded again, and I turned to Gale, who glared up at me. "But one hour, no sooner, Lieutenant. If you leave one minute before that, I swear I will march all the way across Mars and give you a beating that will make that punch feel like a kiss." I shut my visor before Gale could answer, turned on my environment unit, and climbed into the airlock.

Once on the surface, I tried my comm. I kept it on the team circuit, and I checked to be sure Captain Aames wasn't listening in. I wanted this just between us. "Carver. Van. Answer me, damn it."

I listened. At first there was only the static of the low frequency ground wave. Then finally Carver answered, sounding winded. "A little busy here, Smith."

"Carver! I am so glad to hear you. Did you find Van?"

Van der Ven's deep voice answered: "*Ja,* I am here." He sounded tired, but alert.

"Van, what the hell did you think you were doing with this little hike?"

There was a long pause before finally he answered, "Stretching your resources."

"What?"

"My fever is worse. I waste your time, waste your water. Better I should die, so you may live. So I crawl away so you cannot find me."

"You heard Gale."

"*Ja*. It was like a dream, but I hear him. He makes sense."

"No, he doesn't!" I shouted. "Gale's an idiot, he's only thinking about himself. He can't see the big picture."

"*Ja*, that is what Carver tells me. He says the captain has a plan, and it needs all of us. Especially me, he says. Without the *Bradbury*, a meteorologist is vital, he says."

Good job, Carver. "He's right, Van. We'll never make it without you."

"I hope you are wrong." Van sounded depressed. Isn't that normal for amputees? But this was worse. "You may have to get by without me. Without both of us, since Carver refuses to leave me."

"What?"

"The damned leg. It slows me down, and there is not time. From the mountainside, I see signs. Sandstorm is coming. It will bury us. I tell Carver leave me, but he says no."

"Damn right," Carver answered. "We need you, and we're not giving you up. We just have to move a little faster."

"Lieutenant," I asked, "could you go faster with some help?"

Carver's voice brightened. "Sure. We could redistribute the load, take turns helping Van. But I'm not ordering you to put yourself at risk too."

"Try to stop me, Carver." I headed north at a jog. I was confident that Carver's and Van's trails would show me where it was safe to travel, so there was little need for caution. And on Mars a jog was easy, even in a suit. Lunar Survival School taught us how to bend into the jog, keep our center of mass low, and push off to cover territory fast without arcing up on every step. It's a fast way to cover ground on Luna, and almost as good on Mars. But I made it only a couple hundred meters before pain in my ribs made me slow down. The osteo-nanos could heal the fractures pretty quickly, but not if I forgot myself and undid all that healing faster than they could work.

So I loped along, another gait they teach at LSS: pushing off one leg and stretching out the other, then landing and switching. It's not nearly as fast, but there's less impact, and it's still better than a walk. Soon I was at the top of the first ridge. There I had to stop and search to make sure I was still on the tracks. The wind was stronger up there: I could hear the low rumble around my suit, and the tracks were blown completely clean. But looking down the other side, I saw more tracks a ways down, continuing into the valley and up the next ridge.

And there! Not on the ridge, but on the mountainside beyond it, there was movement. I zoomed my helmet cam, and sure enough, there were Carver and Van, working their way down the slope. Van held a crutch—no doubt that was what Carver had used to mark his trail—but the slope was so steep, their progress was slow.

Well, another hand could help there. I loped downhill, feeling each jolting step, but too eager to let the aches slow me down, and then up the next ridge. Carver and Van were halfway to the valley floor, but the terrain was still against them, more vertical than horizontal. Carver saw me and waved. I waved back and continued down to meet them up on the mountainside.

"It's great to see you," I said as I climbed up beside them. "Geez, Van, when you decide to hide, you don't mess around. Why did you climb so far up here?"

"I am a meteorologist," Van said. "From a small child, I watch the storms and try to understand them. So when I planned to die, I said, 'Not without climbing up to see *that*.'" He pointed to the west. I looked: sand clouds were mounting, halfway to Phobos I swear. The winds were picking up.

"Whoa . . ."

Van nodded. "Now you see, at last. Please, you and Carver leave me. I do not wish to die knowing I killed you too."

"No one's dying here today," I said. "We just have to move a little faster. Here." I plugged my spare air tube into Van's environment pack. As I did so, I couldn't help seeing his vitals: 38.1 °C, almost to the danger range. But for now, I was more worried about air; and Van had plenty of air for both of us, at least for a while. I disconnected my own pack, and Carver helped me to remove it. Then I turned my back to Van, he hobbled up behind me, and he and Carver hooked his bodysuit onto mine, using clamps designed for rescues like this. The official term for this was dorsal assist mode, but spacers called it doggy carry. There were, naturally, plenty of doggy jokes made about it.

Jokes aside, it was an effective rescue carry in low gravity, especially with a partner. I picked up my environment pack and clipped it to Carver's. The second pack bulged awkwardly from Carver's back. His load was heavier, less balanced than mine—as long as Van didn't squirm. But both of us were balanced enough to climb, and this way we didn't have to leave behind precious air and water.

We descended as fast as was safe. In training we had scaled far worse slopes, requiring cables and crampons and other gear. By comparison, this was no challenge—except every time I happened to look west, the dust clouds had snuck closer, like they were stalking us. With the Martian air devouring all sound, it was easy to forget there was a storm at all. Then I would glance up, and . . . Wham! The dark-red clouds were that much closer.

Before long, we had to slow down. The first wisps of dust were thick enough to blind us at times and make us misjudge our hand- and footholds.

But just like that, we were in the valley, momentarily sheltered from the worst of the sand. The dark clouds still stalked us from behind the mountain, but for the moment it felt like we were safe.

"Van," Carver asked, "can you walk these slopes?"

"Not in time. The storm will be here soon."

"How soon?" I looked at the time on my comm. "Oh, fuuuuuck."

"What now?" Carver asked.

"I told Elvio to head for pad B if we weren't back in an hour. There's only eight minutes left. We'll never clear both ridges in time."

"Maybe he'll give us more time," Carver said, but he didn't sound confident.

"Maybe." And maybe Gale had talked him into leaving already. "One way to find out, sir: double time!"

Despite the ache in my ribs, I jogged the best I could manage with Van riding doggy. Without any pain to hold him back, Carver ran ahead, perhaps hoping to catch the crawler before they left. But a glance at my comm told me he would be too late. Another glance over my shoulder gave me chills despite my exertion: the storm front was now directly over the mountain, like the biggest wave ever about to crash down upon us. Silent doom was ready to take us.

I looked back ahead, and Carver had stopped at the top of the ridge. Had he seen the doom storm as well? Was he giving up? But he wasn't looking back, he was looking down into the valley ahead. And waving me forward.

I ran faster, crying out slightly at every step; but a little rib pain wouldn't matter soon anyway. Wincing and puffing, I pulled up beside Carver, and I looked down into the valley. There was the crawler, speeding across the valley between the two ridges.

I got onto the local comm circuit. "Elvio."

A smug British voice answered, "Negative, this is your commanding officer, Ensign. Keep moving, we're short on minutes."

Carver and I started our downward jog. I refused to look back. It felt too good to be running toward something, not away from something. So I peered ahead. "You repaired . . . sensor tower."

"Indeed. You ordered us to wait; you didn't say we had to be idle. The repairs are far from perfect, but they'll get us to pad B. Pagnotto's a top-notch engineer, and I can follow instructions. When they're delivered clearly."

I thought about the punch. "Sorry, sir."

"About what? I seem to have had a bump on my head. I do not recall how that happened, but I do see a bit more clearly now. And so does the deep radar. It's about 70 percent effective, good enough for us to find safe terrain and make top speed. Which we'll need if we're going to outrun that sand. So shut up and run."

I shut up. I ran. Before the end, I hobbled. I had cracked the ribs worse than before. But Carver helped Van and me along, and we all reached the crawler ahead of the storm. I looked back one more time, and I saw the storm tower over us like a giant ready to smash us with great red fists. Then Gale punched the accelerator, and we were off to landing pad B.

ASCENT STAGE

The rearview camera showed the sandstorm not far behind us the entire trip. Carver was at the sensor console, running images of the sky; and despite Van der Ven's fever and his weakness, he stood right behind Carver, leaning on his chair and urging him to turn back to the rearview. Van was delighted with that storm, pointing out its features: sand cloud banks, cell formations, and signs of weak wind shear. His only complaint: "I wish the Doppler radar worked. I'm sure I could find cyclones." Me, I didn't even want to think about cyclones, even though I knew they would be harmless in the thin air. A guy I knew once had his entire semi, load and all, picked up by a twister, spun around, and dropped back to the road going the wrong direction. That load was heavier than the crawler! So even weak cyclones gave me chills.

But we crossed the quadrangle without further incident. As we rode into view of landing pad B, Captain Aames came on the comm.

"Don't waste any time, Gale, that sandstorm is on your ass. We'll have the shelter pit open. Drive in and park on the ramp. Now move!"

"Yes, Captain." Gale pushed the accelerator to the max. The ground near the pads was well mapped, both surface and deep radar. There was no risk in speed, especially when we got onto the smooth surface of the landing pad itself. Soon we saw the pit doors standing open, along with two spacers standing ready to close them behind us. The shorter one could've been any of the crew, but the tall one could only be Adika.

Gale slowed so as not to spray the spacers with dust, and then he smoothly turned the crawler in line with the pit and drove it down the ramp. Adika and his companion pulled the giant plates shut behind us. It was a tight fit, but the ramp had been built for emergency crawler parking. Barely. Gale stopped the crawler nose to nose with lander 1, not centimeters between them.

That still left us with a pretty cramped exit: the airlock at the rear of the crawler was less than half a meter from the pit doors at the top, somewhat more at the bottom. I had to back out of the lock and then shuffle sideways to make room for Van and the rest. As I slid free, Adika grabbed my hand and gave it a hearty shake. "Welcome to Mars Shelter One."

I tried to smile through the visor. "Not a very inspired name."

Adika shrugged. "It's descriptive." He turned back to the lock. "Welcome, Van der Ven. Do you need assistance?"

Van emerged from behind the ladder, crutch first, and shook his head. "Thank you, Adika, no. I must learn to use this."

"My apologies. Please, Ensigns, proceed to the bottom of the ramp. We have converted the access shaft to additional shelter." The ramp had no guardrails, and there was only a narrow walkway between the crawler and the edge, so I moved with caution. I thought about just jumping down in the low gravity, but I didn't want to tempt Van to do the same, so I stuck to the walkway.

When I got to the bottom of the pit, I noticed some of the wall panels were missing. Not fallen, like in our pit: these had been deliberately removed and were nowhere to be seen. The panels weren't just decorative, they covered plumbing and wiring and storage, so someone must have had a more important use for them.

Gale, Carver, and Pagnotto joined us, and we entered the tunnel airlock. When we got through the other side, I saw where the panels had been put to use: the lander 1 crew had walled off the rear of the shaft as a makeshift dustlock and suit locker, and they had affixed panels as benches or bunks all up the wall of the shaft. They had turned the shaft into a vertical shelter with room for the five of us. Sanitary facilities, recycling, medical, and the workshop were all in the main shelter, but at least we wouldn't be cramped for sleeping quarters.

At the top of the stairs, I saw a new airlock attached to the exit door. The entire access turret and shaft were pressurized. They must've produced a lot of air to fill this space. Of course, they hadn't had to dig out from an explosion and cave-in—or amputate Van's leg and dispose of Shannon.

Captain Aames stood on the stairs, waiting for us. "No one move," he said. "Let's not get any more dust in here than we have to. That dustlock can only handle one of you at a time, so the rest of you *hold still.*" He crossed his arms and glared at us as Van hobbled into the dustlock. "Now Lieutenant Gale, would you mind telling me why you stopped and made nonessential repairs after I instructed you to make best time?" I cringed, fearing a big blowup.

But Gale was smarter than I expected. I can't say he and I were ever friendly after I punched him. Certainly he never hit on me again. I don't often let my temper loose like that; it gets me into too much trouble. So I had surprised myself as much as I did him, and I still make him nervous today. And he could have made a big deal about the punch, could've made the entire trip look like a bunch of insubordinate crew defying him in a crisis. Legally, he would probably have been right to do so.

Instead, for that moment at least, Gale proved he was a spacer, not a space lawyer. He must've decided we needed each other, because he lied through his teeth. That's a big risk with Nick, his one unforgivable sin, but Gale did it anyway. "I understand, Captain; but on further investigation, Pagnotto judged we could do most of the repairs very quickly, and that justified the delay."

Aames glared at him. "It justified the delay."

Gale nodded. "Yes, sir, in my judgment it did. We needed the data."

The captain's eyes widened. "Oh?"

I saw Gale glance at Carver. Had these two cooked something up while I was worrying about the storm? They must have, because Carver spoke up. "Yes, sir, Captain. I think it did. I'll need another orbit to confirm, but I think my mods to the motion detection algorithm have found the *Bradbury*."

With that news, Gale and Carver successfully distracted the captain. Aames practically leaped down the stairs, ignoring safety and Mars dust to crowd in beside Carver and stare at the display on his suit comp. Then I saw something I've almost never seen: Nick Aames, exuberant. "Yeehaw!" He slapped Carver's shoulder, and red dust sprayed through the air. "Martian Springs all around. Carver, Gale, you just put us weeks ahead of schedule." And with that, the subject of our unscheduled stop was dropped. Aames had a plan.

Or I should say, he *already* had a plan, and now he had a better one.

Nick's original plan had been simple: Convert the pad B pit into a shelter for the two teams, tear apart pads A and C for spare parts, and do whatever it took to stay alive while we searched for the *Bradbury*; and if we found it, scavenge it for supplies. If we didn't find the *Bradbury*, then the backup plan was to scrape by, improvise more catalytic compressors for water, try to cultivate yeast using our food rations as seed stock (that was part of mission survival protocols all along) . . . and slowly, inexorably descend into hunger, cannibalism, and death, in the vain hope that some of us would survive until the *Collins* arrived.

If you think I'm making some grim joke, I'm not. I saw the captain's plans in writing, including projections for how much water we could produce, how we would have to ration it, how long the food would last, and when we would start dying. He even had a recommended suicide schedule to maximize the chances for the survivors; and just so no one could question the fairness of that plan, his name was first on that list.

But with the *Bradbury* found, and so soon, everything changed. The captain's original priority had been expanding our air and water production. With eleven people, the shelter would be overtaxed. But now his number one priority was getting back to the ship, and to her payload. She was carrying supplies that would have lasted us all the way back to Earth, with recycling. Food stock. Hydroponics tanks filled with algae and ivy for oxygen as well as food plants. Water. Electronics. Spare parts. Hell, spare *landers*. And most precious of all: the mactory deck, the big disk that extended out from the main hull on a long axis tunnel and spun to create gravity. The machining tools, stereolithography tanks, laser sintering macro factories, and nano assembly tanks in the mactory all worked better with gravity to pull away resin or dust or chips, whatever were the remnants of their work. With that deck full of tools and the raw stock to feed them, us eleven skilled spacers could practically build a city to keep us alive. That had been the whole point of that payload: our mission had been to construct a base for long-term habitation on Mars. We just hadn't expected to do the habitation.

So we had to get back to the *Bradbury*, and the captain decided we had to go as soon as it was safely possible. "We won't get any more rested if we sit around," he explained. "We're going to get more tired, thirstier, and hungrier the longer we wait. So as soon as it's safe, we launch."

The captain's revised plan still gave us time to expand air and water production and to nurture the yeast vat, but our top priority was to build a Mission Control center. We needed to get a team to orbit, rendezvous with the *Bradbury*, scavenge supplies, and land them safely back at Mars Shelter One. Launching would be easy, even easier than it had been for lander 2: Ensign Somtow had already installed plenty of propellant disks from the pad B factory. We had enough power to get to orbit twice, even with a fully loaded lander, and maybe some spare capacity beyond that. We wouldn't have to burn any liquid fuel to launch. But the landers were built for telepilot assist mode and weather reports from orbit. Without those, landing in them could be a disaster, especially if the lander was weighed down by a hold full of supplies. We would need absolutely perfect weather recon and ground radar if we wanted to land in one piece.

So the first thing Nick had us build was an impromptu meteorology station. Pagnotto started the effort, designing a sensor mast that could be raised above the access turret to give us a high platform for scanning.

Once Van recovered from his fever enough to handle the math, he started designing meteorology instruments, and Pagnotto, Somtow, and Roberts started arguing about how to construct them out of available supplies. Captain Aames joined in these discussions, not as an engineer—though on that mission, every one of us had some amount of engineering training; it was a mission requirement—but as a veto. "No, you can't use that backup pressure circuit from the crawler lock. We could lose air if the main circuit failed." "No, you can't take plates from the propellant factory roof. If any dust gets in a propellant disk, it could blow apart an engine." "Yes, you can strip out some wiring from the wall panels, but be damned sure it's from the lights, not the air recirculators."

The rest of us worked on the construction crews, tended the machinery, or expanded Mars Shelter One as Captain Aames ordered us to do. All except Carver: he spent all his spare time on his image processing algorithms, trying to refine his plot of the *Bradbury's* orbit and get a clear image of the ship itself.

It was after four days of code cutting and image crunching that Carver emerged from the access turret and walked across the Martian sands to consult with Captain Aames. We were mounting the new meteorology package on the mast, running it through final checkout before raising the mast, and the captain was supervising—meaning he shouted at us when he thought we were working too slow, and also when he thought we weren't being careful enough. Carver came over, tapped the captain on the helmet to get his attention, and showed him something on his suit comp. The captain looked at the comp, looked closer, and then shook his head (though his helmet barely moved). He and Carver switched frequencies to talk in private, and I saw Aames shake his head again.

Then the captain got on the team comm channel. "All right, people, get moving. I want this mast up and testing in twenty minutes. As soon as it passes mooring and electrical tests, I want it online. No, scratch that, bring it online as soon as it's up, and test while Van der Ven starts scanning for storms. I don't care what it takes, just get him operational. I want accurate weather data an hour from now. As soon as you've got the mooring solid and the tests started, those of you not involved in the tests start cycling downstairs. We'll have a briefing in two hours. Carver just advanced our schedule again."

One hour, fifty-three minutes later, we were all unsuited and gathered in the shelters. Captain Aames and our lander 2 crew were in the access shaft, and the lander 1 crew watched via video from the original shelter. The captain's plans called for a direct access tunnel between the two shelters, but that would depend on what we brought down from orbit.

As soon as we were settled, Captain Aames started his briefing. "All right, people, we have a lot of bad news, so let's get to it. Things are going to get tighter here, and we only have a short time to work before they get impossible. Take a look at this orbit track and projections." Swiping a finger on his sleeve comp, he pushed an image to our own comps. It was a model of the Mars system, the big Red Planet against a black backdrop and its two small gray moons spinning around it, Deimos slowly speeding around at three diameters out while Phobos sped the other way at barely one diameter. The captain tapped his comp, and the image froze. A silver dot appeared, almost as far from Mars as Deimos, representing the *Bradbury*. There were also several transparent dots representing past sightings. A set of thin gray whorls circled around Mars, connecting the silver dots. "You've all done orbital calculations, but that one's pretty unstable. Carver?"

Lieutenant Carver stood and paced as he lectured. "The gray lines are best estimates of the *Bradbury*'s orbit, based on the sightings we've made. It definitely looks unstable. And projecting into the future"— Carver drew on his comp, and a wide yellow band appeared on our screens—"the instability is growing. It's tricky to do precise work with a single lander telescope, but I've checked and rechecked my algorithms. They're solid. That band there is the range of likely paths for the *Bradbury*'s orbit by the day after tomorrow." He drew a pale green band, much wider than the first. "That's the range for five days from now." He added a third band, pale blue. This one covered much of the screen. "That's in a week and a half. Notice that the inner range intersects Mars, and the outer range may very well escape. It will take days to narrow down that range so we can make more accurate predictions."

Gale looked up at that. "More accurate predictions. That implies you have *some* predictions."

Carver's mouth turned down. "I do, and they're not good." He wiped across his screen, and the colored bands disappeared. In their place was a single white dot that moved rapidly around the screen, tracing out new whorls that swung farther away from Mars, then closer, farther, closer. And then . . . "My best prediction is that the *Bradbury* exceeds h-dot-max somewhere in Valles Marineris in nine days."

H-dot-max. Apollo-era slang for a vehicle crashing into a planet.

Gale pointed at the orbit projection. "But how did the orbit get this bad?"

Carver nodded. "The captain asked the same question. Here's the best image I can get of the *Bradbury*, with the best image augmentation I can manage. There's not a lot of sunlight to illuminate it, and it's still more pixels than picture, but . . ." He pushed the picture to our comps, and then started to draw circles to point out features. "This dark blotch here, I think that's engineering. Completely blown out. From that and the captain's data feed, I can simulate the collision." He pushed out a slow-motion simulation video: Lander 2 approaching from the wrong angle, too high and way too fast; the lander ripping through the hull of the bow; the *Bradbury* starting to slide and flex from the impact; the ribs of the hull ripping through the lander's hull in turn, tearing into the engine assembly; the lander's engine exploding, ripping the entire bow off the *Bradbury*—including the mactory deck—and adding more wobble and tumble to the ship; and the lander slipping free, but then colliding with the engineering deck at the aft end, sliding forward and into the fusion reactor, causing a coolant leak and the collapse of the fusion reaction. Seconds later—microseconds in real time—the reactor's magnets let go and exploded, spewing chaff through space and adding one more tremor and yet another velocity vector to the *Bradbury*.

Carver tapped his screen, and the simulation switched to normal speed. The changes in the *Bradbury*'s orbit weren't done yet. The lander, pushed by the exploding reactor, ripped through at least two more compartments before its battered hull ripped free of the *Bradbury*. Meanwhile, atmosphere vented from the bow of the ship, giving it yet another push. Then as the ship tumbled farther, it crossed paths with the lander one more time. This time the battered lander bounced right off the drive bell, cracked, and spun away in two pieces. Meanwhile the ship continued on yet another new path.

We all stared, openmouthed. Finally Gale asked, "How reliable is this simulation?"

Carver looked down, not meeting our eyes. "At least 94 percent. It fits all our data. And . . ." Once again he pushed out his pixelated image of the ship, but this time he put it in motion. With the fuzzy image, it was hard to describe the motion, but there definitely *was* motion. Plenty of it, and in multiple axes. And worst of all, I saw nothing at the bow at all.

Somtow said what I was thinking: "The mactory deck is gone." And then the meeting exploded, everyone talking at once.

But the hubbub ended in only seconds when Captain Aames shouted, "People!" We all went silent. "This is no time to panic. Yes, we desperately need what was on the mactory deck. We also desperately need whatever's left on the *Bradbury*. Until the *Collins* gets here, *every* resource is vital; but there's no sense worrying about what we can't have. Let's get what we can. Now."

"Now, Captain?" Ensign Hsü pulled back up the orbital prediction. "It's at least six days before the orbit decays too far for us to work with. Can't we take time to study and plan our rendezvous?"

"No." Aames shook his head. "Van der Ven, tell them the rest of the bad news."

Van pushed out his own Mars map, this one overlaid with waves of dust clouds. The nearest wave was red and distinct, but the waves behind it were gray and transparent. "Another storm comes," he said. "Our Doppler radar has limited range, we cannot predict exactly. But the radar on the mast, it sees these." He circled the bright leading wave. "The rest I infer from our Martian weather models. Not Carver's 94 percent confidence, maybe, but this sandstorm comes in three days. And when it hits, it lasts at least three more, wave after wave with only brief lulls between. Too brief for landing visibility even if *Bradbury* could help."

"So that means now," Captain Aames said. "Or as soon as we can be ready. Carver, Hsü, Smith, you're my crew for this flight. I want you all to get a solid eight hours of sleep so you're fresh for the launch. The rest of you, I just pushed out a work schedule to get us ready. Priorities are reducing as much mass from lander 1 as you can by stripping out gear and making lots of cargo space. Also, Van der Ven, whatever you need for meteorology, add that at the top of the work orders."

Aames picked up his helmet to return to the main shelter and his bunk, but Gale stood to stop him, holding the helmet down. "Captain, I think I should lead this mission. We cannot risk you."

The captain's eyes widened, and he hesitated before answering, "Negative, Gale. We need a pilot up there, and we need you as a medic down here. You'll be in charge."

But Gale didn't release the helmet. "You might need a medic up there as well. Besides, Carver is a decent pilot, he can fly the lander."

I glanced at Carver, and I saw that he was as surprised as me. Gale didn't make compliments very often.

Then I looked back to Aames and Gale, as the captain said, "Carver's good. If we can salvage any automated landers, he can telepilot them down. But for this flight, we need our best. And that's me." He yanked his helmet away, put it on his head, and spoke through the open visor. "Now if you're done arguing with me, *Lieutenant*, I have a launch window in nine and a half hours." He closed the visor and entered the airlock. Carver and I found our bunks while the others suited up to get to work.

☾

We sat in lander 1, ready for launch. Captain Aames was in the pilot pod in front, hanging from straps with his skinsuit already wired into the ship's controls. Every move he made in the suit would translate into movement of the ship. Well, *almost* every move. Pilots tell a joke about a guy who scratched his nose and accidentally launched a missile attack, but it can't happen. The skinsuit interface only responds to moves you make with your fists clenched.

Behind the captain sat Carver at the comm station, which Razdar and Roberts had adapted into a copilot station. He didn't have a skinsuit, just a computer console, but he could still back the captain up on controls and observation. Carver was damn good with a computer. If anybody could do it, he could.

Behind Carver, Bi Hsü and I sat in the two remaining acceleration couches. Hsü was an older Chinese astronaut, a short woman who had started her space career with the Chinese National Space Agency, then transferred to the International Space Corps when the Chinese finally joined the Initiative. Her hair was cropped short like mine, and some gray showed in the stubble, but she still passed all physicals with flying colors. She looked over at me with a smile, and I smiled back despite the grim situation. For a spacer, a launch is always a thrill.

The captain lowered his legs, and the rear of the lander dropped down upon the adjustable landing gear. The front gear rose at the same time, and soon we sat back at a sixty-degree angle, ready for launch.

"Meteorology?" Aames said.

On the comm, Van answered: "Clear skies, Captain. Sandstorm's moving a little faster than the model, so don't waste time."

"Understood. Launchpad?"

Adika answered, "Pad is clear of debris, sir, and your landing gear reads 100 percent." As soon as we launched, the gear would have to collapse against the hull, so we needed this last-minute check.

"Thank you. Ground control?"

Gale answered, "All telemetry is responding, Captain, and you are green across the board. You are go for launch, on schedule, in one minute."

We sat in silence. A formal checklist and countdown were unnecessary; landers were designed for takeoff with no ground crew at all. But the captain was taking no chances, not after lander 2 destroyed the propellant factory. We sat there and waited for the clock.

"Thirty seconds," Gale said. Then, "Fifteen."

Then, "Ten . . . nine . . . eight . . . seven . . . six . . . five . . . booster igniters hot . . . two . . . one . . . ignition!"

A giant boot kicked me in the ass, right through the thick acceleration couch cushions, and we were airborne as Gale continued his report: "We have liftoff. Forward gear retracting. Forward gear secured. Rear gear retracting. Rear gear secured. We are in flight configuration. Prepare for primary propellant disks in five . . . four . . . three . . . two . . ." And suddenly the giant push from behind us cut off. "One . . . ignition." And the boot was back, kicking harder this time, and we leaped into space. "Primary ignition is green and green. You are go for orbit." Our solid booster propellant came in disks of fixed sizes and power, allowing us to add or discard disks as needed for our flight. It didn't give us the fine control that the liquid fuel main engines did, but it was still better than old-style solid boosters. We would save the mains for navigation and rendezvous in orbit.

"All right, ground," the captain said, "we have this. You get back to work on construction. When we get back to Mars, I want to see a proper landing facility."

"Yes, sir." Gale cut out, and we flew in silence.

Sunlight on Mars is less than half as bright as on Earth, so it wasn't easy to pick out the *Bradbury* as we approached; but Carver's code found it on the scope, highlighting the tiny gray dot with a blue circle. When we got close enough, the lander's spotlights speared out and illuminated the derelict ship, showing us just how bad the damage was.

Carver's model had been too optimistic. The *Bradbury* was now a cylinder with a long gash through it, several cabins ripped open to vacuum. The mactory deck was gone, as we had feared, along with most of the bow. So much for Chief Maxwell: he would've been in the copilot pod, right in the bow, and would've been lost in the first moments of the crash. The drive bell at the aft end was crumpled, with a giant tear, probably left by lander 2. It hung from the ship at an odd angle, almost detached, cut loose by the explosion of the reactor. Three of the four cargo landers were still docked, but the fourth docking port was lost in the long gash. Landers 3 and 4 were nowhere to be seen. The antenna package amidships was undamaged; but the ship tumbled rapidly around two axes, too rapidly for the directional antennas to lock onto any signal. Even if anyone on the *Bradbury* had somehow survived, there was no way to reach Mars without the directionals. Or Earth, for that matter.

But as close as we were, we didn't need directionals. The captain spoke into the comm: "*Bradbury*, this is Captain Aames on lander 1. Come in, *Bradbury*."

The comm was silent for seconds before a warm female voice responded. "Lander 1, this is *Bradbury*. Be advised, your approach is unauthorized. Withdraw to a safe distance."

"Deece? This is Captain Aames. Report your status."

This time the response was faster. "Lander 1, this is Decision Control *Bradbury*. All contact with Captain Aames was lost seven days ago, and he is presumed dead. Your identity cannot be confirmed. Be advised, your approach is unauthorized. Withdraw to a safe distance, or we must take defensive measures."

"Deece!" The captain's shout echoed through the lander. "This is Captain Nicolau Aames. Override sequence: one; code: one-one-A. Now report, damn it!"

But Deece remained as calm as ever. "Lander 1, your override is rejected. All override controls were reset upon the death of Captain

Aames. Your attempt at override constitutes hostile action against this ship. Withdraw immediately, or we must take defensive measures."

"Carver!" The captain twisted in his harness to look back at the copilot station. "What's the matter with your damn program?"

Carver punched furiously at his console as he answered, "It's a total security reset, Captain. I'm trying to open command channels, but they're all blocked. I think Deece has had a breakdown."

"A breakdown? She's a program!"

"She's an AI, Captain. She operates on situational models. When the models deviate from reality, she can get weird; but when they get too far out of line, she 'regresses' to a known state. That warning she's issuing is from models clear back during her construction phase, when unauthorized access could be a spy satellite or a saboteur."

"And what about these defensive measures? We weren't armed."

"We weren't; but in the orbital construction zone, she could summon fighters. She still thinks she can. Don't worry, she's toothless."

"Toothless and useless. I was hoping she could test the attitude jets. If they're still working, at least we could null that tumble. We can't dock like that; and even if we could, it'd be hell working in there."

Carver tapped at the screen some more, but then shook his head. "It's no good, Captain. I could bypass her locks pretty easily from inside, but not by remote."

The captain paused before responding, "All right, everyone suit up with maneuvering units. I'll get as close as I can. Smith, you'll go aboard as search crew. Your top priority is survivors."

I knew not to argue with Captain Aames, but I couldn't stop myself. "Captain, you can't expect—"

"I don't give up on people, Smith. Ever. We don't 'expect,' we find out. So look for survivors as you're looking for salvage. Find anything fragile or perishable. Try to get it into a cargo lander. And anything that can survive vacuum, whatever it is, we'll find a use for it. So toss it out the nearest hatch. Hsü, you play catch: Whatever Smith throws out will be on a random vector; you'll chase it down and throw it to the lander. Carver, you get to the main controls, straighten out Deece, and get me control of my ship. If you can."

That may sound like a desperate plan, but not if you're a graduate of Advanced Orbital Survival School—and we all were, as part of our training for this mission. Boarding a derelict is a standard exercise in OASS, and we had practiced it until it was routine. A two-axis tumble made it trickier, but the computers in our maneuvering units could handle that. You just lock the MU onto your target site—in my case, an open cabin where I could get hold of a hatch and enter the main vessel from there—and let it study the tumble for a minute or so, and it would calculate a perfect approach path, bringing you to a dead stop relative to the site. Then you just grab on, and you've matched course with the target. You'll still get quite a jolt as the tumble hits you, but at least you won't collide with the derelict itself.

So imagine my surprise when, on my approach to the cabin, I saw the hull of the *Bradbury* twist and sway and swing toward me. Suddenly my approach angle was all wrong, and I was headed for a bone-breaking crash. I opened my mouth to shout.

But before I could draw breath, Carver's arm snaked around my waist, and a burst of MU jets pulled us away. Carver called on the comms, "Good news, Captain: we can confirm that the attitude jets *are* still functional."

"I can see that, Lieutenant," the captain answered. "And your AI has teeth."

"She does, sir, but I'm still smarter than her. We'll get in, sir."

"Make it snappy, Carver. We're on a time clock."

"Will do, sir." Carver braked at a safe distance from the *Bradbury*, and then he turned me to face him. It wasn't necessary for a comm conversation, but it was a common courtesy. "So, Smith, are those bull-fighting rumors I hear true?"

"It was bull *riding*, Lieutenant, not fighting. But what do you have in mind?"

"Deece is an algorithm. Whatever she does, she does to a pattern. If I can see that pattern, I can defeat it. But one observation doesn't show me the pattern."

I nodded. "So you need to see how she reacts when someone approaches."

"Yep. She doesn't have a lot of choices here, only a limited number of jets to fire. She's also constrained by the existing tumble. If I can see her react a few more times, I'll be able to predict her next move."

"Understood, sir." I turned back to the *Bradbury*, and I called out, "*Toro! Toro!*" I fired my MU and dove toward the hull.

Behind me, Carver called, "Keep your eyes open, Smith. Don't get too close."

I had no intention of getting too close, but I did appreciate his plan. That bull-riding contest hadn't been a sanctioned event, just a bunch of drunken spacers camping on a ranch near São Paulo, but we had to do much the same thing: bait the bull, figure out his moves, and find a chance to leap aboard. Not smart, you say. Did I mention we were drunk? Pretty risky, you say. Did I mention we were spacers? We thrive on risk, or we wash out. Besides, no one was hurt, not even the bull.

So I made a few passes at the ship. Once I knew what to look for, it wasn't nearly as dangerous as that bull: like Carver said, there were only so many jets, and they could only do so much to change the momentum. It was easy to see the signs and dodge out of the way.

Of course, just as I was feeling smug, the ship made an unexpected turn. Instead of trying to sideswipe me with the hull, it spun on its core, swinging the antenna package around and hitting me with the big Earth antenna like a giant baseball bat. The spin wasn't that fast in itself, but my own momentum added to the impact. I was stunned by the hit, and by yet another stab in my damned ribs—just when I was sure the osteo-nanos had finished their work—and I twirled away in my own unexpected tumble.

Before I could recover my senses, Carver caught me. "Are you all right, Smith?"

I caught my breath so I could answer: "All right . . . sir. Just winded, and a little twinge. Give me a minute, and I'll make another pass."

"No need." Carver pushed a program to my MU. "I've got her pattern figured out. This program will guide us through a tandem approach. We'll enter through different sites, and that will confuse Deece. Her reaction to you will be canceled out by her reaction to me, and vice versa. She'll probably kick at the last moment; but if you grab something and hold on tight, she won't be able to shake you. You'll be entering through the engineering deck in the aft. I'll be up in secondary command."

I couldn't probe my ribs through the bodysuit, so I couldn't tell if there was more damage there, but my suit diagnostics were green. I nodded. "Let's do this, Lieutenant."

Carver tapped his comp, and our jets fired microbursts, separating us. When we were about thirty meters apart, our jets turned and fired again, hurling us toward the tumbling *Bradbury*. For a moment I doubted Carver's coding as I sped straight for the unyielding hull; but then the ship tumbled some more, and the giant gash turned into view, and I was headed straight for the aft end. But still too fast! I held back my panic, trusting Carver; and sure enough, the jets fired again to slow me down and align me with the ship.

And oh, Carver was *smooth*. Just before I impacted inside the gash, the jets fired sideways, pushing me through the hole in the engineering bulkhead and onto the engineering deck. Half a second later, just as Carver predicted, the deck *kicked* toward me, catching me unawares and bouncing me off a wall; but instead of knocking me out into space, the move merely knocked me to the far wall, where I was able to grab a handgrip and hold on tight. The ship tossed three more times in different directions, like a horse trying to shake off a rider, but my grip held. And after the third kick, the ship settled down into a dizzying but steady tumble.

I opened the comm channel. "Lander 1, Smith. I am aboard the *Bradbury*."

An immediate answer came: "Lander 1, Carver. Same here. Repeat, we are aboard and secure."

"Expedition, lander 1," the captain answered. "Good job. Now don't waste time. If you can null that roll, it will buy us lots of time and lots of cargo. But watch your backs. Deece may have more surprises for you. Go!"

My bull-riding experience served me well that day. The wall tossed and twisted, but I held on as I got my bearings. The engineering deck was almost unrecognizable: the main reactor was gone, and in its place was a charred mess where fire had fought to catch hold but had failed as the air fled the deck. But the chaff from the exploding magnets had been as bad as any fire, shredding the engineering consoles into unrecognizable tangles of metal, glass, and wires. On the plus side, that included the security monitors. Deece couldn't watch me in here.

I didn't have many landmarks to orient myself with, but I had enough. The remnants of the reactor told me where I was on the deck. I had bounced off the inner wall and landed on the outer wall. The inner wall had a hatch to the main shaft, almost directly opposite from the reactor. Since the shaft itself had survived the explosion, surely the hatch had as well.

Timing the tumble, I leaped back to the inner wall. I might not be as precise as an MU computer, but I was good enough after months in zero G on the trip to Mars. I hit the wall with a bump, just enough to rattle me, but I grabbed another handgrip and started working my way around the shaft, one grip at a time. A few times I felt a stab in my ribs as I twisted in an odd direction, but nothing near as bad as jogging across Coprates quadrangle.

As I rounded the shaft, I saw that it had indeed sheltered the far half of the deck from the worst of the reactor explosion. The consoles and systems on that side looked mostly functional: air and water recycling, waste processing, and reaction jets. Maybe if Carver couldn't shut down Deece, we could manually control those systems from here.

I worked my way around to the hatch, and I checked its readouts. Automatic access was offline—Deece controlled that—but all hatches had manual controls as well. The readouts showed no pressure on the other side. That made things easier, since I didn't have to try to enter against pressure. I opened the cover on the manual controls, pulled out the handle, and gave it a twist.

The hatch sprung open, throwing me violently across the deck. Damn Deece! The readouts had been a lie. I was glad the hatches were designed with hydraulic brakes to slow them down. Otherwise the hatch could've hit me hard enough to crack my bodysuit. Still, it had been fast enough to cost me my hold. I slammed into the wall, bouncing off and right back at the hatch. I held my left arm up to shield my visor, while with my right I scrabbled for a hold. I barely got a grip on the hatch edge, but that was enough to slow me down. I lowered my left arm, reached inside the hatch, and grabbed the inner controls. That gave me a better grip, good enough to swing my legs up and pull myself into the main shaft, even against the push of escaping air.

If I'd had to pull the hatch shut, I could never have done it. Interior pressure on the *Bradbury* was one atmosphere, 14.7 pounds per square inch, and the hatch had a lot of square inches. Adika himself couldn't have pulled it shut without help. Fortunately, I had help, more hydraulics. I grabbed the close lever and pulled on it, and the hatch sealed itself.

I was breathing heavily from the exertion, but I got on the comm. "Carver, don't trust readouts. Deece is using them to mislead us. I just opened a hatch under pressure, thanks to her."

Carver sounded better than me when he answered, but he also sounded concerned. "Smith, Carver. I read you. So does she. Think."

Damn, that made sense. Anything we said on the comms, Deece would know. We would have to stay off comms unless it was critical. So Carver was on his own, and I was too. I turned off my mic. No sense in letting Deece hear anything.

Captain Aames wanted the perishables first. More than anything else, that meant Hydroponics, which was just two decks fore of engineering. Hydroponics split that ring with storage, and most of the storage cabin had been torn open by lander 2. I was pretty sure that the Hydroponics cabin would be undamaged, but I would have to go in to find out. Our survival could hinge on whether Hydroponics was intact or not. If we were really lucky, that cabin was full of racks and racks of Lada gardens: Russian-designed automated garden units with self-contained environments and systems for circulating nutrients and air. And there should also be more soil and nutrients. If it survived, it would be our own little slice of Eden. If it didn't . . .

When I got to the cabin door, the readouts looked bad. Way too bad: *Vacuum. Radiation Hazard. Biohazard. Fire.* Fire in a vacuum? "Ah, Deece," I said to myself, "you're a lousy liar." That was a known fact; Carver had taught me that once: AIs were all about drawing correct inferences from limited models, so deliberately incorrect inferences were hard for them to formulate. Deece wanted to scare me away from Hydroponics, so she raised the alerts. All of them, as contradictory as they were.

But maybe *one* of them was true. I couldn't be certain. A fire would destroy the hydroponics and maybe cook me in my suit. So it was with caution that I pulled the manual hatch controls and slowly looked inside.

No fire. No signs of rushing air. I would take my chances on biohazard and radiation. But what I didn't expect was that all the Lada gardens would be dismounted from their racks and packed for shipping.

"What the hell?" And then I saw movement at the far corner of the cabin, a figure bobbing near one of the Lada gardens and pulling lettuce out. I quickly pulled myself inside, closed and locked the hatch, and turned on my external speakers. "Dr. Weaver, is that you?"

Anna Weaver, our ship's doctor and telepilot, spun around. She saw me, her eyes lit up, and she leaped across the cabin at me. "Smith!" She wrapped herself around my bulky suit in an awkward hug, and her momentum threw us both back against the hatch. "You made it. Thank God, you made it!"

I nodded, then pulled free of her arms. "Thanks to Captain Aames, who will be glad to see you. We didn't dare hope for survivors. Is there anybody . . ." But my voice trailed off as her face fell. No need to answer.

But she did. "Koertig and Uribe were in the mactory deck, doing maintenance on landers 3 and 4. From the angle, I'm sure the deck was lost." I nodded agreement. "And Max, I heard him scream just before our comms cut out. I'm sure his death was instant."

I didn't react, because I had already said good-bye to Katja and Normando and Max. And Anna. We were all so sure we had lost everyone. All of us except Captain Aames. He never gave up.

Instead I turned to another question. "So how did you survive?"

Weaver swallowed hard. "When Max was sure a collision was coming, he sent me down the main shaft to ensure that all the cabin hatches were secure. He was already thinking about salvage and how much we could preserve. He said Deece was flaky, and we couldn't trust her to secure the hatches."

I nodded. "He wasn't kidding."

Weaver continued, "So I wasn't in the telepilot pod when the lander hit. I was well down the shaft. But the pod was wide open to the shaft at that point. As soon as the pod was cracked, air started whooshing out the bow. I grabbed the first hatch I could find, and I shut myself inside before the shaft was in vacuum. I was lucky it was the hatch with all the food."

"Lucky," I agreed. "But the shaft is under pressure now. The forward emergency hatch must have sealed."

"Under pressure?" Weaver indicated the readouts near the hatch. "It still shows vacuum out there."

"Uh-huh. Deece is more than just flaky, Doctor. She has flipped back into security mode. She thinks we're intruders. Probably you, too, since she has invalidated all ID codes. My guess is she's using the fake vacuum to keep you a prisoner here."

Weaver nodded. "That makes sense. I had no suit in here, so I was stuck. Deece had told me I was unauthorized here, and I hadn't been able to make sense of that. Finally, I turned off her pickups here."

"And then you decided to start packing up the food?" I waved my arm at the Lada units.

"Uh-huh." She pushed over to the units and started inspecting their meters. "I figured there were only two possibilities. You were all lost down there, dead or trapped, and it was only a matter of time until I was dead too. In that case, at least I would eat well until the end, and the Lada units would give me oxygen as well. Or somehow you would survive, get back to orbit, and come for this food." She smiled. "I've served with Captain Aames before. I knew which way to bet, so I figured I would save us time if I got a head start on packing."

I admired her faith. I had known Aames a long time, but I was still learning to trust him like that. "This will certainly save us a lot of time. We should get these to the cargo landers immediately. But . . ."

Weaver looked at me. "What's the matter, Ensign?"

I stared at the hatch. "There was pressure out there before. There might not be now. Deece is trying to protect the ship from us, and she's trying every trick she can think up. The only weapon she has is deception. There might be vacuum out there now. Or she might open a hatch later, and you're exposed. I need to get you a suit."

Weaver agreed, so we moved her and the Lada units as far from the hatch as possible before I carefully opened it. There was no airflow, so

I dashed out and resealed it behind me. Then I went to the suit locker three decks forward, pulled out Weaver's suit, and hauled it back to Hydroponics.

When I got to the hatch, I had a new surprise. The readout screen was blank. I tapped on it, and nothing happened. Swiped the soft reset code, and still nothing happened. Finally I swiped the hard reset code, and the readout rebooted. After a few seconds, the readouts were back to normal, showing standard ship's pressure and temperature inside.

I didn't trust whatever Deece might be up to, so I took a chance and called Carver. "Carver, Smith. Anything I should know about?"

Carver's voice was strange: relaxed, yet terse: "Smith, Carver. No worries. I have Deece in maintenance mode. *Now* she's toothless."

"Good job, Lieutenant Carver!"

"But I'm still busy trying to get control of the ship, so I hope you can handle the cargo without me."

"Oh, I can." I smiled, though Carver couldn't see it. "Dr. Weaver's alive!"

Carver stammered for a few seconds before he answered, "Fantastic! Okay, you two get to work. I'll stabilize the *Bradbury* as soon as I can."

I was ready to sign off, when suddenly it occurred to me: *What if this wasn't really Carver?* Deece could fake audio even easier than video. So I thought, and I made another call. "Carver, when I was in the top of the access shaft at landing pad C, remember that?"

Carver paused, confused. Then he responded. "Oh, I understand, verification. Yes, Ensign."

"I dropped a bolt. What did you say about it?"

"I said it was coated in butter. Now can I get back to work?"

This time I grinned. "With my compliments, Lieutenant. You do nice work."

While Weaver suited up (we still didn't trust Deece), I called Captain Aames to fill him in on all the good news and to get instructions. "Do we still toss gear overboard?"

"Negative. Hsü, get aboard the *Bradbury* on your fastest safe course. Help Smith and Weaver pack the cargo landers, and then pack up everything you can find that will fit in the lander. Ladies and gentlemen, the more cramped we are on our ride home, the better."

We started packing Lada units into the cargo landers, and we made great time thanks to Weaver having prepped them for transport. We were two-thirds done when Hsü joined us; so I left them to that, and I went ahead looking for other items to ship. Just like back in the shelter pit, the captain had given me an inventory of crucial items. I hunted those out first, stuffing them into bags and hanging them from handgrips in the main shaft. Weaver and Hsü followed behind me, Weaver hauling the bags off to the cargo landers, and Hsü inspecting each cabin for other valuable items. Without having to watch our backs for Deece's next trick, the only real challenge was the constant tumble of the ship, but we managed that. It was just like an exercise.

Soon I neared the front of the ship, right behind the forward emergency hatch. Beyond that were our personal cabins, the command deck, and the wreck of the telepilot pod. Those were all in vacuum, so we would wait to try to salvage from them. I turned to the next hatch, Computer Control, and went in.

"How ya doing, Lieutenant?" Things were going better than I had dared hope, and I was in high spirits.

But Carver's brow was creased with concentration. "Still busy here, Smith." He had strapped himself to the main computer station so he could work even as the ship tumbled. The cabin was dark, the way he liked to work on the computer, the only light coming from his monitor and playing across his dark face. He looked far more intense than he had on Mars, more in control.

"All right, don't mind me, I'm just gathering." I bounced around the cabin, shining my light around, but there wasn't a lot the captain had requested from there. Most of the computing power we would need was already on Mars. I gathered up some storage blocks, some tools, and some styluses, and I shoved them in a bag.

While I worked, I glanced over Carver's shoulder. As I watched, I gradually recognized what he was doing: he had disconnected Deece from the ship's controls, and now he was slicing out her historical models, starting from the past and working forward. The current model was like a long thread through time, a series of historical models stitched together. They gave Deece memory, experience, an awareness of time, not just the present. Each historical model was a combination of data from multiple sources: the ship's sensors, the AI knowledge base, mission rules and parameters from the Initiative, and a base model shipped up from Earth. Each new historical model was grafted onto the end and tied in to Deece's knowledge engine, and that's what she used to make her decisions.

Slicing out a model is tricky, especially a middle model, unless you want to do real damage. It leaves a break in the thread. If you don't patch that break, splice together the ends, then the whole model is flawed. Any search against it can produce nonsense answers, or even get lost in a loop. But if you *do* splice the ends together, the knowledge engine will still be misaligned, because some of the conditions will change across the splice. The functionality quotient will drop, and it will take patient work to readjust it. This all takes time and skill, and Carver was one of the few people I knew who could do it well. As long as I stayed out of his hair.

Looking further, I saw that he was splicing the broken end to a model from . . . five weeks ago? But that meant he had sliced out as many as three dozen models already. Why was he going through this?

"Aha!" Suddenly it struck me. "You couldn't fix Deece's current model. It's too tied to all these old models, and there's some flaw in there somewhere."

Carver kept working, but he smiled. "Very good, Ensign."

"You couldn't just slice out her current model, that's tied in to security. There are guards against that. But you can slice out everything *except* the current model, one slice at a time. And that should remove the flaw. You're going to splice her to a known state, and then let her fix any anomalies from there."

"With a little training from me, yes, she can get back to an acceptable functionality quotient. This is a hole in the security system, but you'd have to be aboard the ship to exploit it. *And* you'd have to be the best damned programmer you ever met." Carver's smile turned into a broad grin. I'd never seen him at work on the computer like this. Here he had real pride, and he was confident. If he could get that confidence in other areas, Captain Aames would sit up and take notice. "I had to go back far enough to make sure the model was clean, so Deece is going to wake up with the AI equivalent of the world's worst hangover. She's going to have a lot of gaps to fill in."

I didn't want to disturb Carver, so I hooked my comp into the main system to review his work. The system had recorded every step, so I could watch them, rewind, stop, even watch in slow motion. Maybe I could learn his trick, or at least a bit of it. So I went back to the first model he had sliced out, and I watched the recording of his work. His steps were fast and smooth: shut down the knowledge engine; scan the model thread to find the desired historical model; run a slicing tool to disconnect it from the thread on both ends; run an input probe to find all the matching codelines on the two ends and map them together; build bridgelines where the codelines didn't map well; and then check the splice for minimum FQ. It failed, so he tried again, building stronger bridgelines where he saw problems. This time the splice passed the minimum FQ, so he powered up the knowledge engine and ran it through training exercises until it reached operational FQ. Then he moved on to the next historical.

I moved on as well. A lot of what he did was applying simple, automated tools. Anyone could do that. But how he selected the codelines to splice together, that intrigued me. A codeline was a bit of genetic algorithm, more grown than programmed, and it was hard to comprehend how they worked. They just *did*, because the system eliminated the ones that didn't, and let the power of selection produce the best lines. So how did he identify the splice points? I could ask him, but I wanted to try to figure it out on my own. So I looked at the next slice operation.

Then I saw something familiar: this historical model had come from the Initiative on Earth, and had been grafted in by Gale. I rewound to the first slice. It was also a historical model, grafted by Gale. I fast-forwarded to the third: the same thing. And the fourth, and the fifth, and . . .

"Carver, these models."

"What?" He looked at his screen, swiped something, and suddenly my screen went black. I never knew he could do that. "Forget it, Smith."

"But these models all—"

"Forget them, Ensign. That's an order." He sounded stern, like I had never heard him before. Then he looked up at me, and the light from his monitor glistened from moisture in his eyes. His tone softened. "Please."

"But sir, the captain needs to know this. These models that you're slicing out: every one of them came up from Earth and was grafted right into the thread immediately. By Lieutenant Gale."

"And so?"

"And so? So you're cutting them out! That must mean they caused Deece's malfunction. They caused . . . Gale caused all of this."

"We don't know that, Smith."

"We don't know that? Then why are you slicing them?"

Carver turned back to his screen and continued working. "Because I want to get to the last point where I *knew* things were right. Before Gale started checking in updates from Earth."

"Before Gale screwed us all, you mean. The captain *needs* to know this."

"To know what? That Gale did his assigned tasks according to the recommended procedures?"

"What?"

Carver nodded, bobbing in his harness. "Smith, Gale is a pompous ass, but he's all about procedure, about checking all the right boxes so he looks good to the higher-ups. He did *exactly* what the manual says. He just didn't do any *more*. If I had been checking in updates, I would've done model consistency tuning, because I've found the grafts from the Initiative don't line up with reality like they should. It's probably some damn *bureaucrat* down there who 'knows' that his model is right and keeps blowing off my corrective responses. The variances are small, in the second decimal usually, but I catch them a lot. But I wasn't maintaining Deece then. Gale was cross-training for my post. I told him about the tuning, but I don't think he understood. There's no record he ever did the tuning."

"And that caused Deece to flip out!"

"One more time: we don't know that. It's probably true, but there might be some other problem in these models, something even I wouldn't catch. I sure can't trace down what's wrong now, and I tried. All we really know is Deece was stable at one point, and now she isn't, and we need to regress her back to stable."

"But Gale . . ."

Carver pulled back from his screen and crossed his arms. "Smith, why was Gale maintaining Deece? Do you remember?"

I tried to remember the details. So much was going on in those final weeks of Mars approach. "We were all cross-training. Gale was on your post, I was in medical, and you . . . pilot, right?"

He pointed a finger at me. "Bingo. The captain and Max kept me so busy, I barely had time to sleep. So maybe it was my fault. Maybe I should've supervised Gale better."

"That's not—"

"Not possible? Damn straight it's possible. But like you said, right now, I don't give a damn. I only care about surviving the next eight months until the *Collins* gets here. And the captain has a plan, and it needs everybody, and we can't afford any rifts between us. If we don't work together, we're dead. If the captain and Gale have it out, it won't be good for any of us."

I tried to calm down. "But Carver, it's not good to keep secrets from Captain Aames. He always finds out, and he won't tolerate lying." At that Carver laughed, and I stared at him in surprise. "What?"

Carver rubbed his chin as if he couldn't decide whether to speak or not. Finally he continued, "That time in my pilot training, the time the captain chewed me out so the whole ship heard it. You never heard what happened, right?"

"No." We all knew about the collision, but no hard facts.

"No, you didn't. And neither did the captain. Not the *real* story. The captain read me the riot act for steering my lander too close to Max's and causing a collision. I spent two weeks on lander maintenance for that. But what the captain never knew was *Max* collided with *me*. I made a rookie mistake, clenched up in the pilot pod, and I lost control of my lander. I was on a collision course, almost as bad as"—he waved his arms around, swaying in the harness—"all this. I was on course to *kill* all of us. Scared the ever-loving piss out of me, which only made me clench up worse. So Max kept his cool, he flew his lander into a collision with mine, and pushed me out of *my* collision course. It nearly ruined landers 3 and 4, and it went on my record as a pilot-at-fault collision. But Max never told the captain the real story."

I could hardly believe my ears. "Max kept a secret that huge from Captain Aames?"

"Uh-huh. I was even going to go to the captain, confess my sins, and Max stopped me. 'Anson,' he said, 'don't be a damned fool. You screwed up, but it's a mistake you'll never make again. I'm sure of that. You deserve punishment, but you also need something Nick Aames has in short supply: mercy.' So he gave me his mercy. I certified as a pilot on our next round of cross-training, because Max gave me a second chance. Smith, this team needs Captain Aames pushing us to be our best, but it also needs someone giving out mercy and second chances. The captain doesn't understand that, but somebody has to."

I thought about his words. "So since Max is gone, you're appointing yourself? It won't be easy. You'll have to stand up to the captain, make him back down. Max was one of only a couple people I've ever seen do that."

He let out a long sigh. "Yeah, I think I'm ready. We'll find out when the time comes. Besides, who else do we have? Gale?" At that we both laughed. "No, it's me. I have to figure out this job. I owe it to all of you." He lowered his eyes. "And to Max. So what's it going to be, Ensign? Do we forget what you saw in those models?"

It took me several seconds to decide. Carver was growing. Mars was forcing him into it. And I trusted the man he was growing into. I nodded.

"Good." Carver wiped his hand down his screen, and the room lit up. "And just in time. Deece, diagnostic summary?"

Deece's cool voice sounded from the console, and I tried not to shiver. "Controls are offline, and there is a significant gap in my model thread, but codelines and bridgelines are interpolating the differential. Functional quotient is eighty-one and rising. Eighty-three . . . eighty-four . . . eighty-six . . ."

"That's good enough, Deece, I'm hooking you back into ship's controls. Please analyze and null this tumble with minimal fuel expenditure." Then he switched to the comms channel. "Weaver, Hsü, brace for acceleration in"—he looked at his screen—"seven seconds. Six . . . five . . . four . . . three . . . two . . . one . . ."

The ship's attitude jets started firing. We heard the rumble through the hull, just as we had many times on the trip out; only now they reminded me of the low, quiet, stealthy rumble of a Martian storm stalking me, and I just wanted them to stop immediately. But I held my cool, even as they tossed us here and there as they corrected the tumble. Finally, after over half a minute, the jets cut out. I let go of my grip, and I floated in freefall. I didn't drift toward any wall, I just hung there. We were stable.

Carver wasted no time before getting back on the comms. "Lander 1, this is *Bradbury*. Captain, we don't have enough fuel to correct the decaying orbit, but our tumble is nulled. You're welcome to come aboard."

The captain answered, "*Bradbury*, lander 1. About damn time, Carver, but good work. Now I have two more tasks for you: reestablish ground communications, and find what's left of the mactory deck, wherever it is. And make it snappy, I'm on my way in. Aames out."

The comm clicked off, and Carver stared at it. "Always pushing."

I floated closer and patted him on the back. "You have your work cut out for you, Lieutenant."

I met the captain at the lander dock, and Weaver and Hsü floated behind me, a flotilla of packing crates and bags still behind them. "Shall we finish packing, sir?" I asked as the hatch slid shut behind him.

The captain raised a hand. "Hold off, Smith, that depends on Carver." He opened a comm channel. "Lieutenant, have you finished those tasks yet?"

Carver's response was crisp and confident. He might figure out the captain yet. "Yes, sir. We're sending down weather data now. It's not good, sir. Van der Ven says the storm's coming faster than he predicted."

"We'll deal with that. And the mactory deck?"

"I think I found it, sir, and it's mostly intact, just tumbling like a dervish." He pushed a video feed out to the general comp circuit, and I looked at the image: a large, faint disk shape with a long, bent shaft extending out from the center. The combination tumbled at least three times as fast as the *Bradbury* had. Two blobs on opposite sides of the deck were probably the missing landers in their maintenance cradles.

The captain frowned. "That's more tumble than I expected, but we're stuck with it. How's the orbit?"

"That's not good either, Captain. More eccentric than the *Bradbury*'s, and decaying faster. It might have two, maybe three more orbits before it crashes."

"Well, which is it, two or three? I don't need guesses, Carver, I need data. Figure it out!" The captain looked up from his comp and turned to Weaver. "Doctor, climb aboard. I need you to pilot me over to the mactory deck, so I can board it and salvage whatever we can before the deck crashes. Then you hightail it back here and load up the lander. I'll put whatever I can get into lander 3, and then bring it down to Mars."

"Captain!" I couldn't stop myself from shouting, earning me an instant glare from Aames.

"Ensign, shut up. We *need* those machine tools, people. Our safety margins are practically zero without them. With them we have a very good chance. That's worth risking one person."

"But not you, sir." This time I wasn't ready to back down. "I'll go. We won't survive without you, sir."

"The hell you won't, Smitty. You're a good crew, and I'm leaving you good plans. Follow them to the letter. That's an order. But this mission needs a pilot. Carver's not ready, not for this, and Weaver's too valuable. Having a doctor increases your odds more than a captain does. I've worked the scenarios, and this is how it will be. End of discussion. Weaver, get aboard."

Dr. Weaver had no choice, not with a direct order. She pushed toward the lander hatch. But it didn't open.

Captain Aames reopened his comm channel. "Carver, I thought you had Deece under control."

Carver's face appeared on the comm, and I saw sweat bead up on his dark forehead and hang there in zero gravity. He was up to something. This soon after assuming Max's role, and already he was up to something. But did he have the guts to knock heads with Nick Aames? *Make this count, Carver.*

Carver's hesitation was only an instant, then he calmed down. Some of that earlier confidence reappeared. "I can't let you do this, Captain."

"Carver, you're relieved." Captain Aames turned back to me. "Go pull him away from that console. If he touches anything, break his fingers."

I looked at Carver's face. If he had pleaded with me, I would've followed orders. Instead, his nerve held, and I didn't move. Carver answered, "Captain, I can teleoperate landers 3 and 4 through Deece, just like I locked your hatch. It's not as smooth as a telepilot link, but I can do it. I've already powered up their engines."

The captain looked at me and pointed forward; but I held my ground, so he turned back to the comm. "What good will that do, Carver? Two lander drives won't be enough to stop that tumble. They certainly won't be enough to lift the deck to a higher orbit. You're costing us time, Lieutenant."

"No, sir, I'm buying us time. I can do this, Captain. Watch your screen."

So all eyes turned to the comp screen. Already the deck's orbit was changing: not higher, but lower. Carver was using the landers to put the mactory deck into a dive toward Mars. The captain shouted, "Carver, you fool!"

And then, precise as clockwork, eleven kilometers of rock came into the screen on a fast orbit: Phobos, the inner moon of Mars. And the mactory deck dove in front of it, practically on top of it—close enough that the gravity of Phobos, even weak as it was, grabbed the deck, swung it around, and slung it out into a higher, sweeping orbit.

Carver used the landers to nudge it still higher and to level it out. Even the tumble had slowed, thanks to Phobos's weak tidal forces soaking up some angular momentum.

All eyes blinked. I snuck a look at the comm screen, and Carver grinned at me. I winked back.

Finally Captain Aames spoke, very calmly. "Carver, why didn't you tell me this plan?"

"When I saw the solution, I saw we had only one chance, sir. And it had to be immediate. You would've told me I couldn't do it."

"You're damned right I would've. It was a damn fool plan. And if you'd stopped to argue with me, it was no plan at all." The captain drew a big breath and raised his voice. "All right, everyone on board lander 1. Carver, get your ass down here on the double."

"Sir?" But Carver didn't sound afraid. He had impressed Nick Aames in the only way possible: by being right.

And the captain as much as admitted it. "We'll have three landers at the mactory deck, Carver, so we're going to need three pilots. Apparently you are one. And a damned good one, Lieutenant, and maybe a *good* officer someday. Chief Maxwell would be proud."

"Thank you, sir."

ORBITAL RENDEZVOUS

I could tell you the rest of that expedition: how we intercepted the mactory deck, got the macroassemblers and the nanoassemblers and the machine tools and even the raw stock; how what we couldn't load that trip, we launched into a stable parking orbit; how we returned to the *Bradbury*, packed up the rest of the hydroponics, and launched everything else that we could into another parking orbit; and how by the time we finally returned to Mars, the sandstorm was upon us, and we nearly lost lander 3, but weather reports from Deece and radar readings from the ground brought us all down safely. Oh, sure, Carver and

I had to change course at the last minute and ended up at landing pad C, but we knew we could find shelter there, just like we left it.

And I could tell you how we went up and retrieved our loads from orbit. How we expanded Mars Shelter One, adding the greenhouse and the machine shop and another habitat wing. I could tell you how we used the *Bradbury*'s remaining orbits to briefly reestablish contact with Earth, and also with the *Collins*, so people would know we were still alive. And I could even tell you how we finally lost the *Bradbury* crashing right on schedule into Valles Marineris. I took some great videos of that. I thought it was some important history.

But why tell you all of this, and all the rest? It's all in the mission reports; and it really is anticlimactic, because it all ran according to a plan. Captain Aames's plan. And increasingly Lieutenant Carver's plan. They were still feeling out their relationship and establishing their territory, but they were clearly becoming a partnership. Carver's right: Aames needs someone he can trust as that buffer, someone who sees his worst and then decides how much of it to let through. And deep down, I think Aames knows it too.

Of course, Gale was still technically second-in-command, and he bristled at Carver's expanded responsibilities. It wasn't proper delegation of authority, not by the book at all. But one day he and Carver took a long hike across the quadrangle, and I think they had a meeting of the minds. After that, Gale deferred to Carver any time Carver had an opinion, and we all could tell who was really second-in-command from then on. I never saw any bruises, and only fools fight in suits, so I don't think it was like my little dustup with Gale. Instead I think Carver simply told Gale what we found in the historical models, and how furious Captain Aames would be if he found out. I think he offered Gale a little mercy, but with strings attached. Gale became bearable, and he carried his share of the work.

So we followed the captain's plan, heavily modified thanks to the efforts of Lieutenant Carver, and we survived. We didn't have fancy dinners, but we had food and water and air and shelter. I lost a lot of weight, back to my preservice size, and I wasn't alone in that; but we stayed healthy. We eventually found time to do some real Mars science, justifying our presence there a little bit. And with eight months to kill, we really expanded Mars Shelter One, turning it into a full-service spaceport with assist services so that a wider range of landers can use it. It was Carver who renamed it "Maxwell City," and that name has stuck.

And one night Van came running out from the access turret to join the rest of us out on the plains of Coprates quadrangle. Pagnotto had told him that this new prosthetic leg would work both indoors and outside in a suit, and it worked even better than he'd promised. Van now ran everywhere he could, and he had promised Pagnotto a whole keg of beer in gratitude. The beer would have to wait until we made it back to Earth, but suddenly that seemed a lot more likely.

That night Carver swiped his comp, and each of our heads-up displays lit up with a tracking circle, helping us to pick out the little white dot of an approaching spaceship: the *Collins*. We all cheered and applauded and hugged as closely as our suits allowed.

Adika, ever our most sober teammate, checked the heads-up readings. "Fast. Very fast. Captain, are you sure you can catch that?"

The captain sounded casual, confident. "With the modifications Pagnotto and Somtow made to lander 1? No ordinary pilot could do it, maybe; but I will. Trust me."

And we did; we trusted him, and Carver, and their partnership. They had got us this far. They would get us home. In three weeks, we would rendezvous with the *Collins* as it made its second cycler pass, and we would be on our way home. We all stood in silence at the thought of leaving Mars at last.

Then Captain Aames shook his head and broke the silence. "It's a damn express train."

Carver looked at Aames. "Sir?"

The captain pointed up at the *Collins*. "That. Oh, I don't mean it's fast; I mean it goes from point A to point B on a fixed route, no stops in between. Then it circles around and goes back. I'm glad it'll take *us* to point B, but it never even stops at either end to explore. This proto-type will only make one loop before it goes in for redesign; but they're already working on her sister ship, the *Aldrin*, and that one will be a giant express train from nowhere to nowhere, never stopping. What kind of captain worthy of the title would want duty like that when there are worlds to explore?"

7. The Road to Recovery

From the memoirs of Park Yerim

5 June 2083

"And yet here he is," I said as Smitty finished her story.

She had told the story all through the morning and afternoon, pausing only for Santana and Dr. Baldwin and the nurses to check on us, change dressings, and adjust our medical controls. That happened every hour, at least. During one visit, they removed me from the plastic cocoon, and I was free to sit up and turn my bed so I could watch Smith as she talked. I still wore my dark glasses, but I could see her clearly enough. Her new skin was very pink and tight, exaggerating her natural red coloring. The nurses frowned at her and told her she should rest, but she just kept talking as soon as they removed her own cocoon. I was glad she did. It passed the time, and it gave me something to think about so I didn't focus on my stiffness and pain.

I didn't ask about Adika. After Aames's visit the night before, that subject felt too personal, too risky. But just before noon, both doctors had gathered at his bed, excitement in their voices. I didn't follow all the medical jargon, but his condition had changed; and from the smile on Dr. Baldwin's face, I knew it was a change for the better.

"Indeed, here he is," Smith answered, "lord of all he surveys. Unless you remove him."

I felt uncomfortable about that. Here I was, only in my midthirties, sitting in judgment of a man who had conquered Mars when I was still a teenager. What had I done to compare with that? What right did I have to judge him?

But it was my job, so I had to do it, somehow. I had to know more. "So how did that happen? How did he end up here?"

Smith laughed. Despite talking for hours, she sounded stronger. "He did that to himself."

"What? How did he do that?"

"By being Nick, of course. On the long flight back to Earth, he prepared the most exhaustive after-action report of his career. And he's famous for those reports."

"So he found out—" I lowered my voice. "He found out about Gale and the AI models?"

"Never did, as far as I know." Smith lowered her voice as well. "And Yerim, that was off the record, between roomies, right? I've never told anyone that before."

If I kept this to myself, was *I* choosing loyalty over duty? Maybe Aames had found out. Maybe that had caused friction between him and Gale, and that had led to the current dispute. So maybe I needed to pursue this lead?

But I needed this crew to trust me. And I had given my word. "Off the record, Smitty." I paused. "But maybe, if Gale had been disciplined then—"

"He wouldn't have caused that explosion yesterday? I thought of that. But Carver was right, we just don't know. We know the models were largely to blame—that came out of the captain's investigation. We just don't know if a consistency test would've found the problem.

"But it wasn't just the models," Smith continued. "The captain interviewed every one of us survivors extensively during the months of the return journey. He went through every log, every data recording, every record we had salvaged from the *Bradbury*. He pulled up Initiative reports from Earth, and he pored over them line by line, looking for discrepancies. He reached one inescapable conclusion. The invalid models were just part of a larger problem: the Initiative's insistence on running everything from back on Earth. That had barely worked in the first lunar missions, with a two-and-a-half-second communication lag. It was *impossible* with a forty-minute lag to Mars. Adding Deece was supposed to minimize that problem, like putting Mission Control on-site with us, but she only made it worse. The captain showed, with impeccable logic and data, that every time the decisions were made back at Initiative headquarters, they were inconsistent with reality. Their decisions ranged from too cautious to too risky, and they were off the mark far more often than on. Their schedules were too aggressive, and they ignored the consequences, insisting that work was on schedule when it wasn't. That report was a beautiful thing, a damning indictment of letting central decisions override the people on-site."

Smith paused to take a drink. Then she continued, "And the idiot was determined to *publish* the thing! I tried to talk him out of it. He was right, every last word. But I knew what that would do to his career, since the evidence was so damning of the Initiative itself. I tried to talk him out of it, and Carver did too. We told him the report was career suicide, a political firestorm that would finish him off like Mars never could. We argued with him throughout much of the trip home. Finally we understood: Aames just didn't care. He had the facts, they were right, and he was going to present them to the world. He didn't give a damn about the consequences.

"Aames was more valuable to the space program than Carver or me, so we came up with a plan of our own. I still think it was a good plan, if it had worked, but it ended up being the dumbest move of our careers. Carver hacked in and got a copy of the captain's report. Then we proceeded to edit it, putting our names as chief investigators in place of Captain Aames's. With the changes, Carver was certain that no one could prove that Aames had a hand in the report. Oh, anyone who knew Aames's work could recognize his style and his attention to detail, but there was no proof. And then we blasted the report out ahead of our return. The captain had planned to make his formal presentation upon debriefing when we got back to Earth; but by the time we got home, *everyone* had already heard the conclusions in 'our' report. We had broadcast it, and we hadn't encrypted the stream because we had hoped in that way to get out the word with no chance the Initiative might bury it; and at the same time we hoped to draw any fire away from the captain. We would get blamed for the uncomfortable conclusions, not him."

Smith shook her head and took another drink. "But we hadn't accounted for the captain's stubborn insistence on facts and facts alone. Admiral Knapp contacted Aames via teleconference, full of fury, and demanded our heads. Not just because we broke security by broadcasting the report, but because of its conclusions. Like I said, they made the Initiative look pretty bad—including Knapp himself—so breaking security was just his excuse to hang us. He insisted that Aames confine us to quarters until the Admiralty could get its hands on us and put us up on charges. The captain could've thrown us to the wolves and saved his career. We urged him to do just that. But instead he stared straight into the camera and said, 'They didn't write that report, Admiral, I did. And I stand by it. The Initiative needs to clean up its act before it gets more spacers killed.'"

My eyes widened. "You and Carver had actually expected something else? From all I have learned about Nick Aames, he had to do that."

Smith nodded. "I know that, *now*. Back then, even as long as I had served under him, I didn't realize how absolute he was about facts. Every fact in the report was accurate, everything but the name at the top, and that would've done everything he wanted to accomplish with it. But it wasn't good enough for him, it wasn't the truth. So Carver and I ruined our careers trying to protect his, and then the idiot threw it away anyway."

She sighed, and continued, "We could find work with transport companies, and there were lots of consulting opportunities for designing private Mars missions; but we were done with Initiative missions. We were both decommissioned. I was sure I would never leave low Earth orbit again. Aames was a wreck. He spent a year arguing with officials and avoiding reporters. And drinking, lots of those Brazilian caipirinhas he likes. That got him drunk enough to get into a bad marriage. Not that Hannah was a bad woman, but Aames was a lousy husband. Sullen, bitter Aames is even worse than ordinary Aames. The marriage lasted only a couple years. They barely talk now, though I know Aames still sends holiday gifts to Hannah's son from her first marriage.

"And that might've been the end of his career—drunk and depressed on a Brazilian beach. But that all changed when Holmes Interplanetary hired Captain Aames to command the *Aldrin*. The first thing he did was hire Carver and me. He insisted on that in his contract." Smith smiled at that, pride beaming through her new pink skin. "And so here we are, on an express train to Mars."

Smith settled back, and I thought about her story. There was so much to absorb: not just about Aames, but about her and Carver and Gale. The three spacers who had been so closely tied up in his career. "Thank you, Smitty. You're right, the official reports don't show me Nick Aames as you know him."

She waved a hand, but carefully. "That's nothing. If you really want to understand Captain Aames, the one person you *have to* talk to is Chief Carver."

I frowned. "That's a problem. He's Aames's right-hand man. He's hardly objective."

That remark brought Smith suddenly back to full alertness. She sat up, wincing, and glared at me; and I wondered if I was going to be thrown against the bulkhead. "I like you, Yerim," she said in an even tone. "You're cute, and you have a lot of potential. You're also young and naïve, so I'll forgive you that remark. Once." Her glare grew darker. "But don't ever bad-mouth Anson Carver where I can hear you. He's the most honest, trustworthy man in the entire International Space Corps, and he's worth both of us put together and then some. Captain Aames trusts him implicitly, and so do I. And so should you."

I was flustered. I knew Smith's loyalty to Nick Aames extended to Carver as well, but I hadn't realized how strongly. "Sorry," I mumbled, not sure what else to say.

"Well, you should be." Smith settled back into her bed. The air in the infirmary felt suddenly cold. I was glad I had my dark glasses on, so Smith couldn't see the hurt in my eyes.

Before I could think of something to say, Dr. Baldwin came in from her office and straight over to my bed. She looked at my readings and frowned, but then she turned to me. "Do you think you can get out of this bed, Inspector?"

I leaned forward and braced my elbows behind me. As Dr. Baldwin put a hand behind my shoulder to steady me, I asked, "Is there something wrong, Doctor?"

"Wrong?" She listened to my heart. "We've got dueling admirals, the whole ship is ready to explode, and the only thing that may stop it is if you can convince everyone that you're fit for duty."

"What's happening?"

"Admiral Reed has been on my comm every hour asking for status reports on you. He's getting pressure from Admiral Knapp to declare you incapacitated and unable to fulfill your duties due to your injuries."

I exploded. "The injuries that his men caused!"

Dr. Baldwin frowned at my diagnostics. "He's overlooking that little issue. He's an admiral, he can do that. I've told him you're recovering ahead of schedule, but he says the investigation is falling behind, and he'll take steps to prevent that."

"Falling behind? We've got five months to get to Mars. No one's in a hurry."

"Knapp is. He has ordered Admiralty guards on *all* decks. 'Security measures,' he says. And he's angling to have you replaced with someone who won't hesitate to empanel a court."

I shook my head. "Matt's a good aide, but he's not ready for this level of responsibility."

"No, not Harrold. Knapp pulled out the rule book and found a regulation that allows any command-rank officer to serve in the absence of an inspector general. He's ready to move on that regulation. If you're not on duty within the hour, he's going to demand that Admiral Reed turn your assignment over to another command-rank officer."

"Not Gale!" I shouted, and then regretted it: the repairs in my larynx and lungs were still raw, and they hurt from the strain. I lowered my voice. "There's no way in hell I'll let Gale do my job. He put me in here; and he's such a suck-up, he'll be a rubber stamp for whatever Knapp wants."

"It won't be Gale," Dr. Baldwin said. "He's in the next ward, busted up bad. But Knapp has other toadies."

"Doctor, my uniform, please." I sat up and swung my legs over the side of my bed; but suddenly, I felt weak and dizzy. I feared I might pass out if I bent over to pull on my pants. "Oh, hell, the comm pickup will be from the waist up. Just get me my uniform jacket."

Dr. Baldwin dropped my pants on my bed, and she handed me my jacket and helped me to put it on. She rearranged my two IVs and my nano sump so they ran out under the back where they wouldn't show on the comm pickup, and then she helped me carefully off the bed. She offered me an arm to steady myself, and I took it. Low gravity or not, my legs were still pretty wobbly. "Thank you, Doctor. Can I use the comm in your office?"

Dr. Baldwin nodded. "Are you sure you can do this?"

I thought carefully before I answered. I wondered how I was going to manage *two* angry admirals. "I have to, Doctor. I won't be a party to a kangaroo court." But my voice sounded frail in my ears. As we set off across the infirmary, I was still so tired and weak. It was tempting to let Knapp just have his way so I could rest. But I kept walking, my automated IV stand following behind me.

I stopped, almost to the office, when I heard the sound of a wolf whistle. I carefully turned back to Smitty just as she added, "Nice legs, Yerim." And she grinned, and I knew she was over my comment about Carver. I grinned back, and turned back to the office, feeling recharged.

In the office, I sat in front of the comm pickup and arranged my uniform. Dr. Baldwin found me a comb and a mirror so I could straighten out my hair, which had gotten tangled, even as short as it was. I took off my dark glasses, and I winced: not just at the bright light, but at my eyes in the mirror. They were sunken and red rimmed. I looked like I hadn't slept in a week. I put the dark glasses back on. Regulation or not, I looked more fit for duty behind them.

When I was satisfied that I looked as good as I was going to get, I looked at Dr. Baldwin. "All right, show me my latest from Admiral Reed."

Dr. Baldwin looked doubtful. "Admiral Knapp left orders that he wants to talk to you as soon as you're up and about."

"Screw Admiral Knapp." Just saying that out loud made me feel bolder. There's power in taking a stand. "On this ship, I am the top of my own chain of command, and I answer only to Admiral Reed. If Knapp has a problem with that, he can take it up with Reed."

The comm screen lit up, and I saw a flashing icon for Reed. This wasn't a recording, it was a new incoming call. I pulled it open and spoke to the pickup. "Admiral Reed, Inspector Park reporting, on duty."

The light-speed delay was almost fifty seconds before Reed responded. "Park, I've got complaints from Admiral Knapp, Chief Gale, and others that you are dragging your feet on this investigation, and you're feeding dissent on the *Aldrin*. You've taken no depositions from Aames, and you've taken no depositions from his command crew. They say you've had plenty of time, and the evidence—the *overwhelming* evidence, they say, is clear as starlight—is growing stale while you waste their time. Knapp says there's no excuse for not empaneling a court. And now he says you're not fit for duty, and he's ready to take charge."

As soon as Reed paused, I answered, "Admiral, Dr. Baldwin has certified me as fit to return to my work. Doctor?"

I turned the pickup to Dr. Baldwin, and she nodded. "Admiral, for the record, I am Dr. Constance Baldwin, chief medical officer of the interplanetary vessel *Aldrin*, and as of this date, I have certified Inspector General Park Yerim for all administrative and investigative duties. She is still restricted to light physical duties, but is otherwise cleared for work."

I turned the pickup back to myself. "Thank you, Doctor. Now, Admiral, if the evidence tells us anything at all here, it's that the case against Aames is far from conclusive. The Admiralty's official account is only part of the story. Even now, they're painting only part of the picture. Have you missed the fact that Knapp's team blew up the I Ring?"

After the delay, Reed answered, "I haven't missed that, Park, but that's in the present. What does it have to do with Aames's crimes in the past?"

"Admiral, have we issued any findings yet? No. Until we do, there were no *crimes*, only an incident. And Aames's justification for his actions during that incident was that the Admiralty crew weren't competent to work aboard the *Aldrin*, that they couldn't be trusted with the safety of this ship. *Gale*"—I made a point to emphasize the name—"has demonstrated that Aames was right about that. That puts this whole case in a new light."

When Reed finally heard my words, he frowned skeptically. "What, so he's psychic? He knew that would happen?"

I tried to sound patient and reasonable. I needed to get Reed back on my side, not alienate him. "Admiral, when it comes to this ship, Aames and his team practically *are* psychic. They know it inside and out, every nut and bolt, and they know what their crew can do. Knapp has been holed up in H Ring, issuing orders but not getting to know this crew. He and Gale don't know a thing here. I don't either. If I want to understand what happened during the incident, then I need to understand this ship the way Aames does, the way his crew does, as much as I am able. Am I wrong in that?"

After the delay, Reed shook his head. "No, that's not wrong, that's thorough. But Park, you should know that Knapp is making some noises that you're not up to this job. Your accident is just a convenient excuse, but Knapp was displeased even before that. He and the rest of the admirals are suggesting that you should be replaced."

I smiled. "I'm sure they are, Admiral. They always do whenever the IG Office gets too close to things they'd rather we not look at. You told me that yourself, remember?" I pulled off my glasses and stared into the pickup, knowing my dark, tired eyes would emphasize my point. "*This* is what they don't want us to look at, and I'm not going to let them stop me. If the plenary power of the inspector general can be yanked away anytime it's inconvenient for them, then it's no power at all. That's another lesson you taught me." I took a deep breath. My next statement was risky; but if I was wrong, I would rather learn that now. "If that lesson was a lie, you'll bow to their pressure and remove me. But if the independence of the IG Office means anything, then I respectfully request that you let me get back to my job. Sir."

Reed's face was frightening when he finally heard my words; but he held back for nearly half a minute after I was done, and his scowl slowly softened. "You're right, of course, Park. You're not the only one under a lot of pressure here, but it will only get worse if we let it divide the office. You have my full support. I'll put that in writing as soon as we're done here."

Relieved, I put my glasses back on, sighing as I did so. "Thank you, Admiral. And, sir, if there's anyone I know who can handle pressure, it's you. Park out."

I waited for Admiral Reed to dismiss me, and then I swiped the comm session closed. I turned the desk chair to face where Dr. Baldwin sat in the office chair. She looked at me and shook her head. "They're not going to give up that easily, you know."

"I know." I smiled. "But I just made it personal with Admiral Reed. Now they're not stepping on *my* toes, they're stepping on *his*. He kicks back, and he has some very large boots. They had better guard their shins. And that reminds me, I have some kicking of my own to do."

I pulled open a channel to Admiral Knapp's office in H Ring. His aide, Commander Curry, answered. Her face was perfectly neutral, perfectly noncommittal as she said, "Admiral Knapp's office, can I help you?"

"This is Inspector General Park Yerim." She knew perfectly well who I was, but Curry was a stickler for protocol. "Let me speak to the admiral, please."

Curry remained neutral, though with just a hint of a grin. I suspected she enjoyed obstructing people. "I'm sorry, Admiral Knapp is busy. He left orders not to be disturbed."

I, on the other hand, made no effort to hide my grin. "That's all right, you can pass him a message for me. I have heard a rumor that he has stationed Admiralty guards throughout the *Aldrin*. I'm sure that must be some sort of mistake, as it would directly contravene my orders confining Admiralty personnel to G and H Rings except for official duties."

That wiped the impassive look from Curry's face and replaced it with shock. "Ship's security *is* an official duty."

I shook my head. "Not in my judgment." I emphasized that last word, rubbing my IG ribbon with my fingertips. "I'm sure that once the admiral has time to straighten out this misunderstanding, he'll find that some junior officer overstepped their bounds. I think ten minutes ought to do. Please inform your guards that they have ten minutes to return to G Ring. After that, I'm sure Commander Adika's security crew would be happy to help them find their way."

Curry started to protest, but I pushed the comm channel closed. "There, one more call out of the way." I felt weak, but strong at the same time. It felt good to take action.

I braced myself to get up, and the automated IV stand backed away to give me room. Dr. Baldwin rushed to my side. "Here, let me help." I decided not to protest; and with her help, I limped back into the infirmary with my IV.

This time as we passed Adika's bed, I had the courage to speak up. "Doctor, how's Commander Adika doing?"

The warmth of Baldwin's smile answered before she could. "He's much better. Thank you. His blood pressure's strong, his muscles are starting to regrow, and his liver's practically clean. Dr. Santana's almost done growing his new lungs, and we'll start surgery this evening. He'll pull through fine. My man is strong as a rhino."

I smiled back, remembering Aames's visit the night before. "Like a rhino," I agreed. I owed Adika my life, and I was glad the price he paid hadn't been his own.

We crossed over to my bunk, and I picked up my pants. "Doctor, can you help me get these on? And where are my shoes?"

Dr. Baldwin shook her head. "I haven't discharged you yet."

Reaching deep, I summoned up a little more of the courage I had needed to face Reed. "Doctor, we just told Admiral Reed that I was fit and on duty. Shall I call him back and tell him we lied?"

The doctor shook her head. "No, but . . . Oh, sit down." She helped me remove my jacket, then gave me a thorough examination. Finally she disconnected my IVs and my nano sump, and she handed me my full uniform. "All right, but light duty, just like I said. And I'm going to prescribe you a physical therapy regimen to get you back into top shape. If you slack off, I'll send guards to drag you back here and strap you into that bed."

"Understood, Doctor. I'll behave."

Dr. Baldwin helped me get dressed, and then she pronounced me fit to return to duty. She went to Adika's bed to check on him, while I turned to Smitty's bed. "Well, roomie," I said, "it looks like you lost our little contest. I'm going to beat you back to duty by at least a day."

Smitty smiled, and I saw that her skin was already relaxing, healing quickly. "We never said what the prize was. So what did I lose?"

I smiled back. "I'll figure that out." I reached out a hand to shake hers, and she took it in both her hands, squeezed it, and pulled it close to her. Then she let go and saluted. "It was good rooming with you, Inspector."

"Indeed it was, Bosun." I hesitantly returned the salute, and then I left the infirmary.

C

I had been days behind in my paperwork before the explosion of the I Ring. Two days in the infirmary hadn't helped me any, though Matt had done an admirable job in my absence. He'd handled most of the mundane matters, leaving only the most critical issues for my decision. Of course that meant I had to review all his decisions, just to be sure he was handling them correctly; but by the time I was done with that, I trusted his judgment pretty highly. I sent Admiral Reed a message recommending Matt for immediate promotion to lieutenant so that I could delegate more work to him. Reed's quick approval made me feel proud both for Matt and for myself: Reed may have had doubts, but now I had his full support.

But I also had too much paperwork *and* a heavy therapy regimen from Dr. Baldwin, mostly a lot of walking to strengthen my legs and my respiratory system. Fortunately she had also given me a way to combine them: the heads-up display in my dark glasses. Back at university, I had mastered the art of studying while walking, with many nights spent studying on the university running track. As long as the traffic was orderly and I turned on the proximity alarm on my comp, I could walk for two or three hours while reading. With the voice control in the glasses, I could also respond to reports, forwarding them as needed or dictating notes for Matt to handle them.

So I spent the next few days at my desk for first and second watches, third watches walking the track in the inner ring, and then having a shower and dinner. The walking time was actually peaceful, so I could concentrate on the more difficult issues that came before me. The track wasn't used much during third watch, and the proximity sensor in my comp was in fine working order, so I had no problem with collisions. As my eyes adjusted, I lowered the polarization on my glasses, but I kept using them for reading.

On the fourth night, my left-side sensor buzzed, so I knew someone was coming up beside me. I shifted to my right—and straight into a runner. We collided, and I tripped and fell flat on my face, my glasses sliding across the deck. Immediately, pain throbbed behind my eyes: they were almost completely recovered, but they were still sensitive. Dr. Baldwin said that would last a couple more days until my retinas adjusted. They still had the sensitivity of infant retinas, but I was working them like old, tired adult eyes.

"Sorry," I said as I squinted and looked for my glasses. "I don't understand, the proximity alert said you were on my left."

"Here you go," a baritone voice said. I felt my glasses placed in my hand, and I put them on. Then I saw the dark, friendly face of Chief Carver leaning over me. "The sensors don't always work in an open space like this ring. The echoes can bounce off the walls." Carver held out a hand. "Can I help you up, Inspector?"

I took Carver's hand, and he pulled me to my feet. I breathed in deep and shook my legs, feeling for any new damage, but there was none. I let out my breath in a sigh. "I guess I've been lucky I didn't hit anyone sooner. Thank you, Chief."

Carver looked at my comp. "May I?" I nodded, expecting him to remove it from my sleeve and investigate it. Instead he looked at his own comp; but my screen started flashing with images and messages. Just as quickly the flashing stopped, and Carver tapped his own screen. "Yes, here's the problem. Your proximity sensor is fine, looking forward. It shows you've avoided fourteen collisions in the past four days. But it's not calibrated correctly for side to side, the echolocation is out of sync. Here, I'll recalibrate it." He pushed more commands to my comp, and my screen flashed another message: "Calibration Complete." Carver nodded. "Respectfully, Inspector, never navigate using uncalibrated instruments. You're lucky you weren't injured."

"Thank you, Chief Carver." I was grateful, but I also felt awkward. I was on the *Aldrin* to decide the future of Nick Aames; but whatever happened to Aames, Carver would share in his fate. I had this man's life in my hands, and here he was keeping me safe. "But I interrupted your run. I should let you get back to it."

Carver smiled, a broad, warm smile, and I could see why so many of his crew trusted him so easily. "No worries, Inspector. I have plenty of time to run these days."

Ouch! Was that a dig? But I didn't hear any malice in his tone or see any in his face. Carver just seemed to be genuinely in good spirits. I fumbled for an answer. "All right, then. But I'm under doctor's orders. I need to keep walking."

"Certainly. You don't want to argue with Connie. Even if she's in a better mood now." That I knew: Commander Adika had come through his surgeries in good health, and he had spoken to her just that morning. "So you'd best keep walking. Why don't I keep you company?"

So despite my discomfort around him, I found myself walking the track with Carver for hours, talking the whole time. And soon I lost all of my awkwardness. Anson Carver was a natural at putting people at ease. I couldn't discuss Aames's case with him, but I found myself discussing practically everything else: the tense situation on the *Aldrin*, the pressure from the Admiralty, Adika's recovery, and the latest news from Mars. I briefly mentioned the foibles of Horace Gale, but Carver diplomatically steered us to another topic at the first opportunity. And from that I detected a pattern: Carver would never willingly say anything bad about anyone, at least in those unofficial discussions. If he had criticism, he always couched it in terms of opportunities for improvement. I thought at first he was simply being polite, but I began to suspect that Chief Carver was just that optimistic. He wanted to find the positive potential in everyone.

And inevitably the conversation turned to Captain Aames. I tried to avoid it, out of principle; but there was no topic on the *Aldrin* that did not eventually involve Aames. Even when he wasn't there, he was there.

I even found myself explaining my theory on Aames. "I understand how people can trust him. He's good, the best in the Corps probably."

"Definitely," Carver interrupted.

"Okay, he's the best. If you want to be safe, to finish your mission, he's your man. And if you want your people trained to be their best, he'll push them to do better."

Carver held up a hand. "Or break them. Not everyone can keep up with Nick's demands."

I nodded. "I can see that. Back in my files I have hundreds of pages of complaints from spacers who feel they got a raw deal from him. He has broken more careers than any three other commanding officers combined. But the crew that survives his pressure have a higher commendation rate than average in the Corps, by nearly a standard deviation. Those who leave for other posts—and that's a pretty low number, compared to other commanders—maintain those high standards. The only major blemish on their records is they keep doing things 'the Aames way' instead of adjusting to their new commanders."

Carver answered, "Yes, we get a lot of return transfers. Our crew discover they miss the community here."

"Yes." I nodded again. "That's the word, 'community.' The crew not only trust Aames, they trust each other. This is more than an assignment for them. And yet, even though I can see why people trust Aames, I don't see how they . . ." I trailed off, not sure how to say what I was thinking.

Then Carver said it for me: "How they can stand him?" He smiled. "How they can stand such a difficult, demanding man?"

Once Carver had said it, I felt safe in agreeing. "Exactly. I'm sorry, I know he's your friend; but even his officers say how unpleasant he is. How uncaring." I thought again about Aames in the infirmary. "But is that the real him? I don't know, and I think I need to."

Carver looked doubtful. "Inspector, I really don't feel comfortable with this. I appreciate what you're saying, but I don't think I should comment without counsel. My career is on the line, too, remember." Exactly. He had brought the conversation right back around to my original concerns. I really needed to stop the discussion right there.

But what had Smitty said? *"If you really want to understand Captain Aames, the one person you* have *to talk to is Chief Carver."* I believed her, especially after this discussion. So once again I found myself pledging secrecy: "Please, Chief Carver. Off the record. Your opinion is vital to me here."

Carver stopped walking, and I stopped and turned to him. He stared me straight in the eye, and I felt like he was weighing my integrity to see if I could be trusted. I hoped I would measure up.

Finally Carver smiled. "All right, Inspector. Maybe if you understand the man, you'll see a way out of this situation. You're right, Nick's not pleasant. He's not friendly or warm. He's not fun very often, although sometimes he can be, if you learn to understand his sense of humor—and if he doesn't turn it upon you.

"But deep underneath all that, he's human," Carver continued. "He cares about his crew and his friends, perhaps as deeply as anyone I know. Oh, he's absolutely lousy at showing it. He really doesn't understand how normal people relate, so he has his own way of acting on it. He can seem cruel, but it's more complicated than that."

I tried to understand. "He cares, so he's cruel?"

Carver rubbed his chin. "I can see that I haven't explained it well. Like I said, it's complicated. But . . ." He started walking again, and I moved to keep up. "Well, let me tell you about the investigation of the Azevedo mission. Maybe an example will help you understand."

8. Murder on the *Aldrin* Express

Off-the-record account of Chief Anson Carver, Chief Officer of the IPV *Aldrin*

Covering events of 27 April 2074

I looked up from the view screen. "Are you sure about this, Riggs?"

Ensign Riggs nodded. "The micrographs don't lie, Chief Carver. There are nanos all over that cable."

I scratched my neck under my stiff gray uniform collar. It was hard to keep my uniform clean with the water rations on the ship. Besides an inescapable slight stink—inescapable because the whole ship had the same stink of bodies confined for months—I was developing a bit of a rash. "But are you *sure*? We're going to have to take this to Captain Aames."

I saw the young British astronaut turn pale, almost as pale as his close-cropped blond hair, and I managed to conceal my amusement. Riggs was new to the *Aldrin*, but already he lived in fear of Nick.

Riggs was understandably nervous: being challenged by the chief officer was bad enough, and bringing bad news to Nick would be even worse. But the ensign hesitated only briefly before he swallowed and answered, "Yes, sir. Take a look."

I pulled Riggs's report onto my comp. I wasn't an expert in nano-machines any more than Riggs was, but I could read the computer analysis easily enough. The frayed S3 cables were infested with dormant nanobots.

Well, I had been hoping for a distraction so I could stop thinking about Tracy. I had managed to avoid her even in the close confines of the Mars cycler, but I couldn't avoid the memory of her without some distraction. This would certainly fit the bill. "All right, then. No sense in delay. Let's go see the captain." As we headed out of my office, I noticed that Riggs still moved with exaggerated care. Eventually, he would adjust—if Nick didn't break him first.

Probably Riggs would break, but I hoped not. He was a good kid, endearingly eager to be in space even if only as crew of a Mars cycler. Most in the Corps saw cycler service as pretty low duty for an astronaut, tantamount to punishment. And working under Nick didn't make that duty any more popular, which added to our attrition rate. I couldn't guess whether Riggs would last or not. Nick couldn't, either, which was why he insisted on testing people until he found out. Nick hated not knowing.

We walked through the ship as I ruminated, passing through one brownish-gray passageway after another. Eventually we arrived at Nick's outer office—empty, since I was the one who usually manned the desk there—and passed through to the command office. The door opened as I approached. I ushered Riggs in, and we stood before the display desk.

A chair was behind the desk, its high back facing us, and it didn't budge as we entered and the door closed behind us. Nick was staring at the stars and probably ignoring us, but it was possible he hadn't heard us. As usual, the office was filled with mellow Brazilian music playing from the beat-up old e-reader, which was the only item on his massive desk. Many of us in the Corps had trained in Brazil and picked up a little Portuguese, but Nick had thoroughly adopted the country and its culture. I recognized "Brigas Nunca Mais," one of Nick's favorites. I always found some irony in that: the title translated roughly as "Never Fight Again," and Nick was a tenacious fighter.

The chair back swayed slightly. Despite the music, I was sure Nick knew we were there. He was just ignoring us. Fine. I would wait him out.

Finally the song ended, and Nick's voice came from behind the chair. "Are you going to stand there all day, Chief Carver?"

"How did you know it was me?" Did he analyze the sound of my walk? I couldn't see how over the music.

"Elementary, my dear Carver. After Margo Azevedo's breakdown at last month's maudlin dinner, I would rather avoid any unnecessary contact with our passengers. That door is currently programmed to open for only one other person on this ship besides myself; and that one other person is you, Chief."

"Someone could have broken your lock program and entered that way."

"True. But there's only one person on this ship whose programming skills are up to that task. And that person is also you. Ergo, if someone intrudes on my solitude, it could only be you. Oh, and Mr. Riggs, of course."

I saw Riggs flinch when Nick said his name. He looked at me and mouthed the word "How?" but I didn't respond. I didn't want to give Nick the satisfaction. Besides, he likely had a camera hidden in his office, so it wasn't any big mystery.

Over the years I had learned the value of having more patience than Nick. It's not easy, but I've done it. He has nearly zero patience when he wants something from you, but nearly infinite when he's avoiding someone. So I just stood silently and waited him out. At last he spoke again. "So what is it, Chief Carver? More of the incessant mourning?

Have our passengers decided they want to regale us with yet more stories of the late, great professor and his botched expedition?"

"No, sir, but it does involve the expedition. Riggs has found evidence that Professor Azevedo's S3 cable was sabotaged."

It's rare that I get to surprise Nick, even with bad news; so I took a secret, perverse delight in the way he spun the chair around and slapped the old e-reader on the desktop. Instead of his usual casual slouch, he leaned intently forward. When he got like this, his energy seemed likely to burst out in a random direction on the smallest provocation. Again Riggs flinched, as if Nick might leap at him or throw something at him; and I had to admit, it had happened to others in the crew.

Nick fixed Riggs with his best contemptuous stare. "Mr. Riggs, synthetic spider silk breaks. It is incredibly strong, but it also breaks when not properly maintained over time. And Paolo Azevedo was notoriously sloppy—exactly as I warned his backers before the expedition, not that anyone listened to me. Half of his maintenance reports never got filed. So I have no doubt he fell behind on S3 inspections, and the cable broke as a result. Why would you suggest otherwise?"

Riggs straightened to attention under Nick's stare, and he stood his ground. I could really get to like the kid. He had spunk. "Captain, I was performing the quarantine inventory, as per Chief Carver's orders." We were less than two days away from Earth orbit, so it was standard practice to scan all transported gear for contaminants—including nanos—since many Earth jurisdictions have pretty strict laws about unlicensed nanomachines. "I inspected Professor Azevedo's S3 cable, and I found a small colony of scavenger nanos. If I may, sir?"

Nick nodded, and Riggs swiped his finger across the comp on his sleeve, pushing his report to Nick's display desk. Nick gestured us closer as he leaned over the electron micrograph, an image of several parallel gray tubules dotted with miniscule magenta specks. Riggs tapped his comp, and several circles zoomed out of the image for more detail. The tubules began to show as a fine matrix; and the specks became a number of small structures, false colored in shades of magenta to stand out against the gray background. "There they are, sir. Scanner says they conform 99.993 percent to the structure of standard scavenger nanos, one of the same lines that the expedition took along for scavenging raw materials. This particular line scavenges salt ions and fixes them to a substrate, manufacturing salts and salt-based compounds. And these"—Riggs tapped the comp again, and small flecks were highlighted in yellow—"are salt ions trapped in the glycine matrix."

Nick sneered at Riggs. "And why are you wasting my time over a bunch of salt ions?" But I knew that sneer from long experience: it meant that Nick was testing Riggs. Nick already knew the answer, and he suspected that just *maybe* Riggs wasn't a complete incompetent. If Riggs could just keep his cool and make a thorough professional report, he might actually impress Nick. And I knew as well as anyone how difficult it is to impress Nick.

Riggs held up under the sneer and continued his report: "Captain, the salt ions depolymerize the glycine, reverting it from a fibrous state to more of a gel. The silk becomes liquid again, Captain, and it stretches like taffy. It pulls thinner and thinner until it just wisps away. If the captain is done with this micrograph?" Nick waved his hand dismissively, and Riggs brought up the next image. "This is the same zone, zoomed out by a factor of ten." There were a number of gray strands, too small now to see the magenta specks; but the strands became progressively more yellow as they approached the upper right corner. They also narrowed dramatically. When the strands had diminished to roughly half their width, they started to bend and warp. And suddenly, almost in the corner of the image, they became a knotted yellow tangle, and they reached no further.

Nick turned one wide eye up at Riggs. "So, Mr. Riggs, you're telling me that although Azevedo *was* an utter fool who had no business leading that expedition, he wasn't at fault in his own death? You're telling me that I was wrong?"

Riggs swallowed before he spoke. "Yes, Captain."

"Good!" Nick looked back down at the desk. You would have to know him as well as I did to see the slight edge of a smile at the corner of his mouth. Riggs had impressed him. "Riggs, it is my job to be right. This ship and all aboard depend on that. It is *your* job to tell me when I'm not doing *my* job. I *will* tear you into small bloody bits when you do, because I'm *never* wrong; and I expect you to do so anyways, because sometimes I *am* wrong, and I will *not* tolerate that. If you can accept that, you might have a future on this ship. Can you?"

Riggs didn't hesitate again. "I don't know, Captain. We'll find out."

This time Nick even let his smile show, though awkwardly, like he was out of practice. "Honesty. Another mark in your favor. Don't ever lie to me, Riggs, and we'll get along fine. So I trust you did research on these nanos. You know how they're activated."

"Concentrated UV light, Captain, of specific frequencies. The light excites certain outer electrons in the structure, ionizing the nanos and initiating a chain reaction that starts them in motion. I'm afraid chemistry isn't my best subject, Captain, so I can explain how to activate them but not the details. The frequency and intensity required are such that they don't occur naturally in the solar spectrum."

"So they can't activate by accident. Someone has to use an emitter." Riggs nodded. "And that's why you believe the break must have been sabotage."

I decided Riggs had had enough of Nick's attention, and it was time to draw some fire of my own. "Yes, Captain, and that's why we had to bring this straight to you. It's your responsibility to investigate, Captain. Secure the evidence, prepare a report for the authorities on Earth, and make sure whoever is behind this isn't a danger to our passengers and crew."

"My responsibility?" Nick turned one glaring eye upon me.

"Yes, sir. And I guess this changes at least one thing."

"Oh?"

"You were wrong about the expedition. The failure wasn't their fault."

"Oh, really?"

"Well, clearly, it was deliberate. It wasn't an accident."

"Oh, really? And what does that change?"

"Well . . . everything." Nick exasperated me. As usual. I think exasperating people was one of his primary joys in life. Defying expectations and challenging beliefs was one of his many ways of testing people.

"Does it change the fact that they didn't plan for adequate backup water? Does it change the fact that they didn't plan for the possible temperature extremes? Does it change the fact that they were completely unprepared for a category 5 dust storm? Does it change the fact that they had no plan for what would happen if they lost their orbital platform *like we lost ours?*"

"Nnnnno." I had intended to needle Nick, but I hadn't expected him to react so strongly. Riggs was squirming. The crew didn't usually see Nick and me duel like this.

"Then I wasn't wrong. They had a poorly planned mission from start to finish. Though I grant you there's one failure even I overlooked: they didn't plan for a criminal on board."

I saw my opening. "And that's *another* reason why only you can investigate this murder. You understand their expedition, and you know what to look for."

Nick sighed, and I knew I had him. "Very well, then, Chief Carver. I guess I must end my exile here and deal with the members of the expedition. Interview them and find out who might have a motive for this crime."

"So should I bring them in, sir?"

"Oh, not all at once, one at a time. That's all I want to deal with. I think we'll start with Ms. Wells."

Tracy! I tried to stall. "Nick, surely you don't think she had anything to do with this."

"What I think is none of your concern. Has she already messed up your head so much that you've forgotten how to follow orders?"

Damn it, Nick, get out of my head. "No, Captain, if that's your order, I shall carry it out, *sir.*"

"That's good, man, because I need to know if you're going to have a problem with this. I need to know if you're thinking with your brain, or somewhere lower."

I had manipulated Nick into taking charge of the investigation, and he was going to make me suffer for that; but I wasn't going to let that impair my performance of my duties. "Sir, I shall carry out my responsibilities exactly as expected."

I left, Riggs in tow, and the door closed behind us. Facing off with Nick must have emboldened Riggs. Normally I wouldn't expect personal questions from such a junior crewman, so his next question hit me by surprise. "Is there a problem with Ms. Wells, sir?"

"No, we just have a history. I've been avoiding her. Too many uncomfortable memories."

"He knows this? And he's putting you in this bind deliberately? He's a right bastard, isn't he?"

"That he is, Mr. Riggs. That he is." We reached the tube to the berthing ring, and I turned off while Riggs continued back to his post. Under my breath, I echoed Riggs: "A right bastard he is."

☾

I had dreaded that encounter, but I couldn't put it off. Three months ago I had looked up the cabin number where Tracy bunked with Arla Simms, another member of the Azevedo expedition. I had managed to stop myself from going there, but the number was lodged firmly in my brain.

And now I stood before 32A and held my finger on the door buzzer. *Nearly four years.* Too soon, and far too long. I pressed the buzzer.

Arla opened the door: a trim young woman in a simple blue jump-suit from the expedition, her blonde curls cut functionally short. We had met several times during the voyage, but never for very long. I had avoided prolonged contact with the passengers almost as thoroughly as Nick had. Arla seemed surprised to have a visitor. "Yes, Chief Carver?"

I straightened to attention, hiding behind formality as best I could. "Begging your pardon, ma'am, but the captain has sent me. He has asked me to fetch Ms. Wells"—I managed not to stammer at her name—"so that he may ask some questions about the expedition."

"The expedition? Is there something wrong?"

"Nothing I can speak of, ma'am. The captain is just thorough." It wasn't precisely a lie. Not that I would hesitate to lie to keep the investigation low-key, but I would stick as close to the truth as I could.

"Well, come in, Chief. Tracy's in here." *Damn.* I had been afraid she would invite me in, and I hadn't figured out a polite excuse to refuse. Arla stepped aside, and I entered the cabin.

Instantly my eyes were pulled to Tracy where she sat on her bunk, a desk folded out from the cabin wall. She was editing expedition videos, and she paused them as I came in. Tracy wore a blue jumpsuit like Arla's, but she had altered the legs to thigh-length shorts. She had always liked her legs free, and I had never minded the chance to see them. She looked just as I had glimpsed her in random moments since the expedition came aboard: a little older than when we had parted, and a little thinner from the tight rations on Mars, and somehow that made her even more beautiful than the day we had met. Her face was the same cocoa shade that I remembered. Her hair was the same black that I knew so well, but pulled back in a bun. The auburn highlights that fascinated me so were only visible when she let her hair flow free, so I was safe from them for the moment. Her deep-brown eyes looked up at mine, and I looked just a bit away.

And her scent. It wasn't possible, but the cabin smelled of lilacs. After months on Mars and more months on the trip there and back, she couldn't possibly still have any of the lilac water she liked so much. I concentrated, and the odor faded away. It had been only a memory.

Tracy still knew all of my tricks too. She shifted her head to meet my eyes. "What is it, Anson?" My pulse leaped. Practically no one called me by my first name, and no one at all since Tracy and I had broken up. I couldn't look away. I didn't want to. I had to—but I couldn't. "The captain is conducting an investigation of the accident, and he has asked me to escort you to his office so that he may ask some questions." There. I had gotten out a whole sentence.

"Certainly, Anson. Anything I can do to help." Tracy folded up the desk and stood from her bunk. I managed not to analyze how her body moved in the low gravity. "If you'll lead the way. I have no idea how to find the captain's office."

Glad of the excuse, I turned on my heel and faced the door. I touched my cap. "My apologies for the intrusion, Ms. Simms."

I left the cabin. I heard Tracy's soft tread behind me, and then the door closed. I waited until she was almost beside me, and then I set off through the passageway.

I knew the silence wouldn't last forever, but I still felt a stab when Tracy broke it. "You said there's nothing you can speak of, so I assume there's something you *can't* speak of?"

I never could fool Tracy. "I'm sorry you heard that."

"'I'm sorry you heard that,' *Tracy*. It's okay to say my name, you know."

I missed my stride, but only by a fraction of a second. I tried for casual: "Why waste words? We both know who I'm talking to."

Tracy sped up, edged around me in the narrow passageway, and stopped in front of me, forcing me to stop as well. "You're *not* talking, not really. You're *avoiding* talking."

Before I knew what was happening, I answered, "We talked four years ago. That didn't turn out so well." I should've let it rest, I knew I should've. This could only get worse.

And it did. "And you're still angry? After four years?"

"Still angry that you left me? Absolutely!"

"I left you for Mars! My chance to film the documentary of my dreams. I couldn't pass up that opportunity. You should know; you did the same to me when you left on the *Bradbury*."

"That was different." I tried to control my emotions, but they were building higher.

"Different? Different how?"

"We barely knew each other then. We had only been together for a couple months. We hardly meant anything to each other yet. Not like . . . not like breaking our engagement."

"I had to break it. It wasn't fair. I was going to Mars for nearly four years with training and travel. I couldn't ask you to wait that long."

"You couldn't?" And suddenly my restraints broke. "You couldn't ask me? Why not? *That* made me angry, the way you just decided without asking me. But oh, I got past angry." That took nearly a year. Then I tried hurt for a while. Hurt and drunk. Then just drunk, and then drunk and bitter. Eventually Nick dried me out and kicked my tail and got me to focus on work again. That's what I have now: my work, and I'm damned good at it. "I ferry passengers to and from Mars now, and that's all that's going on here."

Tracy was silent for almost a minute; and when she did speak, I could barely hear her. "I thought maybe you joined this crew so you could see me."

I looked away. I didn't want to give her the satisfaction of seeing how much that had touched me. She wasn't my reason, though part of me wished she had been.

Trying to keep a steady tone, I answered, "No, I've been on this crew since the first cycle, and you had nothing to do with that. I'm here to serve under Captain Aames."

"Nick? He's a bastard!"

"That bastard is the only reason I'm alive today. Me and the twelve other survivors from the second *Bradbury* expedition."

"Yes, but the way he treats you. How can you put up with that abuse?"

How could I explain it to her, when sometimes I couldn't even explain it to myself? But I had to try. "The safest place to be in this solar system is under the command of Nick Aames—but just outside of shouting distance."

"And inside shouting distance?"

"Third safest. Second safest if you can get him shouting at somebody else."

Tracy smiled. Despite myself, I did too. *Damn it!* I couldn't do this. I had to keep my distance. If I relaxed, if I let myself loose, it would happen all over again. I couldn't take another round of losing her.

I squeezed past her. "Come on. The bastard is waiting."

☾

Nick's door opened, and the liquid notes of a trumpet emerged, accompanied by a soft drumbeat and guitar. It was a sad, sweet tune, "Mue Esquema." Now *there* was a title that suited Nick: "My Scheme." We entered. Nick looked up and silenced the e-reader.

I stood by the door. "As you requested, Captain, Ms. Wells is here to speak with you. I'll be in my office."

"No, Chief Carver, stay. I need your perspective on these interviews."

Nick had me right where he wanted me, but I wasn't going to acknowledge it. "As the captain wishes."

"Ms. Wells, have a seat."

"Thank you, Nick." Tracy had never been big on formality, and it looked like she wasn't going to play by Nick's rules. No surprise there. She casually dropped into the guest chair, settling easily in the low gravity.

Nick stared directly at Tracy, his hands clasped on the desk. "You've had quite an expedition. It's been a long time. How long?"

"Almost four years, as you know. You *always* know details like that."

"Certainly. Attention to detail *is* my specialty. And yours, apparently, is distracting and ruining my best officer."

Tracy held her casual pose, but I could see the rising ire in her eyes. "*I* ruined him?"

"Look at him standing there, all tense, ready to flinch at any moment."

"*I* wasn't the one who talked him out of his opportunity to go back to Mars."

"I did no such thing."

"You know full well you did!" Tracy leaned forward. Despite her resolve, Nick was getting to her. He always did. "When you turned down the liaison post on the Azevedo expedition, you knew there was no way Anson would go with us if you didn't. Of course he wanted to go back to Mars. What member of the Corps doesn't? Three-quarters of your crew were on our applicant list. I've seen it. But not Anson, nooooo! He wouldn't go on any expedition you didn't approve of. He wouldn't leave you."

"Not even to be with you."

"Not even to be with me."

"And that bothers you."

"No, not anymore. It stopped bothering me a long time ago. But it bothered me then."

"And that's why you broke up with him."

"Captain!" I had had enough of the two of them arguing over me as if I wasn't there. "You're supposed to be investigating—"

"Chief Carver, I *am* investigating, and I'll do it my way. I expect you to respect my line of questioning and trust that I have my reasons."

I sighed, but not loudly. "Aye, Captain."

Tracy glared at me. "'Aye, Captain.' It's still like that? All right, if you want to pretend this is germane, I won't give you the satisfaction of fighting with you. I broke up with Anson because it would've been unfair to ask him to wait for me for nearly four years through the training and the expedition. It would've been different if we were together, but you made sure that wouldn't happen. He had to get on with his life, even if his 'life' was following you and taking your orders."

"Taking orders. Discipline. Concepts you never really understood, aren't they? That's why you fit in so perfectly with the Azevedo expedition." Tracy didn't respond, but I could see she wanted to. "Carver tried to warn you about their poor planning, I know he did; but you were Mars-struck. Or should I say starstruck, perhaps? The great Professor Azevedo was going to Mars, the first mission of the Civilian Exploration Program, and he was taking the best of the best with him! Or at least that's what his press releases said. And he chose you, a practically unknown film student, to record his journey! You weren't about to let anything stop you from going. The dazzle of the spotlight blinded you to the actual state of the mission."

"It didn't blind me."

"No?"

"All right, it sounded glamorous and exciting, at the start. All my life, I had dreamed of shooting documentaries on other planets and between planets. I wanted to capture life in space and on ships and space stations. That's how I met Anson, when I was filming at the Initiative one time."

Nick didn't interrupt, but I knew what he was thinking. He had told me often that he thought Tracy had used me as a stepping-stone for her video ambitions. Tracy's admissions came uncomfortably close to proving his point.

"But I took my training *seriously*. Azevedo didn't train us, you know; we had training from the Corps. From *your* protocols. And oh, I took notes, and I *learned*. I wanted to understand what Anson thought was so important, so vital that he would turn down a promotion if he thought the mission was poorly planned. I wanted to learn what made *your way* so important to him."

"And did you learn?"

Tracy paused. I knew her face too well, I could read the reluctance there; but then she nodded. "I did. I learned the value of precision and protocol and observation. And your way *is* right. So I learned."

"Uh-huh. And your proof is?"

Tracy pushed a file from her comp to Nick's desk. "Here's a list of my reports. And notice in particular the variances: every time I observed a deviation from protocols, I filed a variance. Every variance includes a risk assessment as well, and also my contingency recommendations. Every one filed with Professor Azevedo and also with Gale as the Corps liaison. It got so they both stopped reviewing my reports. I was never wrong, but still they just kept doing what they wanted. Despite them, *I* did *everything* by the book. By *your* book, Nick."

"Hmmm . . . We'll see, won't we? These records *do* look impressive. I've had Bosun Smith running an inventory of the expedition gear. It's sloppy, poorly maintained, articles are missing or misplaced. As I expected, most of your team weren't as meticulous as you've been here."

Tracy stared blankly. She was used to abuse and criticism from Nick, but something close to a compliment seemed to baffle her.

When Tracy didn't respond, Nick prompted her to continue. "All right. Tell me about the Chronius Mons trip, and the accident." I relaxed a bit. *Finally* we were moving on from personal matters—*my* personal matters—to the actual subject of the investigation.

Tracy, on the other hand, became less relaxed. As she started into her report, she sat up and looked alert and *serious*, in a way I wasn't accustomed to from her. "As you know, Professor Azevedo selected Terra Cimmeria for the first CEP expedition due to two unusual phenomena observed there, one measured and one inferred. The Mars global surveyor measured large magnetic stripes in Cimmeria and Terra Sirenum, which are hypothesized to be evidence of ancient tectonic activity; and albedo spectroscopy had indicated possible carbonate deposits that could be evidence of ancient life. The professor hoped that by choosing that locale, he would double the chances of a momentous discovery that would bring in new investors for future expeditions.

"But by our hundredth day on Mars, Terra Cimmeria had proven frustrating and disappointing. It wasn't even that we had negative data to report, just no statistically valid conclusions either way. The magnetic stripes didn't conform exactly to any of the three standard tectonic models; but they didn't vary far enough to disprove any of the models, either, nor enough to choose between them. All our data really told us was we would need a lot more data. In the same way, the carbonate deposits were largely albedo specters; and what deposits we *did* find were too small, too dispersed for us to make much sense of. They could've been remnants of ancient biotics, but they could just be natural mineral phenomena."

I managed not to stare, but I was surprised. Tracy had never shown much science knowledge before. Oh, she had always been smart, but she had concentrated on filmmaking and project management. She was an artist, not a researcher, and Azevedo had hired her for her video skills. Somehow, in the past four years she had developed a whole new side to her.

Tracy continued, "So the professor decided to make the trek to Chronius Mons. He . . . Well, it might be easier if I just played back my journal."

Tracy tapped her sleeve comp, and a strange voice emerged. It was *almost* recognizable, but pitched to a high octave like a cartoon character's. "Azevedo Expedition Journal, Day 106. Videographer Wells reporting. After considering my advice—refer to variance report 104-27w—Professor Azevedo has filed a revised exploration plan for a two-day hike to Chronius Mons. He believes we may find—"

"Stop," Nick shouted, and Tracy paused the log. "Enough with the chipmunk log."

"I'm sorry," Tracy said. "I don't even notice it anymore. After five months of breathing heliox, I speak chipmunk fluently." To reduce payload mass, Azevedo's team had brought a helium-oxygen breathing gas mix rather than standard air. It massed only one-third as much, but it had the unfortunate side effect of raising human voices by an octave or more due to the thinner gas. We didn't bother with it on the *Aldrin*, since our orbit required almost zero fuel to maintain; but the choice had made a huge impact on Azevedo's mass budget.

"Well, I hate heliox," Nick said. "For the sake of my ears, I'd like you to summarize. We can skip the journals."

"If I have to do a lot of talking, can I get some water? I got spoiled by the heliox, it's easier to breathe. I'm still readjusting to normal air. My throat *always* seems dry."

Nick looked at me. "Carver, fetch the lady some water." I went to the sink in the corner, poured a glass, and brought it to Tracy. Our fingers touched briefly as she took the glass. I managed to keep my hand from trembling.

Tracy took a drink, and then she resumed. "With the carbonates disappointing and the plate tectonics inconclusive, Professor Azevedo didn't have much to show for the expedition. So he announced a *new* mission objective. I told him that was clearly outside of *all* protocols; but he overruled my objections, as usual, and said we had plenty of safety margin for a trek to Chronius Mons. He said we had spectroscopic evidence of significant and unusual phosphorus outcroppings on the upper slopes. We had no particular theory to test, no reason for scouting for phosphorus. It was data gathering and grandstanding, nothing more. And the spectroscopic assay was *far* from conclusive, as I told him."

"Oh? And when did you get a degree in chemistry?"

Nick's question had been mocking, so Tracy's answer surprised him as well as me. "I started the program during mission training, and then I got my degree on the trip out on the *Collins*. I had to do something to fill my spare time." She glanced in my direction, then looked back to Nick. "Anson always told me how important it is for expedition members to cross-train so that critical skills have backups. Videographer isn't a critical mission skill, even if the professor saw it as such; but a grounding in chemistry made me a backup for a number of personnel."

I actually saw Nick nod at Tracy's answer. That was as close to praise as she was likely to get.

When Tracy realized Nick had nothing to say, she continued, "So Professor Azevedo insisted on Chronius Mons. In truth, I think he was looking for challenge and adventure. He kept talking about scaling the highest point on the Terra and the great panoramas I could film from up there. He wanted something that would make great publicity. This wasn't really for the scientists, it was all for the money-folks and the media back home.

"He also insisted that we could hike the distance in two days and make the climb in two more, rather than risk a lander flight in the questionable winds. We had no ground vehicles, so it was hike or fly or stay at the camp; and he wouldn't consider the last two choices.

"Professor Azevedo selected Lieutenant Gale and Dr. Ivanovitch for the hike, and also myself to record it. Gale selected himself, really: as International Space Corps liaison, he had supervisory authority over any trip outside the bounds of the camp. He didn't always exercise that authority, but he insisted for that trip. Margo also insisted on coming, and the professor wasn't inclined to say no to his wife—especially since she financed much of the expedition.

"We loaded up sleds with supplies. I personally prepared the equipment plan, but then was overruled time and again by the professor and Gale. Still, I think we were adequately prepared when we left. We had three Mars tents—"

Nick's eyebrow raised. "Three tents? For five people?"

"I know, protocol calls for two: a primary for all of us, and a backup. But again, I was overruled. We also had food, water, tanks of heliox, comm gear, spare clothes, the doctor's med kit, a telescope, a microscope, shovels, sample bags, pitons, hammers, plenty of S3 cable, computers, a satellite locator, flare guns, an emergency beacon, a chemical minilab, a mineralogical kit, videography gear, and suit repair kits.

"Despite the frequent stops for photo ops, the hike to the mountain went quickly, and it was pretty uneventful. Even pulling the loaded sleds, it was light work in the Martian gravity. We walked all day and set up camp, two nights in a row as scheduled. Inevitably Dr. Ivanovitch broke out his vodka. I had long since given up fighting that, and he was too professional to drink to excess when he was the sole medic on the trip. But I had to nag him and Gale to see to equipment maintenance before they started drinking each night."

"And did they?"

"Look at the reports, here. I didn't have the opportunity to inspect the gear stored in the other two tents. I encouraged the others to do standard inspections. As you can see, the inspections were spotty; but in aggregate, most of the gear was covered. Except . . ." She paused and pointed.

"Except the professor's climbing gear, including the S3 cables," Aames interjected.

"Mmmhmmm. It hadn't been unpacked since we left Earth, so he saw no need to inspect that.

"And then we reached the mountain. Chronius Mons, the highest peak in that quadrant. We had done mountaineering training in Peru, all in full Mars suits. The mountain was tall, but it looked like only an average-difficulty climb, and even less thanks to the gravity. And I'll give the team credit: while they were lax on most mission protocols, they took the climb seriously. They tested every handhold, double-checked every piton. And so it came as a complete shock to me when . . ." Tracy stopped, her face anguished. Old instincts kicked in, and I wanted to comfort her; but before I had to decide whether to follow those instincts, she gathered her strength and continued, "Professor Azevedo's cable snapped. Any one of us could've been on that cable at that time, but it happened to be him. He fell so slowly in the Martian gravity. He had plenty of time to cry out for help. But even on Mars, one hundred meters is too far. His cries ended in a sickening crunch before his suit comm cut out.

"Margo wanted to rush down to him, and it was all we could do to restrain her so we didn't end up with another casualty. Carefully we rappelled and climbed down to him, taking nearly five minutes. Thanks to his suit's automatic seals and med systems, he was still alive; but the doctor shook his head. He said the professor needed emergency surgery immediately.

"And that just wasn't possible. We had to descend another thirty meters to a ledge large enough to set up a Mars tent. Despite our best efforts, the climb inflicted further injuries. Then we had to set up the tent, pressurize it, and get the professor out of his suit. Dr. Ivanovitch set up for emergency surgery, and Gale and I assisted. The doctor gave his best effort, but it was far too late." Tracy swallowed drily. "The professor died twenty minutes after the start of surgery. He had never really stood a chance."

I was puzzled but impressed. The old Tracy would often be overwhelmed by her empathy. Sometimes I thought she used the camera to put up a layer between her and the suffering she observed. But now she was distraught, but she reported the incident in full, maintaining her composure for the most part. She had grown stronger—but not, I hoped, less empathetic.

As I thought on this, Tracy continued, "With the professor dead, Gale assumed command. Oh, Margo might have contested that if she had tried, but she was in no shape to make any decisions. We bundled the professor back into his suit for transport, and Gale led us back down the slope. There we had to rest for another night. We were physically and emotionally spent. The next day we double-timed it back to the camp.

"The rest is in my reports and covers the remaining month and a half until your pickup. We did our best to continue exploring and sampling, trying to salvage what we could for our objectives. Margo slowly regained enough energy to argue about who was in charge of the expedition. Legally she had the stronger case, but Gale kept arguing that we needed a professional in charge."

Nick nodded. "You did. Too bad all you had was Gale."

Tracy almost smiled at that. "The camp was pretty small, so their arguments made the place very unpleasant, with different members of the expedition lining up with her or with him. Dr. Ivanovitch and I eventually managed to calm things down by appealing to Azevedo's memory. His personality had united the expedition in the first place, and it was enough in the end to keep us alive until you arrived. Like I said, the rest is in my reports."

Tracy took one last drink of water and then set her glass down on Nick's desk. "So that's my summary. Is that what you need?"

"Yes, if you've told me the whole story, then we're done here."

"I wouldn't keep anything secret. That's against mission protocols."

"Ms. Wells, I have learned in my command career that people keep all sorts of things secret when they're trying to protect their own careers and their own reputations. If they have a guilty conscience or they think perhaps they contributed to some mistake, they keep secrets, and they lie. I've learned to ferret out details that people would rather hide. I won't be lied to on my ship."

"You will find that my reports are complete in every detail and as factual as I could make them. I did everything I could, but I lacked the authority to override Professor Azevedo's decisions."

Nick looked over his comp. "I wouldn't have expected it, but it does seem that way. So considering everything, I have to say that perhaps your training wasn't wasted. You mastered the protocols, which is more than I can say for your leadership."

Tracy stared blankly at Nick. I did as well. He had just come very close to complimenting her, at least by Nick's standards.

But she quickly recovered. "Then if you don't mind, I still have videos to edit before we get to Earth." Tracy stood to leave, but she stopped and turned at the door. "Good-bye, Anson." And then she left.

After Tracy was gone, I turned on Nick. "You never once asked her about the cable and the nanos! The murder!"

"I didn't need to."

"What?"

"I heard what I needed to hear. Now I know the basic outline of the trip and Azevedo's death: who was present, what their roles were, and so on. I'll talk to her again later if I need more details."

I knew better than to push Nick. He would keep his secrets until he saw a need to reveal them. Besides, I had something else on my mind. I didn't like it, but I couldn't stop myself from asking: "Did you have to be so hard on her?"

"Yes, Mr. Carver, I did. I have my reasons."

"And you had to drag *me* into it? What was the point of that?"

"Carver, I am conducting a criminal investigation. Didn't you ever read mysteries? Means, motive, opportunity: those are the classic requirements for solving a crime, and a key part of that is motive. I have to understand the people involved and what drives them. So I had to know where she stood in regard to you and in regard to that expedition. I had to know everything about her."

I was in no mood to be mollified. "You just can't resist picking at old wounds, can you?"

"Your wounds or hers? I'm not convinced she has any."

"What did she do to deserve that?"

"What did she do? You ought to remember. Are you going to let her do this to you again?"

"What are you talking about?"

"You are! You're going to let her just use you for whatever it is she's up to: chew you up, spit you out, and leave you crying in your beer. Again!"

"It's not like that."

"It's *always* like that."

"Look, just because *your* wife and *your* kids aren't talking to you anymore doesn't mean it's like that for everyone."

"It was last time."

"It wasn't like that last time either. Relationships just sometimes . . . They just sometimes end!"

"Yep, it ended when she got what she wanted."

"That's not fair. She had the chance to go to Mars, and she took it. I did the same thing when I had the chance. I can't blame her for that."

"Uh-huh. You went with *me*. She went with Azevedo, and now he's dead. That was mighty poor judgment on her part. She's lucky she's still alive."

"That's not fair. You heard her. She studied. She learned *your* mission protocols. She did everything possible to ensure the success of that expedition."

"Yes, she did, didn't she? I have to admit, that surprised me. A chemistry degree? Surprising, yes."

Nick sat in silence, clasping his hands and staring at his fingers. I realized he had gotten to me again. He always probed for weakness, always had to know where someone might fail him. I stood, fuming but patient, determined not to give in to his testing.

At last Nick looked up. "All right, Ms. Wells has given her report, and that's a start. But I need another perspective. Carver, express my condolences, but bring me Margo Azevedo."

I found Mrs. Azevedo alone in her cabin. She had it to herself, a luxury we normally couldn't spare even for important passengers such as her. But on this trip, I had triple-berthed some junior crew to open up a private cabin for her. I figured she deserved some solitude if she needed it. The ship might be too damned crowded for her otherwise.

When I signaled at the door, it took Mrs. Azevedo almost a minute to open it. She was a tall, dark-toned woman with dark hair that showed some gray. In her pre-mission photos there had been no gray, but hair dye was just another luxury not to be found on Mars. Despite the gray, she still looked much like the fashion model she had been in her youth, back before she turned her earnings into shrewd business investments and a major fortune.

Her once-elegant face was lined with grief. She wasn't red-eyed from crying like she had been earlier in the voyage. Five months of travel from Mars had gotten her past the deepest grief. But she still looked very weary, and I felt guilty for having to disturb her. But guilty feeling or no, Nick had his reasons and I had my orders.

Mrs. Azevedo summoned the energy to speak. "Yes, Chief Carver, can I help you?"

"Begging your pardon, ma'am. I hate to disturb you, but I have orders from the captain. He has sent me to request that you come to his office. He has some matters to discuss."

"What's it about?"

"I'm sorry, ma'am, I'm not at liberty to comment on the captain's business." That was a lie, of course, but I didn't want to explain to her that someone had killed her husband. And I didn't want to even consider that she might be a suspect. But as we walked through the ship, I realized I had an obligation to prepare her for Nick's investigation. "Ma'am, you know that Captain Aames can be a bit brusque."

"Brusque hardly goes far enough."

"Ma'am, I don't think you understand."

"Please, Chief, don't treat me like a china doll. This is a rough time for me, but believe me, I'll get by. I've been making my fortune the hard way since before you were born: first on the fashion runways and then on the spaceplane runways. And I saw plenty of ugly corporate battles in between, I survived all of them, and I triumphed. I've faced opponents far ruder than Captain Aames."

Despite myself, I grinned. "There's no one ruder than Captain Aames."

She laughed, and for a moment I saw the charm she had used to win the backing for this expedition. "Nick Aames can be a smug, self-righteous asshole, no doubt. I appreciate your concern. But don't worry. I've handled Nick before, and I can handle him today."

"Of course." I knew the basics, so she didn't have to explain; but she seemed to need to talk, like the silence was too much for her.

"Nick was Paolo's first choice for the Corps liaison for our expedition. I thought it was a done deal, but Nick and Paolo couldn't agree on terms. Nick insisted on rewriting the entire mission plan to his exacting standards."

I nodded. "The captain would do that."

"But his standards were *too* exacting. Too much redundancy, too much expense. Paolo wanted a streamlined mission—still a *safe* mission—so that we could keep to an affordable budget. He said a mission to Nick's standards would never get launched; and Nick said that was fine with him, and he hoped Paolo's mission would never launch either. He said the Civilian Exploration Program couldn't afford to have its first expedition go wrong, and that that would undermine support for it. And now I fear he'll be proven correct." Her face darkened, and I looked discreetly away. "Nick cut us off that day, and we had to hire Lieutenant Gale instead. Gale is a fine officer, and he gave us none of Nick's troubles. But rest assured, I know Nick's moods, and I'm ready for him."

"I hope so, ma'am."

We arrived at Nick's outer office. We entered the command office in the middle of a samba tune. Nick stood to the side of the desk, absently bouncing to the beat. If we had been alone, I would've told him what a lousy dancer he was, even in one-quarter G. That's a common jibe in our ongoing duels (and also unfair: Nick's a far better dancer than I). But I would never disrespect an officer in his official capacity.

The song soon ended, and Nick sat down. I pulled out the visitor chair for Mrs. Azevedo.

Nick leaned on his desk. "Ah, Mrs. Azevedo. Much as I wish otherwise, I'm afraid I've opened an investigation into the tragic incident on your expedition. Some information has come to me about your equipment, and it's very troubling."

Mrs. Azevedo started to speak, looking agitated; then she paused and regained her control. "Captain Aames, are we going to discuss this again?"

"I have some concerns."

"Yes, Nick, I'm well aware of your concerns from before."

"And now you can see that I was right, and Paolo's carelessness has gotten someone killed. At least it was him, not someone who trusted him."

"Nick!" I couldn't help myself. That was over the line, even for Nick.

But Mrs. Azevedo wasn't disturbed. "No, Chief, he's just trying to provoke me. I won't let him do that. Yes, Captain, you predicted a disaster, and it happened. But *none* of your dire predictions came to pass. What happened was something you never foresaw, a freak cable accident and nothing more. I stand by my original decision that your fears were groundless, and you were afflicted with your usual excess of caution and your pathological need for control."

"And I stand by my original decision. I wanted nothing to do with your poorly planned vanity expedition. Only a fool would take your offer, and I'm no fool. But you found one in Gale, didn't you?"

"All right, Nick, if it makes you happy: I wish you *had* taken our offer. Maybe if you had been our liaison . . ." She trailed off, but we all knew what went unspoken: Maybe Nick could've gotten Azevedo safely back to shelter in time to save his life. Or maybe Nick would've prevented the accident in the first place.

Nick's face turned more serious. Perhaps his conscience was tweaking him just a bit. "I'm sorry, Margo, that would never have happened. I can't take a mission I don't believe in."

"And so you stayed here instead?" Mrs. Azevedo leaned forward. "I know there are some in the Corps and in the Initiative who will *never* forgive you for the second *Bradbury* mission, even though the review board ratified your every decision. There were many who told me I was crazy for wanting you for liaison for this expedition. I wanted you anyway. Okay, you turned me down, you explained your reasons. But then, to take *this* job . . . Nick, you're throwing away your talents here. You're better than this. You're more than a glorified subway conductor. If you didn't want to be on my mission, you would've been invaluable in program management."

"And work with fools like Frank Knapp? Not a chance."

"Judgmental as always, aren't you? Everyone in your eyes is a loser or a fool."

"No, not everyone. There are fifteen billion people back there on those two worlds. They're not *all* losers. About 90 percent of them are ordinary folks, minding their own business, going about their day, not causing me any trouble. And there's maybe half a dozen people worth actually spending time with. But that leaves that 10 percent—one and a half *billion*—*idiots, jerks, losers*, and *psychopaths*."

"And so you'll lock yourself up here with only a few."

"Yep. My chosen few, and I'm smarter than all of 'em. And I'm in charge."

"All right. You're the captain, you're in charge here. Are you happy now?"

Nick paused. When he started again, his tone was lower and more reserved. Nick can be respectful when he chooses. "Margo, I know we clash. And I clashed with Paolo too. It's my nature, not anything to do with you. I call them like I see them, and sometimes I neglect how people might feel. So please accept my condolences. I didn't agree with Paolo's plans, but it wasn't personal. He was a good man. I'm very sorry."

Mrs. Azevedo stared down at the floor, but she nodded. "Thank you, Nick. That means a lot. Chief Carver says you have questions for me?"

Nick hesitated again. "This will be difficult, I'm afraid. But I need to hear about the trip to Chronius Mons."

"It's in our reports." Mrs. Azevedo's tone was flat.

"I know. It's important that I hear it in your own words."

She nodded, and then she started slowly retelling the story. She echoed Tracy's version, but without Tracy's critical judgments about mission protocols. In fact she made every effort to portray her husband in a positive light. On the subject of Terra Cimmeria, she saw the site selection as a great success: "Oh, we didn't find evidence to decide among the competing theories, but we have radically improved on the precision of the orbital data. Now we know exactly where we should plan new expeditions to definitively rewrite the geological history of Mars. Paolo already submitted a paper on that before the accident." She similarly saw the carbonate data as eliminating a lot of possibilities, pointing the way to new research.

And then she got to a crucial point: the reasons for the Chronius Mons trip. She saw it very differently than Tracy had. "That was in the back of Paolo's mind all along. That was why he insisted on bringing Wells on the expedition in the first place: he wanted to show humanity the grandeur of Mars, the grand vistas and the sweep of the unknown. He wanted to excite people, ignite their sense of adventure."

"Yes," Nick agreed, "he was a visionary. Or that's how he saw himself, which is visionary enough. It's what worried me about him: that vision blinded him to flaws in his plans. He had this sense that destiny would see him past any problems." Mrs. Azevedo didn't answer, but her face turned down. "And he would tackle any obstacle, follow any path for that destiny. How fortunate for him that he married into enough money to fund his visions."

"Nick!" Again I was stunned that even Nick could be so callous; but before I could say more, Mrs. Azevedo held up a hand to stop me. She glared at Nick.

"So that comes up again." Her tone was bitter. "You said as much during expedition planning. You think he married me for money?"

"Well, there are always many motivations that lead into a decision like that. You were young and attractive, and you bought into his vision. The money was just an added benefit; but as it happened, it was a crucial benefit in order for him to succeed."

When she answered, she spoke slowly, restraining her emotions: "I know you're a cynic, Nick. I know you will never understand what Paolo and I had. But to question it now . . . I didn't think even you could be that cruel."

Nick leaned back in his chair and shrugged. "You call it cruel, I call it diligent. I have to get some answers."

"Fine, here are your answers. I loved Paolo. He loved me. We had problems, everyone does, but we shared so much more than just Mars plans."

Nick looked down at his desk. "So noted. My apologies, but I have to be thorough. Please, continue."

Mrs. Azevedo looked at Nick, seemed to consider what to say, and then went on. Soon she got to the subject of supplying the expedition, and Nick again asked about the three tents. She seemed surprised by the question. "Why is that important?"

"I can't tell what's important," Nick explained. "Details matter. That's what I tried to tell your husband: details matter, and you can't guess which ones. So why three tents?"

"Well, we had them to spare, so why not? Paolo and I had a tent for ourselves. The command tent, as it were. Besides, we were entitled to our privacy. Ivan and Gale shared another tent, and Wells slept in the third. We divided supplies among the three tents so that an accident with one wouldn't affect other supplies. You should approve of precautions like that."

"Hmmm. Yes, I approve of precautions; but protocol here is entirely different. For a mission that size, two tents would have been proper: one for all of you to share, and one as a backup for that. It might be less comfortable to squeeze five into a tent, but it would've given adequate safety margins and less mass to transport."

"Yes, yes, I've read your recommendation. We decided we could handle the mass, and we wanted the comfort. And ultimately it had nothing to do with Paolo's accident, so can we just *drop it*?"

Nick didn't answer. He had made his point, so he let her continue. He also didn't comment when Mrs. Azevedo discussed their stops for the night; but even I could see that Tracy had been correct: the team had performed only perfunctory equipment inspections. Their uneventful time on Mars to that point had made them sloppy—or sloppier, as Nick would say.

And there was something else: something about the expedition had distressed her, and she had difficulty discussing it. She drew out the discussion with a lot of trivialities, stopping and repeating points. It took her twice as long to describe the trip as it had Tracy, and yet she revealed less. Was she just postponing the discussion yet to come? Maybe; but I saw Nick eyeing her carefully, as if he suspected something more.

And then finally she discussed the climb, and then the fall and the attempted rescue. She started to choke up when she got to the surgery, tears flowing; and Nick showed unexpected kindness by stopping her there. "That's enough, Margo. I only need to know what led to the incident. I have a clear picture of what came after. Carver, give her your handkerchief." I did, and she dabbed her eyes.

Nick was being uncharacteristically kind, but I knew it couldn't last. Sooner or later, he would point out again how this was all Professor Azevedo's fault. Before he could get the chance, I spoke up. "Captain, if we're done, Mrs. Azevedo has had a long day. Can I escort her back to her cabin?"

Nick seemed a little distant. "What?" Then he recovered. "Oh, yes, we're done here. But I've summoned Bosun Smith. She can see to Margo. I have more duties for you."

Just then the office door opened, and Smith, whom I knew to have a compassionate side when she needed it, came in. Nick was right: Mrs. Azevedo might appreciate having a woman's support after putting up with him. But he would never admit that was his motive.

Bosun Smith stood at attention. Nick looked at her, a question on his face. "Well?"

Smith lifted her sleeve comp and pushed a file to Nick's desk. "There's my full report, Captain. A number of items are missing, as indicated, and the necessary maintenance reports haven't been filed for much of the rest."

Nick nodded at Smith, then rose. "Margo, again, I'm sorry. If I could've prevented this pain for you, I would've. We'll talk again. Ms. Smith, please see Mrs. Azevedo to her cabin." Smith saluted and then offered an arm. Mrs. Azevedo took it and leaned on Smith's shoulder as they left the office.

When the door closed, I turned to Nick. My questions were the same as before. "I hate to repeat myself—"

"Then don't," Nick interrupted. "Everything is going as I planned."

"This is a plan?" I couldn't see how Nick would learn anything about the murder this way.

"Yes. I'm learning what I need to know. Besides, didn't you hear that undertone? There's something she's not saying, something she feels guilty about."

I hadn't heard it. I mean, I'd heard something wrong, and noted it; but I hadn't picked up on guilt. She was a grieving widow, I expected some distress. But Nick had always been better at reading people than I was. He himself might come across as a one-note scold and a control junkie, but he was excellent at ferreting out hidden motivations and secrets.

"What would she have to feel guilty about?" I asked.

"I don't know. I've no idea. For that I need the help of an incurable gossip. And so I guess it's time to speak with Horace Gale."

☾

I tracked down Lieutenant Gale in the rec lounge. As had been the norm on this trip, knots of expedition crew occupied the tables, and our off-duty crew hung near, each imagining what it must have been like to be down on Mars. But strangely, when I found Gale in the corner with Riggs, they were discussing soccer, not Mars.

"Yes, sir, Lieutenant." Riggs's enthusiasm was all over his face. He was eager to talk about soccer clubs with a fellow Brit. "Absolutely it's Manchester's year. They've been rebuilding for five now. It's their time."

"Well, Karl, I'm not so sure. Liverpool is looking pretty strong."

"Liverpool?" Riggs nearly exploded with laughter. "They'll barely finish the season. They're old and tired."

"You're right, you're right. Still, they have experience."

Riggs raised an eyebrow. "In soccer, sir, isn't that just another word for 'old'?"

"All right, they're old, I'll admit it." Gale laughed. "But just remember: in the Corps, it's not age, it's seniority." Riggs joined the laughter on that line, though I thought his sounded a bit forced.

I cleared my throat, and Gale looked up. "Yes, Chief Carver?"

"Lieutenant Gale, the captain would like to see you, sir."

"Oh, Nick causing trouble again, eh?"

"It's not my place to comment on what trouble the captain might cause, sir." I'm not normally that formal with an old shipmate, even if Gale and I didn't always see eye to eye; but in front of the junior crew, Gale deserved the respect due his rank. "If you'll come with me, please."

"I suppose. I knew this was coming eventually. Well, Mr. Riggs, it has been a pleasure. See you at the SP meeting?"

Riggs raised a glass to Gale. "Indeed, sir. Thank you."

We set off to the captain's cabin. As soon as we were alone, Gale turned to the subject I knew was coming. Despite our differences, Gale saw me as some kind of a friend. Who knows? Maybe I was as close to a friend as he got. Whenever we met socially, he *always* turned to this subject. "So, Carver, have you had enough of Aames and this tin can yet?"

I deflected. "The *Aldrin* is no tin can, Gale. It's a masterwork of engineering, and it gets better every cycle as we add rings and capacity."

But Gale wasn't about to let up so easily. "Yes, yes, but it's still a glorified transport ship. You're a fine officer, Anson, you deserve better. If you had the Space Professionals behind you, you might get a better posting."

The SPs were something of an "astronauts guild," though they never used that term. They advocated for more influence over mission planning. Ideally that would be something Nick would support. His feuds with the Initiative were legendary in the Corps. But Nick had laughingly rebuffed their efforts to recruit him, saying that they were more political than professional. And that included Gale, who had a lot of influence in the movement. As Nick explained it to me: "It's the only way a bumbler like Gale can hope to get work. Before long they'll have work rules that say I can't dismiss any crewmember any damned time I please; and next thing you know, someone'll get killed because of those rules. Why would I be part of that?"

Back on Mars, Nick hadn't been so harsh on Gale, who had succeeded Chief Maxwell as second-in-command. Gale got his full share of Aames's scorn, but Nick had trusted him as a capable member of the crew. But after Mars, most of us lost favor in the Corps because we had made uncomfortable but true statements about the poor planning and management of the mission. Gale, on the other hand, didn't. He played the political game, said all the things the admirals wanted him to say, and came out smelling like a rose. Nick never forgave him for that. And he never trusted Gale again.

So when Gale tried to recruit Nick into the Space Professionals, Nick laughed in his face. (Laughing was better than spitting, which had been my bet.) Since Gale had failed with Nick, he kept working on me, hoping I might influence Nick; but I found Nick's arguments to be irrefutable as usual. There were some good people in the SP, but a lot of them were just looking for more money for less work. I was tempted to answer as bluntly as Nick would; but instead I simply said, "I'm sorry, Gale, but I can't imagine a better posting than this, or a better commander than Captain Aames."

And with that, I opened the door to Nick's office. We entered to the sounds of bossa nova, but this time Nick didn't make us wait, turning off the e-reader immediately. "Ah, Horace." Nick exaggerated the name: *Hor*ace.

"Hello, Nick. So this is where you say 'I told you so'?"

Nick waved his hand dismissively. "Waste of my time. We both know it."

"Yes, but I'm sure you've just been waiting for the chance."

"No, I've been avoiding the lot of you as best I can. I may have to transport you, but that doesn't mean I have to sit here and listen to the mistakes I *knew* would happen."

Gale sat in the visitor's chair while I remained standing. "So, Nick, what's this about?"

"Well, *Hor*ace, we do need some discussion regarding the fate of your ill-planned mission."

"Yes." Gale sighed. "Get on with it."

"That final trip across the desert, it was just the five of you?"

"Yes: me, Paolo, Margo, Ivan, and Tracy."

"So you had five people, and yet you had three Mars tents. Wasn't that a little bit of excess weight to carry? You could've carried more consumables."

I was confused. *Again* with the tents? What did that have to do with the sabotage of Azevedo's cable? But Gale didn't seem to find the question unusual. "The Mars protocols—*which you wrote*—say we should have a backup for every piece of essential equipment. Mars isn't Earth, where we might survive without a tent."

"Yes, so two tents would give you a backup. But three? Those tents will hold six."

"Yes."

"So why did you have three? You didn't need them for storage."

"Well, we did store supplies separately in each tent. 'No single point of failure,' that's in the protocols too. If something happened to one supply cache, we would still have the others."

"Oh, so you didn't even reserve them as backups? You deployed all three tents?" Nick already knew that from Tracy and Mrs. Azevedo. I could only assume he was feigning ignorance to keep Gale talking.

"Yes. Paolo and Margo wanted their privacy, you know." Nick looked up, but Gale shook his head. "No, not for sex, for fighting. They did an awful lot of arguing on the expedition. I'm sure Margo regrets it now."

I nodded. That might explain the guilt that Nick had detected. But Nick showed no reaction and continued his questioning. "So the lovebirds insisted on their own tent. And the three of you remaining needed two tents because?"

"Well, Tracy insisted we should share a tent. 'That's the protocol,' she said, 'and I don't want to write up another variance.' The girl is almost as mad as you, Nick, always writing up variances and insisting on following protocols to the letter. She acted like *she* was in charge, not just a videographer. But Ivan said he wanted more space."

"I see. And you bunked with Ivan."

"Because Tracy was making such a row about protocols, I finally got fed up with her."

"But why, Horace? You knew she was right."

"Of course she was right."

"Then why—"

"*Because I didn't want to keep fighting about it!*" Gale was red-faced. Nick knew Gale's hot buttons; and Nick can never resist pushing buttons, testing to see where your breaking point is. It looked like he had found Gale's. "Why make such a big deal about it?"

Nick steepled his fingers and looked up at the ceiling. "I'm finding I have a new respect for Ms. Wells. If she annoyed you this much, she must've been doing something right." Gale scowled, and Nick smirked. "Same old Horace. You're smart enough to know what the right thing is, but you're too weak to fight for it."

"I heard enough of this from you before the expedition, and I am tired of it now."

"Good! If I provoke you enough, you *can* show a little backbone. But you never seem to when it matters. That's why Paolo chose you as Corps liaison, you know."

"What?"

"You won't argue with the wrong decision, even if you know it might get somebody killed. You're too eager to get along. You're too nice. Space doesn't give a damn about nice."

"If you're going to bring that up again, then I think this conversation is over."

"No. I'm still captain on this ship, and we're still outside the gravipause. This conversation is over when I say it's over. Chief Carver?"

I straightened. "Yes, Captain."

"If he tries to leave, sit on him."

"Yes, Captain."

"Horace, you are a weak man. You didn't used to be, but somewhere you lost your way. I wouldn't send my worst enemy on an expedition where you made the decisions. You won't stand up for what's right, and that may have gotten Paolo killed." Gale's face showed dismay, but not shock. Suddenly I was sure he had already reached the same conclusion, and guilt was tearing at him. I knew from our time on Mars that Gale was an opportunist, but he was a capable spacer, and he had a conscience buried deep inside. And then I was also sure: if he felt his mistakes might be responsible for Paolo's death, and he felt remorse at the possibility, then he couldn't be the murderer.

Gale seemed to rally, mounting a weak counteroffensive. "I needn't worry about sending men on an expedition with you, since no one in the Corps will have you."

"Nope, they won't. Knapp and the rest of the Initiative want a bunch of yes-men and toadies."

Gale sat looking at the floor in sullen silence. Nick let the silence hang for several seconds before continuing, "One more thing. What did Paolo and Margo argue about?"

It took Gale a few moments to answer. Finally he looked up at Nick. "I shouldn't say. It's a personal matter, and it's in bad form to mention it now. But I know you, Nick. You're going to gnaw on this until you get an answer, aren't you?" Nick just stared at Gale. Gale looked away. "All right, Margo was jealous of Tracy. She said several times that she was sure Paolo and Tracy were sleeping together." I winced, but I managed to control my reaction beyond that. "I'm not sure when they would've had the opportunity. It's very close quarters on Mars, and very tight schedules, as you know. But she was sure they were grabbing spare moments here and there. Certainly Paolo showed an excessive interest in Tracy."

"Ah, there we go. A classic motivation for mischief, eh?"

"Mischief? Who said anything about mischief?"

"Oh, I'm looking for motivations. That was one of Azevedo's biggest mistakes, you know. He didn't consider the range of interpersonal problems that might arise. And you didn't help him any." Gale glared again, and Nick returned to his previous tack. "So you have no reason to suspect foul play?"

"No! And especially not Margo! She couldn't have. They fought, but . . ."

"So she couldn't have. And you, no doubt, will proclaim your innocence. You're narrowing down the list of suspects."

"What's all this about suspects, Nick? What, you think some sort of crime was committed?"

"I am *certain* that a crime has been committed. Now I'm just trying to determine by whom. All right, Mr. Carver, I'm through with him. You can let him leave."

Gale stood stiffly and headed for the door. He glanced at me, but he turned away at my impassive response; and then he left.

I looked at Nick. "So I suppose you want me to summon Dr. Ivanovitch next?"

"Oh? No, I have no need to talk with the good doctor."

"You don't think he could've killed Azevedo? Maybe he sabotaged the cable; and then after Azevedo survived, he did a poor job of treating him?"

"No, I am quite certain that Dr. Ivanovitch is much too smart for this crime."

I didn't understand what intelligence had to do with it; but I knew Nick would explain when he was ready, and not until. So I tried another line of questioning. "At last you've gotten around to the subject of the crime; but why didn't you ask Gale about the cable?"

"Trust me, I'm very curious about the cable. But I was waiting to see if he would bring it up."

"What? Why would he do that?"

"Why, indeed? That's what I've been waiting for: one of them to bring up the cable."

"Nick, that makes no sense. The *last* thing the murderer would want to do is draw attention to the cable. That's evidence."

"Ummhmmm." But Nick said no more. He just stared at me as if waiting for me to reach some obvious conclusion. But whatever that conclusion was, it eluded me.

Besides, I had another concern tugging at my mind. "What's with your obsession with their sleeping arrangements? You don't seriously believe that Tracy was . . ."

"Whether *I* believe it or not is inconsequential. And I'm not sure why it matters to you, either, if you're over her like you say you are. But if it soothes your worries any: no, I don't believe it. Unless she's fooling me—and she's not—she has changed. She's too professional to risk the expedition over an affair.

"But what matters is: does Margo believe it? If so, that might have motivated her anger during the expedition, as Gale said; and perhaps it motivates her guilt now. This is a complex case, and it's all about motivations at this point. I understand the crime, so now I just need to understand who had a motive."

"So what now? More interviews? Whom do I fetch next?"

Nick shook his head. "No more interviews quite yet. I need to think. Tell Bosun Smith I have some errands for her, and then you can go about your duties."

Nick didn't bother dismissing me. I knew him well enough to know I was dismissed when he turned on the e-reader, and music started playing. It was another classic, "Parece Mentira," from an old Brazilian saying: "It seems like a lie."

But instead of going about my duties, my watch was over. Not that that really mattered: on Nick's ship, you were off duty when Nick said you were off duty, and not until. And that was doubly true for me as his second-in-command. Still, I had nothing on my schedule; and I had had a long, emotionally draining day already. I needed to unwind like I hadn't needed in nearly four years. So I headed back to the rec lounge.

But when I got there, I knew I wouldn't be able to escape my troubles after all. Tracy was there, and she had a large audience gathered for a preview of the final cut of her big documentary. There was a large mix of expedition members and *Aldrin* crew. Tracy opened with some production notes and then started the show, but she stopped occasionally for more notes or to invite comments from expedition members. Riggs sat in the front, right next to Gale, and he asked lots of questions and took notes on Gale's answers. Gale seemed relaxed and at ease, as if his feud with Nick had never happened. He had always been able to put up a good front.

But my attention was reserved for Tracy. She had cleaned up for this presentation, switching to a freshly pressed jumpsuit. She had let her hair down so it hung around her shoulders the way I always liked it. Again I smelled lilac water, and I tried to shake it out of my memory; but it wouldn't go away. Her eyes lit up as she explained details of the expedition and her filming; and she was an engaging speaker, as always. I knew that wasn't just my heart speaking, as the crowd hung on her every word. But the documentary stood on its own just fine even without her production notes and her enthusiasm.

It was *really* good. She covered the highlights of planning and training. She showed just enough of the flight out on the *Collins* to give the flavor without losing the viewer in the tedium of five months in orbit. She vividly captured the blend of exhilaration and terror of landing in the Ishiro-class shuttles. She showed the camp setup and the scientific experiments, including both the disappointments and the tantalizing hints for the future.

And she covered Professor Azevedo's death. Oh, she had no film of the incident itself. The rescue had taken all their efforts. But she had a computer animation of the scene, with stick figures tastefully substituted for the real participants. She showed exactly what went wrong—except, of course, she didn't mention the salt contamination. Nick hadn't revealed that yet, and if Tracy knew . . . No, I didn't want to contemplate how she might know.

I was still wrapped up in these thoughts, not even noticing that the film had ended, when I felt a tap on my shoulder. Before I turned, the scent of lilacs swept over me. It was Tracy. Old habits took over before I could even think, and I smiled at her. When she smiled back at me, I almost reached out for her; but at least I held that reaction in check.

"So what did you think?" she asked as she sat across from me.

"I . . ." I searched for the words. Then I decided to just be up-front. "It's brilliant. Your best work ever."

"Thank you, Anson. That means a lot."

"Except in your report to Nick, you were so harsh on Azevedo and his team for their poor planning. You didn't miss a note, and you didn't pull a punch. And yet none of that came through here."

Tracy hesitated. I could see that I had caught her in a conflict. "Anson, there are two stories of the expedition: the story of what went wrong, and the story of what went right. A lot went wrong, and that's all in my reports; but even with all the inconclusive experiments, even with the professor's death, he accomplished his primary goals. He showed that Mars is a place where *people* will go, not just an elite group of professional astronauts. And where people go, people will die. People make mistakes. We're not all perfect robots. We're not all Nick Aames. If we let imperfection stop us, we'll never go anywhere."

"Imperfection gets people killed."

"Yes, and perfection can't always save them either. Have you forgotten the *Bradbury*?"

I would never forget the *Bradbury*, and she knew that. We had lost a lot of good crew in that incident. "But don't you feel like this is a lie?"

"No, it's the other side of the story. When we get to Earth, I know the media will be full of reports of the accident again—my *own* reports.

They're going to give Gale and that bunch another weapon to use in their argument: 'Space isn't safe for ordinary people. Leave it to us professionals.' They will find reasons to be safe, to avoid risks. We can't afford that. We need people to take chances. That was the professor's goal and Margo's goal, and it's still my goal. I thought it was a goal you understood."

I understood, but I understood Nick's point of view as well. I felt like they were doing it to me again, forcing me to choose all over again between his caution and her dreams.

I couldn't choose, so I said nothing; and I saw disappointment in her face. Once more, I hadn't chosen her. I hadn't chosen Nick, either, but I hadn't chosen her.

But it seemed she wasn't ready to give up, not again. She pulled her chair around beside mine, uncomfortably close. The lilac water couldn't be imaginary, as clear as the scent was. She must've preserved a vial. I remembered other nights when I smelled it so close, and I squirmed; but Tracy didn't seem to notice. "We were there for seven months. I've got months of footage to work with. This won't be my only documentary coming out of the expedition. There will be one that tells the mistakes quite thoroughly. But this is the one that I need to tell now. The one that shows: *We can do this!*" She opened her comp so I could see it. "Here. This is my *real* last scene. I haven't included it yet because I want to get Margo's approval first. But it's important that you see this, that you understand."

She tapped her comp, and a new scene appeared. It was Mrs. Azevedo in a shelter in the camp. Her eyes were red from recent tears, but she had a defiant look on her face. The shelter was darkened with a hint of red, probably from natural Martian daylight outside; but a mild light shone down on her from above, accentuating the shadows in her face. She leaned forward, directly into the camera. "Am I going to give up? No. Never! If I give up, *then* Paolo is dead. When his dream dies, then I bury him in my heart. Until then . . . No, there is no then.

I won't give up, not ever. But maybe others will. Maybe I'll have no choice. But my words, my money, my time, my power, I'll use them all for Paolo's dream. People *will* come here, they'll keep coming here. And they'll remember Paolo, and how his spirit calls them to come here and live here and work here. And some of them . . . Well, they'll be brave like Paolo. They'll know the risks."

And then the scene rolled back in time and space, all the way back to Earth, back to the earliest days of training. Professor Azevedo sat in a tent that bore a superficial resemblance to the Mars shelter; but the light was bright and blue white, and Azevedo sat back in his chair. He wore a stubbly beard of gray with flecks of white, much like the hair that stuck out from his knit cap. I suspected they were on a mountain trip. He looked into the camera, and he smiled that smile that had won over so many skeptics. "Will people die in this program? Of course they'll die, what kind of question is that? It's the old pioneers' creed: 'The cowards never started, and the weak died along the way.' People die on the frontier, and that's no reason not to go. The ones who survive will be the strong and the smart and the lucky and the just-too-tough-to-kill."

From off screen, Tracy asked, "And which are you?"

His grin broadened. "There's only one way to find out. And no matter what, I *will* find out. Gladly. How about you?" And he laughed. And the screen faded to black, and white letters appeared: "Paolo Azevedo, PhD, Founder of the Civilian Expedition Program. 2021–2074."

I stared at the simple words, dumbstruck. Tracy's video made her argument far more eloquently than her words had. In that moment, I wanted to take her in my arms and tell her I was wrong. I wanted to take her to Mars.

And so, with his usual uncanny timing, that was the moment Nick's voice came from my comm. "Chief Carver, we're almost to the gravipause, and I'm ready to conclude our business. Please bring Mrs. Azevedo, Lieutenant Gale, and Ms. Wells to my office immediately."

I ushered the expedition members into Nick's office. By unspoken understanding, the others left the sole guest chair to Mrs. Azevedo. She sat and looked at Nick.

Nick stood behind his desk. In his hand he held a coil of S3 cable. He looked across the faces and then began to speak. "Well, here we are. One last time together. We're entering Earth's orbit, we've passed the gravipause, so this ship is now back under the authority of the System Initiative. So I guess that wraps up my investigation."

"Investigation?" They were all thinking it, but Mrs. Azevedo was the one who asked, "What investigation?"

"Oh, the investigation into this S3 cable. It has been an internal matter to this point, but now it's time to present my findings to you all before I report to the Initiative. Ensign Riggs has found conclusive evidence that this cable has been contaminated with salt ions, destroying its integrity; and then it stretched until it broke." Mrs. Azevedo turned pale, but Nick gave her no time to interrupt. "Furthermore, there's no doubt that this contamination was *deliberate*."

This time Mrs. Azevedo did break in. "Deliberate? Paolo . . . ?"

But she got no further, and Nick continued, "Someone wanted it to break. It's also clear that the cable is from your trip to Chronius Mons. Ms. Wells's inventory reports are quite thorough, and they document precisely which gear you took with you."

Tracy said, "But Mrs. Azevedo couldn't—"

Nick interrupted her, nodding. "You're right, she couldn't. Oh, people do surprising things, angry spouses especially. Gale told me how Margo was jealous of you, Tracy, jealous that Paolo had his eye on you."

Mrs. Azevedo stood, too fast for the low gravity. "That's a lie!" In her anger, she ignored her unexpected bounce, but Nick seemed amused. "We were past all of that months ago. Paolo convinced me he had no interest in this little *girl*. We made up, and we were closer than . . ." She glared at Nick. "But how could I convince a cynic like you? You always believe the worst of people. What would you know about two people in love?"

That stopped Nick cold, and his face showed something close to sympathy. Then he shook his head. "No, I believe you. A gossip like Horace always exaggerates what he knows. But just because Paolo had no interest doesn't mean *Tracy* had no interest."

This time it was Tracy who was angry. "That's ridiculous! I would *never* let personal feelings endanger the team. I admired the professor, and I was grateful to be on this expedition; but that's *all* there was between us."

"Is it? Did you know, Ms. Wells, that when you broke up with Carver, he wondered if perhaps you had your sights set on Professor Azevedo?"

"What?" Tracy practically shouted; and at the same time I said, "Nick, that's out of line!"

"Oh, he was quite sure of that for a while. He said a lot of bitter things when he was drunk."

"Anson! You didn't believe that?"

"Tracy, I was hurt. I . . . No, I didn't believe it, I just didn't know what to believe. I wanted some explanation."

"And maybe . . ." Nick broke back in. "Maybe he was correct. Motivations, that's what we're after here. Was it perhaps the woman scorned? And that brings us back to this cable." Nick held up the cable for us all to see. "I had Bosun Smith bring me this cable from the lab because there was one piece of information missing from our earlier report: the RFID tag woven into the cable end. And guess what? It's *not* one that Professor Azevedo packed in his gear."

"What do you mean?"

"Ms. Wells, the RFID tag is clear, and your meticulous inventory is equally clear: this cable came from your personal supplies. You had it stowed in your tent each night before the climb. Oh, and Bosun Smith also searched the rest of the expedition's supplies very carefully; and the professor's cable is nowhere to be found. She checked the tag on every cable. Someone swapped this sabotaged cable for his."

Someone swapped . . . And Tracy had packed this cable. And . . .

No. I couldn't believe that. Tracy had surprised me before. She had disappointed me. She had broken my heart. But this? No. I knew that was impossible. I loved her, it couldn't be possible.

But Nick was drawing the conclusions I refused to draw. "So the cable Paolo packed, the cable that would've been in his tent every night where Margo had access to it? That cable's missing. And the cable you packed, Ms. Wells? That cable's sabotaged."

Tracy grew livid. "What are you implying?"

"I'm presenting facts, not implications. Now that we're in Earth orbit, it's up to the Initiative to make decisions from these facts. My duty is to report what I know, not to speculate."

"So what will you report?"

"The facts exactly as I know them. I will report that this cable is not Professor Azevedo's, it is yours. I will report that it was under your control the entire time it was on Mars. Professor Azevedo's cable is missing, and no one in the expedition crew admits to knowing where it is. I will report that this cable has been contaminated with salt-affixing nanomachines. And I'll report all the rest of our findings, and they can draw whatever conclusions they may."

"And I will get a good lawyer to ensure that your accusations never make it into my record."

"I'm not making accusations. The conclusions should be obvious to anyone with half a brain, so I expect the review board to miss them entirely."

"And what are *you* going to do, Captain?" Tracy asked.

"Nothing, and you know it. Now that we've passed the gravipause, my powers are strictly curtailed. I can't hold you. I have no authority here over anyone but my crew."

"Well, that's good news, because I'm innocent. As soon as the funeral's done, I'll clear my name."

I knew that determined look on Tracy's face. Every bit of self-control was at work, holding back her anger, and maybe her tears. I wanted to comfort her, but I had to stand my post. She looked at me, and I almost broke; but then she left for the docking bay.

No one else spoke. Mrs. Azevedo stood. She stared at Nick, her expression unreadable. Then Gale offered her an arm, and they left.

C

I hadn't been dismissed, and I had no orders, so I had nothing to do but stand there and stew over all that I had just heard. Stand and stew and stare at Nick.

Nick ignored me for almost a minute and a half; but finally he spoke. "Don't stand there glowering at me. Can't you make yourself useful?"

"Glowering? Really?"

"It's the perfect word to describe your expression, and I get to use it so seldom. But get over it already. Ms. Wells will be fine. In fact, I've entered a commendation into her record." I must have looked puzzled, so Nick explained, "The silly little girl who broke your heart is gone. That woman who just left here is the only one on that whole team who understands how to properly plan a mission. I can't guess what changed her, but I can't deny the change. Azevedo was an ass. He chose his expedition members for their willingness to fawn over him and for how popular they would be with the press. Plus a bunch of other *entirely* personal reasons: camaraderie, influence, favors, you name it, anything but competence. But with her, despite himself, he got lucky. The only one whom he chose who was worth a damn was Ms. Wells, and even I wouldn't've guessed that. She surprised me."

"What?"

"Look at her reports, Carver. Look at what she's done. Look at everything. Despite my doubts, that woman has shown that the discipline we need in space can be found far outside the Corps. The people who want to go to space, the ones who really *should* be there, are going to do it right. I couldn't have predicted it four years ago; but if I had to staff a mission and my choices were 'professionals' like Gale or an amateur like Ms. Wells, I would choose her without hesitation."

"But I thought— I thought you blamed Tracy. You practically accused her of murder."

Nick sighed, his "you are beyond an idiot" sigh. "There was no murder here, Carver."

"No murder?"

Nick tapped his desk, and the comm chime sounded. "Mr. Riggs, you can come in now." The door to the office opened, and Riggs entered, looking nervous as usual when crewmen are summoned before Nick. I ushered him in, and he stood at attention before Nick's desk.

Nick wasted no time on pleasantries. He sat and looked up at Riggs, who stood neatly at attention. "Ensign Karl Riggs. What do you know about salts in chemistry?"

"Not much, Captain, I'll admit. I know I like salt on my chips!" It was a weak joke, and weaker in Riggs's delivery. Nick had the man nervous, which wasn't unusual.

"Ah, that's right, you said you're weak in chemistry. Unlike Ms. Wells, say. Quite a surprise, that chemistry degree of hers. It gave me a whole new perspective on that discovery of yours.

"Mr. Riggs, a salt is a compound wherein a positive and a negative ion exactly counter each other, yielding a neutral end product. They can be quite useful both biologically and in other reactions, and it's very hard for us to get by without them. That's why we've manufactured nano lines that can scavenge or even assemble the necessary ions from available stock."

"I see, sir."

"But nanomachines don't have *brains*, Riggs. They only have simple chemical sensors, valence detectors particularly. They look for the proper valences, grab the ions, and affix them to other ions or to a substrate. They're really just glorified enzymes in a sense. If they can't find the precise valence signature, and yet they're still active, some of them will grab the nearest equivalent they can find: something close enough to the right ionic properties.

"Ah, but something close electrically can still be chemically a very different salt. For instance . . ." Nick pulled up Riggs's report on his desk comp. "The nanos in these micrographs you took were designed to scavenge carbonate items out of Mars's atmosphere, with its high concentration of carbon dioxide. It's almost 95 percent CO2, did you know that?"

"Well, I knew something like that, sir."

"Yes. And in fact, Azevedo chose his site because of the high presence of carbonates, perfect for these nanos. But if they can't find the carbon ions they're designed for, many of them will find the next closest valence. For example, a nitrite ion would be electrically identical to a carbonate ion, and a nitrate might be close enough for a nano's detectors.

"Now there's something interesting about these micrographs you took. If you look at the chemical analysis attached—as I did when you brought them to me—you will find that the S3 cables have been contaminated with *nitrite* salts, and also a smaller proportion of nitrate salts, *not* carbonate salts. That means that when those nanos were active, they found predominantly nitrogen stock, not carbon dioxide. Nitrogen, you know, the stuff that makes up 79 percent of standard air mix."

Riggs was silent. His normally fair complexion had turned even more pale.

"In fact, since they get much of their stock from the surrounding air, that implies that this contamination happened in a nitrogen atmosphere. Now you won't find that on Mars, as I said. It's nearly all

CO2. And you wouldn't even find it in the expedition's shelters. They used heliox as their breathing gas to lower their payload mass. That, by the way, is why I was so insistent on confirming the details of which Mars tents were used and where and how the gear was stowed. I needed to be *certain* that I knew where these cables had been and what they might've been exposed to; and all three expedition members confirmed for me that the gear was safely stored in the Mars tents every night, in the heliox conditions. There would be trace amounts of nitrogen, surely, but it should be completely dominated by carbon dioxide. There was no chance for contamination there, so there's only one place this contamination could have happened."

I couldn't keep quiet. "On the ship!"

"Yes, on the ship, Chief Carver. And since these cables were very thoroughly inspected and recorded by Ms. Wells—I'm quite astonished at her meticulous records, Carver, you could learn something from her—we can be certain that the cables were not contaminated when they left the *Collins*. And so the contamination could only have happened aboard the *Aldrin*—*after* Professor Azevedo's all-too-avoidable death."

Riggs found his voice. "I see, sir."

"Oh, I'm quite sure you do. And Mr. Carver is starting to see as well, though I think you had a head start on him. I knew right away: I wasn't investigating a murder, I was investigating a frame-up. Someone is trying to frame someone for Azevedo's death, and I needed to know who the someone was.

"So I had to ask myself the traditional questions: Who had means? Who had motive? Who had opportunity? At first I thought Ms. Wells had opportunity. She could've gotten to the cable at any time; and once we learned it was *her* cable, the opportunities expanded. But no, even before that, I learned of her chemistry degree. No chemist would make that mistake with the atmospheric ions. They would know it was a waste of time.

"As for Margo, what would she gain by making Azevedo's death look like murder? Not much. For one thing, the spouse is *always* the first, most likely suspect in a homicide, especially given their well-known fights. Oh, in theory she might have tried to frame Ms. Wells by swapping the cables; but Margo had too much to lose either way. Her whole media campaign is about Azevedo's great judgment, his people instincts that helped him to select an elite team of scientist-explorers, the best of the best. If people think he let a murderer on his crew, his entire myth falls apart. Not that I put any stock in that myth, mind you, but her investors do. She wouldn't do anything to endanger that myth. It would ruin her.

"And Horace?" Nick chuckled. "What would he gain out of it? Cast suspicion on Margo, maybe? Hardly. He needs her. He's a joke in the Corps. Yes, I know he's a bigwig to you SPs, but no one in the Initiative trusts his decisions. He needs this Civilian Exploration Program to succeed if he wants to stay employed. Oh, I considered briefly that Horace might have a motive: if Azevedo's death was murder, then it couldn't be blamed on Horace's poor planning. He could've been trying to duck responsibility. But Horace just isn't that clever. Besides, he may be a damned fool, but he's well versed in the atmospheric chemistry of Mars. He couldn't make that mistake any more than Ms. Wells could."

I broke in. "And that's why you didn't question Dr. Ivanovitch either. You knew his chemistry knowledge ruled him out as a suspect."

"Yes."

"Then why'd you interview Gale at all?"

Nick grinned. "Because it amuses me to rub his nose in his mistakes. *And* I wanted his perspective on the personalities of the expedition. Horace Gale may be a pompous ass, but he's also a political climber. He always knows the gossip.

"But that was before I realized I was looking in *entirely* the wrong direction, because I was only looking at the expedition personnel. If the sabotage happened here, that added dozens of potential suspects from our own crew. Mr. Riggs?"

Riggs was slow to respond. "Captain?"

"Reports are that you seem to be very friendly with Gale."

"Yes, sir. We worked together in the past. I trained under him on my first post. And besides, he's the only other Brit on board. It's nice to talk soccer with someone."

"Indeed. My reports are that you've spent pretty much all your free time with him."

"Can you blame me, sir? It's a chance to talk to a real explorer. Someone different on this ship, you know."

"Ummhmmm. Perhaps you forget: both Chief Carver and I have already been to Mars, on the second *Bradbury* expedition, right along with Lieutenant Gale. I do hope we're 'real' enough for you." Riggs took the rebuke without blinking, and Nick continued, "And you—and you're not alone in this, so don't take offense—you've voiced concern in the past that the CEP is a mistake, and missions like this should be Corps missions. 'Leave space to the professionals,' I believe that's what the SP activists say."

"I'm entitled to my opinion, Captain. As you say, I'm not alone. We Space Professionals have a lot of influence in the Corps command."

"Yes, yes, just what we need: more politics in the space program. Be that as it may, it looks like, despite poor planning and one unfortunate death, *this* expedition met most of their mission objectives. I would hazard a guess that Mrs. Azevedo's investors will be pleased overall, and will invest in further CEP expeditions. Once she buries her husband, Margo still has the clout and the drive and the financing to mount another expedition, and another."

"I wouldn't know, sir."

"Oh, trust me, she does. These decisions are being made politically these days, not sensibly. And I'm sure you believe it as well."

"Y-yes, sir."

"But now *if* Margo were to be implicated in a murder—or for that matter, if any of the senior staff were, it hardly matters who—it would throw everything into disarray. Suddenly there would be investigations, there would be questions, there would be doubts. Investors would get nervous and pull financing. The Corps would feel pressure from the Space Professional contingent, and would likely push to cancel the CEP. The next mission would likely be under Corps command, probably under Horace Gale himself; and he would pick his loyal crew."

Nick still held the coil of S3 cable in his hand, looking down at it, not at Riggs. "I have a report from your supervisor that you may be leaving us."

"Sir?"

"He says you've applied for a transfer."

"Well, yes, sir, just considering it."

"Yes, and a chance to ingratiate yourself with them as well, especially with Horace Gale. Looking at the letters of recommendation you've requested—"

"Sir!"

"Pshht. You think any communication goes out from this ship without me knowing about it? Please. What kind of a captain would I be if I didn't keep up with details on my vessel? So it looks like in fact you're hoping for reassignment to the Mars expedition on their next trip."

"Well . . ."

"And lo and behold, with the news from this expedition, there are sure to be some vacancies on that crew. Azevedo dead, and now Ms. Wells tied up in legal battles, the whole CEP in jeopardy. There should be a complete shakeup. It's likely the Space Professionals will get their way. Gale will end up in charge, and there could be an opening for the right man."

"Well, I guess."

"Oh, most certainly. Horace would want to take his chosen crew with him, men he knew and trusted. And you hope to be one of them."

"Captain . . ."

"Oh, don't deny it. As I was told, three-quarters of my crew applied for that last expedition, you included. But there will be some difficulty with your transfer, I'm afraid." Nick touched the comm control on his desk. "Bosun, come in, please."

The office door opened, and Bosun Smith came in. She carried another coil of S3 cable.

"Well?" Nick looked from Smith to the cable.

Smith nodded. "It was in his cabin, sir, just like you said it would be. I found it coiled up in his pillowcase, crammed in between the bunk and the wall. You'd never notice it without a search. Well, *you* might, Captain, but not the average person." She handed the cable to Nick. "The RFID tag confirms that it's Professor Azevedo's cable."

Nick stood slowly, came around his desk, and stood nose to nose with Riggs. He didn't yell. That's when I know Nick is *really* angry, not just domineering. He gets very calm. He looked at Riggs and said, "Get off my ship."

Riggs swallowed. "Sir?"

"You lied to me, Mr. Riggs."

"Captain, I—"

"Don't bother denying or explaining. We may be inside the gravi-pause; but when it comes to my crew, I am still judge, jury, and lord high executioner. And I do *not* want to hear more lies. I'm a realist. I know people lie for all sorts of stupid reasons. It's part of their nature. But *not* to me, and *not* on my ship. That gets people killed, and I won't tolerate that. Bosun, escort Mr. Riggs to his cabin. Watch him pack his kit. If he tries to go anywhere else or talk to anyone else, slam him into the nearest bulkhead. Twice. Once he's packed, escort him to the docking bay and confine him there until the ferry arrives."

"Yes, Captain." Smith didn't grin, but her eyes did. She was half again as large as Riggs, and she knew how to fight dirty. I think she wanted Riggs to make trouble. But he didn't: he just left, and Smith followed.

My head spun. It was like it had been tossed into microgravity, and all the facts I thought I had learned that day had been tumbled into space and rearranged themselves. I had been wrong. About all of it. And about Tracy. But Nick—I looked at him. "But if you knew this already, why didn't you say so? Why did you let Tracy twist in the wind? Why did you let her suffer? She left here practically in tears!"

Nick sat in his chair, leaned back, knotted his fingers before him, and looked at me for several seconds. "Carver, you may have gotten over what she put you through, but I still had a bit of a grudge to work out. She almost cost me the best junior officer I've ever had. She appears to have grown up since then, but she had still earned a little suffering for that. And I knew *you* would never give her what she deserved, so I had to do it."

"You planned that?"

"It was a simple calculation. I had nothing to gain. It's not like exonerating her is going to endear me to her. It's far too late for that. But I had nothing to lose as well. It's not like she could hate me any more than she already did. So I might as well play the villain."

"So you were cruel to her just because you had nothing to lose?"

"You missed the final line in my calculation: *I* would gain nothing by exonerating her; but if *you* get on that shuttle and present the evidence that clears her name, you're her hero. You'll come in and save her from my vile accusation."

I blinked. Nick playing matchmaker? But . . . "No. I can't play games like that with her. I won't lie to her."

"Oh, don't be a complete ass, Carver. Tell her a lie, tell her the truth for all I care, but don't you *dare* let her leave you behind the way she did last time. That woman is going to space, with or without you. So get going before you miss that shuttle. I don't need you moping around for another six months. Go work out whatever it is you two have to work out."

"Thank you, sir." I leaped for the door.

"Oh, one last thing." Nick halted me on the threshold. "The *Aldrin* leaves Earth for Mars in two months, with or without you. If I'm wrong, and she's not going back to space . . . If I'm going to need a new chief officer, please try to give me enough time to find a replacement who can measure up to your standards."

"Yes, Nick. Permission to go ashore, Captain?" But Nick ignored me, turning his e-reader on instead. Once again I heard "Brigas Nunca Mais." Without waiting for an answer, I was already in the outer office and heading for the passageway.

I *would* be back aboard the *Aldrin*. I was certain of that. And I was just as sure that next time I wouldn't be alone. That would give Nick something to complain about, so everyone would be happy.

9. Grand Gestures

From the memoirs of Park Yerim

9 June 2083

As we walked along the track, I shook my head in disbelief.

"What's the matter, Inspector?" Carver asked.

"I can't see it," I said. "So this man, who you think of as your friend—"

"He is," Carver insisted. "My best friend in the Three Worlds, save only my wife."

"That's just it. He tormented Ms. Wells, the woman you loved, out of some petty sense of revenge. That's a friend? And then said he did it to make you look good, and you believed him?"

Carver slowed his pace, and he shrugged. "Yeah, when you put it that way, he sounds pretty awful. But it all worked out. Tracy and I came back to the *Aldrin*, and we got reacquainted on the trip back to Mars. When we parted that time, we knew it wouldn't be forever. She filmed another documentary and helped plan new Mars settlements; and the next time the *Aldrin* came around, we were married. There were a couple of long years in there, but we were never really separated. Only by distance. I would say Nick's plan worked out fine."

"Huh." I didn't want my skepticism to show through, but I couldn't help myself. "It seems far-fetched to call it a plan. I would say it's just one more example that Captain Aames is a manipulative bastard."

At that, Carver stopped walking, and he laughed. I turned back to him as he said, "You're not the first to call him that. I could make a list." Then he caught his breath. "But I don't think you understand; it wasn't manipulation, it was . . ." He paused. "In Nick's eyes, it was a grand romantic gesture."

At that it was my turn to laugh. "Romantic? *Aames?* Of all the words used to describe him, that's one I've never heard."

Carver nodded. "I'm sure. But in his own way, yes, Nick is a great romantic. And he's especially fond of grand gestures. He can be awkward with them, but he makes the effort if you know what to look for. It's the day-to-day stuff where he slips up."

"I'm sorry," I said. "I just have trouble believing the most hated man in space is some closet romantic."

Carver sighed. "All right, maybe I can make my point with another story. Well, it's really a story of a story, one I told Tracy at our wedding. She had her doubts, just like you, and she wouldn't let up until I told her a story to explain what was really going on with Nick."

10. Brigas Nunca Mais

Off-the-record account of Chief Anson
Carver

Covering events of 24 November 2078 and also 21
June 2050 to 30 October 2052

I hadn't intended to spend our entire wedding reception talking about Captain Nick Aames. Really, I hadn't. But Nick has a way of working his way into events even when he's not trying to, especially events on the *Aldrin*, his ship. I'd be damned before I'd let him ruin our wedding night! So when Tracy asked a bunch of questions about Nick, I figured it was better to get them out of the way immediately, not later when we were alone.

It all started with the reception line. We stood just outside the chapel, a small one by Earth measure, but a pretty large space by the *Aldrin's*, large enough for our sixty guests. The rest of the ship had watched by video. The ceilings were no higher than standard deck height, but the simulated wood grain and some creative use of lighting and pillars implied depth up there. Overall, the chapel felt spacious compared to the rest of the ship. It was decorated all in lilacs. Oh, not real ones, we didn't have the budget for that; but little purple silk blossoms were tastefully arranged on pillars and pews.

By contrast, the passageway outside was just another ship's passageway: narrow and functional and gray, though Bosun Smith had continued the lilac decorations out there. Tracy looked stunning in her dress, a white ensemble that practically floated in the quarter G of the *Aldrin*'s main habitat ring. Her veil was clipped back behind her dark, elegantly styled hair, and her deep-brown eyes were aglow. The corners of her eyes were lifted by a smile, and I couldn't stop staring at her. If I could see only one thing for the rest of my life, I would want it to be Tracy's smile. And if I could smell only one thing, let it be the lilac water she wore.

Like the rest of the officers, I was in white as well, my dress whites, which never felt quite right to me: more like equipment than clothes. I was awkwardly aware of all the places where it didn't fit the way it was designed.

I saw someone who was perfectly comfortable in *her* dress whites; but then, she had been wearing them for a lot more years than I had. Admiral Morais, my former commander, had rearranged her schedule literally for months so that she could join us on the *Aldrin* as it swung around Mars. I was honored beyond words, and I beamed when she came up through the line. "Admiral." I snapped a salute.

Morais returned my salute. "At ease, Chief Carver. You can relax for a day. You're off duty."

I relaxed as much as I could in full dress—maybe 5 percent or so—and I got Tracy's attention. "Tracy, honey, this is Admiral Morais. I've told you about her. Admiral, my wife, Tracy Wells."

"Tracy Wells-*Carver*, Anson. Get used to that." Tracy smiled more broadly, and I melted. (Would I ever stop doing that? I hoped not.) Then she hugged the admiral, and I cringed. I wasn't sure how this fit with protocol.

But I needn't have worried. Morais returned the hug, with only a slight reserve. If Tracy had breached protocol, Morais was too classy to react. Instead she just smiled back. "Dr. Wells-Carver. Delighted! I loved *Pioneers' Creed*. I can't wait to see your next documentary."

Tracy's smile couldn't get any broader, but I could feel how happy she was. "You've seen *Creed*?"

Morais nodded. "Tracy, everyone on Mars has seen it, over and over. They've seen your whole series. You captured the real Mars experience."

"Admiral." Tracy hesitated, very unlike her. "I'm flattered."

"You deserve it. When this affair is over, I would enjoy a chance to talk with you and Chief Carver in less crowded circumstances."

"Absolutely. I want to hear all the news."

Then they hugged again; and the admiral, mindful of the crowd backing up behind her, moved down the line to Nick. "Captain Aames," she said. You would have to know Morais well to detect the amusement in those words. She knew Nick hated formalities like this.

"Admiral." The captain and the admiral saluted, stiffly. While I greeted our other guests, half my attention was reserved for Nick and the admiral. Nick clashing with the brass was as predictable as an orbit, but I hoped he would be on his best behavior for Tracy's sake. He had been reluctant to attend at all, only agreeing to be my best man after I had harangued him for weeks; but he had cleaned up nicely for the occasion. His red-gray hair and beard had been trimmed neatly, and *his* dress whites fit precisely, like he was born in them. He was slightly short, but I almost never noticed that. Nick acted tall—a tall presence, even around senior officers like Morais.

"The *Aldrin* is a very fine vessel, Captain," Morais said. "I see the new habitat rings are completed."

"Completed and half-booked. It's getting a bit crowded aboard." Nick was proud of his command, but he didn't like many people. The more the *Aldrin* grew, the more he huddled in his black-walled office and let me deal with passengers and crew. "I would offer you an inspection tour, but—"

"Orbital mechanics waits for no man," Morais replied with an old cliché of the space business. "Still, we'll have time for a fine reception, and for our dance."

Nick's face was stony. "I'll have to pass on the dance. It was bad enough Carver got me into this suit. Dancing wasn't part of the agreement."

The admiral shook her head. "I must insist. Protocol demands an officers' dance; and as senior officers present, we must set an example. Plus it would be good to test those legendary dance moves of yours."

Nick started to steam. "My ship, my rules. Pass."

The admiral's face tightened. She wasn't angry—not yet—but she was heading that way. "*My* gravipause, *my* rules, *Captain*. Anson Carver is one of the finest young officers I have ever commanded, and I will see him shown the proper respect."

I tried to defuse the tension. "Admiral, it's all right, we don't need—"

But Morais would have none of that. "It's *all right*, Chief Carver, because Captain Aames knows he's going to accede to protocol and my request. We *will* show proper respect to you and your lovely bride. And we'll do it without my having to make it a formal command and an incident in his record. Won't we, Captain?" She stared directly at Nick.

I expected Nick to bristle even further. The only records he cared about were safety and mission objectives. Threatening his personal record usually made him laugh.

But Nick surprised me. He stared right back, never breaking the fiery eye contact, and answered, "As you wish, Admiral."

☽

Tracy and I had twenty minutes of privacy between the receiving line and the reception: just enough to build up anticipation, not enough to do anything about it. Not properly, anyway. But we did spend five of those minutes embracing, kissing, and enjoying the anticipation. And the quiet! I had never imagined how chaotic a wedding would be.

But then Tracy pulled away. "Sorry, Anson, you've messed up my hair. I need to touch this up before we go in."

"Allllll right." I sighed. "If you're sure you don't want to just sneak away to our cabin."

Tracy giggled. "After the point Admiral Morais made about protocol, do you think we dare miss our own reception? She scares Nick Aames! She's certainly more than *I* want to tangle with. So let me work."

Tracy started adjusting her hair in the mirror, and I stood back and gazed at her as she worked. Removing her veil and reaching for a brush, Tracy continued, "So Nick is certainly in an extra sour mood tonight, isn't he? I know he and Hannah had a messy breakup, but does that have to put him down on *all* marriage?"

"It's not marriage," I explained, "it's weddings."

Tracy paused. "Oh?"

"Hannah was his first marriage, but his second wedding. The first one was a disaster, and he has been sour on weddings ever since. He and Hannah ran off to a justice of the peace, and he had to get half-drunk even to go through with that."

"A disaster? How bad could it have been?"

"Tragic, really. But Nick never talks about it, and it's not really my story to tell."

Tracy put her veil back on, adjusted it in the mirror, and turned to face me. "Oh, come on, Anson. Now that you've started, you know you're going to tell me eventually." She reached her arms around me; but at the last instant, she jabbed her fingers into the ticklish spot beneath my ribs, and I jolted off the floor in the low gravity. "So you might as well tell me now," she said as I settled to the deck, "before I really make you jump."

"Oh, you think so?" I grabbed her wrists, and I wished we had the rest of the night to ourselves. But we didn't. "All right, all right. But I wasn't actually there. This was before I ever served under Nick. This is just the story as Bosun Smith told it to me." And slowly, as the evening's celebrations played out, I started telling Tracy the story Smitty had told me about Nick. And about Rosalia.

C

Nick was a lieutenant in the International Space Corps at the time, stationed at the new São Paulo Spaceport and overseeing component tests for L2 Farport. Smitty was a petty officer at the port; but the Corps was pretty new then, and fraternization rules were pretty lax. Smitty was . . . well, not Nick's friend—he didn't make friends easily even then—but a close acquaintance. And his occasional dance partner in the nightclubs of São Paulo. Smith always had a way of dragging people out of their shells. In Nick's case, she did so through dance. I joked about Nick's dancing, but he's actually not bad, and very enthusiastic. It's one of his very few passions outside of his work. These days he only dances alone, and only in the privacy of his office. I'm one of the few people who has seen him dance in years. But back then, he had quite a reputation in the Corps.

Of course, Nick also had a reputation as a bit of a martinet. Oh, not like he is now that he's in command. He wasn't as moody as he is now, with his cabin all in black and him never leaving it except on duty. The dark moods came later, after all of this. But he was just as much a stickler for procedure and safety and attention to detail. He never hesitated to write up any infraction that he saw, no matter how small. But his first introduction to Rosalia, the new ensign at the port, was when *she* wrote *him* up.

Smitty was an astronaut first class then, attached to Commandant Birch as an administrative aide, so she was there for their first meeting, recording the minutes. She said Nick showed up just at the appointed hour, summoned by the commandant to discuss his inspection of a cargo rocket bound for high orbit. He paid little attention to Rosalia, standing at attention along the wall. She was in perfect duty order, her long dark hair rolled up into a bun behind her cap, her blue Corps uniform neat and trim. Nick sized her up as a Brazilian local, correctly as it happened, and so he didn't consider her worth his attention. The locals in the Corps then had a reputation as token spacers, enlisted merely to satisfy Brazilian politicians, and expected to wash out before they ever saw orbit. Nick didn't know it then, but Rosalia was determined to shatter that reputation.

After Commandant Birch returned Nick's salute, he called the review to order, and he started asking Nick questions about the cargo rocket. Finally he got to the crux of the matter: "So on 5 May, you performed a readiness inspection on cargo rocket 54-17?"

"Yes, sir, I did."

"And you found eleven exceptions that caused you to issue a hold on preparation for launch?"

Nick glanced over at Rosalia. "I did, sir. I'm sure the ensign did her best to prepare the vessel, but—"

Birch interrupted Nick to say, "You are under a misimpression, Lieutenant. The ensign was not in charge of preparing the cargo rocket."

Nick twitched under the commandant's gaze, but he chanced another glance at Rosalia. The corner of her mouth was turned up in just a hint of a grin. "Oh?" he asked.

"No, the ensign was in charge of the readiness inspection of 6 May. Ensign, tell the lieutenant what you found."

"Yes, sir." Rosalia stepped forward. "Sir, in addition to the eleven exceptions reported on 5 May, I found two loose safety covers on an environmental system."

Nick couldn't stop himself from interrupting. "That's impossible. Someone must have been in there between the inspections."

The commandant shook his head. "We have the access records. No one entered the rocket or the area between the inspections. And, Ensign, what would be the consequences of these loose covers?"

"If I may, Commandant?" Birch nodded, and Rosalia pushed a simulation from her comp to his desk display. The inside of the rocket appeared. "I simulated the most likely scenario. The covers would have shaken loose during launch"—the image started shaking with a simulated launch—"and crashed around the cabin." And the simulated covers smashed back, bounced around, and broke instruments everywhere they tumbled. "The results would be tens of thousands of dollars in lost time and equipment."

Throughout her simulation, Nick had leaned over the desk. Occasionally he openly glared at Rosalia, as if enraged that she had the temerity to report *him*. But at the end, he shook his head. "Hundreds of thousands. Depending on which instruments were broken, possibly the entire payload." He straightened up and snapped to attention. "Commandant, I have no excuse. I await your discipline."

And then Birch actually laughed. "Relax, Lieutenant. We caught the problem. And we would have caught it before launch, regardless. You had so much to report, you just lost track. This will go in your record, and that will gnaw at you: a blemish on your spotless record. That will be enough to make you twice as careful in the future. Dismissed, Lieutenant."

As Nick turned to leave, he stole one more glance at the young ensign. This time, with Nick blocking her from the commandant's view, she openly grinned at him.

The incident became a mark on Nick's record; but in the eyes of his fellow lieutenants, the mark on his reputation was even larger. No one had ever caught Nick in such a large mistake before. No one had *ever* made Nick back down. But the new ensign, a local girl who had worked her way into the officer ranks of the Corps, had done both in one day. In one move, Rosalia had become Nick's rival for the top officer at the port.

Nick had been dead wrong, he'd been caught, and he took his lumps. As you might guess, it motivated him to be more careful in his own work; but it also drove him to be more ruthless in his reviews of others. Sure enough, about three weeks later he found something to report in Rosalia's work. It was a minor thing—Smitty didn't even remember what it was—but Rosalia took her lumps better than Nick had. She was always much more good-natured than him. Sometimes that made her a little sloppier, but it made her easier to deal with as a person.

And then the inspections became almost a game for them, tit-for-tat reporting on each other, but a game with strict, fair rules: they only reported legitimate infractions that actually belonged on a report. They never made up anything just to score points on each other. Their commanders were amused, but also annoyed, because the infractions they reported became a paperwork nightmare. Also, the game became frequent fodder for the rumor mill, and a few joked that Nick and Rosalia should just get a room already. But most assumed it was rivalry, not romance, the two of them bucking for promotion—Rosalia earned lieutenant in record time—and each seeing the other as the most likely obstacle in their path.

And they were probably right, up until that night in Porco Cego, a nightclub near the hotel where many of the junior officers stayed. São Paulo was a pretty small port then, and there was a shortage of on-base housing, so junior officers and senior enlisted were encouraged to find billets nearby. Smitty had a room there, too, and she said it was a great way to meet the locals, particularly at dance clubs like O Porco.

That night, Nick was cutting moves on the floor, drifting from partner to partner and dance to dance. Smitty says he was in a rare, relaxed mood, enjoying the release of just moving to the music. Locals and Corps, he danced his way through them all.

Then a beautiful, graceful, dark-haired Brazilian woman tapped him on the shoulder for the next dance. It took two takes for Nick to recognize Rosalia out of uniform, her hair down around her bare shoulders, decked out for a night of liberty.

"What do you want?" Nick asked in his usual blunt fashion.

Rosalia laughed. "If you don't know, then you're probably too thick-headed to keep time, but I'll give you a try anyway. Dance, Lieutenant?"

Nick started to turn away; but he turned back and looked her over, her golden skin set off against a sleeveless blue peasant blouse and a flowing white skirt. He shrugged. "Oh, what the hell? I've danced with everyone else tonight."

And then, Smitty says, magic happened. Between Nick's enthusiasm and Rosalia's grace, they made the perfect partners: swinging around the floor, changing steps and styles with the tempo changes as if they could read each other's minds. They anticipated every step, every spin. Smitty thinks it was another form of testing each other, challenging and assessing one another; and they quickly learned what they could do together, daring themselves to new heights with every song. There was no more trading that night: Nick and Rosalia had found their partners. They finished with "Brigas Nunca Mais," a slow, languid, romantic tune that's great to listen to but nearly impossible to dance to. The tempo's just wrong, not quite a fast song, not quite a slow dance. But they did it, turning it into a sensual mix of pulling away but not quite out of reach, drawing swiftly together as if tugged by a gravity well, and then spinning slowly around, locked in each other's arms. When the music finally stopped, the onlookers applauded.

Smitty tells me that Nick never made it back to his hotel room that night, the first time that had ever happened. But it became a pretty regular occurrence after that.

☾

Though the reporting game continued, the tone changed, at least for Rosalia. It became more about giving Nick points that he could work off on the dance floor. But for Nick, it remained as serious as ever; and Smitty says eventually Rosalia realized: this wasn't a game for him, it was rehearsal for the deadliest challenges imaginable. Yes, that's exactly what it's supposed to be. They drill that into us so we can't forget it. But that message struck Nick more deeply than it did the average astronaut. Obsessively, you would have to say. And so he kept right up on the smallest infractions, the smallest details, reporting them with that cynical, critical view he has.

Mind you, Nick wasn't being an ass just for the fun of it. L2 Farport, the jumping-off station at LaGrange Point 2 beyond the moon, had recently been approved by the System Initiative; and everyone knew they would be staffing construction crews in the near future. São Paulo started receiving a lot of visits from brass and diplomats, and everyone assumed the teams there had a good shot at L2. Nick made no secret that he planned to turn that good shot into a sure thing.

Even though Rosalia agreed with Nick in principle, and even though she wanted the L2 assignment as much as he did, she grew annoyed with Nick's obsession. Smitty thinks Rosalia decided she wanted to find Nick's fun side, somehow. On the dance floor, out on the town, in bed. She wanted to lighten him up, to show him he could enjoy life and still live within regulations, still advance his career. One night, she took it a little too far. She always did take more risks than Nick. That night, after Nick fell asleep, she logged in to the hotel computer and canceled his morning wake-up call. Smitty says that she heard the consequences the next morning from three rooms away.

"You did *what*?"

"Lighten up. It's not like you have important duty today."

"It's *duty*. It's *all* important. People rely on us. The brass are *watching* us. I've got twenty minutes!"

"No problem. You woke up even without a call."

"I woke up fifteen minutes *late* without a call!"

A door slammed, and Smitty heard Nick's running feet in the corridor outside. She says that morning's report showed Nick at his post on time—but out of uniform in three particulars, a record for Nick.

Outside of official duties, Nick and Rosalia didn't speak to each other for five weeks after that.

And Nick was miserable! You'd have to know him well to tell the difference between Nick's usual acerbic manner and his new bitterness, but Smitty said it was unmistakable if you knew the signs. It was the difference between a gleam in his eye as he pounced on a mistake, versus a frown and a tone in his voice that indicated despair that anything would ever be right. He even stopped talking about L2.

Finally Smitty and some of the other trainees took matters into their own hands. A brash move, perhaps, but they hoped to get Nick to let up on them just a little. Plus I've always suspected Smitty was a closet romantic under her party-girl exterior. She showed up at Nick's hotel room one night, dressed for a night on the town. When Nick answered the door, she smiled and asked, "Join us for liberty, Lieutenant?"

Nick shook his head, face turned down. "Not in the mood, Smith. Pass."

Nick moved to shut the door, but Smitty held it open. "Come on, Lieutenant. It would be good for you to bond with your team a bit. You know the L2 selection committee puts a high value on unit cohesion."

Nick glowered. "Who cares what the selection committee thinks?"

"Begging your pardon, but you do, Lieutenant. You've just forgotten for a bit."

Maybe Smitty was convincing, or maybe Nick was just in a mood to be convinced, but he went along. Once at Porco Cego, she wheeled Nick out onto the dance floor for a few numbers; but he was sulky and unenthusiastic, just going through the motions. Finally Smitty made her move: when a new song started, she grabbed Nick's arm and spun him around. Behind him stood Rosalia, equally trapped by Ensign Matsuura. "Sorry, Lieutenants," Smitty said, "but you two need to talk. For the sake of unit cohesion." And she backed away, sure that Nick and Rosalia couldn't avoid their overdue confrontation.

And if you believe that, you don't know Nick Aames. Without a word, he stalked off the floor, through the bar, and out into the warm Brazilian night.

But as stubborn as Nick is, he had met his match in Rosalia. While he pulled away, she determined to draw back together, whatever it took. She chased after Nick. Smitty and the others had the good sense not to follow, but they heard the shouts from outside, even over the music. They were sure Nick would be an absolute terror in the morning, and they wondered how they had screwed up so badly.

Then, just as they were imagining the horrors of their next duty shift, they noticed the shouting had stopped. And the music had stopped. Rosalia was crossing the dance floor, storming for the exit and her home; but Nick was up at the DJ stand, handing over a credit chip as the DJ swapped songs. Rosalia slowed when she heard the opening guitar notes of "Brigas Nunca Mais," pausing just long enough for Nick to dash across the floor, grab her hand, tug her back to his arms, and twirl her into a blur of hair and skirt and flashing limbs. They spun around each other, pulling closer and closer until they clung together as one. As the song trailed off, they leaned in for a kiss. The song meant "fight no more," and that was the effect it had. That dance, their song—those always drew Nick and Rosalia back together.

☽

"But Anson, what about the wedding? I still don't see Nick's problem here."

I had a panic impulse to hush Tracy—probably not the smartest move on our own wedding day. I looked around, and was grateful that Nick was nowhere within earshot. We were in the passageway outside the assembly deck, waiting for Bosun Smith to formally announce us to our reception within.

I lowered my voice and hoped Tracy would follow my example. "You can't really understand what went wrong with the wedding without understanding how they got there. Trust me, Nick and Rosalia's relationship was a tangled knot from the start; and the wedding disaster was a consequence of that.

"But for a while, things were knot-free. After making up on the dance floor, Nick *did* lighten up. Smitty says you wouldn't recognize him. Instead of his cynicism being locked on all the time, it was like a rheostat that he only dialed up when he needed it to make a point. The rest of the time, he almost gave up his snide remarks, as if the world suddenly measured up to his expectations. Smitty even saw him smile at odd times for no reason at all, something Nick rarely does. Rosalia made him a different man, she said, a *complete* man like he never was before. Or since."

Tracy smiled wistfully. "I think I'd like to meet that Nick."

"So would I, my love, so would I. But I fear that Nick is dead."

Just then, I heard Smitty's voice boom through the door: "Chief Anson Carver and Dr. Tracy Wells-Carver!" And the door opened with a roar of polite applause. We entered our reception; but throughout the night, whenever a private moment presented itself, Tracy pressed me for the rest of Nick and Rosalia's story, starting with how they went to orbit.

☾

The reporting game continued in earnest, and it had one more side effect: it brought up the performance of their entire unit. You've seen how Nick is: He drives away or breaks or pisses off anyone who can't measure up to his standards; but the ones who remain, even if they don't like him, are prepared for any challenge. The entire unit got better, with individual and unit commendations far above the norm. They supervised preintegration testing of the L2 environment units; and they found and diagnosed so many problems, they practically bankrupted the supplier. That caused a construction delay, but it also saved lives *and* the schedule in the long run.

So it was natural that, when the time came to staff the construction team for the L2 Farport, a large contingent was selected from the São Paulo Spaceport. Smitty made the cut—even though she was more junior than command was looking for—because of recommendations from both Nick and Rosalia. Anyone who thinks that was a matter of personal bias doesn't know Nick.

What followed was eight months of mission training in simulators and neutral buoyancy tanks. Nick and Rosalia both drove the team to the highest marks on record. Then came the blastoff to orbit, transfer to Luna, and then finally a transport out to LaGrange Point 2. When the transport delivered them to the L2 construction site, those demanding standards really began to bear fruit. Sixty-thousand kilometers beyond Luna, with nothing around but temporary habitats and the growing shell of Farport, the team had to rely on each astronaut getting each thing right. Captain Leeds was one hard-nosed son of a bitch, as bad as Nick in a lot of ways, although for him schedule and budget were as important as safety and detail. He had a timetable, he had a spending target, and by damn, he was going to hit them. He drove the construction team harder than any earthbound, downside officer ever had; but he seemed to have an internal micrometer that could measure precisely where the team's breaking point was, and then he stopped just short of it, before stress would make them sloppy. Accidents would cost him valuable, trained personnel and untold lost time and money. Though Nick was never as concerned about the budget, he worked well with Leeds. Soon he had a promotion to lieutenant commander, and he was on Leeds's advisory staff. They often clashed—this *is* Nick we're talking about—but Captain Leeds appreciated Nick's independent voice and his focus on the mission. Nick also got command of one of the four construction shifts.

Farport then was just a hint of what it is today. The Prime Module was there, of course, the original construction platform that served as their habitat and base of operations. It had the massive engines they used for occasional orbit corrections. The Prime was mated to the long docking axis; but the axis was still only a framework, not closed in yet, and they were just starting to assemble the first habitat ring. You would need a lot of imagination to look at that skeleton and see Farport today, with its growing stack of habitat rings and the new extensions added every year. But even then you would see a lot of traffic: suited astronauts, one-person construction hoppers, and the larger mobile platforms that served as ferries and transports between the docking and assembly points and the port itself. A lot of modules were assembled far from the port, so that stray parts or any other problem couldn't threaten the port itself. Then the hoppers would grapple and tug the modules to dock with a mobile platform, and the MP would ferry it and maneuver it to attach to the port's skeleton.

Soon Rosalia had command of another construction shift. She got along with Captain Leeds, of course. She was always more in touch with the human side of the Corps. When Leeds wanted an opinion on whether he was pushing the crew too hard, it was Rosalia he asked. He knew she would have a better read on crew morale, which mattered to him because it could affect their performance and his timetables.

Morale building was actually a line item in Leeds's schedule and budget. So as soon as the first habitat ring was spun up to one-quarter G, he announced a gala in celebration. It wasn't much of a gala by Earth standards, not even by the standards of our wedding here on the *Aldrin*; but for a weary crew of astronauts stationed at humanity's farthest outpost (at the time), it was a much-needed chance to unwind and cut loose. And to explore the possibilities of dance in low gravity. That was something only old Luna hands had experienced before then. Rosalia hadn't served there (and Nick's Lunar Survival School stint had left no time for dancing), so this was a new challenge for them. You know the Coriolis catch, that move we can never get right? You can't do that move on Luna, can't do it anywhere but a spinning habitat. I'm supposed to toss you so high that the Coriolis effect takes over, so you'll land somewhere downspin; and then I slide across the deck on my knees and catch you when I land. My knees still ache from the last time we tried. Well, Smitty claims Nick and Rosalia *invented* the move at that gala, Nick catching her and wrapping her in his arms as if they'd practiced it all their lives. Then they would hold that embrace through the end of the song, as if trying to make that moment last forever.

The gala wasn't the only place that Nick and Rosalia danced. With habitat ring 1 spun up, Leeds was able to accommodate a larger construction crew, so all the schedules and assignments got reshuffled. Rosalia was assigned as lead hopper pilot on mobile platform 1; and as second-in-command of the construction project, Nick was the pilot on MP1. If it had been the other way around, it would've never worked. Nick wouldn't have been happy going from a shift commander to command of just a hopper squad. But Rosalia loved to pilot above all her other duties, and lead hopper pilot was enough command to satisfy her. When they worked together, she and Nick turned her hopper and the mobile platform into a delicate duet, each anticipating the other's moves, launching and rendezvousing with unparalleled elegance. Given their relationship, a few in the Corps grumbled about the two of them working so closely together and in two such prime positions; but their efficiency ratings were absolutely top-notch, so Leeds left them where they were. Later he would come to question that decision.

Working the same shifts and in a small, remote station, Nick and Rosalia became closer than ever. Smitty didn't think that was possible, but they became almost of one mind on most things. Oh, they still clashed sometimes, and some of their shouting matches were legendary; but it was always about the safest, most effective way to perform the mission. And once one of them was clearly proven right, they united again to carry out their decision with utmost precision, as if the shouting had never happened. They never really reached "fight no more," like they did on the dance floor; but they had found a way to fight only over what mattered, without losing what *mattered*.

So no one was too surprised when Nick and Rosalia showed up one day wearing matching gold rings, each on the right hand in the Brazilian engagement tradition. With boost costs as high as they were, it had probably cost Nick as much to lift those rings up from Earth as the rings themselves had cost, a few months' pay altogether. But Smitty says the sparkle of the gold matched the sparkle in Rosalia's eyes. Like I said, Smitty's a closet romantic. She really believed Nick and Rosalia were fated to be together. If only she had been right.

☾

"Anson, don't you *dare* think you're going to stop there."

"*Tracy!*" I whispered, putting down my napkin. "They're about to call us out for our first dance."

"Good! It's a long, slow song. You can whisper in my ear, and no one will be the wiser."

"But . . ." I hesitated. "You know I'm a lousy dancer, I don't have Nick's moves. I have to concentrate, or I'll be all over your feet."

Tracy giggled. "Sorry, hon, but you're all over my feet even when you concentrate. It's okay, it's a quarter G. My feet can take it. Now tell me about the wedding."

I glanced over at the officers' table. Nick seemed to be in some argument with Admiral Morais—a polite argument, but I could see fire in his eyes again—and I figured he wouldn't hear. So I continued, "Rosalia chose a wedding date to fall within the grand opening ceremonies for Farport. The System Initiative had scheduled a week of celebrations to mark the port's opening to civilian personnel, researchers, and tourists. The wedding wouldn't be the opening night, of course, nor the closing night. Those were slated for massive diplomatic and public relations parties. But Captain Leeds had grown quite fond of Rosalia. He said she reminded him of his daughter. He also said she was an excellent officer and too good for Nick; but the captain pulled some strings, and he arranged for the wedding to take place on the second-to-last night, when there would be plenty of brass and friends to attend. He even agreed to officiate.

"In the end, maybe that was the mistake. Maybe they tried to cram too much celebration and too much work into too little time. Maybe if Nick and Rosalia had scheduled their wedding for later, everything wouldn't have gone so horribly wrong . . ."

☾

Or maybe not. So many small things had to go wrong to create the disaster. Afterward, despite his pain, Nick dispassionately documented every one of them, defining causes and assigning blame in an incident report that is still taught in the academy today as an ideal after-action report. But even Nick couldn't have foreseen everything that went wrong.

It had started nearly sixteen months earlier, at Darwin Spaceport, when a technician transposed two digits while setting up a test for a fuel injector. The injector was tested at more than twice maximum pressure, and it developed a hairline crack; but because the readings all fit with the transposed digits, the test "passed." So the injector was certified and placed into inventory on superorbital transport *DeMarco*, and there it sat in a parts locker for sixteen months. But when the *DeMarco* was bringing a contingent of System Initiative bigwigs and other civilians up to Farport, there was a fault in the starboard engine. The *DeMarco's* engineer, showing admirable caution under ordinary circumstances, chose to overhaul the entire starboard engine while they were coasting to their next burn. She was absolutely correct per maintenance protocols; but in the process, they installed the faulty injector. The unit lasted through initial testing and course correction burns; but when the *DeMarco* went to a full burn to settle into a matching orbit with Farport, the vibrations caused the cracked valve to break wide open. The ignition chamber flooded with far too much fuel, and with a horrifying whump, the entire starboard engine blew out, venting gasses and causing the ship to spin. The port engine automatically adjusted to compensate, but not enough. The *DeMarco*, crippled and tumbling, sped ahead on an altered trajectory. They couldn't make orbit, and they couldn't return to Earth. All they could do was fly deeper into space and hope someone was in position for a rescue.

And fortunately, someone was. Even though they had a wedding scheduled in less than twenty-four hours, Nick and Rosalia and their MP1 crew were on duty, picking up modules that had been dropped by a cargo rocket. They had insisted on keeping up with their work right up to their final shift before the ceremony. So when the SOS went out from the *DeMarco*, Nick got on the comm. "Transport *DeMarco*, Farport mobile platform 1, Lieutenant Commander Aames commanding. We're in your neighborhood. What's your vector?"

The comm screen lit up, and a young, blonde female astronaut appeared. "Mobile platform 1, transport *DeMarco*, Captain Austin commanding. Our vector is still changing. We're trying to use our remaining engine to get control. Sending our control feed now."

A blinking light on Nick's console told him the feed was connected. He looked at his navigation screen and nodded. "*DeMarco*, MP1. Affirmative, we have your feed. Nav comp says it's tight, but we can catch you if we start immediately. My computer and yours will work out the approach maneuvers. What's your situation, Austin?"

"MP1, *DeMarco*. We're shaken, Aames, but surviving. We have six crew, ten passengers. No casualties, but the erratic boost led to some injuries. Our chief engineer suffered some nasty burns while ejecting the damaged engine. And I think the engine may have ruptured our O2 lines. We're losing pressure, not fast, but steady. The assistant engineer's suiting up for an outside inspection, but he doesn't sound very confident."

Nick took his thumb off the comm switch long enough for a quick, "Damn." Then he thumbed the switch again. "*DeMarco*, MP1. Understood. I'll tell the computer to prefer a fast pickup. MP1 out." By that time, the nav comps of the two vessels had worked out a solution. Without a load to haul, the mobile platform had power to spare. It wasn't graceful, but it was fast. Nick punched the "Execute" button, and MP1 started boosting for the *DeMarco*.

Then he switched over to his command circuit. His hopper team was deployed, and he didn't have time to wait for them. "All hoppers, MP1. As you've heard, we have to make an emergency rendezvous and pickup with the *DeMarco*. I've already started a low-thrust course for them. As soon as you all dock, I'll switch to high thrust and catch that transport. So if you don't want to get stranded in the cold, boys and girls, vector on me and haul ass. Burn your tanks to empty if you have to, but I can't wait around for you. You're going to have to catch me. Signal your approach solutions."

And Nick watched as the hopper status screen showed solutions coming in: Hopper 6, hopper 3, 4, 2, 5 . . . but not 1. Nick switched to hopper 1's channel. "Hopper 1, MP1. Where's your solution, Rosie?"

It took several seconds for Rosalia to respond. "MP1, hopper 1. I can't work a solution. Recommend you proceed without me."

"Nonsense. Burn the tanks dry. You've got enough fuel to catch me."

"Nick . . . No, I don't."

"What?"

"Nick, I didn't refuel on my last docking. I had plenty in my tanks, more than enough for our pickup schedule. I just forgot."

"You *forgot*!"

"Remember, you called, just to talk. And then the caterer called, a problem with the dinner menu. By the time I worked that out, there was no time for refueling. I was still within safety margins, on the low side, but within. So I'm sorry."

"Sorry?" Nick fumed. "Fine. I'll wait for you. I'll find another intercept solution."

"Nick, you can't. I've worked the numbers, by comp and by hand. Orbital mechanics waits for no man, Nick. Or woman. If you don't keep boosting, you'll never catch them; and *you'll* run out of fuel trying."

Nick paused and ran some numbers of his own. "Okay, I'll jettison some oxygen tanks. That will lighten my load, make me faster, and then you can pick up the tanks and have enough air for a rescue."

"Nick, you *can't*. With sixteen more people on MP1, and with their own O2 leaking away, you're going to need every kilo of air you have. It does no good to rescue them if you all suffocate from CO2 buildup. Now go!"

"Rosie, I can't leave you out here."

"One of me, sixteen of them. No choice, the numbers don't add up. Now go get them, *Lieutenant Commander Aames*."

Nick worked at his computer furiously, looking for a solution, his frown deepening as every second pulled him farther and farther from the hopper and his bride. Finally he smashed his fists against the keys several times. When he looked back at the comm screen, Rosalia was shaking her head, tears in her eyes. She whispered, "Go get them, Nick."

Lost for an idea, Nick just stared at the screen. Finally, his voice choking, he said, "Brigas nunca mais, Rosalia."

Rosalia answered, "Nunca mais, Nick." And she cut off the comm screen.

☾

"So then she died?" I saw tears welling up in Tracy's eyes. "On their wedding day? Oh, poor Nick."

As Tracy had asked, I'd continued telling Nick and Rosalia's story right through our first dance as husband and wife. She had gotten caught up. Like I said, Nick has a way of ending up in the middle of everything, even when he's not there. Now in the middle of the officers' dance, with all my superiors and peers circling around us like a sea of white, Tracy had insisted on more.

I shook my head. "Died? No. Nick made some quick mass calculations, came up with one more wild idea, and made Leeds see it was the only option. Leeds detached the Prime Module from the docking axis. Freed of the mass of Farport, those giant engines made Prime into one hellaciously fast rescue craft. It wasn't efficient, but by burning fuel like they were giving it away, they found a solution where MP1 could hold up for Rosalia, reach the *DeMarco* before they ran out of oxygen, *and* make rendezvous with MP2 when it launched from Prime with enough spare fuel to bring both platforms back. Then Leeds brought Prime around and back to Farport, tanks nearly empty. The docking was rough—it shook the whole port; but mostly thanks to Nick's determination, everybody lived."

"But then—"

"And then the wedding had to wait. It took two weeks of double shifts for all crew to stabilize the port and correct all the orbits. And then another five weeks for Nick and an investigative team to prepare that marvelous after-action report. And by the time that was done, the wedding was off."

"But why?"

"Because in that incredibly detailed report, alongside the tally of millions of dollars lost due to overtime and structural repairs and expended fuel, alongside the point-by-point enumeration of the direct causes of the incident and the parties to blame, Nick included a thorough list of secondary causes; and at the top of that list was Rosalia's failure to perform basic maintenance due to distraction by personal issues. Second on that list was his own personal call that was a direct cause of her distraction. They both got summoned before the review board to answer charges."

Tracy paused and glared at Nick as he gracelessly suffered through the officers' dance with Admiral Morais. "That bastard!"

I shook my head. "I like to think of him as a calculating bastard. He calculated that he could lose her by following the rules, or he could risk *really* losing her someday by letting up on the rules. He couldn't face that again. His way, she would live. She would hate him, but she would live."

Tracy frowned, trying to see things through Nick's eyes. "But then what happened to her?"

"At first, there were some who used the incident to dredge up the old prejudices about Brazilian astronauts. I hear Nick got into a few fights trying to quash those rumors; but they stung Rosalia, and she took them personally. She was *hurt*. But after the review board confirmed every one of Nick's conclusions—and after Nick himself suffered a demotion as a result—Rosalia eventually, grudgingly, saw that it wasn't personal. She was still angry at Nick, but she moved on, and she grew from the incident. And she realized that her career wasn't completely washed up. She could still make Brazil proud of its native astronauts. So she took her lumps, and then threw herself into her work with a nearly Nick-like zeal; soon she got her rank back, and she rose up through the Corps, proving herself to be the fine, dedicated officer Captain Leeds always told her she was. One of the finest officers in the Corps."

"But did she ever forgive him?"

The music stopped, the officers started to clear the floor for more guests, and I shrugged. "No one's really sure. Some people say yes, some no, but the two of them . . . Well, at least in public, they act like none of that past ever happened. Like they're practically strangers." Then I heard the opening guitar notes of a familiar Brazilian love song. Smitty up to her old tricks, no doubt. I turned Tracy around. "But you'll have to judge for yourself."

Admiral Morais stopped, her back to Nick; and with one quick move, she let her hair down in a distinctly nonregulation fashion. There was some gray in it, but it was mostly still the dark hair of a young lieutenant, and it still flowed in the low gravity. As the music picked up, she pranced lightly away from Nick, but one hand trailed behind her, beckoning. Nick leaped after her, clasped her hand at the last moment, and drew her gently back into his arms and a twirling, laughing embrace.

The other dancers, seeing two true *artistes* at work, yielded the floor to watch them move; and for three and a half minutes, Nick and Rosalia whirled around the floor as if all the years had never passed. She fled, and he pursued. He ignored, and she enticed. They circled each other like two fighters, looking for weakness; then they embraced and twirled, stronger together than when they stood apart. And they clung to each other, swaying and leaping in the low gravity as if they were one.

Just like on Farport, they reached the climax of the music when Rosalia ran and leaped at Nick; and he sidestepped, turned, caught her at waist and thigh, and propelled her higher, so high that the deck of the *Aldrin* spun beneath her, carrying her downspin. Her hair streamed behind her like a triumphant banner. And Nick continued his step into a leap of his own, a downward leap ending with him sliding across the deck on his knees. His face shone with a light I had never seen there before as he slid to a halt almost in front of Tracy and me, exactly where he had to be to catch Rosalia when she needed him to catch her; and he folded her in a loving, protective embrace. The guests rose to their feet in thunderous applause.

But from our place right next to Nick and Rosalia, Tracy and I saw what the other guests couldn't. Nick bent in to kiss Rosalia; but the admiral turned her face away, shaking her head. *No.* I saw the light fade from Nick's face.

Without missing a beat, as if nothing was wrong, Nick rose with her still in his arms, and he set Admiral Morais back on her feet. Then he snapped a salute; and without waiting for a response, Nick Aames stalked back to his dark, empty office.

11. Under Pressure

From the memoirs of Park Yerim

9 June 2083

As Carver finished his story, I heard running footsteps behind us. I turned just as a dark figure in blue running shorts and a matching blue shirt leaped into the air. I recognized Dr. Wells-Carver just as she wrapped her slender arms around Carver's neck, leaned her head around, and kissed his cheek.

Carver stopped walking and turned his head back, and their lips met for another kiss, awkward but sincere. The kiss lasted long enough to make me wonder if I should leave. When they finally broke for air, Carver asked, "How do you *always* know when I'm telling that story? I don't tell it to many people; but every time I do, you show up before the end."

Dr. Wells-Carver let go, dropped to the deck, and bounced in front of him. "That's my secret, Anson." She stretched up for one more quick kiss. "If you figure it out, I might miss that ending. I wouldn't want to do that." Then she turned to me. "Good evening, Inspector Park. It's good to see you again."

She reached out her hand, and I shook it. "Good evening, Dr. Wells-Carver. I hope I'm not keeping Chief Carver from something."

Carver looked at his wife, then at me, and then back at Wells. "Wait. You two know each other?"

I looked at Dr. Wells-Carver. She had a warm smile, every bit as welcoming as Carver described it. They were both very good at putting people at ease. "Everyone has seen *Pioneers' Creed*," I said. "And the dean of Aldrin University—one of the most prestigious schools in the solar system—is pretty famous."

"Thank you," she answered, and then turned back to Carver. "A better question, Anson, is why you're telling that story. No offense, Inspector, but I can't imagine Nick wants it spread around. Or Admiral Morais either."

"I kind of forced him into it," I explained. "It's . . ."

Carver filled in for me. "It's something you're not comfortable talking about, because it might raise questions about your objectivity in your investigation." My eyes widened. He was practically reading my mind. I nodded. "But you think it's important that you understand the people of this ship, not just the facts of the case. You think the facts are only part of the picture."

I nodded again. "How did you know?"

"It's not that hard to figure out," he said. "After years of dealing with Nick, I recognize all sorts of investigative techniques. He's not good at personal matters like you are, so you've got an edge on him there."

I was still surprised. "You figured that out just from my questions?"

Dr. Wells-Carver cut in. "Don't let him fool you, Inspector. He's good, but he's sneaky too." She pinched Carver's ribs, and he jumped. "People talk on this ship. Word gets around. We know you've been talking to Nick's friends. Oh," she added when she saw my face, "Anson didn't set up this meeting on purpose. He always jogs this track on Thursday evenings."

I considered that. Both of them could be lying to me, setting me up to try to build sympathy for Aames; but I just didn't believe it. They were both so *genuine*. That was the only word I could think of.

So I accepted them at their word, and I changed back to a different subject. "There's something I still don't understand. I met Admiral Morais on the rendezvous shuttle. She was a little withdrawn, but she was polite enough. She didn't seem so *cruel* as she was in that story."

Dr. Wells-Carver shook her head. "I know, it sounds like she hurt Nick intentionally, leading him on and then turning him away. I thought it was cruel myself at the time, and I couldn't understand it. Anson had spoken so highly of her, and I had liked her instantly. It made no sense, until I learned the missing piece of the puzzle." Wells took a deep breath, and then she continued, "At the time of our wedding, Admiral Morais was recently engaged to Marcus Costello, MD, of Maxwell City."

"Oh."

"Uh-huh. And more than that: Nick knew it. We learned that later."

"Oh." I repeated. In my mind I saw that dance again, only in a whole new light.

"See?" Carver said. "The grand gesture. Somehow, in Nick's mind, that one dance was supposed to make everything right again, make the admiral forget her commitment to Dr. Costello. It's like his entire understanding of relationships comes from old movies."

"Nothing wrong with old movies," Wells said, wrapping her arm around Carver's waist.

"Nothing at all," Carver said. "But sometimes the movie is *Casablanca*, and Rick walks away alone."

"No, not alone." Wells stroked his arm. "He has Louis, and a beautiful friendship."

"I hope that's enough," Carver answered. "Nick's grand gesture did nothing but reopen old wounds."

"I don't agree, Anson."

I looked at Wells. "No?"

"His gesture may not have had 'magic' that night," she explained, "but I think it affected the admiral. Three months later, she called off her engagement. I doubt the timing was a coincidence."

"I see," I said. And I did see, or at least I was starting to. I knew from the rendezvous shuttle that Admiral Knapp distrusted Morais. Now maybe I understood why. My puzzle was still missing a lot of pieces, but I could start to see what those pieces might look like.

It was time to find some more of those pieces. I said my good-byes and headed back to my cabin to get some rest. I had a lot of work ahead of me.

☾

But my hopes for rest weren't going to work out that night. I'd had Matt and my team taking depositions from enlisted crew and junior officers so I could get a good overall picture for when I deposed the senior officers. Those depositions all arrived on my comp that night, and I made the mistake of looking them over before going to bed. Even Matt's summary ran to a dozen pages, and I was still reading it when a call came in from Admiral Knapp.

I pulled open the call, and Knapp wasted no time on pleasantries. "Park, I've been reading your depositions, and this is all a load of horseshit."

I frowned. I tapped a "Forward" icon on my comm, and then I answered, "Admiral, since my findings have not been released yet, I don't see how you could've read anything. But I intend to find out." Great. Someone on my team was leaking information to Knapp.

Knapp's voice grew louder. "Don't change the subject, Park. Why are you wasting our time with all these enlisted pissants and junior idiots? Where are the bridge crew depositions? Where's Aames's?"

I paused, calming my temper before I responded. "Admiral, I will get to those. I want to get the broad picture from the crew first."

"Bullshit." Knapp pointed a finger at the comm. "Park, I've heard what you've been up to. You're getting mighty cozy with the *Aldrin*'s crew. That's hardly objective. And this *relationship* you have with Bosun

Smith is over the line. I've let Admiral Reed know that you're fucking up this entire investigation."

This time I let my temper loose. "Admiral, I have *no* relationship with Bosun Smith, and I resent your implication."

"That's not what my source—"

"Your 'source' is damned unreliable if they're feeding you gossip and calling it facts. And as of now, your source is *done*."

"You can't talk to me like that!"

"I just did. Admiral, I will work according to the method and order I find most effective. I thought we had settled that already. But since you're so eager for depositions of senior officers, I'll schedule a deposition so you can tell me who your source is in the IG Office. Tomorrow at noon."

"I will not!"

"Yes, Admiral, you will. If you have someone on my team trying to influence this case, *that* is hardly objective. I need to know who it is, because now every single deposition they've performed has to be redone by someone I can trust."

"Reed's going to hear about this, Park."

"He already has, Admiral. I'm forwarding this entire conversation to him as we speak. If you think *I'm* upset about your little mole, I can only imagine how he'll react. He takes the independence of this office very seriously. But if I'm wrong, if he decides I'm out of line, he can remove me from duty. Until then . . . See you at noon, Admiral."

I pushed the call closed. Then I sat silently in my cabin and trembled, waiting for the call from Reed that would remove me from duty. I didn't know if I would be angry at that or relieved to transfer my burden to someone else, but I dreaded that call either way.

But it never came. After over two hours of waiting, fiddling with depositions but unable to concentrate, I finally received a brief text response from Reed: *Do it. Looking forward to Knapp's deposition. AND AAMES'S. Reed.*

Then I felt relief. Pressure or no, I wanted to do my job my way. Do it right. And for the moment I still had Reed's support. But not forever. I tried to relax. I turned off my comp and went to bed.

C

But if I thought I was going to get any sleep, I was in for disappointment. It was just about two hours later when my comm buzzed again. I reached to my bed stand and looked at the screen. A blinking icon said, *Incoming call from A. Holmes.* What did Mayor Holmes want now?

So I pulled the call open, but the face I saw was the wrong Holmes. Anton Holmes, one of the hundred richest people in the solar system, was thinner and grayer than his son, but had the same eyes, fiercely determined, and the same set of the jaw. He had the same steel in his bearing. He waited impatiently to see me appear on his screen, and he scrawled on his comp while he waited. It would be almost a minute before he realized I was there. I remembered Dr. Baldwin discussing how valuable his time was, and I wondered how much that minute would cost him.

While it would take a minute for him to notice me, there was no reason I couldn't greet him immediately. I brushed my hair out of my eyes, and I wished I looked more presentable; but it was his own damned fault for calling so late, ship's time. So I jumped into my greeting. "It's a pleasure to meet you, Mr. Holmes."

After the light-speed delay, Holmes started in. "It's about time you—" Then he stopped. "What time is it there? Oh, my apologies, Inspector Park. My aide miscalculated your time zone. Yes, it's a pleasure to meet you. But I don't like to waste time, so I'm glad I don't have to introduce myself. To get right to my point: I understand you're taking an inordinately long time in prosecuting Nick Aames. If there are any resources I can provide to help speed things along, just let me know. This delay is unacceptable! The sooner that man is busted out of the Corps, and a real captain put in charge of that ship, the better. So explain yourself, Park. What's taking you so long?"

"Explain myself?" I sat straight up in bed. "I don't have to explain *anything* to you. You don't get to tell the Inspector General's Office what to do. Mr. Holmes, I answer to Admiral Justin V. Reed of the Inspector General's Office, and he answers directly to the Initiative Council. You are not in my chain of command, so you can take your demands and . . . file them." I didn't say where.

I could tell from Holmes's eyes when my response arrived, and he grew agitated. "Ms. Park, I am the sixty-seventh wealthiest individual in the solar system. That means there are sixty-six people with enough resources to tell me no, but *you* are *not* one of them. I have more influence than you can possibly imagine, both inside the Initiative and out. If you keep up this insolence, I can make life very difficult for you. I have friends on the Initiative Council. People listen to me there. The right word in the right ear at the right social occasion, and you might find your promotion opportunities held up for years to come."

I shook my head. "You do know, Mr. Holmes, that communications with my office *or* with me are routinely recorded. A blatant threat like that looks very bad for you."

After the delay, Holmes laughed. "Record me? Go ahead. At my level of the game, Park, these aren't threats. This is just how the game is played: I forcefully advocate for my position, using all of the tools at my disposal, and so does anyone else who wants to sway the Council. It's easier when we're above board about what we want and what we'll do to get it. Anyone can see what tools we'll use. That way there are no secrets to surprise us nor to be held against us by those who might try to control us."

Holmes looked down at his comp, and then back up at me. "And speaking of tools, my division, Holmes Agro, is the third-largest rice purchaser in Asia. Second largest in Korea. I buy a lot of rice to support my orbital and asteroidal missions. In fact, I purchase 92 percent of the rice grown in Hongcheon. I have people to handle that business, of course, but I do have to be certain which farmers I can trust to deliver on their contracts. If I lose confidence in, say, Park Farms of Hongcheon, I will have to send in quality inspectors to ensure that the farms meet my standards. And my inspectors are *very* particular. We pay a premium to keep our missions supplied, so we have to be sure the crops deserve that premium. If they don't, I may just have to cancel contracts." And he smiled at me, an utterly poisonous smile that made me want to spit at him.

"Mr. Holmes, are you threatening my family? After I told you this was being recorded?"

Holmes must have anticipated me. He answered before he could've heard my question: "Did I threaten? I merely stated my business position: if I have reason to question your judgment, that gives me reason to question your father's as well, and I will have to reevaluate our business relationships. A man in my position has to pay attention to even the smallest details if he wants to *stay* in this position. I made no threats, and I've got very well-paid lawyers to convince a court of that if need be. But if you give me a reason to trust you . . ." He trailed off; but before I could respond, he continued, "It's time you made some decisions, Park. The *right* decisions."

I shook my head, confused. "Mr. Holmes, I don't understand this anger. What do you care about Nick Aames's case? I know you lost a lot of money when you lost the *Aldrin*, but that was over a decade ago. You can't still be holding a grudge. And if you are, why did you endow Aldrin University?" The school's entire initial endowment was built on Holmes stocks and bonds.

Holmes leaned into the pickup and glared at me, eyes narrowed. "That man cost me more than a lot of money. He cost me a small fortune *and* long-term economic leverage that I have *never* recovered. And it's time everybody learns what an incompetent and dangerous commander he is."

I glared right back. I wasn't going to fall for stupid dominance games. "Forgive me for not studying your corporate history, but how did Nick Aames cost you that much?"

"The way he ran that ship, he killed my profit margins. Oh, the *Aldrin* never *lost* money. He delivered on time—he had to, orbital mechanics gave him no choice—and payloads were well maintained. Customers were satisfied. But everything about the transport cost more than I budgeted, thanks to his overblown safety protocols, his inspections, and his constant crew training. Not to mention the high turnover rate among crew that hated his guts."

"But if you made money, what was the problem?"

Holmes sighed, and he slowed down as if explaining to a simpleton. "Inspector, in a business the size of mine, it's not a question of making money, it's about making *enough* money. I invested money in that ship, and I didn't make enough return on investment. I could've done better in modular fusion, or low-orbital habitats, or a dozen other ventures. But instead, I had invested in the Mars cycler program, and heavily leveraged that investment, expecting a certain rate of return. Thanks to Aames and his nitpicking, we never got close to that return. Our costs were too high. Finally I had to unload that tin can and several smaller divisions that I had used to bankroll that operation, and I took a loss on every one. Nick Aames set me back a decade because he can't treat space travel as a routine business venture."

Holmes looked away. I could see him trying to maintain his calm. "And then, after I sold out to the Initiative, suddenly Aames's costs started coming down. He said it was due to efficiencies that grew over time, but I'm convinced he deliberately sabotaged me. He got a kickback from someone, I'm sure. And soon the *Aldrin* was competing against my own fast boats. That cost me *another* small fortune. For payloads that didn't have to get to Mars quickly, their costs were 10 percent of mine. I almost lost the fast boat business as well."

I tried to hide the smugness in my voice, but it wasn't easy. "As you said, sir, you have excellent lawyers. Investigators, too, I'm sure. If there was any proof for your charges, I'm sure you would've found it by now. I think you're just bitter that you gave up too soon, and you were wrong and Aames was right."

Holmes swung back to the screen and shouted, "That man cost me—" But he swiftly regained his composure. "That man nearly cost me everything. Even my no-account son. Anthony was so taken with Mars, he applied to be a permanent colonist. To prove he could make it on his own, he divested of his entire inheritance and holdings. *He* is the one who endowed that fly-by-night 'university,' not me. He *gave* them voting stock! He endowed it in my name, as a sop to my vanity, but *not* with my approval."

"I see," I said. "And so a major voting bloc in your organization is controlled right here on the *Aldrin*. And you want it back under your control." I wondered which loss bothered Holmes more, his son or his controlling vote.

And then I had another thought. "In fact, Mr. Holmes, I suspect that if I asked Admiral Reed to launch an Earth-side investigation, he would find that I'm not the only one to whom you have applied pressure regarding this case. In fact, I wonder if he would find more than words whispered in ears: perhaps financial contributions to politicians, perhaps even to Initiative Council members. And not just to their campaigns, maybe even to their personal accounts. I am just speculating, of course, but I do have to wonder."

When Holmes heard my comments, he smiled. "I won't respond to such base speculations. There's no evidence for any of that, I'm sure of it." But some of his confidence was gone. He wasn't sure at all.

That was all I needed to know to press my advantage. "Perhaps not, Mr. Holmes, but it would be interesting to find out. Sometimes evidence isn't as deeply buried as we think. Admiral Reed is an extremely thorough investigator."

Holmes turned furious. "Young lady, I'm recording, too, and that's slander."

But I saw sweat on his brow, and I knew I had him. "It's only slander if we can't prove it, sir. Are you prepared to take that chance? Because I am." Then I shook my head. "But I don't think it has to come to that. I think things will work out just fine if we let my investigation follow its natural course. And none of this discussion has to become part of the official case record. So if you will *back off*"—I emphasized those two words—"and stop telling me how to do my damned job, I will do a thorough investigation on the merits of this case, and on those alone. I will have no reason to expand my investigation. But if you continue to push me, I will be forced to inform Admiral Reed that your actions are relevant to the case. That will put the case here on hold, potentially indefinitely, while we pore over every detail of your political connections. I think we can agree that patience is the wiser course, can't we?"

Without waiting for a response, I added, "I hope by now I've reassured you about the independence of this office. We don't take pressure, not from you and not from Captain Aames. We don't take it from anyone. But when we need to, we can serve it up. Park out." And I closed the call.

I hoped it had cost a hundred thousand dollars of his time. I was furious. But I made myself calm down. Anger at Holmes wouldn't help my objectivity, and that was going to get seriously tested. I told myself to be happy I had put Holmes in his place, and just leave it at that.

But for the second time that night, I lay in bed and worried about a message from Reed. I was still worrying when I finally fell asleep again.

☾

The next morning, I woke feeling almost as tired as the night before. Between the late night calls and fretting, I had gotten little rest. I felt edgy and irritated, ready to tear into anyone who crossed me. That seemed like the perfect mood for a mole hunt.

When I got to Matt's office, he was waiting for me, as usual; and he had a large cup of coffee ready and a pot sitting on the table behind his desk. "I saw your comm logs from last night," he said. I smiled as I gulped down some coffee, warm and black and strong, and I needed no other explanation. We were starting to learn how each other worked, and I appreciated his diligence. Maybe we could work together again after this temporary post.

We took our cups into my office, with the walls as dark as the coffee, and we started to work. I set Aames's e-reader on a side table, and I tilted up the giant desktop, turning it into a display board so it would be easier for us both to see. I explained about Admiral Knapp's mole in our team, and then I pulled in two piles: the crew depositions my team had made, and my team's own personnel records. We started looking at them and discussing them, searching for signs of the mole.

Of course the first suspect I had worried about had been Matt himself. I never told him that, but he was professional and experienced enough to expect it. I had to consider that he was so helpful as a means to ingratiate himself with me and work his way into my confidence. But I had reviewed his record very carefully during my sleepless period the night before. Matt had spent his entire career in the IG Office, and he had a string of favorable evaluations, quite impressive at his young age. There were no irregularities in his finances, and Admiral Reed himself had used him as an aide on three cases. If there was any smudge on his record, I couldn't see it. Still, damn Knapp for making me so paranoid. I felt awful having to suspect Matt, but Knapp had left me no choice. I had to suspect everyone.

Now, more awake and recharged from the fresh coffee, I felt more confident about Matt. My trust in him grew. As we worked through the records, I really came to appreciate his sharp mind: he didn't think like me, but he made a nice complement to my methods. I picked out motivations and behaviors, while he was skilled with numbers and connections. Between the two of us, we could tear apart a hypothesis and see if it would break.

And so by 1030 hours, we had narrowed down our suspects to a list of five. By 1110, we had it down to three: Ensign Debra J. McCall, Lieutenant Henrik Kooistra, and Lieutenant Christopher Decker. Each had spent years in the Admiralty offices before transferring to the IG, two of them having worked in Knapp's headquarters. That made sense: Captain Aames wasn't the only officer who could inspire lasting loyalty in his subordinates. For each of them, Matt found possible indicators that they were drawing a salary beyond their IG pay. We pulled out the depositions they had performed, and scheduled those to be redone. I also set up interviews with each of them. I was confident that face-to-face, I could determine which of them was hiding something.

We wrapped that all up with ten minutes to spare before Admiral Knapp's deposition, so I was feeling pretty pleased with our work. When 1200 rolled around, though, Knapp was nowhere to be seen. Instead one of his aides had come down from H Ring. Matt ushered her into my office. The young junior lieutenant looked nervous as she entered, as if she expected fireworks.

I looked at her, and I let contempt slide into my voice. "Yes, Lieutenant?" She didn't deserve it, she was just Knapp's pawn, but I was too cranky to be forgiving.

The lieutenant's voice shook as she answered, "Begging the inspector general's pardon, ma'am. Admiral Knapp expresses his apologies that he will be unable to provide a deposition at this time as he is overseeing certain personnel transfers. As these transfers involve a member of your team, he was sure you would understand. He says this will explain." She handed me a message pouch, then stood at attention and waited for me to dismiss her.

I used my thumbprint to open the pouch. Inside was a data stick marked "CONFIDENTIAL." I looked up at Matt and the messenger.

"At ease." Then I pulled my earphones from my personal comp, stuck them in my ears in case Knapp's message had an audio component, and inserted the stick into my comp.

I needn't have bothered with the earplugs: the message was text files only. The first was a transfer order: *Effective 1000 hours this date, Lieutenant Henrik Kooistra is transferred from the Inspector General's Office to the Admiralty office, with a promotion to lieutenant commander. Transfer order signed by Admiral Franklin P. Knapp.* The second was a computer access record: every file Matt and I had accessed this morning, the precise times they were accessed, and the narrowing trail leading to Kooistra. The third was an encrypted message, requiring my ident code to open; and it self-deleted as I read it: *You had damned well better be this thorough in investigating Aames.* And then the file was gone.

I looked the lieutenant right in the eye to see if she would blink. "I see. He's too busy to meet with me."

"He expresses his apologies," she repeated.

"I'm sure he does." I sighed. "All right, tell the admiral I appreciate his message. And here's my message in response: I understand that he's busy, and I understand how important this personnel transfer is. I am *postponing* his deposition at this time."

"Postponing, Inspector?"

"Yes, postponing. Tell him that I reserve the right to depose him in the future as I see necessary in this case. When the time comes, I'll expect him here in A Ring at *my* convenience. Tell him that *exactly.*"

"Yes, Inspector."

"You're dismissed, Lieutenant."

Matt escorted the aide out of his office, and then he came back to mine. He looked at our display board. "I assume that does *not* end our mole hunt, Inspector?"

I smiled at him. I really did like how his mind worked. "Not on your life, Matt. Knapp wouldn't hesitate to sacrifice one mole to protect another. Continue looking into the files of McCall and Decker, and oversee the repeat depositions for all three. In the meantime"—I looked at my comp—"it looks like I have a little unexpected time in my schedule. I should check my message queue. Keep me apprised of what you learn."

"Yes, Inspector." Matt returned to his office, and I folded the display board back down into a desk. Then I set Aames's e-reader back on the corner. I had gotten used to having it there. It just seemed right.

I could've filled the opening Knapp's strategic retreat left in my schedule with work, but I was still too edgy about the mole to concentrate. I hoped that going through my message queue would distract me and let me calm down so I could get back to work.

The queue hadn't changed much from previous days, new messages but the same topics: more demands for updates from the Admiralty; notes from Reed's office on our reports from the previous day; new crew depositions from my team; and a pile of reports on minor conflicts between the Admiralty guards and the *Aldrin*'s crew.

Then I found a surprise: a message from home. Father and Mother had kept their calls to a minimum, since they didn't want to distract me from my work. Their most recent call had been during my convalescence, wishing me good health. Another call this soon was unusual for them, so I eagerly pulled it open.

But the look on Father's face in his recording changed my mood from eager to worried. His hair was grayer than I remembered, reminding me that I hadn't been downside to visit them in too long. And now I was on a voyage that meant over two years before I would see them again. For as long as I could remember, his face had been weathered from decades on the farm; but now it looked like wrinkled leather, with his eyes narrowed in concern.

Father started speaking. "My daughter Yerim, I hope this message finds you well, and does not cause you concern. Let me assure you in advance that we have matters under control. This morning I have received a visit from the local representative of Holmes Agro." I nearly dropped my coffee when he said that. "He expressed grave concern about your performance in your job and in how, he claims, you are failing in your responsibilities. He told me that if he cannot trust the daughter, perhaps he cannot trust the father."

Holmes wasn't messing around. Despite my clear warnings the night before, he was putting pressure on my family. I opened a call window to record a reply, but Father continued, "I told the representative that anyone who would question the integrity of my daughter was a man whose judgment *I* could not trust, and he did not need my rice. I have canceled all our contracts with Holmes, and I am placing my rice futures on the open market." Father looked down at his comp, and then looked back at the pickup. "I suspect he is spreading rumors to blackball me. The only bids I have so far are below last week's prices." That would be bad. Holmes usually paid a premium above market so as to ensure their supply. Now Father would not only lose that premium, he wouldn't even make market rates.

Again I reached for the reply window, but Father's words stopped me. "Again, daughter, do not let this concern you. The honor of the Park family cannot be bought at any price. I do not know what you have done to upset Mr. Holmes, but I trust that it was the right thing, and your mother and I will be proud of you when we learn it. Do not waver now. There are always hungry people in the worlds, and I shall find buyers for my rice. We shall never find another daughter like you, Yerim. Park out."

I choked back tears, and I found my voice to record my reply. "Father, I am your daughter. I cannot do less than the right thing. Thank you. I love you and Mother. This will be a long voyage to Mars and back, and I will think of you the entire time. I will not let you down. Park Yerim out." I pushed the message to the "Send" queue.

I felt awful that Father was going to lose money due to my work, but I felt so proud that he wouldn't back down. Anger, regret, and pride warred within me, and I sat there shaking with growing fury and weeping with pride. At last I pushed a copy of Father's message to Admiral Reed, along with a comment: "Admiral, based on this and last night's conversation with Mr. Holmes, I recommend an investigation of Holmes and Holmes Agro for interference in this case and for whatever else we can pin on them. Holmes Agro is outside the defined bounds of my plenary power for this case, so I can't make that call myself, Admiral; but if you choose to pursue an investigation there, I volunteer for the case."

I breathed deeply, calming myself. I was moved by Father's trust in me, and I was determined to be worthy of it. Admiral Reed could tell me how to do my job, but I wouldn't allow anyone else to try.

At last I relaxed enough to continue through my message queue. My very next item was a picture message: Adika, sitting up in bed and smiling through a breathing mask. There was no text attached, but I didn't need any. "Matt," I said into my comm as I rose from the desk, "if anyone needs me, I'll be in the infirmary."

☾

When I got to the infirmary, Adika was sitting up, and the breathing mask was gone. Head Nurse Lloyd leaned across the bed and fed Adika through a straw. Adika saw me come in, and he spit the straw out. "Please, Carl, the broth is delicious, but I can eat later. I have a visitor." He wore the same warm smile he had had in his photo message.

Lloyd turned and saw me. "Hello, Inspector." He looked down at his comp. "You're on the approved visitor list. But please, keep it short. He still has a lot of resting to do. And Commander"—Lloyd pointed a finger at Adika—"don't get too excited. Those lungs are still under warranty, but we don't want to replace them again anytime soon." Lloyd put Adika's breathing mask back on, and then he went into the next ward.

I walked over to Adika's bedside. I wanted to touch him, to shake his hand or press his shoulder or somehow make contact with the man who had saved my life. Probably saved the ship. I wanted to feel that he was real, that he was alive and would stay that way. But he had too many wires and tubes attached, and I didn't dare touch anything. Lung replacement was a common emergency surgery these days, but it was still a major shock to the system. So I just stood close, and I smiled.

Adika's voice was muffled by the breathing mask. "Inspector. I am so glad to see you are well."

I laughed at that. "Me? You're the one with the new lungs, Commander."

He tried to shake his head, but all the tubes made it difficult. "Inspector, we have shared an adventure, and an infirmary. You must call me Chuks."

I smiled. "Only if you call me Yerim."

"Yerim. That suits you."

"But Chuks," I continued, "I didn't know if I'd see you again at all."

Again he tried to shake his head. "Constance is the finest doctor in the Three Worlds, and all the spaces in between. I was in good hands, in the best possible place to get treated."

"I'm still relieved. I'm so glad that I can finally thank you, Chuks, for saving my life."

"You're welcome. But I was only doing my job. These tubes, this surgery, they are just part of the job." He sighed. "And now I will get a long vacation, though Constance calls it physical therapy."

"Yes." I could only imagine what his regimen would be like, far longer and more extensive than my own. "I'll miss you during your 'vacation.' I may need someone to knock some heads together, and both you and Smitty are on restricted duty. I'm not sure Matt's up to it."

Adika's face grew stern. "Then perhaps, Yerim, you must learn to knock your own heads together." But he couldn't hold his scowl, and he laughed. Then he started coughing. Lloyd stuck his head in from the other ward, but Adika raised a hand and waved him off. Lloyd returned to the other room.

When Adika's coughing subsided, he continued, "From what I hear, you are managing the situation on this ship just fine. We had that one rough patch, but you are now firmly in control."

"I'm trying," I said. Father's message was still on my mind, giving me confidence. "You were right, there's a lot more happening here than one can find in official reports, and I'm trying to understand it all. That's another reason that I owe you thanks."

"Again, it is nothing," Adika continued. Then he paused. "But if you do feel a need to show your gratitude, you could dismiss the charges against Captain Aames." My eyes grew wide, and he quickly added, "I joke, Yerim, I joke. You must do your job as you see fit. I know that your honor is no more for sale than my own. Please forgive an invalid for a small bit of humor."

"I forgive you, Chuks." But inside I burned. Adika was probably telling the truth: he had just been joking. He hadn't meant to reignite my anger, but that was exactly what he had done. One more person telling me what to do—and someone I had come to think of as a friend. I nodded agreement as I strove to keep my anger inside. I was sure he hadn't meant anything by it.

But I still felt the pressure. I did owe this man my life, but I couldn't let that sway my decisions any more than I would let Knapp or Holmes.

As I pondered all these forces bearing down upon me, Head Nurse Lloyd appeared at my side. "I'm sorry, Inspector, time's up. The commander needs his rest."

"Yes, Nurse." I turned back to Adika. "Thank you again, Chuks. And please get better soon. This ship needs you. We're all pulling for you."

"Thank you, Yerim. Bed: down." Adika's bed flattened out, lowering his head so he could rest. Lloyd led me out of the infirmary.

When I reached the passageway, Dr. Baldwin was there waiting for me. She pulled me aside and into her office. "Inspector," she said, "I'm going to be short here, and blunt, because I don't have a lot of time. So

I'm sorry if this comes across as pushy, but Chuks was right. And he might have been joking, but I'm not: you owe him, and you owe me. That man and this crew saved your life, and we did it according to protocols we learned under Captain Aames. Because of his training, this is the best crew in space, and I don't care what the damned admirals say."

Again I felt my fury building. "Doctor, are you telling me how to do my job too?"

Dr. Baldwin shook her head. "No, I'm just trying to get you to think. Think about what you've seen on this ship. Make your decision based on that. Just do what you have to do. Let Captain Aames go, let us do our jobs in peace. Or if this crew isn't good enough for you, if our commander isn't up to your standards, then charge him already, and to hell with you."

I couldn't find words to speak, and I came up empty. Dr. Baldwin took a deep breath, and her scowl softened. "I'm sorry, that's too harsh. Blame it on the fact that I've spent the last week stitching my husband together from pieces. But I'm tired of this thing dragging on. I've already patched up enough bodies for this cycle. Tensions are through the roof. The longer this goes on, the more likely things will blow up even worse. So whatever you're going to do, just do it already."

I couldn't answer without shouting, and I didn't want to upset Adika next door. So I pulled away from Dr. Baldwin, and I stormed out of her office and down the passageway. When I was a quarter ring away, I finally let out a scream. If one more person told me what to do, I was ready to test the limits of my plenary powers by having them clapped in irons.

And then I laughed at the notion. I was getting as bad as Aames, thinking I had the powers of an old British sea captain to put men in irons. I imagined the look on Reed's face when I announced that punishment, and I laughed even harder.

I was still laughing when Smitty came upon me in the passageway and asked, "What's so funny, roomie?"

Without thinking, I wheeled on her, my temper let fly like a rocket off the pad. "Oh, it's your turn now?"

"What?"

"I see a pattern here. It's like the entire crew of the *Aldrin* is lining up to take turns telling me to lay off of Captain Aames."

"Wait a minute—"

"No, you wait a minute! I am tired of all this pressure from every person I meet, and I am not going to put up with it anymore."

Smitty's face turned as red as her hair. "You're outta line, Inspector. I don't know what's crawled up your ass, but it has nothing to do with me."

I stopped. Considering, I realized Smitty hadn't said anything wrong. The problem was all mine. I had projected my frustration onto her. "I'm sorry, Smitty."

"That's Bosun Smith to you, if you're going to behave like that, Inspector. But as long as you've brought it up, I do have some advice for you: get that stick out of your ass and stop worrying about what everyone else thinks you should do. That's their problem, not yours, so stop hiding behind it and just do your job."

Just do your job. That's really what it came down to: all this pressure from all these directions, they were a sideshow. They weren't my job. "You're right, Bosun. You really are. And I really am sorry. I was wrong, entirely, and you didn't deserve that."

Smitty's voice dropped in volume, but her face remained flushed. "Well, don't waste time apologizing when I'm still mad. It won't do you any good. Save it for later, after I've had time to kick a wall or two." And then she gave just a slight smile, and I felt better. "But what's got you so angry that you're attacking random people in the passageway?"

So I explained: not all the details, nothing that I shouldn't make public, but enough to show how many people were pushing me in one direction or another. "I blocked every one of them, but it's like the pushes are coming faster and faster. I'm getting too tired to keep pushing back."

Then Smitty showed me that maybe I was forgiven after all: she reached out and patted my shoulder. "Poor Yerim, they're going to keep pushing you as long as you give them a reason to try. As long as you haven't made a decision yet, they're going to try to make you decide their way. And I can't blame them: if I thought I could get away with it, I would bully you into clearing the captain."

"Smitty!"

"But I can't. I know you're stronger than that, even as tired as you are. But the only way to stop the pushing for good is to finish the damn job. I appreciate what you've been doing, trying to understand the context, not just accept what's in some reports. But it's time for your next move."

I looked at Smitty. In her own way, she was pushing too. But it was in the right direction.

"You're right, Smitty. Thank you." I lifted my comm and pulled open a call. "Matt, this is Park. Contact Chief Carver, extend my apologies for the short notice, and tell him I expect him in my office for a deposition in an hour."

12. MUTINY ON THE *ALDRIN* EXPRESS

Deposition of Chief Anson Carver in the matter of The System Initiative v. Captain Nicolau Aames. *Questioner for the Inspector General's Office: Inspector General Park Yerim. Court Reporter: Lieutenant Matt Harrold. Questioner's comments and questions appear in italics. Deponent's responses appear in plain text. Deposition taken on 10 June 2083.*

Q: If you're ready, Chief Carver: please describe your assignment and location on 7 March of this year.

On 7 March I was assigned as the chief officer of the interplanetary vessel *Aldrin*, serving under Captain Nicolau Aames, a position I had held for the preceding nineteen years.

Q: Hold up a moment. The reporter shall include a copy of Chief Carver's service record as Attachment Carver 1. Continue, Chief.

On the date in question I was at my station on the bridge of the *Aldrin* as we made our return approach to Earth.

Q: Please describe the events of that date as you observed them from the bridge of IPV Aldrin.

Begging the inspector's pardon, I suggest those events will be more comprehensible if I present them in context.

Q: In context, Chief?

The events of 7 March were just a link in a long chain of events. They didn't transpire in isolation. I think that to truly understand the events of that day, you need to understand the entire chain.

Q: This is unorthodox, Chief Carver. I would remind you that I am running this deposition, not you. But this office is willing to grant you some leeway. Proceed. But stick to relevant events. I don't need you to retell the entire history of the Aldrin.

Thank you, Inspector. The roots of the incident in question can be found in the *Aldrin*'s prior Earth-Mars semicycle, during mission planning for the upcoming Mars-Earth semicycle. The *Aldrin*'s mission plans are always a combination of routine transportation and shipping with unique scientific missions. On some cycles, however, we also upgrade our infrastructure, adding new rings or new levels on existing rings. Those take extra effort from our crew, in coordination with the orbital construction factories that build the new infrastructure. Those additions are part of our long-term infrastructure growth plan.

[Sound of coughing.]

Excuse me, my throat's a little dry.

Q: Reporter, pause recording and bring the chief some water.

Q: Is that better?

Yes, thank you, Inspector. So, our long-term infrastructure growth plan . . . The *Aldrin* is more than just a transport ship, it's an ever-growing platform for Earth-Mars transport and commerce. Besides our transport capabilities, we have workshops and laboratories, we have hydroponics and recycling, and we even have our own university. We have a number of civilian permanent residents who work full-time in the laboratories, and others who provide goods and services to support the crew and the ship. Many of the crew have families aboard the ship. And this is all expanding under the long-term plan: new rings and new levels to grow the habitable space of the ship. New levels are assembled from components we pick up during planetary rendezvous; but new rings are assembled in the Farport orbital shipyards and boosted to speed so that we can rendezvous with a ring all in one piece, dock with it, and integrate it as a permanent addition. Because the *Aldrin* is driven primarily by orbital mechanics, not by reaction engines, the ship can grow without excessive worry about fuel consumption. Our ship is analogous to a pendulum swinging back and forth between Earth and Mars: the pendulum swings the same distance at the same speed regardless of whether it is heavy or light. Of course, our cycler orbits are vastly more complicated than a pendulum, so we have to make minor course corrections during each cycle. Those do take more fuel and become more expensive with each added ring, and it takes a lot of fuel to boost a new ring into a rendezvous vector; but the small additional cost is more than compensated for by the additional commercial opportunities we get from the added space.

That had been our long-term road map, and we had successfully grown the *Aldrin* from its original two rings up to seven, and also added levels to our existing rings. But that new mission plan represented a new phase in Earth-Mars commerce: all our earlier rings had been constructed and launched from the Farport yards, but H Ring was under construction at the new Ares yard in Mars orbit. Its successful launch and integration, immediately following the integration of G Ring, would be a major political and public relations coup. It would demonstrate that the Initiative could greatly expand Earth-Mars commerce on a short schedule. There was a lot of pressure to make it a success, no matter what the cost.

And anyone who knows Captain Aames knows that he doesn't give a damn about politics or public relations, and he doesn't bow to pressure. He won't turn down a mission if it can be done, but he's better than anyone at poking holes in a mission plan and showing when it's doomed. The usual plan for adding a new ring was to dock it and integrate it as part of the Earth-Mars semicycle, and then at Mars we power it up and open it for partial occupancy as a pilot effort. We run it through shakedown during the longer Mars-Earth semicycle. By the time we reached Earth, it would be ready for full-time occupancy, and the pilot occupants would get first priority on the new space. But that mission would have to be accelerated: we were still integrating G Ring during that Earth-Mars semicycle, and they wanted to dock H Ring before we were even sure that G was stable. Then we would have to shake down *both* new rings by the time we returned to Earth.

Captain Aames had his senior bridge crew review the plan, and we came to a unanimous conclusion: it couldn't be done. The risks were too high. The captain reviewed our findings, and he concurred. He informed the Initiative that the crew did not have time to perform docking, integration, and *two* shakedowns in the Mars-Earth semicycle. He did not leave room for doubt: he said it was absolutely impossible.

The Initiative Council tried to argue him out of his position, but he wouldn't budge. They tried to bargain with him, and he laughed. I laughed, too, at the idea that Captain Aames could be paid to violate his principles. A few council members tried to have him relieved of command, but his original contract from when he signed up with Holmes still protected him. The Council even tried to flat-out order him to accept the mission; but in that they were blocked by their own Admiralty office. Despite the captain's frequent disagreements with admirals, they were all too professional to ignore his data and his arguments. They refused to issue orders that they knew would put the ship in jeopardy, and the Council couldn't override their refusal without generating more bad publicity than they wanted to handle.

Finally the Initiative found another way to throw money at the problem: they couldn't bribe Captain Aames, but they could hire an additional construction team to supplement the *Aldrin*'s own crew. The cost would be high, but it would save them the embarrassment of having Ares yard fail in its first major contract. When they proposed this alternative, Captain Aames had us reanalyze the numbers just as thoroughly as before. We concluded that this plan was still risky, but within acceptable margins. Captain Aames reluctantly accepted the plan, with the proviso that all terms of his contract still applied: between the gravipauses, he had the power to change work orders as he saw fit for the safety of the ship, its passengers, and its crew.

The cost for this new plan was pretty high. It was difficult to hire skilled spaceship construction workers on Mars—the Initiative had to entice many away from Ares yard itself—and it took a lot of fuel to get them into rendezvous shuttles to match orbit with the *Aldrin*. Comptroller Lostetter chewed the captain out when she saw what our share of those costs would be. The *Aldrin* by that point was fiscally self-sufficient, supported by tariffs and transport fees while paying an agreed-upon share of maintenance and growth costs. It was her responsibility as ship's comptroller to make sure that we *remained* fiscally self-sufficient, and she said this added cost was more than our reserves could cover.

Their discussion took place on the bridge, right in front of the senior crew. After so many years, we understood that the captain preferred open disagreement over private disputes and schemes. He expected us to stand up to him and prove him wrong when we could; but this time he didn't even look up from his comp as he asked Lostetter, "So we'll burn through our reserves, and it will cut into our net; but will we lose money on this semicycle? Net?"

Lostetter frowned, but she had to answer, "No, Captain."

"Then I don't care. As long as we can pay our bills, we're doing this. I made the Initiative back down until they found a way to reduce the risks. I can't tell them no again, not over mere money. Besides, they'll owe us a favor after this. Find a way to keep us in the black."

The comptroller didn't like his decision, but she knew better than to argue with the captain unless she had new data. So she kept quiet.

I wish she hadn't. Maybe she could've talked him into turning down the new ring, and all of this mess could've been avoided.

Q: Chief, that sounds more like a conclusion than an observation. Please avoid any findings of fact. That's the inspector general's job, not yours.
I'm sorry, Inspector. I'll be more careful.

So that was our revised mission plan for the Mars-Earth semicycle. It would still be a lot of work for our team, since they would have to divide up to do their own work *and* supervise the new crew. Captain Aames insisted on that, since there were too many things that an inexperienced team could get wrong. I think Chief Gale's accident on the I Ring demonstrates—

Q: Recorder, strike that about the I Ring. Chief, that sounds like another attempt to slip a finding of fact into the record. I will decide when and how the I Ring incident relates to this case. Are you going to stick to your observations? Or are you going to make me regret granting you this leeway?
Again I apologize, Inspector. I'll be more careful with what I say.

The problem started . . . I'm sorry, it is my opinion that the problem started with the new construction team. As I said, the Initiative had a limited pool of trained personnel from which to draw, so they had to hire who they could get. Normally Captain Aames is careful to screen new crew for problems. Not that he can override the Admiralty's crew assignments, but once they're aboard and we leave the gravipause, he can decide where they get assigned and what additional training they undergo. While the new crew was being selected and shipped up, we were all tied up with final integration on G Ring. Some tasks we might have left for the next semicycle now *had to* be done before our second passage of Mars. So in a rare moment of weakness, Captain Aames gave the Initiative's list a cursory examination, and he approved the roster as they presented it to him.

So what we ended up with was—and this is not a finding of fact, Inspector, I'm just reporting Captain Aames's words—"a team of SP clock punchers." Every single one of them was a member of Chief Gale's Space Professionals.

Q: Objection for the record. The Space Professionals are not Chief Gale's.
I stand corrected, Inspector. Chief Gale is an organizer and an officer and spokesperson for the Space Professionals, a certifying and credentialing organization that has many members in the International Space Corps, but he is not in any sense an owner of the SPs.

Due to several past conflicts with the Space Professionals, Captain Aames is no fan of them. The Admiralty won't let him dismiss a crewmember for SP membership, but he gives them extra scrutiny to make sure they measure up to his standards. The SPs advocate for more control of their work rules and more say in the chain of command, and that's absolutely unacceptable to the captain. He has to have final say on his ship, period.

So the captain has a habit of weeding out SPs, and the SPs have learned that it's less hassle to avoid the *Aldrin*, and everybody's happy. But on that semicycle, we had a critical mass of SPs. And sure enough—I should say, inevitably *in my opinion*, they started making trouble by trying to do things their way instead of the *Aldrin* way. First, and this was no fault of theirs, there was the fact that they were making a considerable premium for doing the same work our crews were doing. That was the Initiative's decision, not theirs. They just reaped the reward (though the SPs had negotiated precisely what that premium would be for unscheduled work like this). But second, their work wasn't up to our standards. They got paid more, *and* our crew then had to come in behind them and correct their work as needed. And third, by SP work rules, seniority in space accrued with time in space, period, no matter what the posting. On the *Aldrin*, only two things counted: your time on the *Aldrin*, and your record on the *Aldrin*.

So we had a higher-paid crew doing lower-quality work, making more work for our own crew *and* trying to tell them what to do. That created significant morale problems by itself, in my judgment, but it was only half of what went wrong. The other half was that the SPs tried to sign up new members among the *Aldrin* crew. The captain and I never saw that one coming. We could understand the problems with pay rates and work rules, but we never imagined that the SPs would dig up low-level resentments—you know, the usual gripes you find in any work environment, stuff that usually works itself out over time—and then promise to solve them. They promised other changes, too, stuff that was beyond their power to deliver. Under normal circumstances, maybe these promises would've had no impact; but with the crew stressed and overworked, they were more open to persuasion. And the ship's officers were too busy keeping operations running smoothly for us to recognize the problem until it started affecting progress of G and H Rings.

Q: Chief Carver, this really seems to be getting off the track. I trust you'll tie it back to 7 March soon.
I'm sorry, Inspector, but it really does bear on those events. I'll get there.

Q: I trust that you will. We'll reach Mars in four months. I would hope to be done with your deposition before then.
Understood, Inspector.

Q: So you say the crew had complaints. In your judgment, was there any merit to these complaints?

Inspector, when you command a large crew like the *Aldrin*'s, you learn two things: there are always complaints; and if you dig enough, you can always find *some* merit. If you're fair-minded, you can always see the other side and see why they're complaining. You probably don't agree with their view, or you would've fixed the problem already, but you can see how they see it. Part of my job as second-in-command was to watch for those complaints and head them off before they turned into critical issues. People bring things to me because they know the captain doesn't want to be bothered. Frankly, he doesn't understand the problems most of the time. He just doesn't see things that way. So he trusts me to deal with most of them; and he knows that if I bring one to his attention, it's serious enough that it *needs* his attention.

I guess you could argue that I dropped the ball in that area: I got so busy with the extra crew that I lost touch with these low-level complaints.

Q: I appreciate your willingness to take responsibility, Chief, but that's another finding of fact.

I'm sorry, Inspector. So we knew we were falling behind schedule, and we knew we had morale problems, but we were unclear just how large our problems were. We lost even more time ferreting out the root causes. When we finally understood the issues, we took two steps. First, we reassigned the SP crew to administrative tasks. They weren't happy with that, but they had no choice: despite their protests, we were between the gravipauses, and Captain Aames's word was absolute. When the SPs took their complaints to Chief Gale, the captain called their bluff: he informed the admirals that the SPs could do their assigned work, or their pay could be cut off. Over Gale's objections, the admirals reluctantly conceded that the captain had that power, and the

SPs went back to their assignments. They were surly and unproductive, but they were in jobs where we could tolerate that.

And then our second step was to gather our regular construction crew for a meeting, and the captain listened to their complaints, answered their questions, and got them back to work.

Q: Excuse me? The captain just talked with them and he changed their minds? That doesn't sound like Captain Aames.

Inspector, I don't think the details are relevant to the events of 7 March.

Q: I have to disagree, Chief Carver. You opened the door to this topic, and now I expect you to tell the story. The whole story.

All right, Inspector. To be precise, *we* didn't gather the construction crew, *I* did. I asked them to meet with me up on the exercise track, one of the only places we could get all those spacers in one room. Then I asked for their complaints, and I listened, particularly to Bosun Walker, the construction boss. I soon got the larger picture, and I could see how broken their morale was. It would be a challenge, it might take another month, but I was sure we could patch up these differences. Meanwhile the schedule would continue to slip, but that was the best resolution I could imagine. I hoped it would be enough.

Then I heard the one voice I didn't want to hear: from the access ramp, I heard Captain Aames say, "Out of my way, Ensign." I looked toward the ramp, and Ensign Franks looked like he was about to lose control of his bladder as the captain pushed past him and onto the deck.

Walker crossed over to the ramp and pulled Franks aside. "It's okay, Eddie, I got this." Then he turned to Aames. "Captain, you're not wanted here."

Aames pulled himself up to his full height: nearly a head shorter than Walker, but Aames always carries himself as if he's taller. "Walker, are you telling me where I can and can't go on my own ship?"

Walker loomed over the captain. "This is a private meeting. Sir."

From across the deck, Ensign Cho shouted, "Ah, let him through, Walker. He might as well hear: we're sick of this mess, and we're gonna fix it. We've made up our minds."

"You've made up your minds?" Aames crossed to the middle of the crowd, shouldering his way through. His body was tightly controlled, but fury grew in his eyes with every step. "You've whined to each other, you've bitched to the SPs, and you even dumped on Carver. But not one of you chickenshits had the balls to bring your beefs to *me*."

Walker stormed after the captain, got right up in his face, and said, "If you weren't an officer, I'd—"

But Aames interrupted him. "You'd do what?" The captain pulled open his jacket, stripped it off, and tossed it down the ring. "There's the bars, on the floor. It's just you and me, no officers to be seen here. Now what are you gonna do?"

Walker shook his head. "No, sir, I'm not stupid. I take a swing, and next thing you know, I'm on charges for assaulting an officer."

Aames laughed. "So, big man, you're suddenly afraid of the rules? Fine, we're between the gravipauses, so *I* make the rules here. You're all witnesses, we have a new rule: anyone who the captain calls a chickenshit gets a free shot at him. No consequences, no charges, no questions asked. So, Mr. Walker, I say you're a chickenshit. Are you going to take a swing at me?"

I expected Walker to mouth off some more, but he was smarter than that. Without wasting any more time, he wound back his fist faster than I could see, and he landed a solid punch on the captain's jaw. In the one-quarter gravity, Aames flew backward and crashed into Franks, who had come up behind him. Aames slid to the deck, and then he gathered himself to his feet.

He rubbed his jaw. "Not bad, Mr. Walker. You got another one like that in you?" Walker took another swing, but this time Aames dodged it easily. "Uh-uh! I said the *first* one was free. You want another one, you're gonna have to earn it. Come on, Walker, show me what you've got."

The crowd backed away, leaving Walker and Aames with room to maneuver. In the low gravity, Aames dropped into a low, easy crouch. Walker did the same, and they started circling each other. Nick's capoeira came out: he danced around, in and out, slapping and kicking Walker, and then springing out of range. The blows weren't painful, but they were embarrassing, and they pissed Walker off. Oh, sorry.

Q: You just quoted Captain Aames saying "chickenshit" three times, Chief. It's too late to worry about language in the court. Go on.

Walker landed a few shots, and eventually his powerful right hook connected again, sending Aames flying once more. But this time the captain used the momentum to spring off the wall, dance back, and land kicks on Walker's face and gut. Slowly Aames wore Walker down, slap and kick and punch and dance away, until Walker found his second wind. He made a charge at Aames, but it was actually a feint: when the captain tried to dodge, Walker was there with a left jab that caught him a good one right in the ribs.

Aames went down. This time when he stood back up, he held up a hand. "Enough, Mr. Walker. Not bad at all. I guess you're not a chickenshit. All right!" He raised his voice until it echoed around the track. "Any of the rest of you chickenshits want a shot at the old man? Franks?"

Franks took a step back. "Ummm, no, Captain."

"No? Okay, we'll come back to you. Lenard!"

Lenard, almost as big as Walker, hopped forward into the open space. Walker tried to hold him back, but Lenard shook his head. "No, I've been waiting for my shot at this for a long time."

Just as Walker had, Lenard took a surprise shot with no warning; but Aames didn't give him the free shot this time. They went through the dance again. Lenard was nimbler than Walker, and Aames was more tired. After several exchanges of blows, they ended up in a grapple on the ground, with neither having a clear advantage. The captain landed one solid blow to the face, splitting Lenard's lip, but Lenard refused to give in. Aames finally had to tap for release. Lenard let go and rolled away, and Aames helped him to his feet. "All right, you're not a chickenshit. But you're bleeding all over my deck. Medic! See to Lenard. All right, who's next?" He turned to me. "Carver! You've been listening to these chickenshits bitch about me for months, but you never brought word to me. That makes *you* a chickenshit in my book. Come on! This is long overdue."

I approached the captain, leaned in, and whispered, "Nick! We can't do this."

Aames reached out and slapped me. Then he grabbed the back of my neck, pulled me in close, and whispered back, "Make it look good, damn it." With that, he shoved me away, knocking me to my ass.

I let that get the better of me, and I got angry, though I didn't want to. I leaped back to my feet, and I charged at Aames, fists swinging; but at the last moment I stepped right, pivoted on my left foot, and swung my right foot in a roundhouse kick that caught him square in the chest. The kick sent Aames down to his knees, but only for a moment before he popped back to his feet. He came at me, and this time I punched him with my right fist in the solar plexus. Aames caught his breath, leaned in, and whispered, "Didn't . . . have to look that good."

Then the shock of what I had done settled in. I stared at him; and Aames, being the dirty fighter that he was, took the opportunity to box my ears.

And it was on. I tried to knee him in the groin, but I caught his inner thigh. He pulled back, and he snapped a kick at my knee, but I was out of the way already. I might not have Aames's Brazilian dance moves, but I could take care of myself, and he had already been through two fights. Soon I got a grip on his arm, and I turned that into a hip throw that launched him ten meters down the track, spacers scrambling to get out of his way.

Aames rolled to his feet, turned back to me, and sneered. "I guess you're not a complete loser after all, Carver." I was unsure how to take that until he winked. "All right, who's next? Are the rest of you too chickenshit to take your shot?"

And for the next twenty-five minutes, one spacer after another lined up for a shot at the captain: young or old, male or female, new crew or grizzled veteran. Franks redeemed himself, landing three good punches before the captain knocked him off his feet. (I think the captain went easy on him.)

The captain won a few bouts, but he mostly lost. He wore down slowly, but the end was never in doubt. Even his strong will wasn't enough to sustain him through that many bouts.

Q: I'm confused. When you started, I thought you were going to tell some preposterous story of the captain beating his crew into submission. You're telling me he let them beat him?

Oh, he didn't 'let' them. He fought back hard, but against ridiculous odds. They mopped the deck with him. And Aames took it. Some of it was playful combat, some was serious beatings, and he just took it. He got back up every time, but only to take some more. By the end, the mood had changed. He was bruised and bleeding and exhausted, but he wouldn't give up. The spacers saw that, and the ones who were left didn't attack in anger, they just wanted to get their shot, and maybe prove themselves against the capoeira moves they had heard about so often.

Finally, when there were no more challengers, Aames looked around. "Is that all you've got? Is that the lot of you?"

Walker looked around. "I think that's it. Captain."

Aames staggered around, found his jacket, and put it on. As he fastened the buttons, he addressed the crew. "So you've all had your shot. Some of you"—he looked at Lenard—"gave me some pretty nice bruises."

Walker looked at Aames as the captain brushed dust off his braid. "So now what? You throw us in the brig?"

"In the brig?" Aames shook his head. "Hell, no. You beat me, twenty-two to four."

"Twenty-three to three, sir," Cho interrupted. "I still say I got the better of our bout."

Aames raised an eyebrow. "That bruise on your eye says otherwise, Cho, but why don't we settle it with a rematch next week? But no, you all won fair and square. No one's going to the brig." He raised his voice to reach around the track again. "No, you're going *back to work*." Then he looked Walker in the eye. "And in the future, when you have a beef with someone on this ship, you will bring it to me. Not to the Admiralty. Not to Horace Gale and his chickenshit SPs. You bring it to me, or Carver, or Bosun Smith, or your superior officer. We are the goddamned IPV *Aldrin*, and we settle our problems ourselves. Is that clear?"

There was some general rumbling, mostly positive, but not what Aames was after. So I shouted, "Is that clear?"

"Clear, sir!" they shouted in unison, shaking the ring walls.

Q: All right, Chief Carver, that's a good story, but I must insist: What does it have to do with the events of 7 March?

Inspector, that was the day that turned the tide on our mission. That was the day our team returned to the G Ring, and they worked their asses off to get it into shape. Oh, it didn't hurt that the captain had another public fight with Comptroller Lostetter, and he wrung from her a promise to pay bonuses to our construction crew, and to hell with the profit margin for that semicycle. But what really made a difference was that, in a rare fit of practical psychological insight, the captain reunited our team and got them to see him as one of them. That was what got them to work at an energy level we had never seen before. They wore themselves out—they're still practically burned out today—but by damn, they had G and H Rings shaken out and ready for full occupancy by the time we reached Earth.

And that was when the Initiative announced the new project for I and J Rings on an even more aggressive schedule during the next Earth-Mars semicycle.

Q: And that *was what led to the events of 7 March?*

Yes, Inspector. The captain didn't even consult with his command crew. When the mission was received at 0930 hours on 7 March, we all stared at him there on the bridge, stunned. And he sent back his answer: "I'm sorry, Admiral Knapp. It can't be done. We reluctantly decline this mission."

It took eight seconds for Knapp to hear and respond. When he did, his face grew red. "You decline? You can't decline."

Captain Aames pushed a file out alongside the call. "Yes, I can, Admiral. I don't even need my contract for that; it's just regulations." The captain recited without looking down at his comp. "*Standard Space Mission Protocols*, revised, chapter 1, section 3: Grave Risk. 'In all cases not involving an active war or an emergency rescue, it is the responsibility of the commander of the vessel to decline an otherwise lawful order if, in the commander's sole discretion, said order poses a grave risk to the safety of passengers or crew, or if said order poses a grave risk to the permanent integrity of the vessel and its ability to safely return personnel to the nearest port, or if said order poses a grave risk to the occupants or integrity of other nearby vessels. This responsibility may not be overridden by the ship's artificial intelligence, by local port masters, nor by higher ranking officers who are not physically aboard the vessel. If the commander judges that a condition of grave risk has arisen, the order in question must be declined as it is considered to be an unlawful order.'" The captain continued to stare at the admiral. "I am Captain Nicolau Aames, lawful captain of the IPV *Aldrin*, and it is my judgment that your order poses a grave risk to the safety of the personnel of this vessel and to the integrity and safe operation of this vessel. Therefore, I must decline the order issued by Admiral Franklin P. Knapp on 7 March, instructing me and my crew to add two new rings to the *Aldrin* on our next semicycle. For the record, Admiral."

Knapp was already hearing the start of Aames's message before the captain finished, and his eyes grew wider as he listened. But his voice was cold and controlled when he said, "You recited that as if you had it memorized, Captain."

Aames shook his head. "I didn't have to. You gave me a lot of desk assignments after the second *Bradbury* expedition. I was on the committee that revised the protocols."

When Knapp heard that, he almost smiled. "Touché, Captain Aames. Well played." Then the almost-smile slipped away. "But it's irrelevant. Aames, we need those I and J Rings operational before you reach Mars, and that's final. We have some very large contracts waiting for that capacity, and the Initiative Council has no interest in waiting another full cycle. This is going to happen, so you just have to accept it."

Aames folded his arms. "Chapter 1, section 3 says otherwise. My crew is exhausted and stretched to the limit by your last big push. Truth is, Admiral, I think you owe us for getting *that* impossible job done on an impossible schedule. But instead you're pushing for more? It's not going to happen, Admiral. That would be a grave risk to my crew and my ship."

When Knapp heard that, his smile returned. "Oh, is that all you're concerned about? I can take care of that. Aames, your crew can relax, enjoy themselves. I've arranged a secondary construction crew to board and do all the integration work on I and J."

"No," the captain answered.

But Knapp kept talking without waiting for an answer. "I hear through channels that you benched our crew from Mars. You let top-notch, credentialed Space Professionals sit idle while you worked your team twice as hard. I don't know why you did that, but *that* is why your team is exhausted, I'm sure. I'm going to be blunt, Aames: I don't think much of your crew, and I think that the expansion effort has gotten to be too much for them. Now it won't be your concern anymore. You and your crew can just worry about day-to-day operations. As soon as Gale gets over there with his SPs, I'm assigning him as permanent infrastructure officer, in charge of all expansions to the *Aldrin*."

Aames rose from his bridge chair. "Horace Gale!" He threw a pen across the bridge. "No, Admiral, I won't have it. That man is an arrogant, scheming idiot. *He* constitutes a grave risk by himself. You can send your crew, Admiral, and you can send Horace, but you can't make me put them to use. Once we leave the gravipause, I'll reassign the lot of them to scrubbing the Hydroponics deck."

Knapp sighed. "I had hoped for once you wouldn't be difficult, but I should have known better. Aames, you'll use my crew. You won't have anyone else to use." He pushed a file into the call stream. "Captain Aames, that is a transfer order for the entire crew of the *Aldrin* for reassignment to Earth duty. *Ground* duty." Knapp waved a hand as if brushing aside an objection he knew was coming. "Oh, it doesn't apply to *you*. Your contract is so tangled, my advocate office tells me it's not worth trying to break it. But that contract only applies to *you*, not to anyone else. Not even to Chief Carver."

I looked at the captain, but he ignored me, staring at the screen as the admiral continued, "Effective immediately, your crew is to stand down, start packing, and prepare to disembark for Earth. I'm afraid this will show as a demotion in most of their records, but that can't be helped. Meanwhile another full crew will board, a crew I can trust to be more loyal to the Admiralty than to you. Chief Gale will be your second-in-command."

Knapp finally paused long enough for the captain to respond. "You can't do this. You can't possibly get the transports and the—the substitutes in place in time for rendezvous." Each end of our trip required high-speed rendezvous shuttles because our speed was fast by in-system standards. There weren't many rendezvous shuttles, certainly not enough to swap out the crew.

But Knapp pushed another file. "Those are additional transfer orders, ship construction records, and pilot assignments. Some of us have been preparing for this for years, Aames. You were too much of a maverick for us to trust a major Earth-Mars commerce route to you. We knew sooner or later the maverick would have to be roped in. Branded." Knapp smiled, a wide, wicked, toothy smile. "Gelded. We've been preparing for this, and now it's our chance. When you reach turning point one, your crew of troublemakers will disembark, and we'll see how you operate with a professional crew."

Aames sank back into his chair. He looked more tired than he had after fighting the construction team. For the first time, I glimpsed what it would be like if Nick Aames were defeated.

But it didn't last for more than a couple of seconds. The captain sat back up in his chair and pulled open a ship-wide communications channel. "Attention all personnel, this is Captain Aames. It is possible that you have received transfer orders from the Admiralty. *All* of you. They want us to add *two* more rings to the *Aldrin*, and I told them you can't do it. And if you can't do it, no one can. But the Admiralty in its wisdom has lost confidence in me as your commander, and in you as a loyal crew. They aim to replace you all with a bunch of damned SPs who will be more compliant with their whims."

The captain paused for breath. "They may have lost confidence in you, but I *have not*. You are each and every one of you part of the finest crew it has been my pleasure to command. It is unfortunate that their intransigence, which is aimed primarily at myself, is now tarring your reputations as well."

Looking straight at the admiral, Aames continued, "And I won't have it. Consider those transfer orders revoked under *Protocols*, chapter 1, section 3. It would be a grave risk to this ship if it had to operate under any other crew but you."

The entire bridge crew was staring at the captain by that point. Then the impact of what Aames had done hit me. He had just defied the Admiralty, and he had roped us all into his defiance as well. If we stood with him, there would be trouble, but we would live up to the faith he had shown in us. If we abandoned him, we might salvage our careers, but he would be ruined. No one moved, as if the choice before us, the struggle between Aames and Knapp, had us locked in place. I wondered which way the crew would turn.

Then I decided: I didn't care how it went, I knew where my loyalties belonged. I felt damned proud to have earned the trust of Captain Aames, and I wanted everyone to know it. I started clapping, slowly and loudly.

Then Navigator Seth Howarth joined me, and I started clapping faster. Engineer Sakaguchi Nora whistled and joined us. In moments the entire bridge crew was standing and applauding. Comm Officer Ken Baker thought quickly, and he pushed the scene to every comp on board. In a few seconds, monitors lit up with scenes of crew and passengers standing and applauding throughout the ship. I swear I felt the *Aldrin* vibrate with the sound.

Captain Aames raised his hand, and the applause trailed off. Then he continued, "Thank you. You make me proud. One more thing: if any of you have any business that requires you on Earth, any sort of hardship, please inform your superior officer. We'll find a way to get you downside. But aside from that, Admiral, the *Aldrin*'s docks are closed to all vessels except as personally authorized by myself."

Knapp's face was stern, unmoving. "So that's your final word, Aames? You won't accept a replacement crew."

Aames didn't blink. "Final word, Admiral. Chapter 1, section 3."

"Shove your section 3, Aames." Knapp looked down at his comp, and then back up. "Very well, since you have refused a direct order, and the *Aldrin* has been within Earth's gravipause for five minutes, I formally charge you with violation of orders from the Admiralty. Thus

I find you to be in breach of your contract. And now, sir, I order you to relinquish command of the *Aldrin*. You are relieved, Mr. Aames. I'll command from here until Chief Gale arrives, at which time I shall issue him a field promotion to captain, and he shall take command of that vessel."

The captain pointed his finger at the screen. "Admiral, you can give up on that idea right now. Horace Gale will *never* command the *Aldrin*. He's a walking section 3, and I won't have him on my ship. Aames out." He pushed the call closed.

Q: So you don't deny that Captain Aames, within Earth's gravipause, violated a direct order from Admiral Knapp?

Inspector, you have the recordings from that day, both from our bridge and from Admiral Knapp's office. I don't deny the events thus recorded. But I deny that the admiral's order was lawful. The captain has claimed that it wasn't, under chapter 1, section 3. You're the one who will decide that claim in the end; but for me, the claim is self-evident, based on our experience with the Mars crew. Not to mention the I Ring and—

Q. But you couldn't resist mentioning it anyway, could you? Chief, you cannot argue that an incident which had not yet happened was justification for Captain Aames's actions.

No, Inspector, but I think it demonstrates that the captain's risk assessments were more accurate than the admiral's.

Q. Chief Carver, you may rest assured that I shall give the incident on the I Ring due consideration when I issue my findings. But it remains irrelevant here.

Understood. But let me give you a more direct answer to your question. Inspector, I don't deny that Captain Aames acted as I describe, but I deny that he was defying lawful orders when he did so. As far as we were concerned, the Admiralty had just declared war on the *Aldrin*.

Q: Chief Carver, you seem quite agitated. That's very unusual for you.
Inspector, I was agitated then, and I still am now. Our crew performed excellently. That assignment should've been impossible, but they pulled it off. And that was our reward? To have them spit on our effort, tell us we were incompetent, and transfer us all out like a bunch of failures? No, thank you! And when Captain Aames stood by us against the Admiralty, we stood by him. If they wanted a war, we would bring them one.

Q: Chief, I understand your emotion, but it's not helping in this deposition. I'm not your counsel—
I don't need counsel.

Q: That's your decision, but I should tell you that you're making statements that could be considered incriminating. If I find they have bearing on this case, I cannot ignore them. Even if part of me sympathizes with them.
Inspector, the truth is the truth. I've learned that attitude from Captain Aames. Usually I try to express it in more diplomatic terms, perhaps, but I'm not ashamed of it. And maybe I'm just tired of being diplomatic, since it hasn't gotten us anywhere.

Q: Still, Chief, I think it best if we take a two-minute break so that you can calm yourself. Reporter, stop recording and get the Chief another glass of water.

Q: All right, Chief Carver, let us resume. You were telling us that the Aldrin *had just declared "war" on the Admiralty.*
No, Inspector, you have that backward: they declared war on us. Not a formal declaration, but it was as clear as starlight from their words and their actions. And if they thought we were just going to roll over and take it, they didn't know Captain Aames. Or his crew.

But it was a strange war. The *Aldrin* isn't a warship, we had no weapons—

Q: I've heard rumors to the contrary, Chief.

I cannot confirm those rumors, Inspector. As you reminded me, I shouldn't make incriminating statements.

Q: But I would point out that a ship full of smart spacers, including engineers and designers and machinists, can come up with weapons from materials at hand.

Again, Inspector, I choose not to make incriminating statements. *Officially* we had no weapons; and the Admiralty's Orbital Defense forces were in no position to engage us, not so far out on the way to Turnaround One. So there weren't any shots fired. Yet.

So without weapons, we were fighting an information war. The captain and I and Comptroller Lostetter put our heads together to work through the economic issues and consequences we would face and how best to mitigate them. Then the comptroller got on the comm to contact our customers and our suppliers and our agents. She assured them that no matter what they heard, we had the law on our side, and we would come out of this better than ever. She conceded that we might have some delays in physical deliveries, but she insisted we *would* deliver; and she guaranteed that data deliveries would continue on schedule. She also made our suppliers agree to keep up their deliveries. She let everyone know that the situation was not under our control, and any complaints should be taken up with the Initiative; but she also had to give back significant percentages on every deal, with both customers and suppliers. When she was done, she cursed Captain Aames, showing more skill with profanity than I had ever imagined in such a quiet woman. But she cursed the Admiralty more.

When the Admiralty realized what we were up to, they attempted to jam our transmissions. We got a laugh out of that one: our comm techs made a game out of finding relays we could bounce signals off and frequencies they hadn't jammed. Plus we had a lot of allies who were willing to help out. A lot of independent transport operators have no great love for the Initiative and the way they try to control commerce. The independents understood exactly what was being done to us, and they could imagine it being done to them next. Plus both the Grand Nation of the Celestial Arch and the United Cities of Free Luna have long-standing grievances with the Initiative. Both were still paying off debts from before they gained their independence, and they weren't happy with how the Initiative manipulated those debts to the independents' disadvantage. If they could've, they would've resupplied us, but our cycle orbit was too fast for them to match up. But they were happy to rebroadcast our messages and make jamming more difficult. Some even started broadcasting opinion stories on what was happening and all the regulations the Initiative was breaking—including regulations against interfering with communications in space. None of us had considered a propaganda front, so our allies really helped out there.

So then the Initiative decided to fight the propaganda front as well, smearing Captain Aames in the news (with the help of some journos and publishers who were closely allied with Initiative Council members). They painted him as a modern-day Captain Bligh, a cruel commander driving his crew too hard and risking their lives and their mission. They called him everything short of a mutineer. They stopped there, because they knew a charge like that could only be made through your office. But they clearly implied it, and the opinion channels weren't so restrained. Surely you saw some of those shows?

Q: I'm in the fact business, Chief. I avoid the news and opinion channels. We saw them all, and we got a lot of laughs out of how inaccurate they were. The captain's favorite was *Nick Aames: The Man Who Stole Mars.* The producers of that one even tracked down his brother, Derick, for an interview. The captain had a strange look when he saw Derick. I asked him why, but he just whispered, "I hope they paid you well, Dek." He wasn't talking to me.

On 23 April, we were on approach to Earth. A ship was matching velocity with us, burning fuel like it was free. Her transponder identified her as the transport *Poling*. Captain Aames looked at the main screen. "Right on time," he said. "Howarth, is she alone?"

Howarth swept his hand across his console, pulling open every instrument he had. "No comm traffic on any channels, Captain. Nothing's showing up on the scopes or the radar. She's alone."

"All right," Aames said. "Baker, open a comm channel to the *Poling*."

The main screen lit up with the image of a female captain, her face lined and her blonde hair going gray, but her eyes still sharp and her bearing straight. She wore a gray uniform like ours, the most common uniform in space transport. "Captain Austin," Aames said, "it's good to see you again. How are things aboard the *Poling*?"

"We're crammed to the limit, Captain Aames," Austin said with a smile. "I figure I owe you some air and water after the *DeMarco*. We've got plenty of both, plus the cargo you've contracted for Mars delivery, all ready to off-load."

"Will you have any trouble docking?"

"No, Captain, no trouble at all. We have sufficient fuel for maneuvering, as long as your docking cradle is working."

Aames nodded. "They tell me it will break down later today, but it should be good for one more rendezvous." Captain Aames pulled open a ship-wide channel. "This is the captain speaking. All ashore who are going ashore. Those of you with appointments in the Earth-Luna system, your ride is approaching the *Aldrin* now. I expect you to be ready to board the moment those docking hatches open, and I expect every one of you to carry as much outbound cargo as you can. We're not going to have any minutes to spare, so say your tearful good-byes now. Bosun Smith and her team have instructions to shove you through the hatch if you can't move fast enough under your own power."

Captain Aames switched to a more private channel. "Cargo crew, we have passengers handling the outbound loads. Your job is the inbound. Austin's crew will be dumping crates out their cargo hatches as fast as they can move. I want you in the main cargo bay, maneuvering units all checked out, and ready to *chase that cargo*. Remember: without those payloads, I can't sign your paychecks. Get the crates fast, and don't miss any. Captain Aames out."

Then we waited as the *Poling* made her final approach to the *Aldrin*. Since our ship has all the maneuverability of a city block, we can't do anything during docking except wait for the other vessel to approach the lead end of our central tube. When the other vessel comes within reach, we latch on to it with our docking cradles, extensible arms that have tunnels for cargo and personnel. We depend on the piloting skill of the other captain to bring the ships safely together without wasting time or fuel.

Fortunately Captain Austin was an excellent pilot. She brought the *Poling* in ahead of schedule, and then she killed the relative motion perfectly. The three docking cradles were able to grab hold of the *Poling* with only a very slight tremor as the grapples locked down.

Again Captain Aames got on the ship-wide comm. "All right, we're docked. Move it, move it, move it!" On one monitor, we saw the massive cargo-bay hatch open. The bay was already in vacuum for this transfer, and the cargo crew immediately sped out to start chasing crates. On other monitors we saw the first passengers—the ones who had actually been in the docking cradles during attachment, a risky move that Aames frowns upon under ordinary circumstances—climb through the *Poling*'s hatches as soon as those opened. They fanned out, guided by signals from their comps, as more pushed in behind them.

We needed to move everything, personnel and cargo, *fast*. Howarth and Austin's navigator agreed that we had an eleven-minute window before the *Poling* would have to launch again to make their next rendezvous, given their available fuel. Otherwise they would be stranded in space, out of fuel and in need of rescue. Besides the risk to the personnel, that could give the rescuers—Admiralty ships, most likely—a salvage claim on our outbound cargo. We would miss our deliveries, our contracts would default, and our credit rating would be destroyed. The added scandal of stranded passengers would make it nearly impossible to find new customers, which would ruin our credit even further. A bankruptcy could ruin us just as surely as the Admiralty could. So Captain Aames wanted the entire operation done in nine minutes. If that meant some inbound cargo would be left in space and would have to be chased down later, so be it. The schedule was more important than any individual crate.

So the captain and I and Loadmaster Kelly and others watched the monitors, looking for trouble and calling out suggestions where people and cargo weren't moving fast enough. Eventually Bosun Smith and her crew really did have to shove people through the hatch, like pushers on the old Tokyo subway system. At six minutes they had every traveler transferred to the *Poling*. Then they started passing in the remaining outbound crates, one after another like a bucket brigade. Meanwhile, outside the *Poling*, Kelly's cargo team zipped around in their vacuum suits and maneuvering units, intercepting crates and steering them toward our large cargo bay, which was temporarily open to vacuum. Catchers in vacuum suits waited in the bay, snagging crates with hooks and grapples and dumping them into the automated stacker.

At seven minutes, ten seconds, the last of the inbound cargo had been intercepted. Kelly contacted the captain. "We've got them all, Captain," she said. "They match the manifest 100 percent."

"It appears that we *will* make payroll," Aames said to me. Then he turned back to the comm channel. "Austin is ready to drop free. Get your people into the bay and close the main hatch. I don't want anyone caught in her jets."

"Yes, sir." Kelly gave her orders, and the last of the cargo crew sped into the bay, squeezing in just before the giant bay door snapped shut. "We're in, sir," Kelly added.

Aames changed to another channel. "Smith, clear?"

"Clear, sir."

"Kelly, release the docking cradles," the captain ordered; and on the screen, the cradles unfolded and gave the *Poling* a gentle push away. "Captain Austin, you are separated at eight minutes, forty-seven seconds."

Austin reappeared on the main screen. "Very good work, Captain Aames. We've started our boost back to our target trajectory. My compliments to your team. That's the most efficient transfer I've seen in years, especially under such time constraints."

"I'll pass along your compliments." Aames nodded. "And I have a message for all of our friends who are taking passage on your ship: 'Good luck, take care, and if the Admiralty gives you any trouble, tell them to talk to me.'"

Austin smiled. "I'll pass that along. Good luck, Nick."

"Good luck to you too," Aames answered. "And that goes double for you: if they give you any trouble—"

Austin interrupted. "If they give me any trouble, I don't give a damn. You saved my life and my passengers, so I owe you. And I think what they're pulling on you is pure horseshit. A lot of us in the Corps agree."

At that the captain almost smiled. "Now if only more in the Admiralty did. Did they give you any trouble?"

Captain Austin shook her head, and her face looked puzzled. "No. They tried, but it was a really lame effort."

Aames's eyes grew wider. "Lame? How?"

"Well, they had two Orbital Defense patrol boats in position that *could* have made things difficult for us. If they had taken after us right away, they could've caught us pretty easily. I expected them to intercept and try to board us. I thought I would have to dump cargo to get light enough to stay ahead of them."

Aames leaned forward, looking intently at the main screen. "But they didn't try to intercept you?"

Austin shook her head. "They started on an intercept vector, but then they got orders to return to base and refuel. It made no sense to me: those patrol boats *always* maintain enough fuel for a chase. That's what they're stationed out there for. But someone back at their base decided they needed to top off. I don't know who, but they made it impossible for those boats to catch us. They did us a big favor."

At that, the captain broke with the usual comm protocols: he just pushed the call closed without signing off. Then he sat and stared at the blank screen, but his eyes were unfocused, as if looking at something no one else could see. I crossed over to see if something was wrong, just in time to hear him whisper one word: "Rosie."

Q: I assume by that he meant Admiral Morais?
I'm not a mind reader, Inspector, and he didn't explain himself. That would be my assumption as well, though. Admiral Morais was in charge of Orbital Defense at that time.

Q: So you're suggesting she deliberately prevented those patrol boats from intercepting the Poling.
I'm suggesting nothing, Inspector. Again, I don't know. And you wouldn't want me to speculate on matters I know nothing about, would you?

Q: No, Chief Carver.
Then I won't. But I *can* tell you that Captain Aames immediately placed a call to Admiral Morais in Orbital Defense Headquarters. And that call was refused, as were the calls he placed hour after hour in the succeeding days. But it wasn't just Admiral Morais; all command channels

were blocked to us. "Baker, keep trying," the captain said. "Find some way to get through. I'll be in my office." He left, and I took command of the bridge for another shift.

That started the last approach of our orbit. Throughout, our passengers and crew did their part to step up the information war. Every antenna on the ship was flooded with comm calls to friends, relatives, anyone with influence or even just a loud voice. The Initiative tried again to block our signals; but in so doing they fell right into our trap. Our agents on Earth were ready for that moment, and soon the networks were flooded with questions. "Why has the *Aldrin* gone silent?" "What doesn't the Initiative want us to know?" "Our families have a right to talk to us. Has the Admiralty locked them up?" "Did the Admiralty destroy the *Aldrin* and her passengers?" "Doesn't this jamming violate fundamental rights?" After a few days of growing outrage, the Initiative gave up and stopped jamming us.

But they didn't stop their counterpropaganda. The network programs were full of lies about life aboard the *Aldrin*: They painted the crew as a bunch of human traffickers, preying on gullible passengers desperate to reach Mars; and they painted the passengers as virtual slaves. We countered that with reports from Maxwell City on Mars. Many of the citizens there had traveled on the *Aldrin* to keep their costs down and learn along the way, and they were happy to set the record straight.

The Initiative's proxies also called us pirates and accused us of taking the *Aldrin* from her rightful owners. That was a complete lie, of course. First, aside from just the smallest bit of maneuvering capability, we couldn't "take" the *Aldrin* anywhere: she was in her orbital trajectory, and there she would remain. We could adjust course a little to find the optimum cycler trajectory; but if we veered too far in any direction at all, we would lose our cycler completely. Then we could either drift in space until the Admiralty declared us a derelict, or we could hire every tug in Earth-Luna space to try to pull us back into the cycler. The costs of that would bankrupt us for sure, so we would lose either way.

But beyond that, we were not endangering the owners' assets at all. Thanks to Captain Austin, we would still make all our contracted deliveries to Earth—and to Mars, once we got out of this little war—so we would stay current with all debt and dividend payments to our investors. Plus once the Admiralty stopped jamming us, we were able to deliver our data cargo: months and months of astronomic and planetary data from Mars and from our trip back and forth. The highlights of this research were beamed from Mars back to Earth on a continual basis; but the raw data sets, the bulk data, were too massive to send from Mars on the narrow bands available between planets. So we carried copies of the raw data with us, and we started transmitting them as soon as we were in range. And the companies and institutions that supported all that research paid us for every gigabyte transferred.

So no, the *Aldrin*'s owners were under no financial risk. Lostetter assured us that if anything, the owners were making a better profit margin than we were on that cycle. If they lost a single credit in this affair, it would be through costs imposed by the Initiative, not by us.

Not that it mattered. The Initiative would be the ones judging those costs, so no one expected we would get fair treatment in that department.

Q: Ahem.
I'm sorry, Inspector, that was what we expected. But now we have complete faith in the impartiality of the Inspector General's Office.

Q: Now that you're left with no choice.
Yes. Well, the Admiralty had stopped trying to jam our messages (other than on command channels, which remained closed to us). And they continued their counterpropaganda, but it became repetitive: the same shrieking heads repeating the same refuted lies every night. Our agents

reported that the journos weren't persuading anyone new; they were just keeping the Initiative's supporters from wavering in their calls for our heads. That effort was running on automatic, but we were sure the Initiative had another plan in the works. All we could do was wait to see what it would be.

It was Navigator Howarth who first learned the horrible news. When we were a few days from our closest, fastest approach to Earth, he called out from his station, "Captain, our travel lane isn't clear."

Aames looked up at Howarth. "What? Traffic regulations require that our lanes be cleared when we pass through the system."

"I'm picking up visual and radar readings, all from our Earth perigee. It's faint, but I'll put it on the main screen." Howarth pushed his telescope image to the screen, and the comp added faint blue rings to highlight the unexpected objects. "I don't know what they are, sir, but for us to pick them up at this distance they have to be pretty massive. Larger than freighters. Maybe supply barges."

"Barges?" Aames asked. "All passing through the same space, by coincidence, all at the same time?"

"No, sir."

Aames frowned at the screen. "But they can't be in a stable orbit there, that's not possible. This isn't a bad video, things have to orbit, boost, or fall. They can't just sit there."

Howarth nodded. "Let me reverse the image and then speed up the motion, Captain." The image suddenly jumped backward half a day, according to the timestamp. "Now that I know what to look for, this is the earliest point we could see them. Now watch." The image started advancing at 100-times speed. The computer enhancement showed the dots darting out under power, and then slowing, stopping, and falling back. Each dot followed its own trajectory; but every one of them, when it fell far enough, boosted back out again.

"Station keeping," the captain said, his voice flat.

"Yes, sir," Howarth said. "It must be hideously expensive in fuel cost, but they're as close to 'hovering' as you can get in space. See here?" He pushed a new program to the screen, and red circles appeared, highlighting smaller dots. "These must be fuel carriers. They come in, dock with the larger dots, and then return to Orbital Defense HQ."

"That's ridiculous," I said. "We're over a week from perigee. They can't keep this up."

"They don't intend to, Carver." Captain Aames pointed at the main screen. "Those are sabers. You can't hear them rattling in space, but that's what they are. This is their way of threatening us. They expect us to knuckle under. If we don't, they're promising to let us ram into those objects."

"They can't do that." I thought of all the crew, all the innocent passengers. "That would cripple the *Aldrin*, maybe destroy her. No one would win then."

"They can do it, and they want us to know it. Will they, though? That is the question. Would they rather lose the *Aldrin* than let me run this ship the right way? Or is this all a bluff?"

"It has to be a bluff," I insisted. "They're not insane." I was trying to convince the captain. Or at least myself.

The captain stared at the dots dancing on the main screen. "Carver, never underestimate how far an admiral will go to prove that he's in charge. I don't believe Knapp is the type to bluff. Call a meeting of the senior staff. It's time we devised some more active defenses."

Q: Active defenses? So you did *have weapons? You were prepared to attack Admiralty ships?*

Again, I cannot confirm the existence of weapons, Inspector. I can only confirm that we discussed defenses, and we made emergency plans should the Admiralty fire on *us*.

Meanwhile, the dots—as we drew closer, we could see that they were barges, as Howarth had predicted—settled into a high orbit around Earth. They were no longer burning fuel, and they were no longer in our travel lane; but we knew they could be redeployed in a matter of a few hours.

When Captain Aames wasn't busy with our defenses, he was pushing Baker. "Have you reached the admiral yet?" "Any word from Orbital Defense yet?" "Get me through to Admiral Morais, damn it!" But we were still jammed on all command channels. Baker tried routing through every civilian alternative he could find; but every time he found an opening, the Admiralty shut it back down.

We were just under two days out from perigee when the supply barges started breaking out of orbit again. This time we were close enough to watch the elaborate dance in operation: barges boosting into our lane and back out, fuel carriers meeting up with barges so the dance could continue. The barges were small compared to the *Aldrin* as a whole, but large compared to any single ring. An impact with a barge would smash right through a section of a ring, and then our own rotation would tear the ring to shreds. The stresses from that would twist the central shaft. When the barges had our lane thoroughly blocked, we would be powerless to avoid them: our own inertia would pull us right through them. If we started maneuvering immediately, we *might* avoid them, but only by falling off our cycler orbit.

And just in case the barges weren't enough of a threat, Howarth reported that Orbital Defense fighters were deploying from their base into a higher orbit, one that would intercept our course right after perigee. To finish the job.

That was when the command channel suddenly opened, with an incoming call for us. Captain Aames turned to the main screen, his eyes bright. I turned as well, sure that Baker had finally gotten through to Admiral Morais.

But instead we saw Admiral Knapp. His gray hair and his angular face framed his cold, unforgiving eyes staring out at the captain.

"Aames, you are ordered to stand down and turn command of the *Aldrin* over to me. Now."

Aames stared right back. "Admiral, move those barges, or we'll move them for you. Aames out." He cleared the screen.

"Captain." I tried to calm down. I could tell Knapp was beyond reasoning, but I still might get through to Aames. "We can't let them do this. The passengers . . . the ship . . ."

The captain turned his stare on me. "Carver, I don't believe it. They're not going to attack this ship. They just want me to back down."

I tried not to sound desperate. "And you will, right?"

"Not on your life." His eyes were wide. I think he was *enjoying* the confrontation.

Q: Chief Carver, are you implying that Captain Aames was mentally inca-pacitated? Is this some new defense angle?

No, Inspector. The captain was as sane as ever, he was just sure he was right. He was confident that he had final control of the situation.

Then he turned back to the comm station. "Baker, did that new channel pan out?"

Baker leaned over his display. "Sir, I think so. I should be able to give you a few minutes routed through weather satellites. Here you go, Captain."

The main screen lit up again, only this time it *was* Admiral Morais. Her face was lined, there were dark circles under her eyes, and her uniform was shockingly disheveled; but I would still recognize her anywhere—one of the two best commanders I had ever served under.

The captain's voice softened. It sounded odd in the harsh environ-ment of a ship's bridge at war. "Admiral Morais. It's good to see you."

I listened for Morais to respond in kind, but she went straight to business. "Captain Aames, I strongly urge you to stand down. You have no doubt scanned the supply barges in your path."

The captain nodded. "We picked them up days ago. We have some surprises in store. We think we can shoot a few supply barges out of our way."

The admiral shook her head. "They're not barges, Captain, not anymore. They've been equipped with extra fuel, and they've been stripped down for maneuverability. They're not going to sit and wait for you. Those are torpedoes, and they'll be headed your way any minute."

Over the years, I had seen many expressions on Captain Aames's face: anger, determination, sorrow, scorn, even a smile every year or so. But that was the first time I had ever seen shock. "That will destroy the *Aldrin*, tear her apart. We can launch lifeboats, but a lot of people will still die. And they'll still lose the *Aldrin*. That won't help *anyone*. It will cripple Earth-Mars commerce. It may lead to starvation on Mars."

The admiral shook her head again. "No, it will make opportunities for Holmes and his fast boats." I realized then: losing the *Aldrin* might actually be profitable for Anton Holmes. And for his friends in the Initiative Council. Maybe even for some in the Admiralty.

Captain Aames didn't seem to want to believe it. "That's insane. There aren't enough fast boats for the cargo they need to haul, and the fuel costs will put nearly every load into the red. This makes no sense."

But Comptroller Lostetter spoke from her console. "It's possible, Captain. Holmes has been expanding their fast boat fleet. And if the loads are in the red, they can just raise their transport fees. It's not like Mars can afford to do without resupply. They're ten years away from self-sufficiency."

Admiral Morais said, "My contacts tell me the same thing. Holmes can do it. But this is about more than money, it's about pride and power. Nick, you've made enemies of too many people, and the wrong people. They *have to* stop you, to save face and to make an example of you. If the cost of that is the *Aldrin*, they just don't care anymore. They'll tell everyone it was your actions that led to her destruction. And they'll convince enough people so that they themselves will escape without consequences."

But Captain Aames wasn't ready to give up. He leaned closer to his comm mike, and he spoke in a low voice. I don't know if anyone on the bridge could hear him besides myself. He said, "Admiral, please. Call off those ships."

"I can't, Captain."

"You're in charge of Orbital Defense, Rosie. You don't have to go along with this. You can fight Knapp and Holmes with me. People are going to die. Call them off!"

"Nick, I *can't*! I've been relieved of command."

"What?"

The admiral nodded. "I'm not even supposed to be talking to you. I have a friend in comm services who may face charges for letting me use this channel. Nick, they've reassigned anyone who ever served under you, given them busywork to keep them away from this assault. And me . . . Well, they flat-out accused me of having divided loyalties, so they kicked me aside. My career is as finished as yours."

"You? That's ridiculous. You're the only one in the Admiralty with any brains, and no one is more devoted to the Corps than you. Tell them they're wrong, grab control, and stop this madness."

"Nick." Admiral Morais looked down at her hands. "They're not wrong."

They both went quiet at that, and the silence stretched out. Finally Aames said, "So you can't stop this."

Morais looked up. "And they *won't* stop this, I'm sure of it, Nick." Aames said nothing; they just looked into each other's eyes. Tears pooling in hers, Morais continued, "Captain, you break every rule, you defy every authority, you do whatever you must to bring your people home safe. Now they've pushed you into a corner. They've lied to you, and you hate that. But don't let that make you rash. Don't let them break you." The admiral started weeping, giant round bubble tears rolling slowly down her face in Luna's low gravity. "You're the only one who can stop this. Save the *Aldrin*, Nick. Save your people."

Captain Aames turned his back on the bridge. I heard a catch in his voice when he said, "Lieutenant Baker, contact Admiral Knapp. Tell him I want to discuss the terms of my surrender."

13. The World According to Gale

From the memoirs of Park Yerim

10 June 2083

Chief Carver finished his testimony, and then he sat silently, waiting for more questions. I stared at Matt's transcript on my comp, but too much was running through my mind. Carver had been right: the events of 7 March and later 9 May made more sense when you put them in context. I had had the facts before, but only facts as reported by the Admiralty. Carver's story sounded like something fabricated just to shift the blame away from Aames. But after my call from Holmes . . .

I couldn't leave the chief waiting while I thought. "Thank you, Chief Carver. That's enough for now. If I have more questions, we'll contact you."

"Thank you, Inspector." Carver rose from the guest chair and saluted me. I was flustered by that: saluting isn't common in the IG Office, and I had more experience giving salutes than receiving them. But I realized that Carver was right: as the inspector general on a vessel where the chain of command was in dispute, I was de jure the senior officer on board until the dispute was settled. Knapp didn't act like I was, and no one else seemed to. Even I hadn't been behaving like it. Carver and Admiral Reed seemed to be the only ones who understood the protocol here.

I stood and returned the salute. "You're dismissed, Chief." Carver turned and left the dark office, and Matt followed, leaving me alone to recall how my life had changed immediately after Aames's confrontation with the Admiralty.

☾

It was 9 May 2083, a date that had started as nothing special. I first knew everything in my life was changing when a call came in on my earpiece.

"Junior Inspector Park, this is Admiral Reed. Get to the shuttle deck immediately. Do *not* miss the rendezvous shuttle with the *Aldrin*. I don't care if you have to knock people out of the way to get there, just move."

I rose from my desk and looked around my office on Farport Station. The slate-blue walls were covered with photos of my family and my few friends from school. "The *Aldrin*? Mars, sir? Should I bring anything?"

"I said *move!*" So much for my photos; I grabbed my desk photo of Mother and Father as I left the office. Reed continued speaking in my ear pickup: "Effective immediately, you are promoted to full inspector general rank. But if you miss that shuttle, I'll bust you down so low, they'll have to invent new scut work to keep you busy."

"I'm moving, Admiral." I ran through the administrative ring of Farport, dodging around Admiralty staff as well as personnel from Space Corps and other branches of the Initiative.

"Good. Move faster. I need you to oversee the mess on the *Aldrin*, so you've got seven minutes to catch a rendezvous shuttle. If you miss it, the situation there could explode."

Seven minutes? "Clear the passageway!" I shouted. Ahead, people turned, saw me pick up speed, and stepped out of my way. Soon I reached the access tunnel to the central shaft. An elevator tube ran up one half of the shaft, while a ladder went up the other. I looked at the elevator controls, but the car was up near the top of the shaft. I could climb faster than it could get down and back. I would smell pretty sweaty by the time I reached the shuttle, but it couldn't be helped. I started up the ladder. Again I shouted, "Clear the shaft!" There were only four people climbing, and they looked down and got out of my way, clinging on to handholds near the ladder. As I climbed, the gravity lowered from a half G down toward zero.

Admiral Reed continued my instructions: "I had that new kid, Harrold, stop by the quartermaster and pick you up some spare uniforms and your new rank insignia. Plus dress uniform and off-duty gear. Sorry, you'll be roughing it for a while, but you're the only one from the IG who can make this rendezvous, and we can't wait another seventeen months to handle this case."

At last it was sinking in: I was going to Mars. "Sir, you're assigning me the Aames case?" I was torn between pride that the admiral was trusting me with such a high-profile case and fear that I would screw it up.

"Yes, Park," Reed answered. "You and Harrold and every investigator we have there. I'm clearing out the IG offices on Farport so you'll have staff for this mission. A dozen clerks and investigators. Good people, but you're the only one I can trust to run the thing. So you're promoted, with immediate increase in pay, including hazardous duty pay and off-Earth bonus."

I was making faster time as the gravity dropped. "Sir, I wasn't worried about the money."

"You're going to earn it, Park. That madman Aames has finally knuckled down and surrendered to the Admiralty, and we've been ordered to prepare recommendations for a possible court martial. The Admiralty is pushing for charges of mutiny—"

"Mutiny?" It's not smart to interrupt an admiral, but I couldn't contain my surprise.

"Yes, against him and possibly his entire crew. But this whole thing stinks, Park. There's more going on here than they're telling us, I'm sure of it. If I had my way, I would be there personally to ferret out the truth. But orbital mechanics waits for no man, so it's your chance in the hot seat. I'm counting on you, Inspector."

I pushed into the central shaft. I was never comfortable in weightless environments, and I overcompensated and collided with the far wall. My left shoulder hit hard, and I bounced off. My eyes clouded with tears, and I bit back my pain as I grabbed a handhold. "Just myself and a staff of twelve, sir? To prepare cases against the entire crew?"

"Never mind the crew," Reed answered. "Admiral Morais brokered Aames's surrender, and Aames insisted as part of the terms that we hold off on any crew investigations until his own case is settled. Aames and his command crew can be charged, but no one else."

"Sir, you taught me never to go into an investigation with my hands tied by some bureaucrat's agreement." I started pulling myself toward the docking end of the station, wincing when I tried to pull with my left arm. I would have to make the best time I could, using only my right.

"This is a special case, Park, special rules because we need the crew's cooperation. Morais got the Admiralty to see that the *Aldrin* couldn't get to Mars with her entire crew under arrest. Admiral Knapp said he had a replacement crew ready, but there was no way to get them to rendezvous in time. He'll be there, along with his command crew and some troops. Also Admiral Morais and other likely witnesses. If you decide to empanel a court, Knapp wants enough officers to try the cases right then and there. But he won't have a full replacement crew. So if you find any specific instance of malfeasance on the part of any crewmember, you pursue it. But for the specific crimes alleged here, you concentrate on Aames and his command crew. Your team can depose the crew, but I want you personally to handle any investigations and depositions of Aames and his officers."

"Yes, Admiral." I'm afraid I couldn't keep my doubts out of my voice.

"Don't sound so put upon, Park. Your hands are anything but tied." The admiral chuckled. "If you find cause, investigate anyone you have to. Not only that, I'm invoking *Protocols*, chapter 12, section 1."

"Sir? Plenary power?"

"Yes. The Initiative Council, after some rushed but very intense debate, has agreed that the plenary power clauses apply in this case. It was a very close call, but I just got authorization two minutes before I called you. Then they almost revoked it when they realized that orbital mechanics meant I couldn't be there to exercise the power myself. Downside dunderheads will never truly grasp how difficult it is to make rendezvous and insertion windows. But I told them you were the best IG in my entire command, and I convinced them you were fully capable of exercising plenary power responsibly. So don't make me regret it, Park."

"I won't, sir." I felt immensely proud that Reed had fought for me—and immensely terrified at the responsibility. "So I'm there as your agent, sir?"

"No, Inspector, you're there to make the right decision. How many times have I told you that you can't investigate by proxy? I only trust eyes on-site. Eyes that are far away can never see the entire picture, not even mine. You and your team will report to me, and I expect you to consult with me; but Park, on this mission, you *are* the Inspector General's Office. *You* wield the plenary power."

I swallowed. "I won't let you down, sir."

"I know you won't, Park. But you're going to be under immense pressure from all sides. And whatever you decide, there will be those who will fight you and try to discredit you. There's never been a case like this before, and the ramifications run from here to Mars. You've just been thrust into a precedent-setting case, like it or not, so whatever you decide will be picked apart for years to come. I'll defend you from that as much as I can, using every resource at my command, but you had better prepare yourself for it. You get it right, and you'll go into the history books. You get it wrong, and your career is sunk. Probably mine too." Then Reed's tone softened, and I heard a little of his humor creep in. "There, see? The pressure has started already. But Park"—he turned serious again—"do *not* let it get to you. I expect you to do your job right, as you see it, and I don't give a damn who tries to push you around. Until you issue your findings, you're top dog on the *Aldrin*. Is that clear?"

"Yes, sir." I tried to sound confident, but part of me was wondering if my injured shoulder could somehow get me out of this duty. It was a huge leap to go from Reed's aide at Farport to IG over an entire ship *and* a mutiny case.

But just then I floated out into the main departure dock, and I didn't have time to think about backing out of this assignment. The dock was a large open space, as long as the central shaft's diameter and half as wide. The walls were all painted in shades of gray, but on the far wall were a number of different hatches of different sizes, and each was color coded to identify the vessel docked on the other side. Most were shaded black, indicating an empty dock, but there were seven colors in active use.

There was a large crowd of spacers filing through two large red-coded troop hatches. Their uniforms were a mix of Admiralty black and services gray. My dozen IG staff in their navy blues were almost lost among the black uniforms. But one waved to me, and then detached himself, pushing away from his handhold and floating over to me. He pulled two travel bags in his left hand.

"Congratulations, Inspector General Park," he said as he caught a handhold with his right hand and came to a stop. He was much more at ease in zero gravity than I was.

"Thank you, Ensign Harrold." I thought his name might be Matt, but he was still new on the station. Like myself, Harrold had worked directly under Admiral Reed in his last post. I hadn't worked closely with him before, but I trusted anyone who had learned under Reed.

Harrold handed me a travel bag, and suddenly I recognized it. "I hope you don't mind, Inspector, but I swung by your cabin on my way here. I grabbed your ditty bag and your travel bag. And I called the quartermaster on the way and had them pack whatever you usually brought for off-duty wear. I only had a minute to spare, so I hope this will suit you."

I smiled. "Ensign, just having my own toothbrush will be a blessing." My right hand was holding a grip, so I reached out for the bag with my left; but I let out a sharp breath as my left shoulder stabbed in pain.

Harrold saw the look on my face. "Is something wrong, Inspector?"

I shook my head, my body swiveling slightly in response. "I injured my shoulder, but I'll get by. Here, give me my bag."

"No, Inspector, I'll carry it for you."

"All right, then we had better get aboard. Lead the way."

This time Harrold shook his head, but he kept a steadier control over his body. "No, Inspector. I'll be traveling with junior officers and enlisted. With your promotion, you're now a senior officer. You'll be forward in officer country. That's a different hatch." Harrold gestured with the travel bags. I looked where he pointed, and I saw another hatch just lighting up red. Three figures floated near it, all in Admiralty black. "And if I may, Inspector, you had better hurry. I'll have your bag sent forward to you."

Damn. I had wanted to discuss the case with someone I could trust, and Harrold was the only real choice there. But I knew how strict the Admiralty could be on protocol. So I just answered, "Thank you, Ensign." Then I waited until Harrold pushed off toward his hatch before pushing off toward my own. As I floated closer, the hatch opened, and three stewards in gray uniforms popped out to help the officers board. First aboard was a tall, gray-haired man I had seen around Farport on previous investigations: Admiral Knapp. He looked tense, and he shook off the stewards' hands as they tried to help him aboard. He pulled himself through the hatch, leaving his luggage for the stewards to fetch.

Behind Knapp was a woman, another admiral according to her insignia, but I didn't recognize her. She nodded politely to the stewards as they helped her aboard, and then she turned back to accept her luggage from them.

The stewards started loading Knapp's luggage, so the third officer, a chief, turned and surveyed the deck as he waited for his turn to board. He saw me floating toward them, and he reached out his right arm for me to grab. His left hand clung to a grip. Together we slowed my approach until I floated motionless next to him.

"Welcome," he said with a smile. He had an upper-crust British accent. "You must be Inspector General Park. I'm Chief Horace Gale. It looks like we shall be cabinmates for this cruise."

"Oh?"

"Excuse me, Inspector," a steward interrupted, "do you have luggage?"

I knew better than to try shaking my head again. "No, my aide has mine, thank you."

"Here's mine." Gale unclipped four bags from a nearby baggage hook, and he handed them to the steward. "There's a good lad." Then he turned back to me. "Yes, I'm sorry to say. Oh, not that I'm sorry to have the company of such an attractive officer." Gale smiled at me, but I didn't like it. It looked like the smile was something he wore, not something he felt. "I'm just sorry to inconvenience you like this. This shuttle only has three cabins for visiting officers. Admiral Knapp must have his own, of course, and Admiral Morais hers. So that leaves the two of us sharing the remaining cabin. I shall endeavor not to snore." Then he laughed, but it was no more convincing than his smile.

A steward floated up to me, a tether floating behind her and back to the hatch. "Can I help you board, Inspector?" Before I could say anything, she took my left arm: gently and respectfully, but still too much for my injured shoulder. I cried out, and she looked worried. "Is something wrong?"

Without thinking, I shook my head again, twisting my body in her grip, and my shoulder jolted me. "No." I gasped. Then I caught my breath. "I mean yes, but we'll deal with it later. Just help me get aboard, but watch my left shoulder."

"Yes, Inspector," she answered. "Jimmy, over here." Another steward floated closer, and then tugged on his tether as he clasped her hand. "The inspector has a left shoulder injury. Please help her aboard, but carefully."

"Certainly. Inspector, can you grab your belt with both hands and pull your arms in?"

I tried, and my shoulder only hurt a little. "Yes."

"All right, just let your legs trail out behind us." Jimmy grabbed my right shoulder and turned me halfway around, stopping me with another tug on his tether. Then he grabbed the rear collar of my jacket while pulling on his line. I swiveled in midair, and sure enough, my feet swung behind us as Jimmy pulled us along and into the hatch. Looking back, I could see Gale following close behind us.

When we were inside the hatch, I said, "Thank you, I can take it from here."

But Jimmy ignored me. "Begging your pardon, Inspector, but it's faster if I keep on guiding you. And fewer bumps for that shoulder." And he certainly knew his job. He pulled me into the rendezvous shuttle and around a corner. He deftly lifted me over the third steward as she went back to secure the hatch. Then he pulled to a stop at one cabin, the hatch opened, and he pulled me in. Never once did he jostle my shoulder.

Once inside the cabin, Jimmy pulled me over to the outer wall. "If you could hold on here, Inspector." I grabbed a grip while Jimmy let me go and pushed off to the rear wall. There were two doors in that wall, each larger than a person. He pushed a button near the outer door, and it slid into the wall. Underneath was a large cushion: a combined bed and acceleration couch. "This is your bunk," he said. "Unless you're certified for level 6 boost operations, you'll want to stay in it for most of the trip. Especially with that shoulder." Jimmy pulled me over to the couch and helped me to settle into it, strapping me down to prepare me for acceleration. Last he helped me to adjust the pillow under my head.

Meanwhile Gale was preparing his own bunk. He unstrapped his pillow and handed it to Jimmy. "Put this under her injured shoulder."

Jimmy shook his head. "I'm sorry, Chief, but you'll need this for your safety."

"Are you questioning my orders, Ensign?" Gale's voice lost some of its BBC quality, and now it had more of a cockney edge. "For your information, *I* am certified for level *10* boost ops, so I know what I can handle better than you do. I'm also a certified medic, and I want some extra protection for that shoulder. Do I make myself clear?"

Jimmy's voice shook a little as he took the pillow. "Yes, sir." He turned to me and lifted my shoulder to try to place the pillow under it. But though he tried to be careful, I screamed in renewed pain.

"Bollocks, give me that." Gale pushed Jimmy to the front of the cabin, where the steward grabbed the wall grip and stopped himself. He had let go of the pillow, and Gale plucked it out of the air. "All right, Inspector, tell me what happened, and where it hurts."

I explained the collision and the pain I had felt when I tried to use the arm, and Gale nodded. Gently he probed my shoulder with his fingers, pulling back any time I showed signs of pain. "You'll need a doctor and an X-ray to be sure, but I think you've bruised the ligaments in the socket, and then pulled on them when they were already traumatized. We won't be able to do much until we get you aboard the *Aldrin*, but this should get you through boost." He looked at the pillow. "I'd say this is a little thick. If you have too much under that shoulder, you're like to get bedsores during boost. Too little and you'll inflame it more."

Gale rolled the cover of the pillow between his fingers. "That's pretty thick. Maybe . . ." He turned the pillow over and found a seam. He grabbed the cover on either side and pulled; and with surprising strength, he ripped it open. Then he pulled out the inner pillow and smiled. "That's the ticket. Now, Inspector, this shouldn't hurt. You've got no weight now, so I can move you very gently. But should it hurt at all, it will be only a moment. Ensign?" Gale gestured Jimmy over. Then he unfastened my acceleration straps, slid his right hand under my waist, and pulled me slightly away from the couch. I was impressed with his light touch, as I felt no pain at all. With his left hand Gale slid the pillow in behind me. Then he used gentle pressure on my waist and my right shoulder to press me back against the couch. He held me down as Jimmy again strapped me in.

Gale smiled at me; and this time his smile looked genuine. "How's that, Inspector?"

I smiled back. "No pain. Thank you, Chief."

"Right, then. Jimmy, let's get me strapped in so you can get to your station." Gale was jovial again, all troubles forgotten, and soon he had Jimmy smiling with him. They strapped Gale into his couch, and then Jimmy left. The cabin door slid shut behind him.

Jimmy had been gone for less than a minute when I felt my bunk start to shift. "Whoa."

Gale laughed next to me. "First time on a high-boost shuttle, Inspector?"

My throat was suddenly dry, but I answered, "Yes."

"Don't worry," he said, his tone soothing. "You can't lie flat at high boost. It's too hard on your knees. The couch automatically adjusts."

Once Gale explained it, I recognized what was happening: the lower end of the couch was bending out, putting me in more of a sitting position with a leg rest supporting my knees and calves. "Does this mean we're launching soon?"

Gale started to answer, but a ship's speaker cut him off. "Attention, all stewards: departure boost in one minute. Secure yourselves. Departure boost in one minute. Level 6 boost alert."

"There you go," Gale answered. "It won't be long now. You let me know if that shoulder gives you any trouble during boost. We're not supposed to move around in a level 6 boost, but I *am* level 10. Why, one time . . ."

Gale was still telling me stories when the ship started to shake and roar. Suddenly the wall became a floor, and we were lying back upon it as the shuttle sped off for rendezvous with the *Aldrin*.

The trip to the rendezvous point took nearly two weeks, and most of it at too high of a boost for me to move around much. I was glad, though, that Gale was free to move around more and go visit other parts of the shuttle, because it gave me some much-needed rest. Traveling with Gale was difficult. He was a conundrum. As a spacer, he knew his stuff. As a medic, he was pretty capable. Once we dropped to level 4 boost, he called in the shuttle's medic, and they conferred on my shoulder. They agreed that I needed it immobilized, and that I needed painkillers. So the medic fitted me with a sling to keep it immobile; but he kept looking to Gale for confirmation. I think he recognized that Gale was a better field medic than he was.

But as a person? Gale was annoying in so many ways. First, he was something of a letch. We get those in the services, just like in civilian society, but it can get pretty difficult in the close quarters of a station or a ship. Gale never openly leered, but his *not* leering was pretty obvious, like he was making an effort not to look when the medic applied a dressing to my shoulder. And in casual conversations, he kept "accidentally" dropping comments about my appearance. I'm sure he thought he was charming, and maybe many women found him so. I don't know, but *I* didn't. I finally had to point out that he was making me uncomfortable.

After that he watched his words more carefully, but I still felt like he was trying to charm me.

And second, Gale seldom stopped talking, and a lot of his talk was boasting about himself and all his missions. I had no real reason to doubt him, but it just seemed so unlikely that one person could be the hero of so many adventures. So I took everything he said with a grain of salt.

Still, there was one mission Gale never talked about, the one mission he was famous for. So late in the voyage, when there was a lull, I asked him, "Chief, how come you never talk about the *Bradbury*?" Gale was silent for so long, I worried about him. "I'm sorry, Chief, did I say something wrong?"

Gale cleared his throat. "No, Inspector, it's just that's the mission where I served under Captain Aames. I didn't want to say anything that might prejudice your investigation."

"Oh. I see." I appreciated Gale's reticence, but he sounded uncomfortable, like that wasn't his entire reason. He had piqued my curiosity, though. I wanted to know his other reasons. Besides, it would give me the opportunity to determine where I needed to dig deeper for facts and possible secrets. "I can keep my objectivity, Chief. You don't need to worry."

Gale hesitated again, but then he continued, "Please understand, Aames was a good man once. There's no denying that he saved our lives on the second *Bradbury* expedition. With a little help from me, of course, and the rest of our crew. But he just lost his way, he didn't keep up with the times. He took a desk job after that, for some reason, and I think it made him bitter. More bitter, I should say, and even more arrogant. I stayed active in exploration, and I applied the lessons I had learned from him. The most important of those was how vital it was for spacers to have a say in their own missions. We're the ones who have our arses on the line, after all, so we should decide where that line is. Captain Aames never shut up about 'eyes on-site' and 'local control,' so he should've been a big supporter when I and a bunch of senior spacers decided to set up a certifying body. Our Space Professionals should have been perfect for him, a chance for spacers to speak to the Admiralty as a unified voice with credibility and respect. He should've been thrilled that spacers would have a say in planning their missions, not just have everything run from central command."

Gale paused and took a drink. "But Aames would have nothing to do with us. He turned us down flat. He said, 'That would be trading one central command for two. That's a step in the wrong direction.'

"I argued, 'You're missing the point completely, Nick.'

"But he refused to listen. 'I understand just fine, Horace.' Lord, how I hated the way he pronounced my name, always full of scorn. 'Your Space Professionals will become a damned guild, standing between me and my crew.'

"I tried to reason with him. 'You don't have a crew, Nick, you have this bloody desk. And we're not a guild at all, just a certifying body. We're trying to raise the level of professionalism in space.'

"Aames glared at me. 'You can call it whatever you want. I judge it by what it does. It's still protecting people who don't know what they're doing. Stand in the right line, fill in the right forms, put in the right time, and bingo. Get the right rewards, whether you've earned them or not.'

"I said, 'But putting in the time *is* earning them.'

"But Aames shook his head. 'Bullshit. Putting in the time means nothing if you're not learning and growing. It doesn't mean you know what you're doing. That's not certification, it's clock punching. I see a lot of reports come across this desk, so I know all about the Everett case. If I had been commander of the *Hercules*, Everett would've been busted down to astronaut third class. Instead he pled to your SPs, and they interceded with Captain Milton. So Everett was still in a position to screw up again, and he lost a leg that time. Yeah, that showed a lot of professionalism.'

"'That was just one case,' I objected.

"'One of many,' Aames answered, 'and that number is growing. And worse, I hear some in the Admiralty are starting to endorse your group. It's easier for them to accept your word than to do their own evaluations, and they get less trouble if they go along with your so-called certification.'

"I was getting offended, but I held my temper in check. 'Nick, if you doubt us, check out our certification exams. We could use someone with your reputation.'

"'You could use me?' Aames asked, and I nodded. 'Then let me write the standards, and oversee their administration.'

"'Absolutely!' I was pleased to finally make some progress with him. 'We can put you on the committee—'

"But Aames cut me off. 'No committee, just me. If I want a committee, I'll form one from people I trust.'

"At first I was struck dumb at his arrogance. At last I answered, 'We cannot accept that, Nick. Others in the organization might not approve of your standards. They might find them too harsh, and they would never vote to support them.' I couldn't imagine his standards ever being too lax.

"Aames stared at me, a satisfied sneer on his face. 'That's what I thought: for you, it's about voting, it's about politics. It's not about outcome and results, it's about consensus and protecting members. Your certifications won't be worth spit. Pass, Gale.'

"I reached my limit. I stopped trying to persuade him, and I fell back to arguing. 'What, so we're all supposed to trust you?'

"The sneer remained on Aames's face. 'Hell, no. Trust the data. Trust your team and their training and their eyes on-site. I'm not the one who thinks it's smart to let spacers certify themselves. I think that will end up no better than we have now, but with more layers of trouble in the way. But if you want me to trust your standards, then you start by trusting me.'

"'And who designated you the authority?'

"'You did, when you decided you could use me for publicity. My name, my reputation, my visibility, those come with a steep price. If you really need me, you'll pay it. But you're not ready to, so count me out. It's not like I need you.'

"My anger grew, and I found it hard to control my words. 'Someday, Aames, you'll find that you *don't* run everything.'

"'Fine with me, Gale. When that day comes, somebody better will be in charge. But it sure as hell won't be you.'

"I was furious. I wanted to break something. But I calmed myself, and I thought of one more tack to try. 'Maybe you do need us, Nick. And maybe you have another price. If you were part of the Space Professionals, you would have our backing. We could maybe get you out from behind this desk, and back in command of a mission, where you belong. And this time, with a qualified SP crew, maybe the results would be different.'

"Nick's stare turned cold. 'Gale, get out.'

"'What?'

"'Get out before I kick your teeth in. When I get out from behind this desk, it will be my doing, on my terms. Don't you *ever* think you can *buy* my support.'

"And that was the end of our discussion. I swiftly got out of his office, for fear that he might really attack me. I've met with him occasionally since, and he has only gotten worse. I hesitate to diagnose without a license, but he strikes me as having narcissistic personality disorder. The man's ego knows no limits. And he draws in good people—like his second-in-command, Chief Carver, a fine officer back in the day—and he leads them down the wrong path. They become just like him, no good for ordinary duty."

"Thank you, Chief," I said. Then when Gale had nothing to add, I lay in silence and thought about what he had said. I had heard stories about Aames's arrogance, of course, but never from someone who knew him so well. I wasn't sure I was ready to meet the infamous Captain Aames.

☾

I still wasn't sure I was ready, but I could see no more excuses for putting it off. I pulled open a call to Matt's office. "Matt, please inform Captain Aames that it will be my pleasure to depose him in half an hour."

14. An Immodest Proposal

From the memoirs of Park Yerim

10 June 2083

The door to Matt's office opened, and Captain Aames walked into mine as if it were still his own. Ignoring me, he strode over to the sink, poured himself a glass of water, and took a long drink. Then he poured another, walked over to the guest chair, and gently dropped into it. Finally he looked at me. "Good afternoon, Park." He took another drink, and then raised his glass in my direction. "Best water on the ship. I clean the filters personally. I hope you're enjoying my work."

From that point forward, Aames's eyes never left me. He didn't look at the desk, nor the e-reader on it, nor even the giant view window behind it. He didn't glance once at the São Paulo door. He kept his gaze on me, studying me like I was his next test subject.

Matt came in behind Aames, pushing an extra desk chair; and behind him came Chief Carver. The chief stood at attention behind the chair.

I frowned. "Chief Carver, I didn't request you for this deposition."

Before Carver could answer, Aames did. "I asked him here, Park. I'm entitled to counsel of my choice at this deposition. *Protocols*, chapter 11, section 3. I choose Carver."

I shook my head. "He has a conflict in this case. Depending on my findings, he could end up as a defendant right alongside yourself."

Aames laughed, a dry, scornful sound. "And who on this ship *doesn't* have a conflict? The Admiralty staff? They want my hide nailed to a wall. My crew? My passengers? There's not a one of them who could be any more objective than Carver. Surely you're not suggesting one of your own staff?" I shook my head, and he laughed again. "I would be happy to postpone this whole business until we reach Mars, so we can find some independent counsel—assuming you can find someone there who isn't backing one side or another in this affair—but I had the impression that Knapp was already fuming about delays. If you try to put him off for another four months, he'll find some excuse to get you removed. So no, Park, I think the smart thing to do would be to allow me the counsel that I choose: Chief Anson Carver. He has an exemplary record, and he's more than qualified to serve as counsel. If he has a conflict at all, it's *against* me. If I don't object, I don't see why you care. So let's continue."

I was flustered. In less than one minute with Aames, I was in danger of losing control of my own investigation. I looked at Chief Carver, and he looked back with a pained expression. I would get no help there.

But I still knew the regulations. I looked back at Aames. "Captain, I must insist that you have counsel that—"

Aames interrupted, "'Counsel that can zealously pursue my interests in an adversarial court or investigation.' *Protocols*, chapter 11, section 3, sub A. And my response is: *Protocols*, chapter 11, section 3, sub D, 'Any subject deemed mentally competent may waive the right to claim incompetent counsel as part of any future appeal.' I so waive. If you'll check with Dr. Baldwin, my most recent psych evaluation shows me to be as competent as I ever was, so my waiver is valid. You've done your job to protect my rights, Park, and now I expect you to accept my choice of counsel and get on with this. Carver, sit down already."

Again I looked at Carver. He remained standing at attention, no longer looking at me. I sighed and tried to regain control. "Lieutenant Harrold, please take your seat and start recording."

"Yes, Inspector." Matt sat and opened his comp. "Recording, Inspector."

"Very well. Deposition of Captain Nicolau Aames in the matter of The System Initiative v. Captain Nicolau Aames. Questioner for the Inspector General's Office: Inspector General Park Yerim. Court Reporter: Lieutenant Matt Harrold. Appearing as counsel for Captain Aames, under waiver as per *Protocols*, chapter 11, section 3, sub D: Chief Anson Carver. You may be seated, Chief." Carver sat, and I turned back to Aames. "Now Captain Aames, for the record, your waiver please."

"Really?" Aames asked. I nodded. "Very well. I, Captain Nicolau Aames, have been advised by the Inspector General's Office that my choice of counsel, Chief Anson Carver, does not meet their standards of competence or objectivity. Under *Protocols*, chapter 11, section 3, sub D, I waive my right to future appeals on the grounds of incompetent counsel. Harrold, attach my psych profile from the latest records to confirm that I am competent to make this waiver."

Matt looked at me, and I scowled at Aames. "Reporter, attach the captain's psych profile. Captain Aames, I remind you that I'm running this deposition. You shall refrain from instructing the reporter. Continued disrespect of this office and its procedures may open you up to contempt charges."

"Contempt?" Aames laughed again. "Of course I have contempt! Oh, not for you, Park. My people tell me you're pretty diligent and scrupulous. Carver speaks very highly of you, and I trust his judgment." I looked at Chief Carver, and he winced. "But face it, this deposition is a joke. You already know all the facts in this case, and all the events surrounding it. You can drag this out from here to Mars, but nothing you learn is going to change what you already know. Make your decision now, and save us all a lot of time."

I stood up, so angry I practically flew into the air, catching myself on the desk only at the last instant. "Captain, that is *enough*. I will *not* have you or anyone else telling me how to do my job."

As I got angrier, Aames seemed to grow calmer. "I'm just trying to save us all a lot of time here. I can see what's going to happen. Like it or not, you could spend years asking questions aboard this ship, and you wouldn't learn anything new that would change the basic facts. Sooner or later you're going to have to make a choice; and when you do, some are going to accuse you of following orders. And you won't be happy, either: no matter what you choose, you'll choose it under pressure. But maybe if I cut through all the crap and lay out your choices, you'll be smart enough to tell truth from bullshit. That will take some of the pressure off you."

I was growing so furious, I didn't dare speak. I was sure I would explode. While I hesitated, Aames took another drink and then continued, "I disobeyed unlawful orders. The Admiralty insists those orders were lawful. They will demand that you accept them as such, in which case you will have no choice but to find grounds for a court martial. You will then have to empanel a court, and thirty minutes later, that kangaroo court will find me and my command crew guilty of all charges. So if you bow to their pressure, we're all facing long prison terms. And you'll be giving control of the *Aldrin* to the people who tried to destroy her so that they could control Earth-Mars traffic. Oh, and you'll find this ship in the middle of passive resistance at best. My people might even openly revolt, I can't say for sure. But regardless, this ship won't meet our contractual obligations without my crew actively doing their jobs. Don't think for a second that Knapp and Gale and their crew can run this ship. There's not enough of them to even try. And if they try to force my people to work, that will get ugly. So one way or another, this ship will fail as a platform for Earth-Mars commerce. And that will be fine with Holmes and Knapp, since they have their fast boats ready."

Aames pointed a finger at me as he went on. "Or you can do the smart thing: clear us of all charges. You know you should. But if you do, the problems aren't going to go away. Knapp will shout so loud, they'll hear him back on Earth. He'll accuse you of being unduly influenced by me and my crew. And even if Reed backs you—I think he will, Reed's a fair man—Knapp and his cronies won't let go of their power so easily. Oh, they can't make trouble here, today. We still retain control of this ship, for all practical purposes. We're permitting your investigators and the admiral's team to wander around at will, but we really don't have to." Aames grimaced. "After what Gale did on the I Ring, I wonder if that was wise at all. Never mind now, though, the key thing is Knapp has tipped his hand, and I don't expect him to give up now. He'll find another way to seize this ship eventually, and that will still cripple Earth-Mars trade."

I turned Aames's arguments over in my head, but it was difficult to think. He had irritated me so thoroughly, I couldn't keep the facts straight. So I concentrated on his last remark. "I can't do anything about what Knapp *might* do in the future. I can only deal with the facts in the record today."

At that, Aames smiled. It wasn't a sign of humor, it was a predator about to pounce. "Ah, but that's what you can do. What you *must* do, Inspector: prevent the takeover of the *Aldrin*, permanently. It's the only answer."

"What?" I couldn't see what he was talking about.

"Inspector, you've seen how this ship functions, the crew and the officers and the passengers. You've seen us pull together in adversity. You've seen our institutions, our growth plan. Is there any doubt that the best word to describe us is *community*?" My eyes widened as I started to see where Aames was heading. "And on 7 March, we received orders that threatened our viability as a community. Prior to 23 April, there was an attempt to blockade supplies necessary to our survival. And on 9 May, we were directly threatened with destruction. We have clear grounds—"

This time it was my turn to interrupt. "Clear grounds to file for recognition as an independent political entity under the precedents established by the United Cities of Free Luna."

Aames nodded. "You have plenary power, Inspector. *Protocols*, chapter 12, section 1. You can issue any finding that resolves this case and doesn't violate the fundamental rights of any individual or group." Aames swiped his comp and pushed a file to my desk. "That's an analysis by Comptroller Lostetter, confirmed by two separate auditing firms. This ship is fully self-sufficient *and* able to repay all investors over time, including a better-than-market return on investment. We also have the ability to meet all debts and obligations and maintain future operations. We meet every criterion necessary under the free cities precedent for you to declare us an independent city-state *retroactive to 7 March*. You do that, and then you can find that every action we took since then is legal."

My head spun. Suddenly I heard the phrase I had heard so many times before: *manipulative bastard*. "You can't be serious."

"Completely," Aames answered. "Oh, there will be thousands of minor claims to be adjudicated, but the courts can handle those. Again, there are plenty of precedents. It's all straightforward once you put in place the framework. So there's your choice: let us get back to work and run our ship, and tell the Admiralty and the Initiative they've got no business trying to run things here."

I glared at Aames. "So that's it? I just give you what you want, more than you had before, with no compromise?"

Aames leaned forward in his chair. "If compromise means I'm going to sit and listen while Knapp or you or anyone not part of this community tells me how wrong I am, then no, we're not going to compromise.

If it means any harm to this community, any chance of breaking it apart, then hell no."

Aames stood from the guest chair. "Park, I've shown you your choices. There aren't any others. Come see me when you decide to be sensible." He turned, crossed the room, and left through the São Paulo door. It slid shut behind him, and I stared at it, openmouthed.

15. Ex Parte Communication

From the memoirs of Park Yerim

10 June 2083

I sat behind the desk, trembling, barely controlling my rage. I had trouble gathering my thoughts. That *infuriating* man, Aames.

Carver looked at me, his face full of sympathy and apology. "I'm sorry for my client's behavior, Inspector, and that he was so disrespectful. He can be a little difficult."

"A 'little' difficult?" I snorted. "And we're on a 'little' trip to Mars." Carver smiled at that, which calmed me down a bit; but I was still agitated. "He admitted to contempt of this office."

"Objection," Carver interrupted. "He expressed respect for you and your work. His contempt was for this investigation."

"Is there a difference?" I saw Carver's point, but I wanted to stay angry. "I can have him locked up for that."

"You can, Inspector. I wouldn't blame you if you did. But it wouldn't make your job any easier. You'd still face the same two choices."

"Two choices? And what about his third?"

Carver laughed once. "That one's audacious even for Nick—I mean, my client. It's also pretty creative. If I were so bold as to offer my advice to the IG Office, I would recommend giving it serious consideration. I think it's the best possible outcome, even granted my self-interest. But truthfully, I'm glad that it's not my place to decide. I don't envy you this responsibility."

"Thank you. But there's still the matter of your client's contempt."

"Yes, Inspector, I would like to plead on my client's behalf."

I nodded. "And what is your plea?"

Carver smiled sheepishly. "I don't really have one. I never prepared for this. I suppose I should have, knowing my client. Once he sees a solution to a problem, he has no patience with further discussion. So I can only plead for the mercy and indulgence of the Inspector General's Office."

I smiled back. Though I had wanted to cling to my anger, Carver was lifting my spirits. And that was letting me think more clearly about what was essential, and what was just getting in my way. "I suppose I could summon guards and throw him in the brig, but why bother?" I nodded toward the São Paulo door. "He locks himself in there all day anyway. Reporter, strike everything after Captain Aames left. This deposition is concluded. End recording. You're dismissed, Chief Carver. You, too, Lieutenant. I need to think."

Again Carver saluted me. This time I was ready, and I smartly returned the salute. Then Matt, seeing Carver's example, saluted as well. I saluted him back, and they both left the office.

When the door slid shut behind Matt, I once again sat alone in the all-black office. With all the forces arrayed around me, all the thoughts swirling in my mind, I appreciated the darkness. It gave me calm, focus. "Lights, off." The room lights dimmed to nothing, and the only light came from the desk. "Desk, sleep."

The desk dimmed as well, and I sat in Aames's chair, surrounded by darkness. Was this how he spent his time? His world was so black and white, all right answers and wrong. Was this his way of shutting out the world, all the people whom he despised for disappointing him? Was this how he hid from it all?

But as my eyes adjusted, I realized I wasn't in *total* darkness. A shadow moved upon the desk: a shadow of me, cast by a dim light behind me. I turned and looked at the giant window on the rear wall. The sun was somewhere to my right, beyond the window's edge, so it wasn't the source of the shadow. No, the light that cast that shadow was from a million stars strewn across the window from edge to edge in an irregular band. Since IGs aren't expected to be explorers, I had had only a basic astronomy course; but even I recognized the Milky Way.

Never had I seen it so bright and so clear, though. Hongcheon was a rainy province, and even when we saw the stars, it was through the thick blanket of Earth's atmosphere. And on Farport, I had been too busy for stargazing. But here the main mass was a white-yellow haze, within which I could pick out many tiny pinpricks of light; but I knew from my course that the entire haze was made up of stars, billions of them so distant that my eye could see them only as a collective glow. Obscuring much of that glow were dark swirls of cosmic dust, like some giant tangle of hair. And everywhere—shining through the dust, standing out against the haze, and scattered around the main band—were brighter stars like jewels decorating the blackness. They were mostly white and shades of blue white, but there were also countless dots in red and yellow and occasionally orange.

Closer to hand was a large creamy-yellow dot. That had to be Jupiter, I guessed. And closer still, behind us but a little to the lower right, was a tiny bright-blue crescent. Near it was a smaller white crescent. Earth and Luna, the sister planets, spinning peacefully on their annual voyage around the sun.

And as I sat there and stared in openmouthed wonder, I knew: *this* was why Aames had his office all in black. It wasn't an escape from society. It wasn't a reflection of his dark personality. It was simply the best way to experience this *miracle* of a universe, where humanity was taking its first cautious steps off our home world. This was where the real Nick Aames lived.

Only thanks to the machinations of others, he had been denied the chance to go there himself; and he refused to settle for a life back on Earth, not after he had walked on Luna and Mars and had flown the spaces between. Instead of an empty existence, trying to forget all that he had lost, he chose this assignment, almost a form of exile. He had made it his responsibility to get people safely to the frontier, but he could never go there himself. He had to stay here, ensuring their safe passage, a glorified subway conductor whose own path ran from nowhere to nowhere in an endless cycle.

But at least in the darkness he could see these stars.

And they had a calming effect on me. My anger at Aames had passed. I could consider his unorthodox idea more clearly now. It was certainly innovative, and I couldn't find a flaw with Aames's knowledge of protocols and precedents. I woke up the desk to go over Comptroller Lostetter's calculations, and they were impressive and thorough. There was absolutely no doubt that the *Aldrin* could function economically and socially and culturally as an independent entity.

But I just didn't see how it could work. Aames had a talent for pissing people off, and too many of the wrong people were too angry to ever let him get away with this. Oh, I could order his plan under chapter 12, section 1. I was sure I could get Reed to back me up. But I couldn't see a way to get enough others in the Initiative and the Admiralty to accept it.

I was still staring absently at the numbers, as if some answer hid within them, when the office door opened. I looked up, expecting to see Matt; but instead I saw a weary-looking woman in Admiralty black, with full bars. I had only seen Admiral Morais from a distance aboard Farport, but I knew her face from my files.

"Excuse me, Admiral," I said, "did Lieutenant Harrold forget to tell me we had an appointment?"

Morais shook her head. "The lieutenant is gone." I looked at the desk, and I realized how late it was. Matt had no doubt left for his cabin. "No one has thought to deactivate my access privileges, since where can I go on this ship? I am as much as a prisoner here. So I used my codes to let myself in. Inspector, I believe we should talk. May I sit down?"

I pushed back from the desk, stretching out my arms to get the kinks out. "I appreciate your eagerness to cooperate, Admiral, but I'm not ready to depose you at this time. I've had a long day already, without a lot of sleep, and I'm still recovering from injuries. And I can't run a deposition without the lieutenant here as a reporter. So I'm afraid we'll need to reschedule. I'm available at 1000 hours tomorrow."

Morais ignored my objection as she walked in and sat down. "Inspector, I'm not here for a deposition. I know what charges I shall face, and I'm ready to face them. But I must explain some things that you need to understand."

I was doubtful, and I didn't try to hide it. "Admiral, *if* you face charges, it will be as an accomplice to Captain Aames; and since I haven't yet decided whether to charge him, I haven't yet decided if there was any crime for you to be part of. You may not even need to be deposed; but if you want to claim extenuating circumstances or extraordinary justifications for your actions, please save that for your deposition, if and when."

"You don't understand, Inspector," she said. "I'm not here about myself. As I said, I'm ready to face whatever charges you may press. No, I'm here to try to explain to you about Captain Aames."

I was intrigued. Aames had surprised me when he had comforted Dr. Baldwin, and again when I understood the observatory that was his office. Behind the acerbic misanthrope, there were depths I still didn't understand. And this woman had known him perhaps as well as anyone. I had heard from everyone else who was close to Aames, so it only made sense to listen to her.

So I nodded. "All right, Admiral, explain away."

"Thank you." Admiral Morais smiled, and suddenly she looked younger and more hopeful. She pulled the guest chair up to the desk and leaned forward on her elbows. She looked at the São Paulo door, and then she lowered her voice in confidence, as if afraid Aames might hear. "Inspector, I have known Nick Aames for a long time. In that time, I don't think he has told anyone else this story, not even Chief Carver. I was deeply touched when he told it to me, and I have never told another soul. But I think it's important for you to know this if you want to understand him and judge him fairly. So I shall tell it to you as he told it to me. It was 20 March 2037, in a little town in Alabama."

16. The Last Dance

Off-the-record account of Admiral Rosalia Morais

Covering events of 20 March 2037

The waltz from von Weber's *Invitation to the Dance* played through the speakers concealed in the crannies between the floral-print wallpaper, the stained-oak cornices, and the beige ceiling. This section, Grandma Ruth's favorite waltz, had been rearranged for muted strings at a slower, somber tempo. Nick sat in the big, soft leather chair in the corner of the parlor, flanked by a pot of lilies on his left and an arrangement of forest greens on his right. Their pungent, woodsy odor enveloped him. The smell of pine usually made him relax, since the woods were the closest thing he knew to a home; but today the scent was overpowering, making his eyes water. At least that's what he told himself: the moistness in his eyes was a coincidence, and had nothing to do with Grandma Ruth lying in the big cherrywood coffin in the front of the room.

Nick itched in his back, armpits, and knees, but he was too respectful to scratch in front of Grandma Ruth. At fifteen, Nick had finally had a slight growth spurt, so the suit was tight and itchy in all the wrong places; but it was the only suit he owned, the only one his family could afford. The suit was a hand-me-down from Dek, and Nick's brother hadn't taken very good care of it; but Nick had spent all morning brushing it clean and stitching up the loose seams. Grandma Ruth would've approved of his work.

Dek—Derick, but Nick had called him "Dek" since Nick was a toddler—wasn't at the funeral. None of Nick's immediate family were. Dek had laughed at Nick for urging him to attend, and then had laughed again at Nick in his ill-fitting suit. Dad had spent his time stoned since he had learned of his stepmother's death. Not that Dad was particularly fond of Grandma Ruth, but he was fond of any excuse to get stoned.

And Mom . . . Nick didn't want to think about Mom. How she had almost smiled at the news of Grandma Ruth's death. They had never gotten along, and Mom resented Grandma Ruth for "indulging" Nick.

Indulging. Yeah, like feeding him nutritious meals and sneaking him treats. Like talking to him like a person, not like a burden. Like giving him a book reader, and all the books he could devour; and then when Dad traded the reader for drugs, giving him another one and helping him hide it. Like taking him in every time he couldn't take life at home anymore and he ran into the woods, looking for anything to distract him from the anger and the beatings and the abandonment, and somehow always finding his way to her house.

Now the only *real* family Nick had ever known lay in the dark wooden box, her slate-gray curls resting on the cream-colored fabric of the pillow. Mrs. Quintana, Grandma Ruth's oldest friend, had picked out her outfit: her best navy dress, the one with the tiny white flowers, along with her beloved pearls. Nick hadn't managed to approach the coffin yet, but he couldn't look away either. Grandma's church-lady friends hovered around, occasionally asking if he needed anything but otherwise giving him the solitude he wanted. That was all he wanted today, solitude. And not to cry.

A rocket plane out of Huntsville roared overhead, and Nick looked up, as if he could see it through the ceiling. For him, the rocket plane schedule was as good as the old grandfather clock near the door: he pored over the launch schedules every week, memorizing launch windows, destinations, anything that was on the public networks. That sound was the 1255 launch to the Holmes Construction Station.

Soon the grandfather clock would chime the hour, and it would be time for the service. Mrs. Quintana approached Nick. Usually she wore colorful floral dresses, and her hair stood in dark contrast to the bright colors. Today, her simple black dress had the opposite effect: her hair didn't look dark, it looked distinctly gray. And her face was pale and lined. For the first time, she looked old to Nick, almost as old as Grandma Ruth.

Mrs. Quintana spoke softly in her accented English. "It is time, Nicolau." She used the Brazilian form of his name, as she always did. Usually he smiled at that, or even joked back: "This is Alabama, Mrs. Quintana, we speak English here." But today he didn't find it funny; he found it comforting. Grandma Ruth had filled out his birth certificate, since Dad had been drunk and Mom had been asleep, and she had filled in "Nicolau," in memory of her time in Brazil.

Nick rose from the chair, again feeling his suit binding. Mrs. Quintana proffered her arm. Her touch made him feel awkward, but Nick took it just as Grandma Ruth had taught him. Then they walked to the front pew, and they sat for the funeral.

☾

Afterward, the church ladies put on a lunch, and Mrs. Quintana shepherded Nick through it: making sure he had a place to sit, making sure he was fed, doing all the things Grandma Ruth would've done for him if she had been there. She also provided a buffer when people came up to offer their condolences. Nick knew there were a lot of them, but he was too numb to keep track. It was all a blur.

But he did start to see a pattern, a split into two groups: close friends and casual acquaintances. Nick recognized many of the close friends, having met them at Grandma Ruth's house over the years. Even those he hadn't met seemed to know a lot about him. They asked about his schooling, and they told stories about Grandma Ruth and how proud she had been of Nick. Mrs. Quintana's son Silvio, a pilot out of Huntsville, spent nearly twenty minutes talking to Nick about transfer orbits.

The casual acquaintances, though, had a different approach. They didn't say it, but Nick could see it in their eyes: they saw him as "just one more of those Aames trash," Ruth's black-sheep step-relations. They were all polite enough—Grandma Ruth wouldn't tolerate them otherwise—but they weren't warm.

Nick was used to that. Grandma Ruth was practically the only warm person he had ever known.

Nick picked at his potato salad. The mustard was sharp, just the way Grandma Ruth liked it. At that thought, he lost his appetite. He kept eating, though, popping a piece of Mrs. Quintana's pão de queijo into his mouth. Nick expected this might be his last meal of the day, if his plans worked out, so he knew he had to fuel up, and he quickly ate two more pieces of the Brazilian cheese bread.

Finally the last mourners left, leaving Nick alone with Mrs. Quintana, the church ladies, and the funeral director. Mrs. Quintana patted his shoulder. "They can clean up, Nicolau. Are you ready to leave?" Nick was too exhausted to speak, so he nodded. They rose, and he took her arm, again feeling like he was doing it wrong somehow. Then he escorted her out of the tiny funeral home, and into the ordinary world of Gurley, Alabama, population 2,306.

Make that 2,305 with Grandma Ruth gone. And soon it would be 2,304.

Outside, it was a disconcertingly bright, cheery day. The breeze was blowing, the scent of fresh-cut hay was in the air, and the sun was doing its best to dry out the hay. The rising and falling trill of wrens was everywhere. It was exactly the sort of day when Nick liked to run into the woods and hide all day, exploring and cataloging everything he found so he could bring his notes to Grandma Ruth for review. But there would be no review today, no notes, and no running. Not into the woods.

Mrs. Quintana led Nick to her blue Subaru truck. It was old and faded, but Silvio kept it in good running order. Often Nick had helped him work on it, learning how all the engine components and electrical systems worked.

Nick held the driver's door for Mrs. Quintana, just as Grandma Ruth had taught him. Then he walked around the car and got into the passenger seat. As he buckled in, Mrs. Quintana asked, "Shall I take you home?"

Nick thought of home, of Dad in a stupor, Dek in a mood to fight, and Mom . . . For the first time, Nick hoped she might be out on one of her "dates," some of which lasted days or even weeks. As much as he was ashamed by her actions, he would rather she be gone today. He didn't want to hear her talking down Grandma Ruth. Not again.

In fact, he didn't want to face home at all, not yet. Not ever. He was done with that place. So he shook his head. "No. Please, I need to go to Grandma Ruth's."

Mrs. Quintana didn't argue, just drove Nick to the old two-story red-paneled Victorian home that had been Nick's refuge for most of his life. But when she stopped the car out front and opened her car door, Nick reached out and touched her arm. She turned to him, and Nick quickly drew back his hand as if burned. He didn't know how, but he had to make her see. "Please, Mrs. Quintana, I have to do this by myself."

Mrs. Quintana shook her head, but she closed her door. She pulled a small paper bag from her back seat and held it out to Nick. Inside he found leftovers from the lunch: nearly two dozen small pieces of cheese bread. "I see today you are a man, Nicolau," she said. "You make your own decisions. But I think it is a mistake. You should not be alone today."

Nick looked away. "Why should now be any different from the rest of my life? I'm good at alone." But he turned to her and forced a smile so she wouldn't worry. Then he pulled out his door key and left the car.

☾

The white walls and polished wooden floor of the entryway seemed barren without Grandma Ruth there to welcome him, without the smell of banana bread baking. Nick closed and relocked the big oak door, leaned back against it, and shook. "I will not cry. I will not." But he didn't want to cry, he wanted to hit something. Strike back against the pain.

Instead, he counted under his breath. "One . . ." Breathe in. Breathe out. "Two . . ." In, out. "Three . . ." In, and out. He was calm again.

"Don't be like your father and your brother, slaves to their rage," Grandma Ruth said. *"You're better than them. I want you to be angry when it's the right thing to do. Righteous anger can be a powerful tool. But rage controls you. Don't let anything control you. Count to ten, and be calm."*

"Yes, Grandma." With practice, Nick had gotten from ten to seven, then five. Now he could calm himself down with three deep breaths.

He looked at the stairs, and then at the living room. Living room first, he decided, entering the place where he and Grandma Ruth had spent so many hours. The room was large, nearly a third of the first floor. The walls were painted a dark-rose color with ivory trim. Nick had helped her to repaint it three years ago, and that trim had taught him to concentrate and not do sloppy work.

But you couldn't see a lot of the walls, because so many of them were covered by bookshelves. Once Nick had asked her why she had all these paper books instead of a reader. She had answered, *"A reader is nice, and it's portable. It's a marvelous invention. Buying books for the paper is like buying beer for the bottles. It's what's inside that gets you drunk!"* And then she had laughed, though Nick had been too young to get the joke. But suddenly she had stopped laughing, looked him in the eyes, and added, *"But some of the bottles are sure pretty."* And she had shown him some of her favorite "bottles."

Nick looked them over now. Precious hardcovers and leather-bound volumes. Lavishly illustrated books, colors deeper than Nick's cheap reader could ever reproduce. Limited editions. A rare signed Torgersen first edition. And science books: astronomy, geology, ecology, physics, and more. Grandma had liked her textbooks in paper so she could write notes in the margins. Nick couldn't understand all the notes yet, but he kept reading and trying. He and Grandma Ruth had spent so many nights discussing space and looking through her big Cassegrain telescope upstairs. She had taught him to pick out the Holmes Construction Station, the colonies on Luna, and the Chinese colony at L5, as well as the stars and planets; and she had encouraged him to read everything she had on the subject. Nick's reader was full of sketches he had made of the scenes in the telescope. He wasn't a good artist, but he tried to capture every detail. *"Details are critical, Nick. Learn to see them."*

He wanted to take the books, take them all. There were so many memories stacked on those shelves. But he needed to travel light, and he had all the words in his reader. Those would be memories enough. So he went to the window seat, lifted the lid with its autumn-leaf padded cover, and pulled out Grandma Ruth's old blue duffel. When Grandma Ruth had gotten sick, when she had finally convinced him that her end was near, Nick knew he could never survive Gurley without her. Never survive his family. He would have to get out, escape farther than he had ever escaped before. And so he had started sneaking out clothes and supplies and stashing them in the big duffel. He unzipped it now and checked inside: clothes, food that would travel, his spare shoes, a small bit of money he had scraped up. He squeezed the bag of pão de queijo into the duffel, right under the most important item: the replacement reader from Grandma Ruth. He couldn't take the books, but he could take the words.

Even if he could have taken the books, what else would he want? The dance floor? The south half of the living room, the half with the big picture windows, had no carpeting, just a smoothly polished floor. With Nick's help, Grandma Ruth had polished that floor until she was just too weak to keep up; and after that, Nick had done the job for her. Dance had been her greatest love, even over books and science; and she had taught Nick to dance, and he had grown to love it like she did. He had as many memories there as in the bookshelves.

He couldn't take the dance floor, but he could take the dance. Nick reached into the duffel and pulled out his reader. Along with Grandma Ruth's books, it contained her complete music library. He navigated to *Invitation to the Dance*—the real arrangement, not the well-meaning but flawed funeral arrangement—and he set the reader on the little black table near the stairs and pressed "Play." The song was difficult, the first waltz composed for listening, not for dancing; but he and Grandma Ruth had loved to dance to it. Nick closed his eyes and swayed to the strings and flutes of the "Moderato" and into the horn fanfare of the "Allegro Vivace." When the waltz section started in, he held out his hands to embrace a partner who wasn't there, and he started dancing around the room. Though it was irrational, he was sure he could feel Grandma Ruth's arms holding him. *"It's all right, Nicky. It's all right. You have to be strong now."*

"I will, Grandma. I will." And remembering Grandma Ruth's final words to him, at last Nick broke down and cried as he danced.

But abruptly the music stopped. Nick opened his eyes and looked to the stairs. Standing there, his finger still on the screen of the reader, was Dek: tall, lanky, dressed in his usual jeans and dirty T-shirt. His greasy hair was lighter than Nick's, closer to Dad's blond than Mom's red. His face was hollow and unshaven, and he wore his customary sneer. "Well, if it isn't the dancing Nit."

One . . . two . . . three . . . The last time Nick had lost his temper had been when he had learned what that nickname meant: the egg of a louse, something to be brushed off with contempt. He had rushed wildly at Dek, arms swinging; and his bigger, stronger brother had punched him three times, once in the nose and twice in the ear, then pushed him to the ground, laughing the whole time. Just like Grandma Ruth had said, Nick's temper had made him weak. He wouldn't let Dek provoke him again. "How'd you get in here, Dek?"

Dek grinned. "I climbed the old oak out back and dropped onto the balcony upstairs. Then I broke a window pane and let myself in."

Upstairs? But no, don't react. Don't give Dek any ideas. Change the subject. "You should've been there, Dek. The church ladies asked after you."

Dek chuckled. "Yeah. Right. Just them pretendin' to be polite, for appearances. All them folks in their Sunday finest, they didn't want me around. Didn't want you neither."

Nick was uncomfortable with those words. Dek was right, at least for the casual acquaintances. So he changed the subject again. "Why'd you come here, Dek? Are you saying good-bye?"

At that, Dek laughed out loud, echoes bouncing off the dance floor. "Good-bye? To what? The old lady never liked me. *You* were always her favorite, favorite little Nit. She and me said good-bye long ago. Everything since has been just more politeness, just empty." For a moment, Dek looked a little blank, like maybe he felt some loss after all; but then his face brightened again. "No, I just come here before Mom and Dad could dry out and come themselves. Soon as they can, they're gonna gut this place, sell everything they can. Then sell the house itself. I wanted to get mine before they thought of it. Maybe they won't even remember this, but I did."

No! But Dek reached back on the landing and pulled out the one thing Nick really wanted, wanted enough to carry wherever he went, no matter how tired he got: Grandma Ruth's big reflector telescope. Dek hadn't even bothered to put it in its case. "You give that here. It's . . . it's mine."

Dek laughed again. "Come and take it, Nit."

"Give. It. Here."

"Come and take it!"

Before he knew what he was doing, Nick rushed Dek, trying to grab the telescope. Normally Dek, being a head taller, would just shove Nick to the ground; but with his hands full, he had more trouble than usual, and Nick kept reaching around him, trying to grab the scope. The scuffle escalated, and Dek had to take a step back up the landing. Finally Dek made a big push, and Nick tumbled down the landing stair and slid across the dance floor.

But while pushing Nick away, Dek lost his grip on the telescope. It flew through the air and struck the corner of the little black table. The eyepiece and the finder scope snapped off, and the metal tube dented. The scope bounced off to the floor and landed hard. Nick heard the mirror shatter, and he was sure the sound was his heart shattering as well. Then the tube spun and rolled, strewing broken glass across the floor.

"You little shit, look what you did!" Dek aimed a vicious kick at Nick's ribs; but Nick scrambled across the floor after the telescope, not sure what to do but wanting to do something, and Dek's foot caught him in the thigh. In his shock, Nick barely felt it. He cut his hands on shards of glass, but he barely felt that either. He caught the tube, stopped its roll, and picked it up, cradling it in his arms and sobbing quietly.

Dek once again stood at the foot of the steps, breathing heavily, glaring at Nick. "It's worthless now. Little shit! What you gonna do now, little shit?"

Before he could think about it, Nick answered truthfully, "I'm going to leave. Get out of this town and never come back." And then, without ever planning it, he added, "Come with me, Dek. You've gotta get out of here too."

And he meant it. Somewhere inside, he still loved his brother, still had a little brother's awe for a big brother, even despite the beatings. Somewhere . . . *"Don't hate him, Nick. Dek beats you because your dad beats him, and he doesn't know anything else. He's frustrated and hurt. Don't make him mad, don't let him hurt you. But don't hate him."* Dek was wrong: Grandma Ruth had never given up hope for him.

But Dek had given up. "I'm going nowhere. You neither."

Nick sighed, dropped the tube, and pushed himself to his feet. "Yes, I am. I'm going."

Dek shook his head in disbelief. "What'll you do? Where'll you go?"

"Someplace far away, without all the idiots around here."

"What, we're idiots? *You're* the idiot." Dek picked up the reader from the table. "Readin' all this shit, it has your head all screwed up."

After the telescope, Nick didn't want anything to happen to the reader, even though it was more durable. He grew very quiet, trying to calm Dek down. "You put that down."

But Dek ignored him. "You're a dumb kid. You can't take care of yourself, and nobody likes you. Where will you go?"

Staring intently at the reader, remembering Grandma Ruth's stories, Nick finally realized the answer. The one place where competence mattered, and idiots weren't allowed. "Space."

Dek laughed, waving the reader around. "Space? You're not an idiot, you're a fuckin' moron! People get killed in space. Is that the kind of shit you been readin'? Ruth sure did a number on your head."

One . . . But that was as high as Nick could bring himself to count. He exploded, barreling into Dek. This time he surprised his brother, knocking him to the ground. "You take that back!" Although Dek was bigger and stronger, it was the first time Nick struck back, sitting atop

his brother's chest and pummeling him with blows. "Take"—punch—
"it back"—punch—"you worthless"—punch—"shit!" Punch. Punch.
Punch. Punch. Punch!

Nick's eyes filled with tears, until finally he couldn't see where to
hit; but by that time, Dek was dazed and sobbing himself, incoherently
pleading for mercy.

Nick picked up the reader and inspected it for damage. When he
was satisfied, he slid off his brother's chest and stood up. "If you're
scared, stay home. But don't make *me* stay home because *you're* scared."
Then he picked up his bag, slid the reader inside, and stormed out
the door. The last thing he saw of the house was Dek on the floor,
blubbering.

17. São Paulo

From the memoirs of Park Yerim

10 June 2083

By the time Admiral Morais finished her story, she was weeping. My own eyes were watering, and I wiped them on my sleeve. "That poor child," I said.

Morais straightened up, surprising me. "Don't. Don't pity the child; he's long gone. But now you understand the man. He ran away from a world where he didn't fit in because he was too careful, too precise for people who just wanted to take whatever they could get away with. I've seen his psych profile. Yes, that's against regulations, but I have my sources." She paused and frowned. "Had. And I didn't learn anything I hadn't already figured out. Nick is obsessed with being right, with trying to control his surroundings by finding right answers, and he cannot understand why other people settle for wrong answers when it gets them what they want. He's socially maladjusted because he grew up among broken people, so he had no examples of normal. Even Grandma Ruth, much as she loved him, left her mark: he picked up her obsessive perfectionism, which makes him good at his job but also dooms him to be disappointed in an imperfect world. He has attachment difficulties, I can tell you that personally. And he has major trust issues. He can only trust systems *and* people if he constantly tests them, always expecting to be disappointed. On those rare occasions when someone exceeds his expectations, he forms a deep bond—in his own damaged way. And trust is also why he reacts so strongly to lying: it's a wrong answer *and* a violation of his trust."

She looked over at the São Paulo door, then back at me. "And damaged as he is, he found a place where he could fit in, where his obsessions worked to his advantage: space exploration. And when his temperament wouldn't let him get along in a world of bureaucrats and clock punchers and other people who didn't approach space like he did, he found a way to end up here. He has built his own little world here, populated entirely by people he can trust, and who can therefore trust each other. It's as close to happy as he has been since . . ." She stopped, blushing. "Well, in decades. But even here, he tests his people constantly."

Morais wiped her eyes. "And I guarantee you one thing, Inspector: right now he's testing you too. He's watching to see how you handle your investigation. I hear from Carver that Nick respects what he has heard about you. Can he trust you?" She looked me in the eye. "If he does, don't let him down."

I wasn't sure how to respond. Finally I said, "I'll try not to, Admiral. Thank you. Is that all?"

Morais shook her head, and she stood. "I also have this file to submit for your records." She pushed a file to the desk.

I opened the file and read it: a full confession. I looked up at her, stunned. "I told you I hadn't decided to press charges yet. Are you sure about this?"

"I'm sure," she replied. "Do with it what you will. My lawyer is preparing a copy to file with the Initiative Council. It's decided, Inspector." With that, she turned and left the office.

Again I sat alone in my office. I looked at the e-reader on the desk, and I thought of the admiral's story. Why had Aames left the e-reader here? He couldn't have forgotten it, I knew that now. Was it some way of clinging to his space, leaving his mark on *his* desk? Or was it just an accident? But I didn't believe in accidents when it came to Nick Aames. *No accidents. People he could trust.*

Suddenly I felt an irresistible urge, one thing I had to do. It felt like the right answer. I picked up the e-reader, walked over to the São Paulo door, and thumbed the door chime. I wasn't sure what to expect, and I thought Aames would likely rebuff me; but I stood and waited just the same. After several seconds, the door slid open, and I walked through.

I had expected more darkness, or maybe just a Spartan command cabin, but I wasn't prepared for what I found: an elaborate simulation of a tropical beach. The deck was covered in a short-pile carpet that was dyed and speckled to look like sand. When I walked across it, it even had some of the give of beach sand underfoot. In place of a bunk there were two metal stanchions painted to look like wooden pilings; and between them was strung a hammock, loosely woven from thick strands of twine. Next to it was a rattan lounge chair.

One whole wall was a giant video display, showing a scene of the ocean at dawn. Gulls circled in the distance, the bright red of the horizon showed the edge of a yellow disk, and waves came rolling to the shore, stopping just short of the wall itself. Over the sound system, I heard the squawk of the gulls, the whoosh of the waves as they rolled in and the hiss of foam as they left, and the distant sound of someone playing a guitar. The illusion wasn't real enough to convince you that you were at a beach—unless you wanted to be convinced.

And the final touch: palm trees, very tiny palms growing in clay pots. The walls of the room were crowded with bonsai pots on tables and shelves, a dozen miniature palms making the room almost a forest. The whole room smelled of damp earth, fertilizer, and a slight grassy odor. The scene around me was unfamiliar, but the scent reminded me of the rice farm back home.

Aames had to know I was there, but his back was to me as he worked on one of the trees. With his left hand he held up a branch, while with his right he reached out with a small pair of wire cutters. Snip. More than half the branch fell to the deck, where I saw four more tiny branches and a scattering of yellow leaves. Then he put down the scissors, picked up a small spool of wire, and methodically wrapped wire around the branch, supporting it up and away from the trunk.

When Aames was satisfied, he picked up the cutters again, and he snipped the wire, bending the end in line with the branch. Then without turning to look at me, he said, "Yes, Park? Have you come to swing the executioner's ax in person?"

"No, Captain, I—" But just then a loud screech interrupted me as a gull flew right at us, swinging away from the wall at the last second. Despite knowing better, I flinched. Then I recovered my composure and tried again. "I thought you should have this." At that, Aames finally turned to look at me. I held out the e-reader. "It has been cluttering up my office for long enough."

"Yes, cluttering up *your* office," Aames said. But he took the e-reader anyway: gently, you might even say reverently. "Thank you, Inspector." Then he sat down in the rattan chair and started thumbing through books. His eyes focused intently on the screen, seeming to gleam. I felt unimportant, forgotten.

I thought there was something more I should say, but I wasn't sure what. So I turned away and went back to the open door.

And when I stood there, right on the threshold between the black of space and the red-gold of the rising sun of São Paulo, I knew what I had to say. When I turned back, Aames was engrossed. I wasn't sure he would even hear me, but I said my piece anyway. "You know, Chief Carver is a very good man."

Aames didn't look up at me, he didn't move; but he replied, "That he is. None better."

I stepped back into space, and the door to the beach closed behind me.

18. Plenary Power

From the memoirs of Park Yerim

11 June 2083

I got no sleep that night, and neither did my team; but I promised them that after the next day, they could sleep for a week. I finally had the outline of a solution, and I needed them all researching facts, regulations, and precedents to be sure I didn't overlook anything. Well, all but McCall and Decker: I still didn't know if I could trust them, so I assigned them to summarize all regulations related to mutiny. That was useful research, and a mole couldn't hurt us on that assignment.

I spent most of the night on the comm with Admiral Reed, discussing my plan. Back and forth we went, working around the 1.2-minute light-speed delay until we almost didn't notice it. Reed would tear my plan apart, and I would rebuild it stronger, sometimes consulting with Matt. Reed would find a hole in my supporting arguments, and I would send new research orders to my team. Matt pointed out the powerful people who would be upset by this, and Reed only laughed: he enjoyed upsetting powerful people and reminding them that they weren't above the law.

And by 0640, Reed could no longer poke any holes in my plan. I had an answer for every objection, ready before he even raised it. Reed spent a solid twenty minutes interrogating me, but not a single argument got through.

At 0700, the desk chimed. We had set that deadline for our decision. I looked at the comm screen. "Well, Admiral, will you back me?"

Seventy seconds later, Reed answered, "Park, your case is solid. This plan is fully within your chapter 12 powers. We can make this stick. The only question is: Should we? We *can* do this, but is this the right thing to do? I can't answer that, Park. *You* are the inspector general in charge. You're my eyes on-site. This is your decision, and I'll stand by it."

I felt my weary shoulders lift, my chest swelling with pride. I looked at Matt, and he sat just as straight. He nodded.

"Admiral, it's right," I said. "If I can get them to sign on. I think I can."

Reed grinned when he heard my answer. "Then why are you asking me, Park? Get to it. I'll start things in motion on my end." Then his tone turned more serious. "And Inspector? Damned fine work. I got lucky: the right person was in the right place at the right time. Dismissed." He pushed the call closed.

I turned to Matt. "Lieutenant, set up an appointment with the parties we discussed. Tell them I shall issue a summary judgment at 0900 in my office, and I require their presence. Then contact Bosun Smith and request as many additional chairs as we'll need. That will give you just enough time for breakfast, a shower, and a clean uniform. We're going to be center stage, so we'll want to look our best."

"Absolutely, Inspector." He saluted. I was starting to get used to that.

☾

When I returned to my office, showered and changed and pumped full of strong coffee, I found the cabin crowded with chairs: one each for Matt, Aames, Carver, and Knapp, plus a space for Gale. The best chair was mine, of course, behind the big desk, but I wouldn't need it; I would stand for my presentation. Standing would add an impression of authority, and I wanted every edge I could get.

So I slid my chair over by the big window. I took the opportunity to gaze at the Milky Way again. It wasn't as clear with the cabin lights up, but it was still awe inspiring. I wished I had time to just stare at it, but not today.

Then I returned to my desk and flipped up the top so that it faced the room. I saw Reed's blinking icon, so I pulled open his call. He looked out from the desktop, larger than life. "Admiral," I asked, "are you ready?"

After the delay, Reed answered, "I'm just here to watch. *You* are ready, Inspector. I can see it in your body language. Give 'em hell."

"Thank you, sir." Then I stood, rehearsing my points in my head one more time. Admiral Reed did paperwork while he waited. I poured myself a large glass of water and set it in a cup holder in the side of the desk.

Promptly at 0850, Matt opened my office door, came in, and sat in the reporter's chair. Behind him filed in Carver and Aames, who sat in the chairs closest to São Paulo. Both wore their white dress uniforms. Aames slouched in his chair and stared out the window at the stars. Admiral Reed looked at Aames, muttered under his breath, but then went back to his paperwork.

At 0857, Admiral Knapp came in and took the last seat, farthest from Aames. Then he nudged it farther away, practically on top of Matt. His Admiralty dress uniform was white as well. The service branches had different duty uniforms, but their dress uniforms were identical save for insignia.

Immediately behind Knapp came a sound like slowly clopping hooves on the deck outside, then softer when it reached the carpet of Matt's office. In walked Gale in a mediskeleton: a large metal and plastic frame that wrapped his body and his limbs, giving him mobility, support, and medication during his extended convalescence. Beneath the frame he wore his dress uniform, but it was mostly hidden by wires and tubes and clamps. What skin showed through was bright and pink, clearly new growth. His scalp in particular was all fresh skin, with a thin layer of brown fuzz just emerging. My sources told me it would be over a month before Gale would leave the mediskeleton. I felt bad about that, but I also knew Adika's recovery would be longer.

Gale marched in, stood in the last remaining space in the office, and tapped a control at his waist. With a pneumatic hiss, the mediskeleton folded down into a sitting position, with extra legs unfolding behind him to form a chair. I gave the man credit for timing: it was 0859.

Then the desk chimed once, and it was 0900. I looked around the room. "Admirals, Chiefs. Captain Aames. Let us begin. Reporter, start recording. This proceeding shall serve as findings of fact in the matter of The System Initiative v. Captain Nicolau Aames. Furthermore, this office has found cause to invoke *Standard Space Mission Protocols*, revised, chapter 12, section 1: Plenary Power, and has filed notice to this effect with the Initiative Council. The Council, after due consideration, has concurred that 12-slash-1 applies here. Therefore this proceeding shall also serve as summary judgment in this case, and no further actions shall be pursued. Presiding for the Inspector General's Office: Inspector General Park Yerim. Court Reporter: Lieutenant Matt Harrold. As representatives for all interested parties are present, we shall begin."

I paused, lifted my glass, and took a small drink. Then I started in. "This office finds that on 7 March, Captain Aames did willfully ignore orders from the Admiralty at a time when the IPV *Aldrin* was inside Earth's gravipause and thus within the Admiralty's jurisdiction." Knapp started to smile, and I continued, turning to look at Aames, "To wit: Captain Aames, on behalf of himself and his crew, refused a construction mission from the Admiralty. Captain Aames further refused the transfer of new personnel to the *Aldrin* along with the transfer of existing personnel to other posts, thus interfering with the smooth operation of facilities across the Earth-Luna system. He also instructed his crew to ignore said transfer orders. Then upon being found in breach of his contract, he ignored an order to relinquish command of this vessel."

I took another drink. "Then on 23 April, after accepting an unauthorized transfer of personnel and materiél from the transport *Poling*, Captain Aames refused docking with three rendezvous shuttles as ordered by the Admiralty. And on 9 May, he threatened to attack Admiralty ships and personnel. Furthermore, neither Captain Aames nor his counsel have disputed these facts. Any of these actions by itself constitutes a serious violation of regulations. Taken together, they constitute sufficient grounds for a charge of mutiny. *If* considered without a larger context."

I turned to Knapp, who was now staring at me, his eyes widening. "But it is the responsibility of this office to consider the entire set of facts, not just those in the Admiralty's complaint. Captain Aames has argued that the initial orders were unlawful under *Protocols*, chapter 1, section 3. He contends that his crew's state of readiness was insufficient to carry out those orders, and that to attempt to do so constituted grave risk."

I paused, watching for Knapp's reaction. "This office sees merit in those claims. After exhaustive review—"

"You can't do that!" Knapp interrupted.

"Admiral Knapp, shall we pause so that I can read chapter 12, section 1 into the record?" Before Knapp could respond, I continued, "I *can* do anything I deem necessary to resolve this case without violating fundamental rights. Furthermore, I can have you removed from these proceedings if you persist in disrupting them. I would prefer not to, since it is better to have a representative from the Admiralty present. But you shall refrain from speaking without first being recognized. Also, you shall address this office properly. This case will be studied and reviewed for decades to come, so let us show proper respect for the process." I paused to see if Knapp would challenge me, but he didn't. "After exhaustive review of the records prior to the incident, this office finds that the crew of the *Aldrin* was already working at an unsustainable pace. And that pace was not through any failing of the crew themselves, nor of their commanders. It was a direct result of earlier decisions by the Admiralty, to wit, a work schedule that was already too ambitious."

I turned back to Aames. "But a grave risk claim is difficult to resolve. The *Protocols* grant the commander sole discretion to determine when a grave risk exists, but subsequent court decisions have muddied the waters there. In some cases that sole discretion has been upheld; but in others it has been overturned after the fact, by distant courts who, while no doubt diligent, were not themselves on-site to face said risk. It is possible, depending on the makeup of the court"—I glanced at Knapp and Gale—"that the assessment of grave risk would be overturned; and just like that, Captain Aames's actions would flip from lawful to unlawful without a single fact changing."

I took a drink. "But Captain Aames has proposed a novel theory of this case: that the crew and residents of the *Aldrin* constitute a viable community, under the precedents established in the matter of the United Cities of Free Luna; and that as a community, they are entitled to decide for themselves what constitutes a grave risk, and to take actions for their own protection; and that the actions of the Admiralty, including those preceding 7 March, constituted a threat to the existence of that community." I paused, thinking: *Here it comes.* "After thorough review of the history of this vessel as well as its financial and contractual assets and obligations, this office concurs. The IPV *Aldrin* must be considered a free city, an autonomous political entity whose citizens and officers have the right to self-governance and to determine their own economic and political future; and although this status was not legally recognized on 7 March, it was as true then as it is today. Captain Aames was within his rights, on that date, to act in the best interest of his city."

Admiral Knapp sprang to his feet and advanced on me, his face right up next to mine. "Unacceptable!"

I stood my ground and stared Knapp right in the eyes. It's always easier to block an admiral with an admiral, so I wished Reed weren't seventy seconds behind us; but I was on my own, and it was time to assert my authority. "Admiral, you will return to your seat and respect this proceeding and this office. Lieutenant Harrold, if the admiral is not seated in the next three seconds, you are instructed to help him to his seat."

Knapp stared back at me—but only for two seconds. Then he returned to his seat. "I'm not finished, Inspector. I shall contest this all the way to the Initiative Council. It is *not* going to stand."

I stepped forward, looking down at Knapp. "Admiral, I have no doubt you will take steps to fight this. It has been alleged that you have a vested interest in shutting down the *Aldrin*, and I find those allegations to have some merit."

"Vested interest!" Knapp moved to stand again, but he thought better of it when Matt shifted behind him.

"There's big money in pushing people around, and that money can end up in the most unusual places. Admiral Reed's auditors stand ready to trace funds related to Holmes Transport, mission planning for the *Aldrin*, and the planning committee. I believe you're a member of that committee? If you *do* have a vested interest, the auditors will find it."

Knapp glared at me. "Do *not* threaten me, Inspector. This plenary power of yours only lasts through this investigation. When it's over, I can make your life hell."

I smiled. "When it's over, Admiral, you will no longer have any statutory authority over the crew and passengers of this vessel. You will, of course, still have authority over Initiative personnel, myself included. You're welcome to try to use it against me, sir, but you forget: this proceeding is being recorded." I looked over my shoulder at Reed's giant face on the desk screen.

Just at that moment, Reed caught up with the start of the confrontation. His voice was harsh as he said, "Sit down, Knapp, and don't be an ass. Harrold, if he doesn't sit down, sit on him. And Knapp, if you're thinking of threatening my officers, *back off*! My auditors have already identified a certain account in the Tycho Under Agro Bank, and are filing papers to connect that account to its owner. If you threaten Park, you threaten me, and we *will* fight back."

Knapp scowled at the screen. I snapped my fingers. "Look at me, Admiral! I'm running this proceeding, not Admiral Reed. He's only here as an observer."

Knapp turned back to me. "I can't believe you people are going to let that *mutineer* get away with this. He steals a ship, defies orders, and you don't punish him, you give him a city!"

"No." I shook my head. "If that's what concerns you, Admiral, let me put your mind at ease." I walked to the far side of the room and stood in front of Aames. "While I find reason to believe that this entire situation has been manipulated by special interests to gain control of Earth-Mars commerce, I have no doubt that those interests would never have succeeded were it not for the intransigence, the arrogance, and the manipulative game-playing of Captain Aames. You and Anton Holmes may have used this situation to your advantage, but Aames created the situation just as surely as he created a community aboard this ship. A better, wiser man could have united the *Aldrin* without antagonizing the Admiralty. In fact, a better, wiser man did. Captain Aames did not cause the events of 7 March, but he contributed to them, and he must face the consequences of his actions. At the close of these proceedings, he shall be dishonorably discharged from the International Space Corps and stripped of all rank and privileges, including pension and other retirement benefits. His contract, formerly with Holmes Interplanetary and currently with the System Initiative, shall be declared void, and he shall have no recourse to invoke the penalty clauses therein. He shall be forever barred from service in any fashion with the International Space Corps."

I shifted my position, standing between Carver and Aames where I could look down on them both. "And as a condition of its grant of independence, the Free City of Aldrin must agree never to elect nor appoint Nicolau Aames to any position of command within the city. He may find gainful employment with whomever will put up with him, but he must *not* have any decision-making power within this city. The grant of independence shall require that the interim governor general of the Free City of Aldrin shall be Mr. Anson Carver."

Carver's jaw dropped. Then he responded, "You can't do that!"

Aames had sat silent as I had spoken, but now he laughed. "She *has* to do that, Carver. It's her only choice, and *your* only chance. I'm a lightning rod for enemies all across the system: every bureaucrat I've shown to be an idiot, every incompetent spacer I've ever dismissed, every business that ever demanded we cut corners and I told them to shove it. As long as I have a say in things here, every one of them will hound you and harry you and make it impossible for the *Aldrin* to succeed. But with me gone, and all the blame with me, you'll have a fighting chance to keep this city running and growing. In twenty years, this will be the most important city in all of space—but not if I'm running it."

Carver stared at Aames as if he couldn't believe what the man was suggesting. "*You* have to be the governor, Nick, not me. That's the only way that makes sense. I execute the orders, I don't issue them."

Aames gripped his shoulder and looked him in the eye. "You connect with people."

"You connect with me," Carver objected.

"I connect with *persons*," Aames said, "individuals that I select according to my exacting standards. *You* connect with *everybody*. People follow me because I keep them alive. People follow you because they like you."

"You're wrong, Nick," Carver answered. "I follow you because I like you *and* because you keep us alive."

Aames sighed. "You're a good friend, Anson. Thank you. But this is no longer about me. Do this. It's what you were born for. Do this, take control, let me be the power behind the throne."

Carver shook his head. "No way. If I do this—" And Aames nodded, for Carver had just conceded the possibility. "If I do this, I'm doing it my way. No power behind the throne for me."

"Fine! Let me be the crotchety old fart yelling 'Get off my lawn, you rotten kids.' But *do this!*"

Carver stared at Aames. Twice the chief opened his mouth to speak, but nothing came out. Finally he turned to me. "On behalf of the people of Aldrin, Inspector, I accept your terms. And your assignment."

"Good luck, Mr. Carver. You're going to need it." I walked back to the screen, and then turned back to face the room. "Our next task, then, is to determine a schedule of debt repayments, interest on investments, dividends, and transfer of assets so that the Free City of Aldrin may remain in good standing with all parties who have a financial interest in the IPV *Aldrin*. We also must determine what customer assets and payments are due to the IPV *Aldrin* as a ship of the Initiative, and which of those outstanding receivables are now owed to the free city. And speaking of payments—and penalties—Chief Gale?"

Gale had been silent to that point, and I wondered if he had fallen asleep from his meds; but he answered instantly and alertly, "Yes, Inspector."

"Chief, it is the opinion of this office that you and crew under your orders were materially responsible for major structural damage to the IPV *Aldrin*, to wit: the explosion and fire aboard the I Ring, and the resulting stresses and wobble in the rest of the ship. There were also significant fuel costs to correct that wobble, extensive damage to the H and J Rings, and loss of atmosphere. Not to mention the costs and trauma of major injuries to myself, yourself, Commander Adika, Bosun Smith, and others. And four deaths." I paused to let that sink in. "However, that incident is outside the purview of this investigation, having transpired while this ship was under control of the Admiralty. This office has no authority to issue findings of fact in that incident. Curiously, however,"—I looked at Knapp—"there appear to be no records that your work in I Ring that day was ordered by anyone. Yet you told Bosun Smith that day—and I have an excellent memory—that she was interfering with orders from Admiral Knapp. Those orders are nowhere to be found. So I must ask you, Chief Gale: did you receive such orders?"

Knapp half rose. "You don't have to answer that, Gale."

I looked at Matt, he stood, and Knapp sat back down. Then I looked back at Gale. "He's right, Chief, you don't have to answer. But I should point out that at some point there *will* be an investigation of the incident on the I Ring. Should you prove cooperative in this matter today, this office shall make a note of that cooperation in your records. That will reflect well on you in future proceedings."

"Gale," Knapp muttered menacingly.

Gale's neck and spine were immobilized by the mediskeleton, so he had to swivel the entire frame to look at Knapp. Then with a mechanical whine, he swiveled back to me. He inclined the frame slightly, forward and back, in a stiff approximation of a nod. "Yes, Inspector, I and my crew acted at the direct order of Admiral Knapp."

"I see." I turned to Knapp. "And do you have copies of that order, Chief Gale?"

"Yes, Inspector. On my comp." He tapped the mediskeleton where his comp was affixed.

"Thank you, Chief. Reporter, summon a forensic data team to take custody of Chief Gale's comp until we can make a verified backup of all its contents." I returned to the screen. "This office finds the Admiralty to be financially responsible for all costs related to damage to the I Ring and related structures, repair thereto, loss of matériel, loss of air, medical costs, and lost time, as well as insurance and survivor's benefits. These costs, to the extent appropriate, shall be credited to the accounts of the

Free City of Aldrin. That should make a significant dent in your debts, Mr. Carver."

"Thank you, Inspector," Carver answered.

I clasped my hands behind my back. "There are hundreds of lesser issues to resolve, but this office believes that this settlement resolves the major issues and establishes a framework for the rest. Admiral Reed, do you have any observations?"

And then we sat, for seventy-four long seconds, as my question and Reed's answer traveled the distance between the ship and Earth. During that time everyone was silent, save for Knapp, who drummed his fingers feverishly upon his thigh.

The time stretched out, and I wondered if something was delaying Reed; but the desk showed precisely seventy-three seconds when he answered, "Only this: Knapp, if you try to fight this, I will knock you down so low you'll need a ladder to climb out of the hole. Go along with this, keep your mouth shut, and maybe we can find a way for you to resign your commission without embarrassment."

"Thank you, Admiral Reed." I looked around the room. "These are the findings and summary judgment of this office in the matter of The System Initiative v. Captain Nicolau Aames under *Standard Space Mission Protocols*, revised, chapter 12, section 1: Plenary Power. Admiral Knapp, we have your objections in the official record. Do you wish to add to them?"

Knapp shook his head, his eyes never leaving Reed's. "No. Inspector."

"Thank you," I said. "Mr. Carver, you have agreed to this judgment. Captain Aames, your agreement is irrelevant. This decision will be made without you. So that brings us to Chief Gale. Chief, if you have any objections either as an officer in the Admiralty or as a representative of the Space Professionals, please state them for the record now."

Gale slowly swiveled the mediskeleton to face Carver. Their eyes met, and Gale said, "No, Inspector. No objections. You made a wise choice."

"Only time will tell, but I hope so. I fear Captain Aames is right, and it may be twenty years before we know for certain." I sighed. "But wise or not, the choice is made. This summary judgment is hereby issued. Reporter, stop recording. Gentlemen, you're dismissed. You, too, Lieutenant." I paused as first Gale and then the rest rose to leave. Then I added, "But not Captain Aames."

Aames raised an eyebrow, and he sat back down as the others filed out. When everyone else had left, and the door had slid shut behind them, he said, "It's still 'Captain' Aames, is it?"

I pulled my chair over from by the window, folded down the desk screen, and sat. "Until we process your discharge papers, yes, it is. I'll need your signature on that, and on the summary judgment, certifying that you understand and accept the terms."

Aames pulled his chair up to the desk. "Why wouldn't I accept them? Gale was right for once: you made a good choice."

I looked across at him. "Of course I did. It was the only choice you left me—the choice you expected me to take."

"Oh?"

"Oh, come off it, Aames. You think I don't know that you manipulated me into this? You set it up so perfectly. I could side with the admirals, even though they were clearly in the wrong, because it would be so difficult to *prove* them wrong—months and months of effort, with command fighting me every step of the way. Or I could side with you, who I knew was in the right; but siding with you would've torn up half the Initiative.

"But then you did everything you could to make sure that I saw Anson Carver as the sensible alternative to yourself. The one reasonable man in this entire affair. The one person everyone respects, everyone likes. He was the obvious choice. Even Knapp will accept him eventually."

"And you think I set all this up to lead you to this conclusion?"

"Captain, if anyone can be that manipulative, you can."

"I'll take that as a compliment," Aames said. "But as long as I'm on a roll, I have one more term before I'll sign your paperwork."

I was shocked. "You think you're in a position to dictate terms?"

"Just one, but I must insist: clear Admiral Morais. Give her back her command."

"I'm sorry, Captain, I can't do that."

Aames leaned back from the desk. "Then I can't sign your paperwork, and you can go to hell."

I shook my head. "You don't understand, Captain: I *can't* do that. It's too late."

"What do you mean, it's too late?"

I explained, "There's one flaw in my plan: I'm not sure the blanket immunity for your crew will hold up. There are a lot of regulations where Knapp might try to trip them up; and if he insists on investigating them one at a time, each as a separate action under this investigation, he can drag this out for almost a decade."

Aames nodded. "And until the last case against the last crewmember closes, *this* case can't be closed."

I nodded back. "And the *Aldrin*'s charter as a free city can't be finalized. Plus if Knapp shops around, he might eventually find an inspector general who's more pliable."

"I see the problem," Aames agreed. "How did you resolve it?"

"I didn't." The puzzled look on Aames's face gave me a moment of guilty pleasure—guilty because I knew I was about to cause him pain. "Admiral Morais did, but I'll need you to back her up on it." I pulled open Morais's confession and started reading: "'I, Admiral Rosalia Morais, do affirm and testify that on 7 March I issued orders to the crew of IPV *Aldrin* to the effect that they were to disregard any subsequent orders regarding reassignments or personnel transfers to and from the *Aldrin*, as well as any orders transferring control of the *Aldrin* to a new commander. They were to consider all such orders to be unlawful, null, and void. I further ordered them that my orders were not to be countermanded, whether by Captain Aames or any other officer, without my personal authorization. I confess to sole responsibility for this order, and for all consequences arising therefrom. Any charges against the crew resulting from this order must be summarily dismissed, as to the best of their knowledge, they were operating on orders from the Admiralty. Therefore I also take sole responsibility for any infraction, accident, injury, or incident arising from their actions, and any charges resulting from this order must be directed at myself. Since this was an order I was not authorized to give, I also acknowledge that this is a violation of my oath of service. I know that the consequences for such a sweeping, unauthorized order are dismissal, dishonorable discharge, and loss of pension and benefits. I accept these consequences under this, my confession to all infractions described above. Signed, former Admiral Rosalia Morais.'"

Aames leaned forward. "That whole thing's a lie!"

I nodded. "Yes, it is, Captain. Sign it."

He shook his head. "I can't lie on a formal report like this. It's a complete fabrication."

"Captain, I've spoken to your crew." I paused for emphasis. "To your friends. They all tell stories where you've shaded the truth for a good cause."

Aames looked down. "Sometimes you have to withhold facts. But never . . . never lie about them."

"Aames, sign it. For the good of your crew, for the good of the *Aldrin*, for the good of Mars. Even of Earth, they need this trade too. *Sign it.*"

"But . . ." I couldn't believe it. Were his eyes welling up? "But she'll be ruined."

"Aames, she made her leap, and you can't catch her. She'll land on her feet or she'll stumble, but she'll do it on her own. You can't save her this time. This time she's saving you. And it's already done."

"What?"

"She turned in this confession and resignation last night, and copies have been filed with the Initiative. It's done. I'm sorry, all you can do is go along with it. If you refuse to cooperate now, she'll still be ruined, but for nothing."

Aames still looked torn, so I tried another tack. "Mr. Carver deserves to run his city without the threat of Initiative action hanging over his head. She has given him that. Don't take that away from him. Sign the paperwork."

Aames stared at me. For several seconds he said nothing. I realized he was trembling. At last he found his voice. "But it's wrong."

I looked on him with pity. In order for him to get the result he had worked so hard for, he had to give up his obsession with truth. He had to accept and *endorse* a wrong answer. I could see how this was tearing him apart, and I felt horrid for putting him through this ordeal; but like him, I had no choice. So I spoke very softly. "It's all right, Aames. Sometimes it's all right to be wrong. For the right reason."

Still trembling, Aames reached out his right hand. I handed him a stylus, and I pushed my judgment file to him. He bent over the desk and signed his name with a shaky hand.

I took a risk. I reached my left hand across the desk and placed it on his shoulder, hoping to comfort him. But he pulled away and stood.

I stood as well. When Aames turned toward São Paulo, I stammered, "Wait. Salute."

Aames turned back, and already he had collected himself. The trembling was gone, the eyebrow was raised, the stress wisped away, and he looked as much in control as ever. "Inspector, that file I just signed says I don't have to salute you, or Knapp, or anyone anymore. I'm a civilian now."

"That's not what I meant. I . . ." I snapped a salute.

At that, Aames almost grinned. "And you don't salute me either. I'm nobody special. But next time you see him, make sure you shake hands with Governor Carver."

EPILOGUE

Nick stood alone in his room, at peace at last. The simulated beach was dark, the "sun" having "set" somewhere behind him. Far out on the waves he saw the lights of a cruise ship. The big diesel horn sounded, far away, barely as loud as the call of the gulls.

Carver *was* a good man, better than Nick. He had everything under control. The Free City of Aldrin was in the best of hands, exactly as Nick had planned.

Well, *almost* exactly.

Now Nick had only one problem: how to occupy his time, how to stay out of Carver's hair. How to not mess up everything Nick had so carefully arranged.

Nick was at peace *now*, but he would soon get restless. What would he do with himself? He honestly had no answer. For the first time in decades, he had no plan at all.

Then he heard a soft footstep behind him. Music started: "Brigas Nunca Mais."

Nick Aames turned around. And smiled.

ACKNOWLEDGMENTS

Someday I will learn to make better notes of all the people who help shape my stories. But for today, I must rely on my faulty memory to recall all the people who deserve my thanks for their inspiration and assistance in this book. No doubt there are some I have forgotten, so let me thank them in spirit first.

My friends and fellow authors William Ledbetter and Michelle Muenzler run the annual Jim Baen Memorial Short Story Award, a writing contest for short science fiction that will inspire the next generation of rocket scientists and space explorers. I've never won—yet!—but in 2012 my story "Not Far Enough" (the tale of the first *Bradbury* expedition, referenced in this book) took second place. The first-place winner, R. P. L. Johnson, couldn't make the trip from Australia to accept his award at the International Space Development Conference; so he asked if I would attend in his place and read his speech. I eagerly accepted, of course. That is how I found myself having lunch with a number of professionals in the space business, including Apollo 11 astronaut Buzz Aldrin. I managed not to embarrass myself during lunch, and later I went to Colonel Aldrin's talk about his unique plan for Mars exploration. I still remember the brief story note I wrote that day: "Something aboard a Mars cycler."

So without Bill and Michelle and the Baen Memorial and Rich Johnson, and especially without Buzz Aldrin, this book would not exist. Thank you all.

It took a couple of months for the first *Aldrin* Express story to form in my head. As I started trying to understand my main character, Nick Aames, I did what I often do for feedback: I turned to Facebook for suggestions. I received a number of good comments, but the clearest and most on point were from my friend and fellow Ann Arbor duelist Robert Chavez. He discussed the history of smart, difficult characters like Sherlock Holmes and Dr. Gregory House, and helped me to see that Nick's friendship with Carver was the key to helping the reader understand and like Nick. So to Robert Chavez, Sir Arthur Conan Doyle, and David Shore (creator of *House M.D.*), thank you for the character insights.

Thank you to Stanley Schmidt, Trevor Quachri, and Emily Alta Hockaday, the editorial team at *Analog* who bought that first Carver and Aames story and brought it to the world in the pages of *Analog Science Fiction and Fact*, and to the *Analog* readers who responded so well to it. In particular, thank you to my brainmate, fellow author Tina Smith (writing as Tina Gower), who convinced me that Nick Aames was a character who needed to return.

And thanks also to the other part of my brain, fellow author Kary English, and my usual crowd of first readers. Bill Emerson provided valuable feedback, as he always does. My mom and fellow author Stewart Baker both argued to keep the novel as close to my original vision as possible, and I thank them for that moral support.

My brother-in-law Mark "Buck" Buckowing is one of the most avid readers I have ever met, and also a chemist. His chemistry assistance provided the vital clue that tied that first *Aldrin* story together. His support, and that of all my family, is something I truly prize as an author.

Jack McDevitt had kind things to say about many of the stories that went into this novel, and has been unflagging in his encouragement for my career. Thank you, Jack. "The Adventure of the Martian Tomb" is coming, I promise.

Besides writing an excellent foreword, my friend Marianne J. Dyson has reviewed this book and helped me to improve the science.

(She is a professional rocket scientist, after all, as well as a great writer of both science and science fiction.) Any errors that remain are despite her help, not because of it, and entirely my fault.

My agent, David Fugate, has once again helped me to connect with a great publisher in 47North. My editor Jason Kirk and the entire 47North team have been a joy to work with. They set a high bar. In particular, copyeditor Elisabeth Rinaldi and proofreader Ariel Anderson showed attention to detail in their fact-checking and proofing that would impress Nick Aames, and my book is the better for them. Thanks to them and David and Jason and the rest of the team.

Many years ago, my mother-in-law, Bonnie Penar (RIP), got me a Barnes & Noble gift certificate for my birthday. To my surprise, I did *not* buy a book with it. Rather, I was entranced by the music playing in the store: "Brazilian Lounge" from Putumayo Music. That led to my fascination with Brazilian music, and thus it became Nick Aames's favorite music. The Brazilian elements of this novel started there, courtesy of Putumayo and Mom Penar. My thanks to them.

A year ago today as I write this, I had an infected sebaceous cyst that was turning septic, though I didn't know it at the time. I ignored it, hoping it would improve. My friend, nurse and fellow writer Emily Godhand, demanded that I go to the hospital if my temperature increased. Tina Smith warned me of the dangers of sepsis. So when my temperature started to climb, my brother Joe rushed me to the hospital. They were able to halt the infection, but only because I got there in time. They also diagnosed me with diabetes as a contributing factor to the infection, and taught me how to control it and to manage my weight and fitness. I am alive today to see this book—and seventy pounds lighter!—because of Emily, Tina, Joe, and the staff of Metro Hospital. I'm not done thanking them for that.

And to my wife Sandy: *Brigas nunca mais.*